The Wedding Cake Tree

Melanie Hudson

W F HOWES LTD

This large print edition published in 2015 by
W F Howes Ltd
Unit 4, Rearsby Business Park, Gaddesby Lane,
Rearsby, Leicester LE7 4YH

1 3 5 7 9 10 8 6 4 2

First published in the United Kingdom in 2014
by Choc Lit Limited

ISBN 978 1 51000 546 4

Typeset by Palimpsest Book Production Limited,
Falkirk, Stirlingshire
Printed and bound by
CPI Group (UK) Ltd, Croydon, CR0 4YY

For Edward

PART ONE

DEVON, ENGLAND

22 MAY

CHAPTER 1

My mother died unexpectedly on the day when the last lingering rose of autumn lost its bloom. The letter I received from her solicitor shortly after the funeral remained in my work satchel for several months, and I would retrieve it, now and again, simply to confirm the unusual details in my mind.

The signatory on the letter, Mr Grimes, requested I make it my utmost priority to visit him at his office – situated on Barnstaple High Street – at ten o'clock in the morning on the 22nd of May the following year. Mum had requested that six months should lapse between her funeral and the reading of the will. Although I found the delay to be a peculiar request, I realised she had done me a favour. I had a stepfather, but no siblings and no extended family, and the thought of spending hours in Mum's study, trawling through her filing system in an attempt to terminate a lifetime of administration, filled me with dread. Content to postpone the inevitable, I returned to London after the funeral, rested my head on the shoulder of my old friend Paul, and threw myself back into my work.

Spring came around relatively quickly and I was glad when the 22nd of May arrived. I could once again retrieve the tatty letter from the bottom of my satchel and begin to plan my future.

I entered the solicitor's office exactly as a mahogany wall clock chimed ten. The room had a musty smell and the dust in the air was clearly visible as it filtered through dank vertical blinds. Grimes, dressed in a finely tailored pinstripe suit, finished with a striking yellow bow tie, was kneeling on his haunches beside a desk. He was feeding a lettuce leaf to a tortoise whose makeshift home was a cardboard box that had once contained Spanish oranges. If pushed I would have guessed he was the wrong side of forty, but the right side of a funeral policy, and he had the face of a sailor – tanned by the wind, taut and dry.

He took the tortoise from the box and placed it on the threadbare carpet beside him, then stood, and turned to offer me a broad, welcoming smile. At a speed and style perfectly in harmony with the reptile, Grimes crossed the room and shook my hand.

'A pleasure to finally meet you,' he said, heartily. 'You don't mind if Terry hangs around for the meeting?'

I glanced around.

'Terry?'

Grimes looked towards the tortoise, his expression full of affectionate pride. Terry looked up and I could have sworn I saw the creature wink.

'My trusty tortoise! You'll see that Terry is particularly useful in meetings'—Grimes leaned towards me with a knowing nod—'few are wiser than tortoises – except perhaps leatherback turtles – but they're not so easy to keep in a small office. Don't you agree, Miss Buchanan?'

I waited for him to laugh, but he didn't. 'Er, yes . . .?'

Grimes returned to take a seat behind the desk, which is when I noticed he wasn't wearing socks or shoes. I also noticed he had only four toes to share between two feet. Trying not to stare, while feeling as though I had somehow stepped into a surreal dream, I took his cue to take a seat across the desk from him, put my satchel on the floor beside my chair (being careful to avoid the tortoise) and we got down to business.

Grimes took a buff file out of the drawer and placed it on the desk in front of him. Assuming the manner of a man about to discuss serious business, he perched his elbows on the desk, crossed his hands, placed them under his chin, and sat in a moment of silence while he gathered his thoughts. Responding in kind, I sat up straight in the chair and waited for him to begin.

'A few formalities to get out of the way first,' he said, looking up with a smile.

'Just to confirm, you are Grace Buchanan of'— he looked to his notes to confirm the details—'57a Gloucester Court, Twickenham?'

Another smile.

'Yes, I am.'

'You'll remember I asked you to bring your passport as proof of ID. I take it you have it with you?

'Yes'—I reached for my bag—'Do you want it now?'

'No, no,' he said with a wave of his hand, 'I'll take a copy later.' He opened the file. 'I'm going to explain to you the instructions regarding the last will and testament of Mrs Frances Heywood of St Christopher's Cottage, Exmoor, Devon. You will note,' he continued, 'that I said the instructions *regarding* the will – rather than reading you the will directly.'

I gazed at him confused and – trying to hide the frustration in my voice – said, 'My mother's name was Rosamund Buchanan, Mr Grimes, *not* Frances Heywood.'

'Buchanan. Ah, I thought there may be some discrepancy here and wondered how much you knew . . .'

He picked up a pen and swivelled it around with his fingers.

'Your mother changed her name some years ago when she moved to Devon. The reason for this will become clear to you later, Grace, but she did not go through the usual legal proceedings to change her name. So, for the purposes of her will, her legal name is Frances Heywood.'

I tried to interrupt but he held up a hand to stop me.

6

'I'm going to fire a large quantity of information your way and I suspect it will come as a shock. I suggest you let me put all of the information I have forward, and then there will be time for questions later.'

Surprised by his sudden firmness of manner I let him continue. If the discovery of my mother's real name was a revelation, it was nothing compared to what I was about to hear.

'First of all, I should state that you are the sole beneficiary of your mother's estate.'

That was no surprise.

'Secondly, I have a letter for you from your mother.'

That *was* a surprise.

He glanced at the file.

'I'm afraid I cannot inform you of the details of your mother's will at present because she left quite clear instructions regarding the actions you must carry out if you are to meet the conditions of the will and, thereafter, inherit the estate. I also cannot disclose exact details of the estate: that will be revealed to you at . . . well, at the end.'

Too dumbfounded to respond, I let him continue with his instructions.

'She left for you a detailed list of actions,' he said, placing the word actions in imaginary quotation marks with his index fingers, 'that you must carry out, and provide *proof* you have carried out, in order to satisfy the qualification requirements to eventually inherit.'

'Mr Grimes,' I interjected forcefully, 'I appreciate you're doing your job, but please can you tell me, in basic English, what on earth you're talking about? What do you mean, *eventually* inherit?'

He removed his glasses. Despite his precise manner I could see by the way his eyebrows furrowed and the way in which he rubbed his fingers along his forehead that he was finding the meeting stressful.

'Your mother was quite a special lady . . .'

He paused – presumably waiting for me to agree with him – but I said nothing, so he continued.

'I visited her at the cottage not long after she discovered her illness was terminal.'

I felt my eyes moisten; the word terminal was a harsh reminder that she was dead.

'She explained to me that she wanted you to learn a little more about her as a person, the person she was prior to your birth that is, before you can take your inheritance. I'm not sure how much you know about your mother's life?'

He said the last more as a question than a statement, but again I said nothing.

'She discovered she was pregnant with you just after she turned thirty and decided it would be for the best if she had a complete change of lifestyle. She decided to base herself in Devon, set up at St Christopher's, and you know the rest from that point on. Towards the end of her life, she began to consider the fact that she had given you little information, if any, regarding any extended family you may have, or any clue at all regarding her previous career—'

Grimes came to an unexpected halt in his dialogue. He bent down to his left side, picked up the tortoise and placed it on the desk so that the head of the tortoise was facing me. It was at that precise moment I realised the adage that pets and owners share facial characteristics was absolutely true. He took a lettuce leaf from his top drawer and handed it to me, smiling. Thinking it unlikely to be a snack for my own consumption, I fed it to the tortoise.

'She realised that her professional life, the life she led before you were conceived,' he continued, settling back into his chair, 'was an enormous part of who she was. I suppose she felt your image of her was incomplete. She wanted to fill in all the gaps in your understanding. For that to happen she wanted you to go on a journey to places that held special significance in her life, and that is what you must do, Grace, if you wish to inherit her estate. There are only five destinations,' he added, as if this was a bonus, 'and you will read a letter from her at each location. She will explain to you, through the course of the letters, all she feels you need to know. Oh, and she wanted you to scatter a little of her ashes at each destination. Does that make it any clearer?'

My face must have held an expression of complete shock. I raised myself up, leaned forwards across the desk and met Terry's fixed, determined glare, which was surprisingly disconcerting.

'Are you telling me that my mother actually wanted me to skip about the country and scatter her ashes in order to qualify for my own inheritance?'

'Yes, that is exactly what I'm saying . . . you'll be setting off today in fact.'

What!

'Today? How long for?'

'Ten days.' Grimes' voice remained irritatingly monotone.

'*Ten days?*' I jumped to my feet, exasperated. Once again, the tortoise stopped eating and glowered at me. I lowered myself back into the chair. 'But that's absolutely ludicrous,' I said in a quieter voice, not wanted to offend the animal further. 'I can't possibly drop everything with no notice. Mum must have been insane – *you* must be insane!'

Grimes remained calm.

'No, she was of sound mind, if not body, and I can testify to that. Again, she simply wanted to put you in the picture regarding the life she led prior to your birth.'

Simply?

'Mr Grimes, you're making it sound as though I didn't know my own mother; although, to be fair, it seems I didn't even know her name. What I do know is, she gave me a very special childhood, in a very special place, and I don't see why I need to know any more information. Children don't need to know every little detail about their parents, I'm not sure I even *want* to know. Okay, so she changed her name, big deal. She already told me all I needed to know years ago, that she originated from Yorkshire, farmers I think, it had been a happy childhood, but like me, she was an only child. She lost her parents when she was in her early thirties. Yes, I queried the whereabouts of my father, but she hadn't wanted to discuss it and I didn't delve. I don't want to delve Mr Grimes. I just want to keep the memories I have and leave it at that. I don't understand why Mum is passing all this on to me now. Why on earth did she wait until she was bloody well dead to start digging up the past? If all this information is so damn important, why didn't she tell me to my face? This is completely out of character for her.'

My voice began to break towards the end of my speech. He waited for me to continue and I tried to regain my calm.

'Look, no offence,' I said, lifting the tortoise and turning it away from the edge of the desk like a clockwork toy, 'but I'm going to have to seek separate legal advice. There is absolutely no way I'm going to be a part of this folly. I haven't the time to go. I just want to inherit my mother's cottage – it's all I've ever wanted,' I added quietly. 'Maybe her illness altered her towards the end, I'm sure she meant . . .' He interrupted me by holding up his hand and opening the file that lay previously untouched in front of him. He removed

11

a small pile of cream A4 envelopes that were bound together by a red ribbon.

'Please try to understand; I am simply passing on to you your own mother's wishes.' He handed me the envelope from the top of the pile, but asked me to wait for a second before opening it.

'Rosamund mentioned you're a photographer?' he said, leaning back into his chair.

'Yes,' I said vaguely, fingering the letter. I wasn't sure how I felt about a letter from a dead person, even Mum.

'You photograph celebrities, film stars and so on? Must be very exciting.'

I looked up.

'No, not really.' I knew where he was going with this.

'I think your mother felt your artistic talents were somewhat wasted on that kind of photography. I understand you were trained in the opera at the London Academy of Music?'

'Briefly, yes,'

He sighed, defeated.

'Look, I'll leave you to read the letter and you will, no doubt, see what I'm trying, albeit fairly badly, to say.'

He stood, took the tortoise and placed it back in its pen, then returned to touch my arm in a kind gesture.

'I'll make you a coffee.'

CHAPTER 2

Hello Grace, my love.

I have started this letter several times but keep crossing things out. I decide to write something else, but then the page is a mess and now there is a significant pile of scrunched up paper by the bin. So this time, I'm just going to keep on writing – if only for the sake of a small Scottish forest.

First of all, please don't read this letter as a missive from the grave. Yes, the fact that you are reading it means that I'm dead and gone, but right now, as I'm writing, I'm sitting in the garden room. It's July. The garden looks beautiful, Grace. The 'Bishop' is such a good doer this year but I do fear for rosa 'Alan Titchmarsh', I'm afraid he's lost his bloom, but hopefully you will see him make a remarkable comeback next spring. Anyway, perhaps you could see it as a long distance phone call, but with quite a long pause between what is said and when it is heard.

I know you will be upset that I didn't tell you

the whole truth about my illness. When I told you about the cancer several months ago I kept the details deliberately vague and fairly positive. What I didn't tell you was the cancer was diagnosed late (you know I don't like to go to the doctors) and it is aggressive. The chemotherapy and radiotherapy has achieved very little. Last month, I was given the news that there is nothing more to be done: it's bloody horrible. I cry, then I'm angry and frightened, and then I'm melancholic. I was always going to have to bugger off eventually, but I confess another ten years would have done me fine. It would have been nice, at least, to see the wedding cake tree put on another layer.

I didn't have the heart to tell you the severity of the prognosis for several reasons: firstly, I didn't want to believe it myself, and decided to fill my head with positive thoughts (no bad thing), but I was blocking out the reality of what I knew in my heart would be the eventual outcome. Secondly, if I told you my time left was limited, then you would have rushed up the motorway like a mad woman every week and I simply haven't wanted to burden you with the stress of it all. I'm desperate to see you, of course, but what if you had a car accident because you were overly tired? Also, you have your own life to live, and you need to live it; every single day is precious.

And so, as difficult as it is, I've decided to

let the next few months run their course. I'm not expected to make it as far through the year as Christmas and I'm hoping that, on the odd occasion you pop home during the coming months, I can pass myself off as having a bad day. If you turn up unannounced and guess the truth, or if you decide to visit during the final weeks, then my plan will have been scuppered.

It all boils down to the fact that I will not put you through the horror of watching me die. We have a lifetime of wonderful memories and that is what I want you to hold on to. I suppose I feel any time spent with you in the future would be tinged with unbearable sorrow. Saying goodbye each time would be soul-destroying – not knowing if it was to be the last. And so I shall simply disappear from your life, and I hope I will have saved you from several agonising months of unnecessary grief; when you have a child of your own, perhaps you will understand.

Right. Enough self-indulgence. Down to business. Unless Grimes has cocked up my instructions you will have heard by now that my name is really Frances Heywood. You will find out later why I had to change it. That brings me to another point Grace: don't try to jump ahead of yourself with the information passed to you over the next ten days or so – relax and try to enjoy it. Anyhow, continue through your life thinking of me as Rosamund; it's lovely to choose your own name, especially when you name yourself after your favourite flower . . . 'rosa mundi'.

By now you must be wondering what on earth I am blithering on about and getting pretty cross. Well, I want you to go on a little trip – see it as a holiday. In fact, here is an idea, see it as the holiday I hinted we take earlier this year but you were too busy with work to go.

There's so much about my life you are not aware of and I realise there is a great deal I want you to know . . . in fact, need you to know. I always thought there would be time to tell you – eventually – in the right way. Well, life has conspired against me, so I have concocted a plan that allows me to tell you all the things I want you to know, and show you all the places I want you to see, without actually being there with you. I also want you to scatter me as you go. I have fallen in love with the notion of having a little piece of me scattered in every place that has been significant in my life. I hope if I reveal my previous life to you in stages – if you walk in my footsteps, so to speak – then you might understand why I made some of the decisions I made, and why I kept you in the dark regarding my life before you were born.

Anyway, I'm afraid I must insist that you take

the next ten days off work. Being freelance, this shouldn't be a problem. Don't come up with some excuse about a 'tip off' or a celebrity wedding. I'm sorry to have added the caveat that the will cannot be finalised until you have carried out my wishes. It is blackmail of sorts I know, but I only do this as I'm certain it's the right thing for you to do now – more certain than I have been of anything. I could have called you back to Devon, sat you down at the kitchen table, and told you everything, but my mind is made up that this is the best course of action – for everyone.

I'm going to take you to places that will set your heart on fire, and hopefully rekindle your creative ardour in the process. You travel the world photographing famous people, living their peculiar lives with them, but what of your own life? I have worried for some time now that you are no longer seeing the beauty around you in this wonderful country of ours – if you took beautiful photos it would be different, but you don't. I ought to mention that you won't be travelling alone, that would be dreadful. To that end, I've asked a good friend of mine – Alasdair – to go with you. He's a Royal Marine and completely dependable. I should also add that I've been worried about him for some time, as I believe him to be on the brink of exhaustion. Put it this way, he needs a holiday more than you can possibly imagine, so please don't fob him off. I know you hate company to be forced on you but just this once, go with it. Oh, one last thing, while on your travels I wonder if you might placate me and perhaps rethink sharing your beautiful voice in some capacity. You have a wonderful gift, try not to waste it, love. Grimes will fill in the rest of the details. Be excited! I wish I was setting off on an adventure at thirty-one.

Well, where did the time go? Robin keeps staring at me from the bird table through the open window. I think he wants me to dig up some worms just as I have always done. It has just this second struck me as I gaze out into the garden that I will die in the autumn or winter; it would have broken my heart to have gone in the spring, just as new life begins once more. That's why I want you to scatter me in May, when I can be part of the newness of it all, one more time.

All my love,
Mum
X

I read the letter once more, and traced my fingers over the words 'Hello Grace' just as the first teardrop landed onto the paper. There was no doubting it was written in Mum's precise hand, and who else could nag so successfully from the grave?

In silent reverie I sat nursing the coffee – lukewarm by then – that Grimes had given me. Before reading

18

the letter, I had been determined to storm out of the office, hire another solicitor, and contest the will. But, reading her words made me believe she was there again, albeit for a fleeting second. Typical Mum; even in death she couldn't resist nagging.

Grimes reappeared and sat down at the desk. No doubt realising I needed to be rescued from my sorrowful inner monologue, he passed me a box of tissues and I managed to dab the rim of my lashes to stem the flow.

'So, Grace,' he said, 'what comes next is up to you. You know where you stand regarding the will and your mother's request. What are you going to do?'

Despite the clarity of the letter, I was unsure whether or not I should adhere to Mum's request. Did I really want to discover new things about her? Although I wanted to inherit my childhood home, I didn't particularly care about any money. But there was the matter of the ashes. No matter what, I couldn't refuse that request. It was her trump card, and I had to smile at the image of Mum as she thought up that little ruse. She was right about the tip-off though, I did have a lucrative shoot arranged for the following day.

I gazed around the tatty, ramshackle room, looked down at Terry (who seemed to shrug, as if to say, 'What have you got to lose?') and sighed.

'Give me your instructions, Mr Grimes. It looks like I'm going on a journey.'

CHAPTER 3

Nestled between an eleventh century church at the top of the lane and an ancient ford at the bottom, there stood a stone cottage. It had a slightly crooked front door framed by an open porch. Blue-tits nested in the porch eaves, content and undisturbed, as the door, swollen with the paintwork of many generations, was too stiff to open. Casement windows sat in perfect symmetry on either side of the doorway – just as a child would draw – and an exquisite flower border, heady with sweet aroma, was bedded down under the front windows. It was a cottage that sat so comfortably in its position – surrounded by rolling Devonshire hills, wild flower meadows and twinkling streams – only a flash of divine inspiration could have created it.

For half a millennium the cottage had taken on many guises. It had stood fast amid fertile soil in times of famine, provided a constant flow of water in times of drought, and a haven of peace in times of war. Whatever material changes that had been made to suit the needs of the various occupants, however, one facet remained the same – the name.

The house was called St Christopher's Cottage, named after the church that sat in protective vigil on the rise above it.

My mother moved to St Christopher's around the time I was born, and from the moment I had independent thought I knew she had chosen perfection.

Most of all I loved to play in the ford that sat twenty yards or so down the lane from the cottage. There was something so playful and adventurous about the ford. Mum squeezed flowers into every crevice of the garden. Flora and fauna had to battle it out at St Christopher's, bustling with and nudging at each other for a little extra shoulder room. Not even the tiniest car could be driven down to the cottage because the lane that led from the road to the house was too narrow and over-grown. A Devonshire hedgerow towered high above the lane on each side, the uppermost branches met like a gothic archway in the middle. Very few people were aware a house actually existed at that spot, which made the atmosphere at St Christopher's all the more idyllic.

Her cutting garden was phenomenal. We had bouquets of cut flowers in every windowsill from April to November. The garden had a wild feel but it was always beautiful, even in the depths of winter. Snowdrops were the first to raise their optimistic little shoots, of course. Then bluebells in the meadow, self-set aquilegia just about everywhere, and pots and pots of tulips appeared in April and early May. Mum grew many different varieties, but in terracotta pots rather than directly into the border. 'They do better in pots here,' she would say. I looked forward to when their little green heads appeared – waiting to be coloured in – and made an annual pilgrimage home to mark the occasion. We called it the Tulip Festival and decorated trestle tables with pretty tablecloths and draped bunting around the summer house. I knew that the Tulip Festival was Mum's way of ensuring I travelled home at least once in the year. Despite my adoration of St Christopher's, I had become so embroiled in my life in London that I barely returned to Devon, and if I could have been granted any wish after she was gone, it would have been to turn back the clock and travel home more often – I thought time would never run out.

Her favourite tree had been given pride of place in the garden. She had even made a seating area opposite in order to view the tree at its best. It was the only Latin name for a plant I could ever remember – *Cornus Controversa Variegata* – the wedding cake tree. So called because, as the years pass, it sends out fresh branches in tiers, hence, a wedding cake. Mum said she bought it when I was born to celebrate my birth, and so it was always known as Grace's tree. She said the tree was a symbol of my life. That – like the tree – my roots would always be firmly entrenched at St Christopher's. Mum loved planting trees. She planted a whole orchard shortly after arriving at the cottage, and over the years established a mini arboretum – she cherished those trees.

Mum was thirty when I was born and, despite being a single parent, she was easy-going and epitomised hippy chic. As a child I asked many questions about the identity of my father, but she was a closed book. Sometimes I wished she would just lie to me and make something up. But with no information forthcoming, I assumed I was the product of either a one-night stand, a bit of a fling or an affair with a married man. Whatever the case, my biological father wasn't around, so by the time I entered into adulthood and moved to London, the matter was closed for good. I asked questions about her family: where she was from? Where had she lived before I was born? But she only revealed that she was from Yorkshire, that there was 'no one left' in the family, and 'Please, Grace, just leave the subject alone'. And so Mum remained an enigma to me – a loving, beautiful, happy-go-lucky, yoga-loving, spiritual enigma, who provided a wonderful home that I cherished.

Mum set up a retreat at the cottage when I was a baby, converting the stables into basic but comfortable accommodation. She encouraged her guests to meditate in the meadow and paddle in the cleansing waters of the River Heddon as it meandered – late in its journey – through the pasture and her beautiful garden. It was impossible not to step into perfect harmony with the world at St Christopher's.

When I reached an age of understanding, Mum explained that, shortly after opening, she secured a contract with the Ministry of Defence. They had asked her to set aside a considerable number of weeks per year for military personnel, and so St Christopher's was a home to battle-weary soldiers.

The soldiers established a trendy commune around the old wooden stables. A veranda was built on the south side and planted with vines and fruit. The couple of acres of land surrounding the house were tended in such a way we were practically self-sufficient in terms of vegetables, fruit and poultry. Guests would enjoy helping out with the chores, which meant much welcomed free labour. In the endless summers of my childhood, visitors cooked on open fires and ate their meals al fresco while soulful tunes from an acoustic guitar gently filled the night air. I would lay in bed with my window open and hear them going about their quiet business, the faint sounds of their industry would lull me into a secure sleep – I always slept soundly at St Christopher's.

Individuals would come and go. Just as I got to know one of them, he or she would leave and might not return for a year or so, if ever. One particular individual came and never left – Jake. A retired soldier, he had been around at St Christopher's for as long as I could remember; it was his guitar I heard so often as a child. He and Mum were partners – lovers. To a certain extent she kept him at arm's length (Mum liked her own space) but there was no doubting how much he adored her.

On the 14th of November I received a phone call from Jake at my London flat urging me to hurry home to see my mother. She had been too weak to talk when I arrived, but she was aware that I was there. I leaned my head towards her, quietly sobbing into the chest that had become so frail so quickly. She gathered enough strength to smile at me – her familiar smile that said, 'I'm glad you are here, my love'. I loved my mother's smile because she smiled with her eyes as much as with her mouth. They were big brown eyes, surrounded by wrinkles that emerged across her tanned face like deep tracks. When she greeted me after any time spent apart she would hold my face in her hands and say, 'My beautiful, perfect child.'

I had known about the cancer for a year. I had intended to travel home monthly but work commitments always got in the way. Two months before she died I spent the weekend in Devon and, despite her efforts to be cheerful, she looked frail. When questioned, she explained her chemotherapy had started again, and it had knocked her back a little, but she would be fine, the prognosis was optimistic. If only she had told me the truth I would have travelled home more often and finished my job to care for her. I discovered from Jake that she had kept the real prognosis from me all along, the reason finally being explained to me in the details of her first letter of course.

Despite the agonising pain cancer can bring, she passed away in peace in her old wooden bed that had been moved into the garden room. Within a moment I had gone from having the subconscious contentment a child has – knowing a parent's love is available when needed – to the realisation that the warmth and security I felt knowing she was there – in her cottage or garden – was gone.

Within moments of her passing, I pushed open the stiff garden room doors and walked towards the end of the lawn to look back at the house. I didn't feel the icy grasp of the November night embrace me, I suppose I was numb. It was a beautiful evening. The house shone brightly in the moonlight and the sky was alight with a million twinkling diamonds. If she was on her way to heaven, I thought, she had chosen the perfect night to get there.

I felt a sudden chill and wrapped my arms around my shoulders to stop them shaking. Looking across the cutting garden towards the retreat I saw that Jake and some guests had established a night vigil around a campfire. He started towards me but, as he grew closer and returned my gaze, he realised she had gone. He ran into the garden room and I heard him exhale a moan of sheer grief as he lifted Mum's limp body into his arms and rocked her.

I wanted to run to Jake and take comfort in the

big old chest that had provided so much support over the years. Nuzzling into him was wonderful because he would listen to my stories and nod gently while I fretted over some teenage angst – but he would say absolutely nothing. The creases of his hands were ingrained with years of tending the land, and there was an aroma of pure earth about him that acted like a calming pheromone of sorts; anyone close to a person who tends the land would understand.

I walked back into the house and paused at the doorway, trying – and failing – to take in the scene. Jake lay Mum down, stepped towards me and tried to offer comfort, but despite the closeness we had built over the years, I felt betrayed and simply couldn't bring myself to fall into his open arms.

Instead, I sat on the edge of her bed and tuned into the music that had been playing quietly in the background to soothe her; I held her hand as my tears fell freely onto her skin as it turned cold. The track was one of her favourites, *Abide with Me*. Eerily, it was also one of the hymns she chose for her funeral, and I hoped as I held her hand that I would not live a life that facilitated the choosing of my own funeral accompaniment.

I stayed in Devon for a week. The guests at the retreat (I discovered Jake had taken over the running of the place once Mum's condition deteriorated) stayed on. They all knew Mum personally and rather than depart early, decided to stay for the funeral.

Although I knew it would hurt him a great deal, I still found it impossible to turn to Jake for comfort. The day after she died I directed all of my anger at being kept in the dark regarding Mum's condition at him. 'She was *my* mother,' I yelled, 'you should have told me earlier!' I simply could not understand why he had waited until she was almost gone to contact me. Jake tried to explain that Mum had been sitting up in the garden only the day before she died; that the sudden turn of her illness had taken them all by surprise.

After my initial tirade, the anger became exhausting. I calmed a little and eventually sat with Jake on his veranda and talked for a while. But it was stunted, factual talk – the banal detail of death.

Waiting for the funeral left me desolate and numb. Even the house seemed to be in mourning. Curtains hung like wilted flowers while family photographs seemed to be of faceless strangers. As I wandered aimlessly from room to room running my fingers over Mum's knickknacks, cushions and little treasured possessions, it was as though I was another person altogether, looking in, and watching the all-encompassing sadness from the outside. Nothing looked or felt the same now she was gone.

I kept to the garden.

Autumn was shifting down a gear into winter. I considered lifting the tender plants and over-wintering them in the greenhouse, but I hadn't the heart, there didn't seem to be much point. Even the weather, with only a gentle breeze and washed-out sunshine, seemed to be respectful of Mum's passing.

I remembered one of my childhood haunts – the ford, next to which there was a giant of an old oak tree that paddled its long toes in the stream. It had a perfect hollow at the base, plenty big enough for me to crawl into as a child. The beauty of the hollow was this: I could see anyone walking on the footpath down the lane from the house and over the ford, but they could not see me – it was perfect. Having stumbled upon a stash of children's books under the stairs, and having chosen a different one for each day, I returned to the tree, wrapped myself in a blanket and read – every day until the funeral. Not surprisingly, the hollow was a tighter fit, but I could still wriggle in there, just.

On the second day a man appeared on the footpath. I didn't recognise him but assumed he must be a newcomer to the retreat. He was a strange kind of fellow. His age was difficult to determine as his face was almost entirely obscured by a beard. He stopped by the ford and sauntered around the base of a nearby hornbeam, systematically picking up bits of old branch only to assess and then discard them. Eventually he found what he was searching for – a small coppiced branch, roughly four-foot long with a curve at one end and thin enough for the span of his hand to grasp around. He sat on the bridge that crossed the stream and seemed to enjoy the dappled sunlight twinkling in the water where he waggled the soles of his boots.

We would have been no more than ten feet apart, so I used all my powers of concentration to sit very still and avoid detection. He took a penknife out of his pocket and started to carve the wood: slowly, methodically, carefully.

And so I watched him work.

He lingered at the ford for an hour or so, working the wood, stopping to gaze into the stream and then starting on the wood once more.

He returned to the same spot at the same time on the next day – as I hoped he would – and then every day until the day of the funeral. I remained hidden, watching, fascinated. His eyes looked down as he carved so I could only catch the occasional glimpse of his face and eyes as he looked up at the flowing water. He had tired eyes, I could tell that much at least, and they were edged with sun-scorched lines. Every day he wore the same outfit. A cap masked the colour of his hair while clothing covered his legs and arms so I had no way of knowing if the skin was worn with age. His beard was an indistinctive blond/brown colour, with a little grey perhaps. Only his bare hands were visible. He was agile, there were no protruding veins and his skin was tight and fresh, so I thought he was, perhaps, a youngish man; had it not been for this fact, I would have assumed him to be older. As it was, I never did decide upon an age for him.

By the fourth and final day his creation was complete – a shepherd's crook. The curve of the handle took most of his time to carve but it was worth the effort. As he stood up to leave for the last time, I could have sworn he looked directly at me through a knot in the tree I always used as a spy hole. I was grateful he had inadvertently stumbled upon me that day in the glade. His quiet company brought me comfort during the worst week of my life. In the coming months I would often think of him and find the memory of him a calming influence – my old man o' the woods.

The church of St Christopher sat at the top of Mum's lane; the view up the hill from the side window in Mum's bedroom looked directly at the chancel. It was a comfort that the funeral service was quite literally on her doorstep, overlooking the garden in which she spent a great deal of her life. She had requested a cremation rather than a burial, which I found disappointing. After the service it felt somehow incomplete to be taking Mum away from the churchyard. Eventually, of course, I would come to understand why.

The only comfort I had was the knowledge that I could keep this little corner of England, and by doing so I would always have her near to me. Jake told me he would be staying on to run the retreat until the details of the will were finalised – it was what Mum had wanted. I asked for no more detail from him, which was unforgivable. I suppose I still wanted to punish him – someone – for my loss. Later I would understand that although my grief was a necessary emotion, it was also an utterly selfish one.

CHAPTER 4

Grimes' mood lightened once I confirmed my acceptance of Mum's mission. Terry was ambling across the desk once more. Unfamiliar as to how a person displayed affection to a tortoise, I gave his shell a tentative stroke.

'So who's this . . . *companion* I'm being forced to travel with?'

I sounded like a petulant schoolchild, but I did not need hours of forced conversation and polite behaviour with a stranger. It would be like being a prisoner at the hairdressers.

'Your mother felt—'

I stepped in.

'What *didn't* my mother feel? Isn't she manipulating me enough with all these'—I struggled to find the word—'shenanigans! I don't need a companion. I travel alone constantly. In fact,' I continued in a lighter note, hoping to get around him with a softer touch, 'I prefer to travel alone, no need for all that chat and forced politeness.'

His steady countenance was unswerving and I realised my objections were pointless. 'Sorry, go on.'

'You may recognise Alasdair. He's been to the

retreat a number of times. He's easy-going . . . in fact,' he added, smiling, 'I bet you'll hardly notice he's there. I agree with your mother that someone needs to go with you.'

I flashed him my best sarcastic glance. He responded with an equally forceful glare.

'If you travel alone then there'll be a temptation to read all of the letters in one go, skip a couple of locations and get back to work in three days. This is simply her way of ensuring that—'

'I know,' I interrupted yet again, 'this is her way of ensuring that the conditions of the will are met. Put it any way you like Mr Grimes, this Alasdair chap is there to provide proof of my cooperation. He's my guard and checker-upper. Mum's starting to appear in a different light to me already. Did she know Alasdair particularly well? I'm not sure I remember anyone with that name at St Christopher's.'

'He's been going there, on and off, for a few years I think. He became very close to your mother – and to Jake in fact.'

A pang of jealousy. My visits to St Christopher's had become more and more infrequent and it was galling to know that my mother had become close to people I had never heard of.

'The good news,' Grimes went on, 'is that Alasdair has made all of the travel and accommodation arrangements already. Rosamund dictated her requirements to him and paid for everything while she was still . . .'

He paused, stood, lifted the tortoise from the table and placed it onto the carpet. 'What I meant to say was, all you have to do is sit back and relax.'

Listening to his last words reminded me of the letter – enjoy it, see it as an adventure; but could I really do that? Could I really put my life into the hands of a perfect stranger for ten days?

Grimes was sure I would get into the flow of it fairly quickly, but when I offered to take the folder (I knew Mum's letters were in there – she had been absolutely right that I would jump ahead) he said, 'No need, I'll give the letters to Alasdair myself this afternoon. In fact, it's time to get out of this depressing old place and get you going; Alasdair's waiting for you at a café in town. I'll tell you where to meet him, you two can get to know each other a little, and then I'll pop by with your mum's letters and drive you to the airport.'

'Airport?'

He smiled. 'Alasdair will explain. Don't worry, everything will work out fine.'

'Well, it's not that easy,' I explained, 'I have to get some clothes together and arrange to put my car somewhere. I take it I don't need my car?'

'No need for all that. Give me your keys, tell me what car you have and where it is and I'll take it to St Christopher's for you. That's where your journey will end. And here'—he turned his back to me as he opened the under-stairs cupboard with a flourish—'are your clothes.'

The open door revealed a bulging suitcase and suit carrier.

'What's all this?'

'Your mother thought it would be nice for you to have some new clothes for your trip. So, she chose this little lot out for you. Hopefully, she chose the right size. She even got you a selection of shoes. I'll bring it all to you later.'

Grimes seemed genuinely pleased with my delight as I fingered excitedly through the carrier. Mum knew I never allowed myself enough time to shop for anything decent – all that rushing around in jeans and a T-shirt with my camera permanently attached to my belt. I shook my head amusedly and smiled at the tortoise; he gave me a final cheeky wink.

'Game, set and match I think. Well played, Terry!'

CHAPTER 5

It was around twelve o'clock when I finally stumbled onto the bustling high street. My eyes were forced to squint after the darkness of the office, so I delved to retrieve sunglasses from the depths of my work bag. I also grabbed my mobile phone. I had an interview-cum-photographic shoot planned for the following day that, thanks to Mum, I needed to cancel. This would not be an easy call. I started down the road towards my rendezvous point with Alasdair, and waited for a familiar voice to answer. Paul, a magazine journalist and close friend, had a tendency to answer the phone hands-free while driving and would immediately spill into a shouted conversation that was the verbal equivalent of machine gun fire – that day was no exception:

'Ah, blondie! I take it you're back from deepest Devon. I was worried you might have fallen into a giant cowpat, or gorged yourself to death on cream teas – I suppose there are worse ways to go. Okay if I kip at yours tonight, that way we can travel to the shoot together. I'll be round your place for about . . . seven? Chicken balti okay?'

'Yes, but I—'

'I'm just about to park, so I'll see you later, sweet cheeks.'

'Paul! Wait! Don't hang up. I need to tell you something . . .'

As expected, the rest of the conversation did not go down so well, and I had crossed two busy roads and completed half the length of Barnstaple High Street before I could take hold of the conversation. But, once I had assured Paul that he could easily get another photographer for the shoot (it was a peach of a job), and placated him with the offer of dinner on my return to London at a new swanky restaurant in Twickenham, he calmed down – a little bit.

'So, let me get this straight in my head,' he said, 'because I'm struggling to comprehend it.' I could imagine him gesticulating into the hands free while trying to park at the same time. 'Your dead mother has insisted you trip about the country with a complete stranger – and a man at that – just so you can inherit that house you're always banging on about? Absolute madness! Was your mother a complete fecking nutcase or what? Get your arse back to London and forget the whole thing. You've got a job to do and—'

I interrupted him, successfully for once.

'I don't need reminding how crazy the situation is. I can assure you that I'm blood-vessel-bursting annoyed as it is, so I could do without any extra hassle from you, okay?'

'Okay, whatever. But you need to kiss this bloke right off! He could be a well dodgy character for all you know. Why don't you just tell the solicitor to sod off? Bugger your inheritance.'

'I know, I know, but I *have* to do it. Not because of the money, but because of the ashes. I can't refuse to scatter her, think how *you* would feel if it was your mum. This . . . stuff, she wants me to know about her life, it must be pretty important. And also, I admit it, as fickle as it sounds, I want my bloody house. It's my home.'

He sighed down the phone. 'Fine. Whatever. It's your life. But just so you know, I wouldn't feel the same way about *my* mother. She wouldn't be sober long enough to write me any bloody letters! One final thing though . . .' He paused for breath.

'What's that?'

'Keep checking in with me every couple of days, just so I know you're okay.' His voice mellowed a little with this final suggestion.

I smiled at the phone. 'Don't worry, I'll text at the very least. You can be quite sweet when you want to, Paul.' I heard him harrumph down the phone. 'And don't worry about this Alasdair bloke, I'm just on my way to meet him now, and I bet he doesn't even want to come. I'll tell him that I'm happy to go alone.' I thought about Mum's letter. Did this man really need a holiday? And with me? Surely he would have other people he would rather go away with.

'Good girl! Dismiss the soldier from his duties,

then read the letters, scatter the ash, and get that sexy arse of yours back to London.' I was only vaguely listening by then.

'I'd better go, and listen, I'm truly sorry for letting you down at the last minute. I'll make it up to you, Paul, promise.'

'Oh, don't sweat it. Anyway, I'm sure I can think of a way for you to make it up to me . . . after we've finished at the new Thai place that is.' His voice became playful.

'I'm sure you can,' I laughed.

'I'll win you over one day. Haven't you heard of *The Tortoise and the Hare*?'

'Please don't tell me you're the tortoise in this scenario,' I said, pausing at a pedestrian crossing, 'because being slow on the uptake is one thing you could *never* be accused of.'

He laughed. 'Only when it comes to you, Grace.'

Grimes had told me to meet Alasdair at the Olive Tree Café. I hadn't required directions as I knew exactly where the café was. 'Our café' was Mum's venue of choice for my meeting with Alasdair, and it struck me that if she had wanted to put me through every emotion someone in mourning can endure, then she had certainly succeeded.

At the café I paused for a moment to remove my sunglasses and put a brush through my hair. With an overwhelming feeling of 'let's get this over with', I pushed the heavy glass door open and stepped into a bustling room.

I spotted Alasdair immediately – not because I recognised him from St Christopher's, but because a small billboard with 'Grace Buchanan' written across it was leaning against a chair. He hadn't noticed me arrive; he was engrossed in a book while making notes on a writing pad. His right foot was perched jauntily on his left knee and the book was being held a significant distance from his face. I thought *that one needs glasses*. A split second later another thought crossed my mind – *Oh Christ, he's gorgeous!*

My immediate reaction made no sense. Rather than behave as I usually would (maturely approach Alasdair and introduce myself) I flushed with panic and rushed to the counter. A waitress tried to catch my eye so I pretended to admire cakes stacked in a glass case. I bit my lip – trying to look as though I was still choosing – and fobbed her off on to another customer. The wall behind the counter was panelled with glass so I took the opportunity to size Alasdair up.

In his late thirties perhaps? Closely shaven, a broad chest (I supposed) and blond, bordering on mousy hair cropped short. His face was slightly tanned and my overriding first impression was that he had a kind look about him.

I stole a glance at myself through the mirror – I looked tired – and lifted my hands to smooth away lines above my cheeks, lines that had only appeared since Mum died. My hair hung unruly around my shoulders and my usual red flushed face had returned; it instantly appeared whenever I felt a trace of embarrassment.

I was about to confront him when the waitress appeared in front of me. What I really wanted was a glass of wine, but decided to keep a clear head. I opted for comfort food instead.

'I'll have the bread and butter pudding please, and tea – just normal tea though, nothing fancy.' My chosen dessert wasn't in the cabinet, but I had been to the café enough times to know it was the best pudding on the menu.

A strong voice with just a trace of a northern lilt breathed over my right shoulder.

'Make that two please, and could you put it on the tab for table seven? Hello Grace,' he continued cheerily, now meeting my gaze through the mirror. 'I believe you're looking for me?'

I turned on my heels, smiled, held out my hand and said, 'Hello.'

We returned to table seven and sat just for a moment in (fairly awkward) silence. I placed my hands under my legs to stop them fidgeting with the table mats.

The billboard with my name plastered across it rested against his chair; I nodded towards it and smiled.

'Don't know how you missed it,' he said with a laugh, but there was a twinkle in his eye and we both knew I hadn't – I flushed again.

'Well, I don't know about you,' he began, 'but

now this is really happening it feels a little bit . . . strange?' He scratched the back of his left ear while talking, his head slightly tilted to one side.

'Yes, I've had quite a morning,' I said, trying to find some semblance of normal conversation, my previous bravado during the call with Paul had diminished somewhat. 'I've only just found out about this whole . . .' I took a deep intake of breath, 'I'm not sure what to call it really. Trip of discovery?'

At that moment the waitress arrived. She looked to be about my age. As she placed the accoutrements on the table she flashed her best smile at Alasdair and leant over – in an exaggerated manner – to place the pudding in front of him. He afforded her a courteous smile, and moved his pile of books to one side to make room on the table, before she sashayed off.

'Shall I just tell you what I know and how I happen to be caught up in all of this?' he said. 'You must be wondering why on earth I'm here. Rosamund's request was a little, well, let's say . . . peculiar?'

'Yes, that would probably be a good idea. Do you mind if I eat while you're talking? I'm starving suddenly. I had a long drive down from London this morning.'

He gestured I should start eating, took a quick sip of tea, leaned forward in his seat and began.

'I've been passing through the retreat for about three years now, on and off. I've got to know Jake,' he paused, 'and your mum was a really good friend. I was there last April and they invited me back for a couple of days in July, that's when they told me their terrible news.'

I felt my expression harden. How could Mum have told this man about her prognosis and not me?

'I know she chose not to tell you about the severity of her illness and if it's any consolation, we both – Jake and I that is – tried to talk her out of it, but she was adamant. She asked me to make myself available for the last two weeks in May so I could go with you on the trip. I said no to her at first, thinking the whole thing was unfair on you, but she could be so . . . persuasive?'

I realised it was the perfect opportunity to explain he need not accompany me on the trip. I put my spoon down.

'It's funny you should say that,' I began, 'because—'

'But after about an hour of toing and froing,' he continued, seemingly oblivious to my attempt to interrupt, 'I agreed to go, obviously. But I've spent the past six months wondering if I should have said no. Anyway,' he sighed, 'to cut a long story short, here I am. And now I'm here, I'm really looking forward to it. I could do with a holiday.'

He smiled cheerily – contagiously – and picked up his spoon.

'Sorry, Grace, you were about to say something?'

43

'Was I?' I lied.

Christ, this was going to be difficult.

'My mind's gone completely blank. You must have thought she'd gone barking mad when she told you her plan.'

'Tell me about it,' he scoffed, 'even my anti-shock watch was surprised!' I laughed, and he added, 'I understand she wants you to discover a little more about the life she led before you were born.'

I nodded.

'Apparently so. But goodness knows what I'm going to find out. This is Mum we're talking about so who knows what she got up to . . . lap dancing? Lion taming? Nothing would surprise me.'

'Well, yes, quite. Anyway, all the travel details are taken care of.' He paused for a second, clearly trying to find the right words. 'Look, I want to say straight off that, although I know Rosamund has written some letters to you and I have a vague inkling regarding the details – locations and so on – I haven't read them. It's just none of my business and I don't want you to think I'm interfering. All I know is that I'm simply to take you from A to B and deliver you back to Devon on the 31st of May in one piece – why are you smiling?' I had just taken a mouthful of pudding, which I swallowed quickly.

'The 31st of May was Mum's official birthday. She chose that date because she said it's always a beautiful day in England on the 31st of May.'

He laughed. 'Official birthday?'

'Mum's real birthday was on the 3rd of January and she hated it. She said it was the most depressing day in the whole year. Everyone unhappy to be going back to work, the rest of the winter ahead, dark nights . . .' He knew where I was going so he finished the sentence for me.

'So she came up with a second birthday for her official celebration, just like the Queen.'

'Yes, just like the Queen,' I said in a more reflective manner than intended. Pulling myself back to the present, I realised it was time to focus all my efforts into ignoring the fact that Alasdair had the most captivating blue eyes I had ever seen, and 'dismiss him from his duties' as Paul had said.

'Listen, I've been thinking. It was wrong of Mum to ask you to give up your holidays just to travel with me. I can easily do this journey on my own. You must have better things to do with your time. Family to see, maybe? More exciting places to go? If you just give me all the details, I'll be happy to carry on by myself.'

I flashed him my best smile. Immune, he frowned and rubbed his chin.

'Hmm, I thought you might say that.' He leant forward again. 'You should know that I owe a great deal to your mother, she was very good to me during my time at the retreat. And regarding your concerns about taking up my leave entitlement, at the moment I'm on a short sabbatical – Rosamund's suggestion – and I've had a holiday at my house in Snowdonia, and done most of the things I

45

needed to do. I know the thought of spending the next ten days with me must seem, well, odd to say the least, but it's what your mother wanted. Please remember that I promised a dying woman I would accompany her daughter on a journey that seemed vital to her, and I *really* don't want to break that promise. So, as bizarre as it is, let's just go with it. What do you say?'

How on earth was I supposed to get rid of him after that? Some pudding fell off the spoon I had been balancing absently over my dish. Trying to think of a response, I moved the pudding around the dish and tried to decide what to do for the best.

Would it really be so bad to travel around the country for a few days with this amiable and attractive (although clearly not the deciding factor) marine?

Suddenly animated, he beamed his brightest smile, sat upright and began to delve into a pocket.

'I know!' he exclaimed, 'I'll show you my military ID, so you know I'm exactly who I say I am?'

I began to feel sorry for him and raised my hand. 'No no – you're a friend of Mum's after all. It's fine.'

He removed his hand from his pocket.

'So, we'll stick together then?' he asked, his expression the epitome of optimistic innocence, 'because I've already planned the whole thing, and I've really been looking forward to seeing some of the places we're going to; they're all great loca-tions, I'm sure you'll love it . . .' His enthusiasm was contagious.

'Okay, fine. We'll go together.'

He smiled a broad sexy smile, looked decidedly pleased with himself and changed the subject, which is when I realised the man had known all along he'd talk me round. I couldn't help but smile.

'And a couple of these,' he said brightly, gathering the books from the table and packing them into a small rucksack, 'are tourist books for the places we're going to visit.'

I leant forward. 'Oh, can I see them? Grimes didn't actually say where we're going.'

'No, no, no. I'm the book holder and each destination is to be revealed only as we move from place to place. Rosamund was particularly firm about that.'

'Seriously?'

'Seriously.' He flashed me a cheeky wink. 'I'll tell you more later, once we've landed and feel like the journey's got going. We're booked on Flybe 109 to Leeds from Exeter. It departs at four o'clock. I was told you would have your passport with you. Please, *please* tell me that's correct!'

I nodded; I couldn't say no, Grimes had seen it, the conniving toad!

'Bob Grimes will be here soon to give me all of the paperwork and drive us to the airport.' I got the gist of why we were flying to Leeds.

'Would I be correct if I guessed Mum was taking me back to her northern roots?'

'I believe that would be a correct assumption, yes.'

I had to smile. He was trying so hard to make this crazy situation work – make me happy and follow Mum's wishes. It was easy to see why she had singled him out to be my companion. I returned to the bread and butter pudding while he gestured to the waitress and asked for some fresh water for the teapots and two clean cups.

'I don't know about you,' he said, 'but I have to have a fresh, hot cuppa with my pudding. All my jabbering has made the last one go cold.'

Whoever this man was, we were certainly on the same wavelength, and although my plan to travel alone had somehow been scuppered before it ventured past the blueprint stage, I had the vaguest of inclinations that this journey might prove to be worthwhile after all.

PART II

THE YORKSHIRE DALES, ENGLAND

22–24 MAY

CHAPTER 6

The flight to Leeds was short – fifty minutes at the most. When the aircraft pushed back from the stand, the steward ended his safety brief by reminding all passengers to switch off their mobile phones. Alasdair tilted his head towards mine but kept his gaze towards the front of the aircraft. 'There is one minor detail I haven't told you yet,' he said.

'Go on.'

He nodded towards the phone in my hand.

'Your mum wanted you to leave your phone turned off for the duration of the trip.'

My head whipped through ninety degrees to look at him directly.

'Why?'

'No distractions.'

I considered this request for a second . . . or maybe even two.

'The answer to that would be no, absolutely not.' I jostled in my seat. 'Turn off my phone? No way, I need it for work. I answer my emails from it. I've gone along with everything else, but no, no way.'

'Hmm,' he muttered. His thumb and forefinger stroked the lobe of his ear. 'Well, how about if we *both* keep our phones turned off, and just check for messages at the end of each day. That's a fair compromise surely?'

'I don't need a compromise, thank you.' I lowered my head to glance through the aircraft window.

'Fair enough,' he said – *that was easier than expected* – 'although to be fair, Rosamund said . . .' He shook his head, 'no, it doesn't matter . . .'

'What? What did Mum say?'

He sat back and sighed.

'She said you would find it difficult to live without your phone, that it was permanently glued to your hand.' I glanced down to the phone in my hand and quickly stuffed it back into my bag under the seat in front of me.

At that moment the pilot powered up the engines and the aircraft began to roar down the runway. Too late to back out now.

When the steward began the drinks service, Alasdair delved into his rucksack and handed me another letter from Mum. I expected a couple of pages of prose, but she had written very little:

Grace.
Time to start living life, not watching it.
Mum
xxx

I looked up from the note – bemused and a little annoyed. 'What exactly has Mum got planned Alasdair? Should I be worried?'

A wry smile emerged across Alasdair's face. 'Worried? Never. Excited? Yes.'

I lowered my head to look down on the British landscape below. 'Excited about spending some time out in Britain? I'm yet to be convinced.'

A young man holding the keys to a shiny Range Rover waited for us outside the airport terminal. It was Alasdair's turn to have his name splashed across a billboard and I realised I hadn't even asked his surname. It was Finn.

After about half an hour we turned down the slip road that led onto the A1. I relaxed a little.

'Is that where Mum's from then, the Dales?' It was odd to be asking a stranger details about my own mother's life.

'Yes.' He offered no more information.

'Oh, sorry, I forgot. You must follow your orders and keep me in suspense.' Alasdair took his eyes off the road to flash me a reassuring smile.

'As I said to you in the café, Rosamund gave me limited information. What I can tell you is tonight we're staying at the Wensleydale Heifer – your mum's choice – and then in the morning I'll take you to your first port of call; it's somewhere nearby. I would imagine the next letter will explain all she wants you to know.'

'And when do I get the letter?'

'At the first port of call.'

'And how do you know where this first port – as you refer to it – is?'

'Because I wrote Rosamund's instructions down in a notebook.'

I fell silent to give him a break from the questions – for a few seconds at least.

'You must admit that this is more than a little bizarre though,' I said, more to myself than to Alasdair, while gazing blankly at the passing countryside.

'What is? What's bizarre?'

'Well, you're a complete stranger to me but I'm asking you questions about my own mother. You seem to know more about her than I do.'

He shrugged and smiled.

'I tell you what,' I said, 'I'm going to try my hardest to just follow you around, ask nothing, and then wait for you to shepherd me to some place significant.'

'Really?' he asked, stealing a glance.

I turned to scrutinise him as he was driving. Paul's comment that Alasdair could turn out to be a dodgy character crossed my mind. I smiled inwardly.

'The thing is,' I said, trying to keep the smile out of my voice, 'I keep telling myself to enjoy the trip, but then I start to panic. I mean, a strange man is driving me about in the middle of the frozen north.' I gestured towards the landscape and he laughed again. 'You could be an axe murderer or anything. But, my mother seems to think this is a perfectly reasonable thing to do, so who am I to do anything but just go with the flow.' I gestured with my arm in a casual flowing motion.

'Typical, that is.' He flashed me a scolding glare.

'What?'

'How come I – the man – am automatically tarnished with being the murderer? For all I know, this could all be a weird set up between you and your mum. You could be intending to drug me, chop me up into bits and feed me to the pigs.'

'Well, firstly,' I retorted with an unfeminine snort, 'as *if*. And secondly, pigs?'

'Best way to dispense of a body apparently. They eat the lot.'

He was clearly an expert.

'And how in God's name do you know that little snippet?'

'Saw it in a film.'

'Oh, it must be true then.'

'We're off at the next junction. Through Bedale, into Wensleydale and then we're there.' He glanced upwards through the windscreen to look at the clouds. 'I checked the forecast this morning. It's going to be sunny tomorrow.'

He was obviously in the need of a little tour operator boost, so I assured him that I could see it was a beautiful landscape – behind the mist, the drizzle and field after field of miserable-looking sheep.

By seven thirty we entered a sleepy village called

West Witton. The car tyres scrunched over a gravel drive and we came to a halt in the car park behind the hotel – a seventeenth century inn, according to the sign. The stonework on the outside of the building was freshly whitewashed and the windows – tiny lead mullions – had a lamp positioned on each of the sills.

We left the luggage in the car and dashed through the – by then – torrential rain, and fell into the hotel through a rear door. The hotel was heady with the scent of burning oak but the effect wasn't overpowering, just welcoming and atmospheric. We followed voices down a passageway and found an intimate, candle-lit bistro. A middle-aged lady with the look of a farmer's wife about her backed through the kitchen door and entered the bistro carrying a tray. She spotted us loitering in the doorway and, after serving a couple their dinner, shooed us back to the reception area to register.

'Mr Finn is it?' she asked with a broad smile; she didn't wait for a reply but bustled breathlessly behind the desk.

'Two nights, two rooms, dinner and breakfast.' A matter of fact statement as she opened the large leather-bound bookings ledger.

Alasdair took the lead and completed the registration form for both of us. I stood behind him like a nervous honeymooner. The lady – June – was completely amiable and not a little bit wink-wink, nudge-nudge. No doubt it was the intimacy of the hotel and the loved-up couple in the bistro that made the atmosphere romantic, and me a little uncomfortable.

We followed June up a tight staircase and waited while she unlocked the doors to adjacent rooms, then stood awkwardly in our respective doorways as she edged her way back down the stairs. Stopping abruptly, she looked back up the staircase and said, 'Nearly forgot; you two still want dinner in your rooms then?'

'Oh, yes please.' Alasdair turned towards me to explain.

'I phoned ahead yesterday to say what time to expect us. I thought you would probably have had enough of me by now.'

'Fine, perfect. I'm really quite tired.' I nodded my approval.

'I'll just pop to the car and get the bags.'

Alasdair was right to suggest we part company for the evening. After dinner I felt weary and flopped backwards onto the bouncy double bed. It had been such a peculiar day.

Just twenty-four hours before, I had been at home in London preparing for my trip to Barnstaple and then, somehow, I found myself cajoled a few hundred miles north to what I presumed to be my dead mother's childhood home – crazy. But, it was turning into quite an adventure already and I had to admit that, despite my reticence, I was enjoying the company and the time away.

I had been pushing myself too hard. In the past

month I had chased from one photo shoot to another, so it was nice to relax and let someone else do the thinking for once. Had Mum known a break was what I needed? Some time away from the madness of my photographic work?

Then there was Alasdair.

Grimes was right, Alasdair was easy company. He had an air of authority about him but in an unassuming way. His manner was such that it was impossible not to warm to him – airport staff, the airline steward, car hire fellow and now June – they all accommodated his wishes with a smile. Although I had been in his company for no more than a few hours, I felt he was the sort of man one could become stranded with in the middle of the Sahara Desert and within twelve hours he would have arranged camels, a Bedouin tent, rations and a little man with a fan.

I grabbed my bag to find my phone (despite my argument to the contrary, I had completely forgotten to turn it on), ignored the plethora of texts and missed calls, and sent a text message to Paul.

Everything fine. In Yorkshire Dales of all places! The marine came after all ;-)

The phone rang within seconds.

'I knew it! You're useless, Grace. He'd better not be good-looking.'

Err . . .

58

'Actually, he's good fun, you'd like him. I suppose he's not *bad* looking, in a rugged kind of a way. I'm having a good time, surprisingly.'

Paul sighed.

'Just hold on there a minute, tiger! Good fun you say? Need I remind you that, just a few hours ago, you were moaning like a stuck pig about the whole damn shooting match, and now you say you're having a good time after all – you're so bloody fickle! Just answer me this, though. Soldier Boy's rugged. Does that mean he's got more muscles than me?'

I laughed.

'*Everyone's* got more muscles than you, even me. But okay, yes, he's got a fit body. I'm trying not to look though.'

'God, I hate him. Is he married?'

'No idea.'

'Ask him.'

'No way!'

'He probably wouldn't tell you anyway,' he quipped. 'A man like that'll have a woman in every port. And if he starts telling you about the time he caught a bullet between his teeth when he liberated a small nation, and then pulled shrapnel out of his arm and then sewed up the wound with barbed wire, just tell him to sod off.'

'Why don't *you* sod off!'

He laughed down the phone.

'Bye, sweet cheeks. And don't forget, tortoise and the hare! I'll get you in the end.'

I laughed again. 'As sweet as your relentless advances towards me are, it will *never* happen. I've known you for what – four years? Go find yourself a nice pole dancer.'

'Would that be a Pole who can dance, or a woman who dances round a pole?'

'Either. London has both. Bye for now, loser.'

I turned the phone off (of course I could live without it for a few days for goodness' sake) and drummed my fingers on the bedside table. My eyes fell on the suitcase Mum had prepared. Although she usually dressed in a fairly bohemian style, Mum had impeccable taste and would try to encourage me to 'do more with my hair' as she tried to scoop it up into a fancy up-do, or she might say, 'Why don't we go shopping for something lovely?' – actually meaning, why are you dressed 24/7 like a boy?

A note sat on the top of the clothes:

Enjoy! You are a stunningly beautiful woman. Perhaps you could just make more of an effort with your clothes?

Typical.

I rose from the bed and took her letter from my bag. Oh Mum, I wondered, what was this really all about?

CHAPTER 7

I woke with a start from a knock at the door and it took some moments to remember where I was. I shouted out but no one answered, then reached across to turn on the bedside lamp. It was eight o'clock – eight o'clock in the morning! A piece of paper had been pushed under the door – it was a note from Alasdair:

See you downstairs. Breakfast is until ten – no rush. You will need your walking clothes on today. Bring your boots down and I'll wax them up for you, it's probably quite wet on the hill. A lovely day though (just as promised). Al

Surprised by my own excitement, I flung back the curtains and raised the blinds to observe the day – deep blue sky. I smiled at the thought of how pleased Alasdair would be that the weather had improved.

With my cracked leather walking boots hanging from my hand by the laces, I padded down the stairs and hoped to bump into Alasdair, but was ushered into one of the snugs by June and fed a full, artery clogging Yorkshire breakfast in front of the fire. Once finished, a slab of black pudding was all that remained on my plate (not my cup of tea at any time let alone at breakfast), so I slipped it under the table to the resident Jack Russell who was waiting patiently by my feet for a taster.

June returned with a fresh pot of tea so I asked (trying to be nonchalant) if she knew the whereabouts of Alasdair.

'He was up at the crack of dawn – sitting just where you are now – and going through his maps and books when I opened up at seven. And he'd already been for a run at that.'

She lingered at the doorway, my breakfast plate in one hand, tea towel in the other, and looked on at me kindly, but quizzically.

'You two just friends then?'

The separate rooms were a bit of a giveaway.

I nodded.

'Such a lovely chap. Nice eyes – a bit of spice in that one I reckon. I have a thing for the quiet smouldering look.' She winked and began to walk away. Alasdair appeared around the door, bumping into June as she left, which made us titter all the harder.

He took a seat opposite me and removed a small tin from the top pocket of his rucksack, before picking up my walking boots and rubbing wax into the creases of the leather.

'So, what's on the agenda today then?'

'Well, first of all, we're taking a walk up Penhill. No need for the car, we can set off from here. When we get to the top I'll give you your next letter.'

'Oh, I don't mind a good walk,' I said. 'And second of all?'

He glanced up from rubbing wax into my boots; the man was all innocence.

'Second of all?' he asked.

'You started your first sentence with first of all, which would imply that there's a second of all, or else why say it?'

He lowered his head and looked at me through his eyelashes.

'Rosamund never said you were pedantic.'

'Hmm,' I narrowed my eyes, 'you're side-stepping. Come on, what's the second of all?'

He handed me the boots and grinned. 'It's a surprise.'

We agreed to rendezvous ten minutes later in the front foyer.

'Pass that here if you like,' he said, looking at my camera as we crossed the road. 'It looks heavy, I'll put it in the rucksack for you.'

I instinctively rushed a protective hand to cover my camera; my precious and very expensive appendage that had become a constant presence in my life.

'No, thanks. I like to have it with me. The shots are more spontaneous that way.'

★   ★   ★

We followed a tarmac lane lined with cottages. The residents seemed to be in cahoots to win a Britain in Bloom prize. The result, particularly in the morning sunshine, was very pretty indeed.

As the road gained in height it narrowed slightly, and our view of the Dale opened out to the north. A horse was whinnying as it was put through its paces in an outdoor arena. The predominant noise reverberating across the Dale, however, was not the whinnying of horses, but the ever-present sound of bleating sheep – like a comforting white noise in the background.

I was suddenly overcome by an aroma I easily recognised. The woodland to our left was carpeted with the little white flowers of wild garlic.

'I love the smell of wild garlic,' I said, 'it reminds me of home. There's a large patch of it just beyond our ford.'

Alasdair hopped effortlessly over the tall post and rail fence that separated the road from the wood and grabbed a handful.

'You probably aren't supposed to pick these, being wild,' he said, pulling a mock guilty expression, 'but I have a feeling you might want to have them with you when we get to the top.'

Remembering Mum's wish for me to scatter her ashes in places significant to her, it dawned on me what the flowers were for – a sharp reminder that we weren't just out for a morning stroll. I placed the flowers as carefully as possible in the pocket of my shirt.

'Is this where Mum wanted her ashes scattered then, at the top of Penhill?'

'Some of them, yes.'

I sobered, somewhat.

'And I have to do this . . . how many times?'

'Three.'

Alasdair's expression was so deadpan, I couldn't help but burst into spontaneous laughter.

'What?' he asked, also laughing. 'At least you didn't have to divide them up into three different containers.'

'What?'

'I didn't want to carry all of the ashes with us to each place in one big pot and then get to the last destination and find we hadn't got any left.' Alasdair acted out the scenario by pretending to shake out a container, look into it despairingly and then shake the empty pretend container above his head.

'Didn't the ash go all over the place when you were measuring it out?'

'You would not believe the trauma of it. All I will say is that it involved a mask, a funnel and quite a bit of booze.'

'Oh, Alasdair!'

After about a quarter of a mile, the path – no longer tarmac but a mixture of gravel, earth and grass – opened out and was edged with an endless line of chest-high stone walls. To our left, Penhill climbed into the skyline, and we stopped to take in the view. The hill reminded me of a scaled-down version of Table Mountain in Cape Town; rising symmetrically at each side with a long, flat edge on the top. The last two hundred feet looked to be a sheer face of craggy shale, while the hillside was divided by mile after mile of limestone walls laid out like a patchwork blanket. We were setting a fast pace so I thought we would probably arrive at the top in about thirty minutes or so.

'Only about an hour to the top,' he announced.

I tapped his arm in mock anger.

'What? I'm not that unfit.'

We stopped for him to show me the map. The image of the hill from where we were standing was, in fact, an optical illusion. Two completely flat plateaus, positioned periodically up the side of the hill, were hidden from view.

'That's so misleading,' I said, scrutinising the route. I also noticed we seemed to be taking a rather convoluted path.

'Why didn't we go straight up?' I placed a finger on the map and traced an imaginary line from the hotel to the top of the hill.

'Because there isn't a direct path from that direction, and even if there was, it would be daft to take it. More often than not, by contouring up a hill, you can keep a good, steady pace rather than stopping and starting all of the time up a steep face, which is why this path has been used for centuries I suppose.'

I rested my eyes on my feet as we trudged on

– I tried to step clear of the sheep dung but there really was no point.

'I still can't believe I'm half the way up a bloody hill you know'—I paused for breath for a second—'with a man I know nothing about.'

He laughed out loud while I continued with my methodical stride up the hill. The gradient had increased somewhat.

'Sorry,' I said, breathless. 'Can't talk for a minute. I need my breath for this steep bit . . . not as fit as I thought.'

'Are you having a good time?' The eagerness in his face for me to answer positively was plain to see.

I glanced back and smiled. 'Yes, of course. This is just what I needed.'

He nodded in agreement.

'Me too.'

Just under an hour later, the path zigzagged for a final few hundred yards and we strode out on to the top of the hill. A tundra of heather moorland stretched out ahead of us. Alasdair tapped me on the shoulder and pointed to the north. I turned around. My face felt tight against the strong westerly breeze. Candy floss clouds crossed from left to right, while the vibrant greens of the fields in the valley below changed to muted shades as the clouds took turns to momentarily shade the fields from the sun. There was so much detail in the vista a soul could sit there every day for a lifetime and notice something different each time.

But, the situation had to be faced; after all, I was there for a particular reason. I looked at Alasdair and raised my eyes to say, *is this the moment you give me my letter?*

He suggested we take a seat ten feet or so back down the hill out of the wind, took off his rucksack, removed our coats that had been purposefully placed on the top, and laid them out on the deep, damp heather. He passed me his fleece again.

'It's easy to chill down in the breeze, even in May,' he said. 'You ought to put this around your shoulders.'

'What about you? I can easily put my coat on instead of sitting on it.' I tried to insist but soon gave up. He draped the fleece around my shoulders.

We sat side by side taking in the view across the valley. Perhaps delaying the inevitable, Alasdair pointed out features of interest across the Dale.

After five minutes I looked across at Alasdair and said, 'It's okay, you can give me the letter now. I'm ready.'

He handed me two envelopes. One said, 'Open me first,' and so I did.

CHAPTER 8

Penhill

Hello, My Love

I can imagine you enjoying a clear and bright spring day. The sky will be a hazy light blue and there will be a slight breeze down in the Dale, but at the top of the hill the wind will blow slightly stronger – am I right? I do hope so. It's impossible to guess how often I have sat exactly where you are now, at the top of the zigzag path, above the crags.

As I told you, my parents were sheep farmers from Yorkshire. They scraped a decent enough living at Bridge Farm, which is situated on the outskirts of a village called West Burton. You can't see the farm from where you're sitting as it's over the moor to the west of the hill. It's a beautiful place, Grace, particularly in the spring. Mum would plant up pots of tulips for a spectacular spring display, and her immaculate roses always won 'best in show' at the village hall – I wish I'd paid more attention to how she managed to obliterate black spot! It all sounds idyllic perhaps, but I can tell you the reality of sheep farming is not all duck ponds and fresh bread. My parents were hard working and tough – you had to be tough to make it through a Dales' winter in those days. Back then, any offspring from farming stock were unlikely to have a proper childhood, well, not one you would associate with. Children were put to work, in some capacity or another, as soon as they were old enough to be useful. Our situation was no different except my parents were not fortunate enough to have a son to share the chores, they had two girls instead. Yes, you have an aunt, she's called Annie, and according to Grimes she still lives at the farm.

After Annie was born my parents tried desperately for another child, but no baby came. Then, out of the blue years later, yours truly happened along. My sister is eight years my senior and there is no question that she had, in the early years at least, a much harder life. She was more like hired help than Mum's daughter while I, on the other hand, was the pretty little child with golden hair. I was encouraged to take my studies seriously while Annie was expected to devote her time to running the farm. I had pretty clothes and a dolls house but I don't believe Annie had any of that. Needless to say, Annie and I were never close, and it's no exaggeration to say that over the years she grew to despise me.

I would try to get into her good books, follow her around, try to help, but she had absolutely no interest in me. It sounds as though she wasn't loved, but nothing could be further from the truth. What I'm trying to say is she had different expectations placed upon her.

And then there was this boy, Ted. He was the eldest son from a neighbouring farm. Ted and Annie were inseparable during their early teens, always out and about with the dogs, or fixing tractors – Annie was such a tomboy. I confess I was always a little jealous of their friendship. On my sixteenth birthday I had a party at home. I made a special effort to look glamorous – older. What with my party dress and a little makeup, I suppose it was the first time anyone had noticed me as a young adult rather than a child. Annie had invited Ted. I noticed him look twice in my direction when he arrived at the party, so I flirted with him a little that evening – more than a little in fact – but he never really took his eyes off Annie. Every time he tried to move away from me I found another reason for him to stay. I knew how it looked, the little sod that I was. When the party was over Annie grabbed me by the arm and pulled me into the front room. She was hysterical and started to sob. 'Why must you always ruin everything for me?' she asked. 'Don't you already have everything you could ever want? Why can't you just leave Ted alone?' I tried to explain that I hadn't thought I was doing anything wrong, that I thought Annie saw Ted as a brother – she knew I was lying. She knew I had gone out of my way to flirt with him. The truth was I wasn't remotely interested in Ted. All I wanted was Annie's attention. It was a stupid, childish thing to do, but I suppose that was the point, I was only a child.

Anyway, the damn stupid folly was a major miscalculation on my part. In my quest for Annie's attention I failed to consider her unforgiving nature – not just towards me, but Ted too. She felt betrayed, even though it wasn't his fault. As a result, despite years of inseparable friendship, she cast him off. He tried to make her see sense, but she wouldn't listen. Mum told me later that Annie had expected Ted to propose at my party. I was devastated. Why had no one told me, or pulled me to one side? Ted eventually gave up on Annie and married a woman from Leyburn. My foolish prank cost Annie a great deal, although her bloody-minded attitude didn't exactly help.

In the months after the party I would take myself off for long walks, just to keep away from the house – which is why I spent so much time sitting where you are now, trying to hold a school book down in the wind, or, in the summer, stretched out across the heather reading a romantic novel. It's also where I dreamed up my future life away from the farm.

Royal Air Force aircraft flew up and down Wensleydale quite often in those days, they probably still do. I would lie on the heather and watch the aircraft whistle past in the valley below or gaze at them practising aerobatics. I fell head over heels in love with the idea of joining the RAF, imagined myself walking around an air station in my glamorous uniform. I even practised saluting. On one particular day I made up my mind to join, tripped down the hill and announced my intention to the family. Annie just scoffed, but Mum and Dad were surprisingly encouraging. And so, I stayed on at school to gain the qualifications required to join directly as an officer.

There is no denying the fact that my decision to leave home was based, in part, on Annie's untiring wrath in the aftermath of the party, but I also wanted to leave her the farm. I knew the day would come when Mum and Dad would no longer be able to run things, and two sisters inheriting one farm would never work. One of us had to go and it seemed right that I should be the one – I think they secretly felt this too. I was no martyr though. I had much more of a sense of a world beyond the Dales than Annie. I found living in such a remote farming community terribly claustrophobic;

everyone knew everyone else's business and Yorkshire folk can be brutishly frank to a daydreaming teenager like me.

I trotted off to the RAF in the April that followed my twenty-first birthday. Mum and Dad sobbed as I stepped onto the train at Northallerton Station. Annie chose not to see me off and stayed at the farm. Although I would pop back to see them from time to time, I didn't go home as often as I should have because I became completely absorbed in RAF life.

Tragically, nine years after I left, my father died of a heart attack. It was shearing time and he'd been halfway up the Dale with Annie when it happened. He was only sixty-three . . . my goodness, around the age I am now. I was on leave in a village called Arisaig on the west coast of Scotland when it happened. The news didn't reach me until the day of his funeral; obviously it was too late to get back.

I rushed home as soon as I could to find Mum sitting in Dad's chair by the stove in the kitchen – a silent wreck. And, as for Annie, she threw years of jealousy and bitterness at me almost the second I walked through the door. Mum begged her to stop but I let her have her say – she needed to get it out. I said nothing (once words are spoken they can never be taken back) and I left the same day.

We weren't aware at the time but Mum was

also suffering from a heart condition and she passed away three years later. I made it back for the funeral this time. Annie decided to turn her fury into silent treatment, and once again I left immediately afterwards. I have never been back to Wensleydale and I have never seen or spoken to my sister since.

I could write reams about the whole sorry saga, but all you really need to know is that I had loving parents who failed to appreciate the consequences of the way they treated their offspring. I lived on a farm and I had a sister who, despite everything, I loved.

However, the main reason I sent you to the Dales is because as a child I firmly believed that Penhill was my very own mountain. I would grow terribly cross when hikers appeared over the brow, breathing my air and taking in my view. I was honed out of the very limestone that makes up the valleys, hills, caves and moorland that is all around you. The Yorkshire landscape shaped me as a person – it was my foundation.

As you look down into the Dale remember your grandfather fished in the River Ure (whenever he had the time), your grand-mother travelled by bus up to Leyburn every Wednesday and your aunt was a shepherdess who walked a million miles over the farm's two hundred acres with her beloved dogs by her side. And as for me? Well, I lived my youth running up and down Penhill, dreaming of another life, in another place.

I would give anything to be a young woman once more – to sit where you are now – to stand at the highest point of the hill, close my eyes and just let the breeze roll over me. In the summer I would sometimes run up the hill after dinner and sit waiting for the sun to set. I do love Penhill so very much, which is why I believe that a little part of me still belongs there.

Enjoy every moment, my darling.

Mum

PS As you travel around the country have a good look at the sky; it's a different kind of blue wherever you go. I'm sorry I never showed you this in person. Oh, and if you see Annie, ask her to show you my tree. Dad planted it for me when I left home; I think it was his way of saying thank you . . . for giving Annie the farm.

PPS You can open the second letter now.

A little bemused, I looked up at the sky, then turned to Alasdair who had perched himself on a boulder a little way up the hill. He mouthed 'Okay?' I nodded and opened letter number two.

A little bit about Alasdair Finn

You must be wondering why I asked Alasdair to travel with you.

As you know, some of the soldiers who go to St Christopher's suffer from combat stress. I have tried to help them all, but have always appreciated the need to remain detached – Alasdair was different. His first visit to the retreat was not for himself. He brought a friend called Alex who had been injured in Afghanistan. They spent two weeks with us and I began to realise that their time away was just as beneficial for Alasdair as for Alex. Over time we became good friends. He would pitch up at the cottage, often unannounced, always insisting that he had just nipped in to see Jake and me (but really, who 'nips' to North Devon?). I tried to get him to open up about some of the horrors he had witnessed during his military career, but he never did – not face-to-face. However, I did manage to persuade him to write a journal (I bought it for him – a beautiful leather-bound notebook). He felt a little odd about it at first, but I told him to write the entries as if he was writing a letter to me – maybe you will see him writing in it while you are away? I hope so.

I never kept in touch with any of the other servicemen, but there was something about Alasdair. Maybe I wanted to mother him as he has never had a proper mother of his own, not a good one at any rate. He spent most of his childhood bunking off school, fishing or poaching. At seventeen he quite literally ran away to the Royal Marines to find a family. He then became educated and progressed through the ranks quickly – you will have noticed by now that he is a very capable man.

Enough from me. The best way to understand your companion is to read his own words. Overleaf is an email I received from him the last time he returned from Afghanistan. I have learned that the best – if not the only – way to get Alasdair to talk about his emotions is through the written word.

Mum xxx

I turned the page over.

From: Major Alasdair Finn
To: Rosamund Buchanan

Dear Rosamund,

Sorry it's been a while since I've been in touch. I could reel off a long line of excuses, but you would see right through them.

Your request for me to escort Grace on this bizarre journey has been playing on my mind, and you can't know how many times I've intended to contact you and call it off (she's going to think I'm nuts). But you played your I'm going to die, Alasdair trump card on me, and coughed a bit, and now there's nothing to be done but take off work for a few weeks and trip around Blighty with Grace (tell Jake I'm not doing it because she's a looker, by the way).

I think you were right when you said I could do with a bit of a break. I'm knackered. The bags under my eyes are getting worse. I've been applying that moisturiser you gave me (do not tell ANYONE) but it's a lost cause. The thought of one more trip to some rancid shithole in the middle of a desert makes me want to vomit, and just lately I've been wondering if the intelligence/special forces route was the best option for me. I've also been thinking about our last discussion (the one about my marriage) and you were bang on the money when you suggested that my marriage failed because I put the job ahead of my ex-wife, Jane; she made the right decision to leave. My biggest regret is that I never gave her children, but 'what's done is done and cannot be undone' – a bit of Shakespeare for you. See, I did go to school (sometimes).

Listen to me! All your chats have turned me soft. Note to self: pull yourself together, Finn, you big bloody softie.

I have a briefing to give in five minutes so must be off. Hopefully I will see you soon, but just in case I don't, I do have something I need to say. I want you to know that you've been a mother, a sister and a friend to me, and from the moment I walked down the lane to St Christopher's, I felt like I had finally found a home – thank you.

Yours aye.

Alasdair

I closed the letter and turned to look at my companion. Seemingly in a world of his own, he was standing with his back to me a few feet away, on the edge of a crag that balanced like a cantilever over the hilltop. His body was strong against the breeze.

'Alasdair,' I shouted into the wind, 'I've finished reading.'

Broken from his reverie, Alasdair took a few steps down the hill and handed me a small colourful container, like an old-fashioned tea caddy with a hinged lid.

'I know this is a sensitive moment,' he said with a warm smile, 'but remember to keep your back to the wind when you tip out the ash.'

CHAPTER 9

As we turned to leave the summit I remembered the wild garlic Alasdair had picked. The flowers were a little battered by now, but I laid them down on the grass and placed a stone over the stems to keep them in place. Alasdair stood waiting on the footpath that skirted along the top of the hill.

'Ready?' he asked.

'Ready.'

We set off across the heather and followed a sheep track that seemed to be going in roughly the right direction and eventually found a path that followed a stream.

'I love playing in water,' I said, 'it must be something to do with all those years running through the ford at St Christopher's.'

'Yes,' he agreed, wistfully, 'the ford is pretty special. I was at St Christopher's during your Tulip Festival last year. Don't you remember Rosamund introducing us?' I shook my head.

'We've met before then – seriously?'

'Seriously.'

'I'm sorry. I just don't remember.'

'No bother. I probably looked a bit different then anyway.'

'Why?'

'I'd been away, lost a bit of weight, you know . . .'

I stopped in my tracks and turned to him.

'Lost a bit of weight? Good God, Alasdair, you must have looked shockingly different at St Christopher's for me not to remember someone as gorge—' My brain caught up with my speech. 'Well, you know. I'm just surprised I don't remember you, that's all.'

Alasdair tried to suppress a chuckle, I blushed, and we carried along on our way.

The path meandered on for half an hour or so and I filled the time regaling Alasdair with anecdotes from home. He seemed happy to listen and laugh and I was happy to think of anything else rather than analyse Mum's letters. The revelation I had an aunt remained a constant presence in the back of my mind, as did the thought of what horror Alasdair must have been part of to have lost so much weight the previous year. It struck me that this was no ordinary man Mum had asked to travel with me, and I realised that the journey she had conjured up wasn't, in fact, just for me, but for Alasdair too. An exhausted special forces soldier with a failed marriage (I tried not to see this as a good thing, but he suddenly became a whole lot sexier, on both counts), an absent mother and who knew what kind of baggage from his childhood – no wonder Mum had wanted to look after him.

But then, Alasdair was the kind of man that you couldn't help but feel affection for.

A half hour later we reached a small wooden gate with a latch, beyond which I was surprised to find a narrow, tarmac lane running downhill from left to right. It seemed odd to come across something modern – even if it was only tarmac – and a little disappointing. Despite the emotion of the letter and the ashes, our time together on the hill was special somehow.

'Let's wander into the village,' he said, 'it's down this road by about a quarter of a mile; we'll find somewhere to sit and have our lunch there.' He closed the latch on the gate behind us.

A blacksmith's forge backed onto the village green. Alasdair stopped next to it and removed his rucksack. He stretched his arms upwards and then backwards and, as his shirt rose up, I found myself admiring his muscular frame and perfectly toned midriff. It was evident he took his soldiering duties quite seriously.

Not bad, not bad at all . . .

For a terrible moment I thought he had caught me looking, so I turned away, tried to hide my blushing cheeks, and pretended to find something in the distance particularly interesting.

Inevitably, our conversation turned to the letter.

'I'd like you to read it,' I said, opening up the tin foil covering a second round of sandwiches.

'Me? Are you sure?'

'Of course.'

I took the letter out of my top pocket, making sure to hand him only the first one, and ate while he read.

'I must confess that I already know you have a relative here,' he said, folding the letter and handing it back. 'Grimes wrote to your aunt to say you would be visiting West Burton this afternoon. He asked your aunt to make herself available at the farm for us to visit'—he looked at his watch—'around about now in fact. I didn't know all the details though, a sad waste.'

'And what did she say?'

'She'll be there.'

I put my hands to my cheeks and stared across the village green. Mum mentioned the possibility of meeting my aunt in the letter, but I hadn't thought she meant right now. I had done without the woman for thirty years, why bother?

'Is this the surprise you were talking about?' He glanced across with an expression that said, 'guilty as charged'.

'Afraid so.'

'Is it part of the will that I go?'

'Not according to Grimes. The only thing I have to confirm with him is that you went to each location, read all of the letters and scattered the ashes.'

'So Grimes is happy to take your word for it then – that I did everything written in your notebook?'

'Er – no. We're to send postcards as proof.' He turned his torso to look around the green. 'I should

84

look for one here actually. I bet they sell them in the little shop over there.'

'If you were a truly good friend, Alasdair, you would be taking me to the pub for the rest of the afternoon rather than trooping me off to see, what's her name . . . Cruella De Vil. I can just imagine the farmhouse. I bet it's like something out of Amityville Horror.'

His face took on a serious expression when I had hoped for laughter. Guessing he was about to say something profound, I began to pull up blades of grass.

'It must feel quite strange,' he said, 'meeting a random woman who sounds to be a bit of a nutter. But we're here, in this place, right now. You may never come here again and you only need to stay there for ten minutes, even if you just tell her to sod off. I think it was probably important to your mum that you meet her.'

I scoffed at his suggestion.

'Yeah, because she rushed to take me to see her while she was alive . . . I don't think so.'

We fell silent. Alasdair lay back on the grass. I stared into space and mulled over his words. I supposed I could pop in quickly – if only to see what she looked like – and then, just as quickly, leave. She was expecting us after all, and we had come all this way . . .

I jumped to my feet, finished the last of the piccolo tomatoes, scrunched up the tin foil from the sandwiches and lobbed it at his chest.

'Okay, fine, I'll go. But if I'm going to walk straight into the clutches of a mad woman, then you're coming with me. God only knows what kind of a reception we're going to get.'

He had begun to unpack his rucksack while I spoke (I was *that* interesting) and I became fascinated by the contents: waterproof clothing, first aid kit, a bit of rope, carabiners, an orange thing that looked like a very small wrapped up tent, bungees, a hip flask – the list went on. Once practically empty (although I suspected there were still some items tucked away at the very bottom) he began to pack up again – this was clearly some kind of ritual.

'Your rucksack is the real life equivalent of the Mary Poppins carpet bag. I wouldn't be the least bit surprised if you pulled a twenty foot ladder out of there in a minute.'

'This is just my day sack,' he teased, 'the ladder is in my big rucksack.'

He looked up at me with such warmth I felt able to take on the old dragon at the farm. I felt able to do just about anything. I held out my hands and helped him to his feet.

CHAPTER 10

'Didn't they have any postcards?' I asked as he stepped out of the shop. He held a scrunched-up paper bag in his hand.

'Yes, they did, but it's the post office as well. She took the card from me as soon as I'd written the address. She also gave me directions to your aunt's farm. It's only about five minutes away. And I got you these.' He passed me the bag. '*Ta da*! I told you there would be little glass jars full of sweets.'

'Oh, Alasdair, thanks. My favourites!'

We left the village green behind and, as the road narrowed, rushing water came into earshot. Down a lane and beyond a converted mill, the most delightful waterfall came into view. I reached for my camera again.

'Of course, you're a photographer aren't you? Funnily enough I knew that too . . . paparazzo aren't you?' Alasdair had obviously been listening to Mum.

'No, I'm not a pap. Not any more. I do staged stuff now.'

After snapping some quick shots I skipped to the far side of the falls to look at the tourist information board. Alasdair was standing on a picturesque wooden bridge that crossed the river.

'They're called Cauldron Falls,' I shouted, 'and you can see why. Just look at the shape and the depth. And they were once painted by Turner, no less.' I beamed across at Alasdair, triumphant with my discovery.

He had placed his elbows on the hand rail and was resting his face on his hands. The term 'wry smile' was most definitely designed for the way Alasdair was looking at me.

'Don't think I'm fooled by your sudden interest in the geology of the landscape, Grace. You're time-wasting. Come on, Annie will be waiting.'

After snapping a cheeky photo of him on the bridge, we crossed a stile and turned left onto a wide cart track. Not for the first time, I felt we had stepped back in time at least a century. A mass of pink campions, also enjoying the clement weather, sunbathed on the verge. A grass path ran down the middle of the track and that was the part of the lane I chose to walk on, popping sweets into my mouth as we sauntered along.

Before long the natural smell of spring was overwhelmed by the natural smell of sweet manure. My heart fell to my boots when I noticed a piece of slate attached to a low stone wall almost hidden from view by bolting grass. Alasdair brushed the grass away from the stone. It was engraved with the words *Bridge Farm*.

'We're here.'

The house was not in the least how I had imagined. It looked like a welcoming cottage rather than austere. It was clearly a working farm though, and as we made our way into the yard, a pack of muddy-legged black and white Border Collies rushed to greet us, announcing our arrival with a yappy chorus.

The door opened with a creak before we had a chance to knock, and I took a nervous breath as Alasdair stepped in front of me. An elderly gentleman stepped out. He smiled warmly, but then narrowed his eyes and tilted his head to one side to analyse my face.

'I'm not staying love,' he said gently, then shouted back down the passageway: 'Annie, they're here.'

He touched my arm and said, 'It was good of you to come. It means more to that old battle-axe than she will ever let on.' He winked and carried on his way.

We turned back towards the house to find a woman with a purposeful gait striding down a long, dark hallway towards us. Highly polished slabs of slate, worn with years of use, lined the hall floor. Her bold demeanour withered somewhat as she approached the door.

'You'll be our Frances' child then.'

I nodded and remained frozen to the spot, overpowered by her presence, like a nervous child on an errand.

'You'd better come in.'

The dogs, eager to try it on, followed us into the house but were ordered out immediately.

'Aren't they allowed in?' I asked, but instantly regretted the question.

'They're working dogs, not pets,' she barked without turning. We followed her through to the kitchen.

'Sit yourselves down. I'll put the kettle on.'

The kitchen was at the back of the house and was large enough to accommodate both a substantial pine table and, resting against the wall at the far end of the room, a sofa covered in a patchwork throw and scattered with old but pretty cushions. Annie put the kettle on the AGA.

I took a seat at the table. The chair scraped with an annoying screech along the floor. Annie flashed me a frown as I sat down. I tried to take no notice, but felt like a naughty schoolgirl who had been summoned to see the headmistress. I glanced around nervously. There was an eclectic mix of very old, old and moderately old paraphernalia scattered about the room. The kitchen had no fitted units, but an arrangement of freestanding sideboards and a large dresser covered most of one wall. There was an inglenook fireplace (large enough for Alasdair to stand inside without bending) halfway down the inside wall, housing the chipped but pristine four oven range. The back door – heavy oak like the front – was propped open by a dog made of cast iron, allowing a welcoming breeze into the room to counter the warmth from the AGA.

Alasdair walked over to a wiry-looking sheepdog. She wagged her tail but refused to move from the comfort of the sofa.

'You'll not get much of a welcome from that one,' Annie scoffed, turning her back to the AGA while waiting for the kettle to boil.

'This dog *is* allowed in the house then?' Alasdair asked, clearly taken with the sloppy Collie who rolled onto her back to allow access for a full belly scratch.

'They all come out of the barn and into the kitchen when they retire,' she explained. 'Although Meg here started edging her way in well before that – little tyke.' An affectionate smile crossed Annie's face and, for a moment, she almost looked . . . human?

She joined me at the table and poured tea from a glazed teapot.

'You don't look much like your mother,' she stated, looking up while pouring.

I didn't care for the sarcasm in her voice, so I replied, pointedly.

'No. You don't look much like her either.'

Alasdair looked up from stroking the dog with an almost imperceptible smile. Even into her sixties, Mum was a pretty lady with a regal bone structure. Annie was tall and thick set, although, to be fair to my aunt, she was a woman of a good age, yet had the agility of a much younger woman. She also had the ruddy complexion of someone who had worked outside all her life. Overall, she looked incredibly healthy.

Annie looked down at her teacup and ran her fingers around the rim. Her shoulders twitched a little.

'Yes, well, Frances was always the pretty one.' She looked up at me, her expression a sad one. 'She was no age to speak of though, poor sod.' She rallied a little before continuing. 'The letter said you're an only child.'

'Yes.'

'No family left then.'

'Just you.'

Her heavy eyes betrayed her sadness. But then she looked up (with the naughtiest sparkle in her eyes and one raised eyebrow) and said, 'Aren't you the lucky one?'

We laughed together – the ice broken.

'I suppose you know you're the spitting image of your grandmother – my mother,' she said, taking a sip of tea.

So that's why they had peered at me at the door.

'No, Mum never said . . . but then she never told me anything.'

'Hmm,' she uttered, frowning. 'I'll show you a picture sometime . . .'

Alasdair joined us at the table. He surprised me by asking knowledgeable questions about sheep farming, and my aunt warmed to him immediately. There was no talk of Mum or the past. While they chatted, she pulled a bowl of apples towards her and had peeled, cored and chopped four of them with big, capable hands in the amount of time it would have taken me to peel just one. She took a roll of fresh pastry out of the fridge and made a pie – just like that – without reference to a cookbook.

I left my seat and wandered to the open door. The garden was enclosed by stone walls on two sides with a privet hedge on another; the house completed the fourth side of the square. A picket gate separated the garden from the more agricultural-looking farmyard, and a number of pretty benches were positioned at strategic intervals around and about. It was less blousy than Mum's garden and had more shrubs and topiary, but was every bit as lovely in its own way.

Noticing my interest, Annie offered to show us around the farm, but not before putting the pie in the top oven using the edge of her apron as a mitt.

Meg was cajoled off the settee and came with us for the exercise. She seemed happy to keep only a striding pace from Alasdair's legs.

Pointing out as much of the land belonging to the farm as we could see – which took up a great swathe of Penhill above and below us – Annie explained she had taken the decision a few years before to rent out most of the fields and had reduced her sheep stock significantly.

'I have just enough sheep to keep the dogs active and my bones from seizing up. In the winter I have to get some help in, but it keeps me going.'

After about twenty minutes we turned back towards the house, but it was too beautiful a day to rush back inside, and I hadn't explored enough of the farm to satisfy my curiosity. I asked Annie if she would mind if we stayed outside a while longer.

'If you like,' she answered, and I thought, just for a second, that she was pleased with my request. 'You could take Meg down to the river,' she added. 'She enjoys a good belly soak on a day like today, and it looks like she's really smitten with your man there.' We both glanced with affection towards Alasdair who was larking about with Meg a little way down the hill. Annie bustled back to the house, anxious to take the pie from the oven.

'If you are going to have a smug look on your face then save it,' I said to Alasdair as we sauntered down to the river.

'Not quite Amityville Horror then.' He glanced at me with a kind smile.

'Er, no. I must admit it, I was wrong about that. I got a bit carried away after Mum's letter. Actually, it's a wonderful place. Don't you think so?'

'I do indeed.'

He sat down on the river embankment and threw stones into the water for Meg who barked with delight. I busied myself tiptoeing over rocks and boulders – an opportunity not to be missed. The sun was directly in Alasdair's eyes so he lay back and closed them. It struck me as he lay there in

94

silence on the deep grass that he looked quite weary – handsome – but definitely weary. Meg stepped out of the stream, shook her coat and lay in the sun by his feet. It was at that moment I had the repeated sensation that perhaps I did recognise him, in some vague way.

'Don't you just love the intermittent sound of bleating sheep?' he asked, his eyes still closed. 'Sheep in the Dales sound . . . different. I swear they have a more relaxing *baaa*.' He stretched out his limbs in the afternoon sunshine. '*Baaing* sheep and lush green fields . . . my idea of absolute heaven.'

I stepped out of the stream and plonked myself on the grass beside him.

'Well, relaxing or not, I suppose we ought to make tracks.'

'Do we have to?' he moaned. 'Just leave me here for the next forty years and I'll be perfectly, *perfectly*, content. All I ask is that you pop down to the river now and again with some apple pie, and maybe a cuppa, and I'll be absolutely fine.' He lay back on the grass and closed his eyes.

'Okay then,' I said, getting up. 'I'll tell Annie you don't want any of her apple pie. And cream. And tea.'

He opened one eye. 'Would that be pouring cream, Ms Buchanan?'

'Maybe . . .' I started up the hill at a run. Alasdair shot past me with Meg barking wildly at his feet.

'You'd better get a wiggle on then or there won't be any left.'

'Hey,' I shouted. 'Wait for me!'

Alasdair slowed and turned with a grin as we approached the house; the enticing aroma of hot apple pie shepherded us on towards the kitchen. The man from the doorway had returned and was sitting in a large wooden carver by the AGA. I wondered if it was my grandfather's chair.

He turned to smile as we walked in.

'This is Ted,' Annie said with an indifferent flash of her hand in his direction.

Ted stood, smiled broadly, and shook Alasdair's hand.

Ted? The Ted from Mum's letter?

Alasdair glanced at me. We were clearly thinking the same thing.

I sat down at the table, careful this time to lift and place the chair rather than scrape it along the floor.

'I run the farm next door,' he explained. Annie stopped midway between the table and the AGA – a fresh pot of tea in her hands.

'You mean your *son* runs your farm, you live in a cosy little barn he converted for you, and you fill your useless days sitting in *that* chair and getting in *my* way.' Annie was a blunt teaser, but he smiled and seemed to revel in it. I wondered what their relationship was now; where was his wife?

We enjoyed the pie, cream and yet more tea, and

the afternoon passed by pleasantly. We rose to leave at a suitable juncture, but just as we set off down the passageway towards the front door, I remembered Mum's letter, and turned to speak to Annie.

'I don't suppose you could show me Mum's tree could you?'

Taken aback for a second, surprised but not annoyed, she directed me once more to the garden. The apple tree was just a few feet from the kitchen window and was awash with pale pink blossom. Annie stood staring at the tree as she spoke.

'Your grandfather brought this tree home the week before Frances left to join the RAF. It was no more than a couple of twigs then. I remember him saying to her as he dug the hole to plant it that, no matter where she wandered, this was her very special tree and it signified that her roots would always be here, in the Dales. She would trip home, happy as Larry, and the first thing she would do was measure her tree. Dad loved it. She always knew how to make him happy. The apple of his eye . . .'

'Do *you* have a special tree, Annie?' I asked softly.

'No love, they never got me one, and there's been a lifetime of bitterness eating away in me, just because they never bought me a bloody tree.' She laughed scornfully and turned to take a seat on a bench positioned in the shade of the tree.

'Such a waste. My fault though, no one else's.'

I remained silent.

'I drove her away, lass. I knew it was wrong at the time but I kept it up. Pure badness.' She paused for a second. 'Frances was supposed to watch this tree grow, but once our parents were gone she never came back. Wasted years and for what? My own terrible bitterness. I always thought there would be time to sort things out but . . . she's gone now. Life goes by so bloody quickly.'

Annie exhaled a deep sigh of pure regret and put her hands to her cheeks.

I took Mum's letter out of my pocket.

'I think you should read this. It's a letter to me from Mum, and it describes her time here . . . and everything.'

Surprised, she took the letter, but then waved it in the air impatiently.

'My bloody glasses are in the kitchen. Read it to me will you love?'

Silent tears fell down Annie's cheeks as I read. She lifted the corner of her apron to dry her face as I finished.

'Thank you.'

'Did it help?' I asked hopefully.

'Yes, it did.' She smiled at the memory of Mum. 'She was such a Dolly Daydream that mother of yours.'

I thought of something.

'Annie, if your dad had bought you a tree, what would you have wanted it to be?'

She let out a laugh.

'I always wanted a plum tree . . . the sour old

fool that I am. Do you know, I've never planted one single fruit tree in this garden, and all because of my daft, self-centred ways. What a waste.'

She turned to me on the bench and cupped my face in her hands, just as Mum would have done; the unexpected demonstrative affection was enough to bring my own pent-up emotion to the fore.

'You must have felt so utterly alone after she'd gone,' she said, 'and by God I know what that feels like.'

I nodded; tears were streaming down my cheeks.

'Well, I've no children of my own and a lot of years to make up for. So just you remember this, lass – there'll always be a home for you here if you ever need it.' I nodded and felt a great wave of peace and comfort wash over me.

Annie's innate northern-ness kicked into gear and she rallied.

'Come on now, lass, that's enough tears from both of us. Let's dry those pretty brown eyes of yours. I was wrong to say you don't look like your mother, those eyes are carbon copies.'

She smiled at me with tremendous warmth and, after she wiped away my tears with what was possibly the last dry part of her apron, we hugged thirty years of hurt away, on the bench, under Mum's apple tree.

Ted drove us back to the hotel. An idea crossed my mind.

'Ted, I don't suppose there's a garden centre somewhere nearby is there?'

'There's a nursery near Leyburn,' he answered. 'Why do you ask?'

'I'd like to buy Annie a tree, a plum tree. Will you take me there?'

He took his eyes off the road to smile at me. 'Of course, but we'll need to put a bit of thought into it.'

'Why?'

'Any tree needs to be suited to its new environment. And with fruit trees you have to be extra careful because you may buy one that needs a pollinator close by; so you may have to buy two, or it won't bear fruit.'

'How come Mum's apple tree has fruit then?'

'That's different. It's self-pollinating.'

I thought of something suddenly.

'So, if my grandparents had put a little more thought into it, and bought two interdependent trees (one for each of the girls), rather than one independent one . . .'

He finished my sentence for me.

'. . . life for Annie and Frances may have worked out differently?'

'Yes.'

'And for me too . . .'

'Let's have dinner together tonight,' I said as we walked up the stairs to our rooms. Alasdair paused on the staircase.

'I'm sorry, Grace, I can't. I have things I really have to do. I've had a message to contact work.'

I narrowed my eyes.

'A message? You bloody charlatan, Alasdair. I thought you'd turned off your mobile phone. I, on the other hand, have been really good. You may have noticed that I didn't even *touch* mine today.'

His lips twitched.

'I *did* turn off my phone, but I have to have a bleeper for work. Didn't I mention it?'

I smiled. 'Strangely enough, no, you didn't – and that's cheating Finn.'

He played with the zip on his fleece and grinned.

'Well, only a bit. Why don't we meet up in the snug later, I have another letter for you tonight.'

'Really? But I've already had the letter for here.'

'How about nine o'clock?'

'See you there.'

CHAPTER 11

I felt restless in my room so I sauntered back downstairs and took some magazines from a table in the foyer. It had been an emotional day and I didn't feel like sitting alone – I would only mull things over.

I asked June for an early dinner and made myself cosy in the lounge. *Yorkshire Life* had a number of properties advertised in the Dales area. There was a cottage for sale in West Burton – Annie's village – and I found myself wondering what it would be like to live there permanently. Truth be told, I had fallen in love with the farm, and felt a small part of me belonged there too.

Glancing through the ancient mullion window, the imperfection in the bubbly glass distorting the view into a wobble, I noticed that the crags on the top of Penhill could just about be made out above the roofline of the cottages opposite. I thought nostalgically of Mum dashing up there to catch the sunset and was thinking of doing something equally as impulsive when June walked in with my coffee.

'Your friend's having his dinner upstairs again I see?'

'Yes. I think he's busy on his laptop.'

'Oh, shall I set the fire alarm off, smoke him out for you?'

'Don't worry, I'm meeting him in the snug later.' I hoped this would placate her, but no.

'Well, don't let the grass grow under your feet, lass. I reckon he might just need a bit of a push in the right direction.'

The woman was incorrigible.

A beautiful day had merged into a glorious evening, and I returned to my previous thoughts. It was 6.40; I reckoned I could be at the top of Penhill by eight o'clock, watch the sun set and then run back to the village before night set.

Stuffing the after-dinner chocolates into my pocket, I ran upstairs to grab my waterproof jacket, but remembered it was in Alasdair's rucksack.

Damn.

I didn't want to disturb him when he had made such a point of needing some time alone. Alasdair's fleece was strewn across the bed, so I grabbed it and, having nabbed my boots from June's drying room, headed off across the road and started up the hill.

The route was fairly easy to remember and – pushing myself hard – I made it to the top in just over an hour. The colours across the dale were muted in the evening sun; a golden glow rested on the patchwork of fields that carpeted the valley.

I sat in the same spot Alasdair and I had rested at earlier, and was thrilled to see the wild garlic still in position under the stone. With no coat to sit on this time I felt the moisture in the heather permeate through my trousers almost immediately. The wind skimming my back from across the moor strengthened and cooled. I took the fleece from around my shoulders and put it on to block out the evening chill. The light was fading now; it wouldn't be too long before the edge of the sun kissed the earth on the horizon.

My thoughts turned to Mum's letter, and I gazed down the Dale and thought about my grandparents. I imagined Mum there all those years before, and felt an immediate and heart-warming connection to her – to the landscape. And I realised that although people had changed with time, the landscape had not, and it was comforting to know that I had a connection with such a beautiful part of the world. Glancing at the river once more, I was reminded of Mum's favourite song, *Moon River*. I knew the words by heart of course, and pleased to have a moment alone, sang her song to my heart's content, happy in the knowledge that no one else but Mum, perhaps, could hear.

My childhood at St Christopher's was filled with music: classical, operatic, old songs from Fifties and Sixties musicals, although nothing particularly modern. Not surprisingly, I grew up singing and playing the piano. By the age of twelve Mum reckoned it was impossible to tell if there was a soundtrack of *The Sound of Music* playing in the background, or if I was singing away to myself in the living room. I was asked to sing at school assemblies and commandeered for the village choir. The problem was, I was impossibly shy away from home. Over time I was able to sing within the local community without my face becoming too much of a burning inferno, but for me shyness and singing were to remain inexorably linked.

Academically, I was average bordering on bright. I passed my exams at sixteen with fairly good grades and was considering where to take my life from there. My music teacher suggested I stay on at school and study for advanced music. Mum paid for additional singing and piano tuition, and took me to a Russian woman – who was an opera singer when she was young – every Saturday for a year. I was persuaded to join the local amateur operatic society to broaden my experience and increase my exposure to singing in public. To my surprise the society was good fun, not too serious, and I thoroughly enjoyed it; which was why I auditioned for a place at the London Academy of Music. I was offered a place on a three-year course and, the following September, I began my new life in London.

It took me a while to settle in at the Academy – if indeed I ever did. My lifestyle became the exact opposite of the easy-come, easy-go life I had known in Devon, but that wasn't really the issue. The real problem lay in the fact that I was living in the fast lane musically but didn't believe I had the talent to pull it off. Singing became something to be endured rather than enjoyed.

I stuck at it for a while but towards the end of the second year I literally could no longer face the music. My shyness became marginally less with increased exposure, and I realised that, even if I was good enough to audition for opera or musical theatre when I finished the course, I would never have the confidence to perform on a grand scale. Much to Mum's dismay, I dropped out of the Academy at the end of my second year.

On the plus side, I moved into a flat with friends outside of the Academy and began to enjoy my social life in London considerably more. Although the easiest option would have been to run home to St Christopher's (and part of me wanted to), it was time to become financially independent, so I stayed in London and made a concerted effort to find a good job. Initially I worked in retail but eventually landed a job with prospects in the civil service.

One of my flatmates – a man whom I believed at the time to be the love of my life – was a professional photographer. He worked at a studio nearby. He had started a sideline as a paparazzo photographer and made a tidy profit selling gossip-worthy photographs to the tabloids. This aspect of his work expanded and, in doing so, encroached on his time in the studio. He was torn between his 'inner artist' and cold hard cash. He taught me the fundamentals of photography, bought me a good camera and, whenever there was money to be made in the London area and he was busy being artistic, I would make an excuse to leave the office and take the shot. I took an advanced photography night class, got a few letters of qualification after my name and, over time, developed my own network of contacts and became good enough (with a little more coaching from my friend) to make it a full-time concern.

Not remotely interested in climbing the greasy pole of promotion, I left the civil service at twenty-six and eventually became a respected style photographer. My musical career, or lack of it, was the only thing Mum ever nagged about. Several years on, she would often say, 'In the grand scheme of things, a year was nothing'. But to me, a whole year of being a second rate under-achiever at a first rate establishment was too much to bear and, although singing would always be my first love, I never regretted my decision to leave.

Music remained in my life, but on my terms, my way.

My stroll down memory lane was interrupted by a flash of grey. It was followed by an almighty, glass-shattering roar. A military aircraft had crept up on me from deep within the Dale. I watched the nose jerk upwards through ninety degrees; the burners in the engines glowed a hellish orange. Within seconds the aircraft had disappeared through a hole in the clouds.

Clouds? Where had they come from? I felt a tingling sensation on my skin. It had started to rain.

I glanced around to look in the direction of the prevailing wind and to my horror saw black clouds whipping up over the moors. Not only that, but the sun had set without me noticing and it was getting dark.

No damn coat.

Darting down the zigzag path I realised that the encroaching rain was moving faster than my legs could carry me. Within five minutes the hillside became engulfed by low-lying mist, and somewhere in the distance I feared I could hear thunder.

I stopped for a moment to take in my position. The rain had glued my hair to my face and my trousers were sodden. Alasdair's fleece was keeping my core dry but it wouldn't be long before I was completely soaked. Droplets of rain dripped from my hair and onto my neck, only to move on to soak the back of my shirt.

Looking across the plateau, the initial stages of the path were easy enough to make out – even in the mist – but it was disheartening to know how far from the village the path veered before turning in the right direction. I knew that if I carried on, straight down at a right angle to the side of the hill, then that would be the quickest way back – wouldn't it? I remembered Alasdair's lecture regarding contouring, but guessed the concept would only apply going up a hill, not down. I reckoned it would take about half an hour to get back to the hotel if I took the direct route. My hands felt brutally cold, even though they were tucked into Alasdair's oversized sleeves.

Decision made: direct route.

Before too long my path was blocked by a stone wall – not surprising considering my location. Squinting through the mist, I peered down the length of the wall for any sign of a gate or a stile. There wasn't one. My only option was to climb over. The stone felt like wet sandpaper but it was relatively easy to scale. The next field was steep and I was elated to be losing height rapidly. I started to run. Another wall – over – another steep field, and so my rapid descent down the hill continued. I hit the second plateau within ten minutes of leaving the path and realised I could just about make out the village in the distance – a dim light from a cottage window appeared like a beacon through the low cloud and rain.

The lightning was frighteningly close though, and a decision had to be made; find myself in the middle of an open field in a storm, or hanker down. I tried to remember a TV programme I had seen recently about thunderstorms. *Crouch down beside a stone wall? Was that what I should do?*

With my body now completely soaked, I carried on. I couldn't believe how cold I was. It was spring, and yet I felt like I'd been shut in the freezer. Only my feet were warm and dry.

I sprinted across the fields as if chased by a pack

of wolves. The mist closed in again and I could no longer see more than ten feet in front of me. My right foot became caught in a rabbit hole and I fell forwards, landing hard on the sodden grass; a sharp pain darted up my wrist. With no time to lick my wounds, I jumped up and carried on running, but before too long my path was blocked by another wall. I decided to push on – up and over. Although it was easy enough to gain a foot-hold in the stone, I only had one good hand to steady me – my other wrist was still throbbing from the fall – so I gritted my teeth and hurled myself up, allowing my legs to take all of the strain. I managed to throw one leg over the top and twisted my body to face the wall on the other side. Relief washed over me as my foot touched the earth on the other side, but as I turned to continue my run down the hill, I stopped, petrified.

On turning I noticed a dilapidated barn; a fraction of a second later I caught sight of an enormous ram, furious at being disturbed from his shelter. He postulated aggressively, lowered his head to display his horns, and snorted whilst grinding his hooves.

With my back to the wall I stood, frozen; unable to act, unable to think.

The ram edged closer. It would be suicide to just stand there, but he would be impossible to out-run. Trapped, I edged a foot backwards to try and gain a hold in the stone behind me. Maybe I could clamber back up the wall?

A voice cried out from the mist.

'Grace! Don't move unless he does. Stay still.'

It was Alasdair. *Thank God.*

What happened next was both a blur and a miracle. Alasdair flung me over his shoulder and hurled me – albeit as gently as possible given the circumstances – back over the wall. I landed on my injured wrist and cried out in pain.

The falling rain had geared up to something like an Indian monsoon. Lightning pierced the earth around the valley at increasingly regular intervals while the acoustics of the Dale made the claps of thunder horrifyingly loud. I huddled with my back against the wall. Alasdair also crouched low and hurried to unclip his rucksack.

He strapped on a head-torch and took out the orange plastic sack I had ribbed him about earlier. He removed a large circular nylon sheet from the sack that was also bright orange.

'Come and sit by my feet,' he shouted, 'quickly!'

He lifted the sheet above his head and tried to control it by holding the edges as it flapped wildly in the gale. He squinted away from the fierceness of the wind. Water dripped from every crevice of his face.

'It's a survival sheet. We need to shelter and get you dry.'

We crouched together and Alasdair pulled the sheet over us. He pushed the edge of the nylon under me so that I was sitting on the sheet rather than on the saturated ground. Our bodies made

111

the framework of the makeshift tent, our heads the tent poles. He grabbed a telescopic walking pole that was strapped to his rucksack, lengthened it and, sticking it firmly into the ground, created another apex. His rucksack made up the fourth corner and also had the sheet tucked underneath it. He rifled through his rucksack and pulled out an entire set of dry clothes – his clothes – and took care they didn't also become wet.

'Get that lot off and put these on,' he ordered.

I pulled the soaked fleece over my head while Alasdair unfastened and removed my boots. My feet were dry but my fingers were stiff from the biting wind, which made unbuttoning my blouse difficult to the extreme. Alasdair turned away while I struggled to pull his T-shirt over my head. He then gave me my own coat.

'Get your bum up. I need to pull your trousers off.'

Under normal circumstances I would have either laughed at such a comment or slapped him, but I was in too much pain, wrestling my injured wrist into a sleeve, to offer any comment. And anyway, Alasdair looked far from pleased.

'What's wrong? Why are you wincing?' he asked.

'I fell on my wrist.'

Alasdair took hold of my wrist and manipulated it to assess the damage.

'Is it broken?' I tried not to cry.

'No.'

Within minutes I was dressed and dry, but still

shivering a little from a mixture of cold, shock and the injury.

'You'll start to warm up in a minute,' he said. Taking in my crestfallen expression, he added, 'Don't worry, you'll live.'

I managed a smile. Alasdair delved into his ruck-sack once more.

'Ah, here it is, I thought I'd got it with me.' He unfolded a large green and black scarf.

'What is it?'

'A shemagh. It's from the Middle East, useful piece of kit this. Let's get it on your head and stop all the heat from escaping.'

He leant behind me, stretching the survival sheet upwards as he did so, and wound the shemagh around my head just as an Arabian salesman might have done in a Middle-Eastern souk.

'Let's get you warm and then we'll get back to the hotel once the storm has passed. Put your hands under your armpits.'

He positioned his body so my back was cupped into his chest, and opened his coat so I could benefit from the full warmth of his body. It was like cuddling up to a radiator. The intimacy of our closeness should have been either sexy or embarrassing, but the dankness of the survival tent, combined with the condensation from our breath, the raging closeness of the storm and the fact that I was shaking like a jelly put paid to any possible notion of romance.

'I will never tease you about that rucksack ever

again,' I joked. Although I couldn't see his face, I could feel his smile and was relieved he hadn't remained angry at me for my naivety on the hill.

'You know what? It's nothing short of amazing,' I said, turning my head slightly towards him.

'What? That you stumbled across a ram in the Yorkshire Dales?' He knew what I meant.

'No, that you just happened to stumble across me in the middle of nowhere. Were you out for a walk yourself or were you actually looking for me?' Similarly, I knew what the answer would be.

'June came to see me when the rain came in. She'd noticed a nasty squall passing through, had seen you leave the hotel and noticed your boots were gone. I remembered I still had your waterproofs in my rucksack and realised you would be drenched. So I came to look for you, just in case.'

'But I could have been anywhere.' I turned my torso so that I could face him. 'I can see how logic made you assume I had gone back up the hill – Mum's letter, sunset and all that – but how did you know I would veer off the track?'

'Because I knew.'

Our conversation came to an abrupt halt when a perilously close flash of lightning illuminated the nylon of the makeshift tent; our faces glowed bright orange for a second, and then darkness. The only chatter between us afterwards was to count the seconds between thunder and flash.

After about half an hour the storm abated, my bones no longer shook and my wrist throbbed less aggressively. Alasdair took the executive decision to lift the sheet from our heads. I blew into my hands and danced on the spot whilst Alasdair packed the sheet away. It was completely dark and I wondered what would have happened if Alasdair hadn't found me. I shuddered at the thought.

'Still cold, Grace?'

'No, not too bad now. I was just thinking about what that ram might have done if you hadn't turned up.'

'Probably nothing,' he said, hurling his rucksack onto his back. 'Their *baas* are worse than their bites.'

His head torch illuminated a wink and I chuckled all the way back to the village – the long way that time.

CHAPTER 12

It was around ten by the time we reached the hotel, and I had never been so happy to reach a destination in my life. June fluttered around me like an anxious mother hen, got the local vet who was drinking in the bar to look at my wrist and, satisfied I had survived without any broken bones, ordered me upstairs to take a soak in the bath. I looked back towards Alasdair as I mooched up the stairs.

'I'll wait for you in the snug, if you're not too tired.'

Looking down at his amiable face, I couldn't believe how patient he had been. I must have looked worn out, standing as I was, like a scare-crow in Alasdair's over-sized clothes, because he changed tack suddenly.

'Actually, maybe the next letter can wait till tomorrow.'

'No way, I need a drink!'

'What about your wrist though? You should take some ibuprofen or that sprain is going to hurt like hell in the morning.'

I gave his advice precisely one second of thought.

'Mine's a brandy and ginger. Give me precisely ten minutes.'

I started up the stairs but heard his voice shout out after me.

'Grace!'

'Yes?'

'Although it really suits you, maybe Yorkshire isn't quite ready for the shemagh look just yet.'

I turned around to see Alasdair pointing at my head. My hand instinctively rose to touch the fabric of the scarf. I laughed – I had forgotten I was wearing it. I removed the shemagh in one fluid movement and threw it down the stairs for him to catch.

'You're right, Alasdair. A shemagh *is* a good piece of kit.'

After my bath I sauntered back downstairs to meet up with Alasdair, but I noticed someone who caused my eyes to pop out on stalks. I needed to grab my camera, and quick.

Ten minutes later – looking particularly pleased with myself – I stepped into the snug and found Alasdair sitting alone by the fire; my brandy was waiting on the table.

'No June?' I asked.

'She's shut up shop for the evening. We're to help ourselves at the bar, write down what we've had and she'll tot it up in the morning.'

I sat down on a high-backed chair at the other side of the fireplace to Alasdair and smiled a contented smile.

'What's up?' he said. 'You look like your lottery numbers have just come up.'

I took a swig of my brandy. 'And so they have, Alasdair. So they have! You will never in your life guess who I've just seen in the bistro!'

'Who?' he asked, smiling, clearly intrigued.

'I just saw – and you're never going to believe it – the wife of a *very* prominent politician,' I winked, 'and she wasn't alone. She was all dewy-eyed, holding hands across the table with someone who was definitely *not* her husband. And I would know, I did a photo shoot of the two of them at their house last year.'

Alasdair was nonplussed.

'So . . .'

'So? *So*, I shot upstairs for my camera. I just need to find some way of downloading the picture.' I hoped Alasdair would offer me the use of his.

'Maybe you'll be able to send it at the next place.'

Not the response I was hoping for.

'Maybe, but it's hot news right now, not tomorrow. You don't seem at all interested.'

He took a swig of his brandy.

'I'm not. The fact that some random woman is staying at a hotel with a man that isn't her husband is not something I would ever be interested in, hotel staff must see it all the time.'

I was gobsmacked, he didn't care a hoot. 'But her husband is a politician—'

'Her husband, yes. Not her.'

'But what *she* does reflects on him, surely.'

118

Alasdair sighed.

'Does it? You don't know their background. You might not judge her if you were looking at her apparent affair through her eyes. In fact, if you knew the whole story you might just decide to leave her alone. Anyway, I thought you had given up the pap business?'

'I have, but there's no point throwing good money away. A photo like that is worth quite a bit.'

Alasdair tapped a drink mat on the table. He looked disappointed.

'Fair enough,' he said. 'I would offer the use of my laptop but it's a military one, sorry.' I decided to change the subject. I planned on phoning Paul from my room later to give him the scoop.

'Well, day two complete. Quite a day, eh?' I said, settling further into my chair.

Alasdair visibly relaxed.

'It certainly was. You've had an aunt thrust upon you out of the blue. I liked her, by the way – fantastic farm. Also, let's not forget the revelation that your mum was in the RAF. And finally – and in *my* book the most important part of today's adventure – you were nearly garrotted by a bloody great ram.'

We laughed again at the thought of it all. Alasdair jumped up.

'Now then, what can I tempt you with, young Grace? A cocktail? Champagne perhaps?'

I rose from my chair with a purposeful jolt and

stood to face him across the bar. Beaming my broadest smile, I decided to probe a little. The letter from Mum had revealed just enough to make me want to know more.

'How old are you, Alasdair?'

He laughed out loud, amused by my direct question as he poured the brandy. 'Thirty-eight.'

'And you're a Royal Marine.' I decided not to push the special forces bit. I had spent enough time at St Christopher's to know what questions could – and couldn't – be asked.

He rested his back against the optics, took his wallet from his trouser pocket and removed a small plastic card out of one of the flaps. He handed it to me and returned to his seat.

'Terrible photo!' I joked. I read his name aloud and returned to my chair. 'Major Alasdair Finn. I've never seen Alasdair spelt with a 'D' before, I like it.'

'Mum was Scottish,' he said blandly. Remembering Mum's letter I would have liked to have pressed him for more, but his tone and expression said some things were best left alone.

He returned the card to the transparent sleeve of his wallet.

'Speaking of work, I'm afraid my sabbatical has been cut short,' he said. 'That was the message. I'll still be able to complete this trip with you, but then I have to get back.'

'Oh, that's a shame. You haven't got to go anywhere dangerous, have you?'

He smiled. 'They aren't sure yet, but we need to plan all the same.'

I returned to my seat and gazed blankly into the fire for a while, only to look up at the clock and notice – to my absolute surprise – that it was past eleven.

'It's really late. I should get on with reading Mum's next letter.'

'Why don't you wait until tomorrow to read it, after all—'

'Why *not* read it now? My head is already full of so much clutter. More information can only help rather than hinder, surely.'

He prodded the embers of the fire while I read.

CHAPTER 13

Hello Grace, my love.

How are you enjoying the Wensleydale Heifer?
I haven't been there in years but Jake found
the details on the internet for me and it looked
as though the owners have maintained the
'olde worlde' charm, so hopefully you are both
having a lovely time. I also hope the weather
was good to you for your walk and for the
visit to the farm. How was the old place? As
wonderful as ever, I hope.

You're probably wondering why you're
reading this letter in the hotel rather than at
a specific place. Well, the next destination of
significance to me is RAF College Cranwell
– it's in Lincolnshire. I considered sending
you there but, after deliberating long and
hard, I decided Lincolnshire is rather feature-
less, and all you would be able to do is stand
at the gates and look in at the college from
the outside, so you might as well stay in the
wonderfully cosy pub and read about it
instead.

As you know, I took myself off to RAF Cranwell when I was twenty-one, and my goodness I loved absolutely every single second of it. The College is where the RAF trains its officers. I shan't get bogged down with too much of the detail, suffice it to say, over the course of sixteen weeks, I threw myself into my new life and thrived on the training.

The day I graduated from Cranwell was one of the happiest of my life. I was on cloud nine and brimming with confidence. I was earning my own money and making all of my own decisions – what a confident, headstrong little so-and-so I must have been in those days.

There were only a handful of girls on my course and, as you can imagine, we all received quite a lot of attention from the boys. There was a man called Geoffrey Heywood on the same course; he was tall, dark and unbearably handsome. Besotted, I set my cap at him from the off and by the fifteenth week we were an item – he didn't stand much of a chance, poor man. The course came to an end and I moved on to another RAF station in Lincolnshire to start my training as an intelligence officer. Geoff stayed on at Cranwell and began his flying training course.

I would pootle back and forth to Cranwell in my little car and, over time, we managed to build a strong and loving relationship – not easy given the circumstances. We married on the 31st of May 1974 at Cranwell, in the lovely church that sits within the grounds there. It seemed fitting to marry at a place that was important to us. You won't be surprised to hear it was a beautiful day. Mum and Dad were there and had a wonderful time. Annie came (surprisingly), and was just as sour as usual.

And that, I suppose, is all there is to tell you. Cranwell was a place of great significance in my life. Most importantly it was where I met a man who became my husband. It was the beginning of the rest of my life. I was young and free and full of adventure. Forget all this modern chatter that says 'forty is the new twenty'. I tell you this: twenty is twenty, thirty is thirty and so on and so forth. In your early twenties your real, independent life is just beginning and no other time is ever the same – good or bad. With no significant emotional baggage behind you (hopefully) everything ahead is fresh like the bright green growth of spring. It's a time full of possibilities and I tried to grasp each and every one of them.

With all my love, my love.

Mum

CHAPTER 14

I took my turn to stoke the fire while Alasdair read the letter.

'Well, at least you know the real reason why the 31st of May was so important to her.' He said, handing the letter back. 'Did you even know she was married?'

'Not a clue. This last letter has brought me down a bit, to be honest. I didn't know her at all really, did I?'

'Her story isn't over yet.' He paused for a second. 'Can I give you some advice, Grace?'

'If you like . . .'

'Rosamund may have been your mother, but first and foremost she was a woman in her own right, and I get the impression that it's this side of her personality – her life as a woman rather than your mother – that she's going to reveal to you. So, just for now, I wouldn't think of her as Mum, but as Rosamund.'

'Don't you mean *Frances*?' I asked, with a slight edge to my voice.

'Exactly. You have four more letters to read, so maybe, by the end, you'll come to see what the point of it all is.' Alasdair stared into his swirling brandy before slugging it back in one go.

'What do you *know*, Alasdair?' There was something in his expression that led me to believe he was possibly hiding something. 'What did Mum tell you when you went down to Devon last year?'

He looked up, his expression softened as he smiled.

'All I know, is you'll be glad you came on this trip by the end. Yesterday you told me you were just going to sit back and enjoy it all. You seem deflated after this last letter. So,' he added brightly, 'Rosamund told me you were trained in music . . . and I confess to having heard you sing.'

'Oh my God, when?' I felt the blood rush to my face and my hands followed suit.

'You were upstairs at St Christopher's. I was passing the back of the house on my way to the coop for some eggs. The window was open and there you were, singing away, happy as a song bird.'

'How embarrassing! What was I singing?'

'Amazing Grace.' He smiled at the memory. 'Got to give it to you, you can really bang out a tune.'

I removed my hands from my face.

'Amazing Grace is the song Mum always sang to me at bedtimes. Anyway, my musical career is well and truly over, thank God. I shan't charge you for the impromptu performance if you don't sue me when you lose your hearing later in life.'

'Don't you like to sing any more?' he pressed on. 'Seems like such a waste of talent.'

There it was again, the lost boy look, all questions and innocence.

'Aren't you sick of hearing about me or mother by now?' I paused. 'Would you like to talk about your family rather than mine? It sounds like you've had problems of your own.'

His face hardened.

'No thanks, Grace. I wouldn't waste oxygen discussing my family. Come on, tell me all about it. How come you ended up taking photos rather than singing?'

I yawned. 'It's so late though. What time do we need to get up in the morning? Actually, where are we going tomorrow?'

'So many questions young Grace. Okay, we need to leave here by nine and, I'm delighted to tell you, we're going to a fantastic place.'

'*Where*? For goodness' sake, Alasdair. Just tell me!' He was so infuriating.

'Tomorrow, Grace Buchanan, we're going to Scotland.'

He said the word with such aplomb I could tell he was excited at the prospect. I felt like saying, 'Bloody Scotland! What the hell's bells was she doing up there? It'll be freezing.' But I decided against it.

'Flying again?' I presumed.

'Yes. To Inverness this time.'

'I'll tell you what then,' I sighed, lifting my weary

bones from the chair. 'Seeing as you have been so gracious and have given one of your little secrets away – i.e. a precious destination ahead of schedule – I'll do you a deal. You stoke up the fire and I'll break into the kitchen and rustle up some hot chocolate. It could be a very long night.'

'It's a deal.'

Over the hot chocolate I told him the story of my short and disastrous musical career and how I stumbled into my job as a photographer, and so it was far later than I care to remember when we meandered up the stairs and eventually said good-night. I was just putting the key into my room when Alasdair glanced across at me from his own doorway.

'Grace . . .'

'Yes?'

He smiled. 'About the politician's wife – it's your business, not mine. Don't pay any attention to me.'

I nodded, but instantly realised that, in point of fact, it wasn't my business at all.

'Goodnight, Alasdair.'

'Goodnight.'

I sat on the bed, grabbed my camera and selected the photo of the lovers (if that is what they were) taken at range through the window of the bistro. I zoomed in to look at the expression on the woman's face; she looked happy. I selected the rubbish icon on the Nikon, and a fraction of a second later the photo disappeared from the screen. Let the woman have her moment, I thought. After all I wasn't a paparazzo any more and, like Alasdair had said, I may not know the whole story.

PART III

THE CAIRNGORM MOUNTAINS, SCOTLAND

24–28 MAY

CHAPTER 15

I felt surprisingly chipper the following morning. My wrist ached of course, just as Alasdair predicted, but a couple of high-strength ibuprofen soon sorted that out.

After a rushed morning – packing, eating, driving and then flying – we arrived in Scotland just after 12.30 p.m. The view of the Highlands from the air was breathtaking. Alasdair leant across me and pointed out key landmarks during the final minutes of the flight – the massif of the Grampian Mountains to the north-west, then Black Isle, and finally the golden beaches of the Moray Firth to the east.

On leaving the airport the routine was as slick as it had been at Leeds airport, and I had to admit, to myself at least, that I was having a wonderful time.

Once again, Alasdair seemed to know exactly where he was going and, once again, I only referred to the map briefly to glance at the route he had highlighted in yellow. He explained we were heading into the Cairngorms National Park, to a place called Nethy Bridge.

Having never stepped so much as a toe into the Highlands before, from the moment the car headed south from Nairn and towards the mountains I realised this was a travesty. The glorious spring sunshine had travelled north with us, and the first thing that struck me as we drove into the Highlands wasn't the carpets of heather or the drama of the towering mountains beyond, but the colour of the sky. It was ethereal, like the blue of a water-colour painting.

'Mum was right – about the sky, I mean. Haven't you noticed how different the light is here? The sky is definitely a different shade of blue, and it's brighter too. Everything seems clearer.'

He took his attention off the road for a second to peer into the sky, nodded and let me continue with my thoughts in peace.

Roughly half an hour after leaving the airport, the Cairngorm Mountain Range became omnipresent in the distance. It was a view that couldn't fail to lift the spirits. Beyond Grantown, although the mountain range still dominated the view, the fore-ground opened up into an unexpected plateau of pasture fields. The scenery was further honed to perfection by the presence of a broad, curvaceous river that meandered its way through the glen. Wide, flat fields abutted the river on either side, and a smattering of Highland cattle swished their tails while chewing cud. If I had been an artist I would have stopped the car immediately, taken to my easel and sketched the scene for posterity. Instead, I ushered Alasdair into a convenient lay-by, withdrew my camera and lens filters and began to shoot.

We crossed a rickety-looking bridge that spanned the River Spey, then stopped at a T-junction. Alasdair looked across at me. His hand hovered next to the indicator – I could tell an idea was brewing.

'There's something I'd really like to do, as we're here,' he said.

'What?'

'I'd like to nip to Loch Garten, to see the ospreys. They nest there at this time of year.'

The next question had to be asked.

'Are you into birds then . . . of the two winged variety?'

He laughed.

'If you're asking if I'm a twitcher, then no, I'm not. Not full-time anyway. The ospreys are special though, do you mind if we go?'

'No, not at all.'

He started at the door handle after parking at Loch Garten. 'Wait a second will you, I'll just nip and get changed.'

'Why, what's wrong with what you've got on?' I had noticed he was looking especially attractive that day, in a rugged 'I'm just going to nip out and liberate a small nation' kind of a way.

'If you come to somewhere like this,' he said in all seriousness, 'i.e. *twitcherville*, then it's regarded as bird watching etiquette to dress appropriately. I need to put my camouflage gear on. I've got something in my bag you can wear if you like.'

'Seriously?'

'Grace, you're so easy to wind up.'

'Oh, thank Christ for that.'

He opened the door with a flourish.

'I'll go and see if we have to pay to go into the hide. I'm so excited.'

'Oh no, Alasdair. You really *are* a twitcher!'

With a contented exhale of breath, I grabbed my camera from the back seat and walked the short distance to the edge of the loch. Surrounded by pine forest and overshadowed by mountains, it was a photographer's dream. Loch Garten epitomised peace on earth: serene and completely still.

Alasdair appeared by my side ten minutes later.

'What are you photographing?' he asked, looking down at me. I was prostrate on the floor. I laughed, took the photo and stood up.

'You wouldn't believe me if I told you.' I nodded towards two pairs of binoculars swinging from his neck. 'You look the part.'

'Don't I just.'

We walked down a narrow road that skirted the loch. In all honesty I didn't expect to get much of a thrill out of sitting in a hide for an hour, but it was something Alasdair wanted to do so I tried to feign real interest. As we approached a fifteen-foot square wooden box covered in camouflage netting, Alasdair stopped and took my shoulders in his hands.

'Now then, the whole point of sitting in the hide is to make sure the ospreys are unaware of our presence. I promised the woman in the visitor centre that we would be quiet as church mice and as still as the grave. Do you think you can do that?'

'Okay, David Attenborough, no need for the lecture. I get it.'

'So, do you think you can sit still for more than five minutes?' he persisted.

'Of course. How difficult can it be?'

'The thing is, you have a tendency to fidget.' We were standing outside of the hide by now.

'How do you know I fidget?'

'Because I know.'

The hide was empty except for a long wooden bench screwed to the floor just in front of and parallel to the line of a narrow slit that formed the viewing hole. It was dark inside and smelled of a mixture of woodland air freshener and musty socks. Alasdair handed me a pair of binoculars. As we took our position on the bench I removed my camera from around my neck and replaced it with the binoculars. I looked across at Alasdair. His eyes were already pressed to the lenses and his elbows were propped on a shelf fixed to the wall below the slit.

'What happens now?' I asked in a whisper.

'We sit very still, wait and watch. The ospreys have been on the nest all morning so hopefully we should get to see one of them in action pretty soon. Apparently, once the chicks have hatched, the male will dedicate himself to hunting for the family until they're six weeks old. The female stays with the chicks to brood them.'

'She's got her priorities right. None of this women's lib stuff, get your feet up love.'

Alasdair had morphed into a professional twitcher and failed to respond to my attempt at humour.

'You can't see the nest from here, but they have a camera fixed on it in the visitors centre. I had a quick look, it's fantastic,' he said, keeping his eyes on the lenses.

'Oh, great.'

I wasn't sure how long I could keep up the enthusiasm. I was determined to prove Alasdair wrong though. I was not a fidget.

'So, what stage are we at now? Eggs or chicks?' I asked.

'Eggs. Let's *ssshhh* for a moment.'

'Okay.' I whispered, taking up position as Alasdair had done.

At least a minute passed by until, 'You're fidgeting,' he murmured, through slightly gritted teeth.

'I'm not.'

'I can *sense* you fidgeting,' he continued, quietly but pointedly. 'We'll never see them if you keep moving.'

'I'm not moving.'

'Your head keeps twitching.'

He was right. I sat upright and looked across at him.

'It's these bloody binos. They're not set right but I didn't want to adjust them because you would say I was fidgeting and also my wrist still hurts so I'm trying to balance them with just my left hand.' Alasdair sat up on the bench and let his binoculars hang down onto his chest. He breathed a deep but good-hearted sigh.

'If you get your binoculars sorted out will you sit still?' he asked, a little softer.

'Yes.'

'Go on then.'

'You're being bossy by the way.'

He flashed me a half-smile while I adjusted the focus and fiddled with the width to try to get them to sit flush to my eyes. We returned to our viewing positions but I just couldn't get myself comfortable. The binoculars still didn't feel right and I had left a boiled sweet in my jeans pocket – which was now digging into my right buttock.

'You're doing it again,' he said, becoming quite cross with me now. 'I promised the woman we would be good, Grace.'

'Sorry, sorry. Look, I'm going to ditch the binos and use the view finder on my camera.'

'Fine.'

I took the sweet out of my pocket, placed it on the bench, took the lens cap off the camera and propped it on the ledge. The camera wasn't set up correctly for light and focus.

'Just a couple of adjustments. Won't be a second.'

Alasdair didn't move. I couldn't even see him breathing, but I did hear him sigh as my lens moved in and out of the camera until it focused on the loch.

'Right, finally. I'm ready. This is fun, eh?' I didn't really want an honest answer.

I probably lasted a good five minutes, but nothing was happening: no red squirrels, no pine martins, not even a mouse. The boiled sweet was staring at me from the bench. I licked and pursed my lips. We hadn't had lunch and I was starving. The sweet became an obsession. I edged my hand in fraction-of-a-second movements down to the sweet and slowly raised it onto my lap to unwrap it.

'Grace . . .'

'What now?'

Silence.

I popped the sweet into my mouth and tried to suck it as quietly as possible. The hide came alive with the sound. I must have looked like a camel.

'Grace, please—'

'All right, I'll spit it out.' I popped the sweet back into the plastic wrapper. Alasdair sat up.

'I knew you couldn't do it,' he said.

'I can. I'm ready now, honest.' Alasdair got to his feet and took the binoculars from around his neck. 'Oh no!' I cried. 'Let's stay. You were so excited. I promise I'll be better.'

'We *are* staying. I'm going to teach you how to sit still for just a moment.'

He hopped over the bench and took up position behind me.

'Budge your bum forward a bit,' he ordered.

'That's the second time you've said that to me within twenty-four hours, Mr Finn!'

He positioned himself on the bench behind me and straddled his legs either side of mine, my back rested gently on his chest. I felt my shoulders and arms tense. Being taller than me he could rest his chin on the top of my head, but he moved his head down to my right side to talk to me in a whisper.

'Right then,' he said as his breath brushed against my ear, 'forget the binoculars, forget the camera and relax.'

'Right,' I answered, trying to hide my frisson of excitement at the feeling of his breath on the back of my neck.

'You're not relaxed.'

'I am!' I said, forcefully.

'You're not,' he replied just as forcefully (we were never going to see any ospreys at this rate), 'I can *feel* how tense your shoulders are. Relax into me and concentrate on the water. Look at the water and push everything else from your mind. If any other thoughts come to you, put them to one side and become engrossed in the ebb and flow of the water.'

'Okay, relax . . .' I said, 'I can do that.' I let my

shoulders drop a little, sighed and leant back into his chest a tiny bit more.

'So,' he continued, 'being in a relaxed state is all about being in tune with your breathing, in tune with nature. Listen to the sound of your own breath and slow it down. Feel your pulse slow down while you control your breathing. Breathe in . . . and out. Slow . . . and calm . . . and relaxed . . .'

Yes, I certainly could feel my pulse, but it was racing like a runaway train.

Okay, Grace, you can do this. Concentrate on the breathing – in out in out in out.

'I think I'm hyperventilating.'

I felt his smile.

'No, you're not. Try this. Breath with me – fold your arms.'

He raised his arms and wrapped them around mine. I nestled my head into his neck and, for a moment, felt him lower his face into my hair.

Oh God, the man's actually smelling my hair.

'Right, feel *my* breathing rhythm and follow it,' he said, 'nice and calm and relaxed.'

I eventually calmed down (miraculously) and we watched the water in silence. Alasdair would lift his binoculars from time to time and then, eventually, bingo.

Only twenty yards away, towards the edge of the water but a good hundred feet above it, an osprey was hovering. It was the epitome of grace – still, waiting, watching. A species perfectly designed for purpose: a symbiosis of beauty and function. I tensed up, my breathing short and shallow. Alasdair didn't flinch; his breathing and pulse exactly the same . . . slow, steady, in tune. In a whisper of a heartbeat the wings retracted, the bird dropped at a phenomenal speed into a dive, and at the last moment, a fraction of a second before striking deep into the water, the legs came forward displaying murderous talons. With hardly a ripple in the water, the osprey dived in, then reappeared and headed back to the nest clutching a prize for his mate.

'Wow!' I said, still in a whisper. 'Now that was worth the wait; talk about extreme fishing.'

'Shall I tell you a story?' he whispered.

'Won't the sound of your voice scare them away?'

'Do you want the story or not?'

'Yes please.'

He continued to whisper the story into my ear – it was difficult to concentrate.

'Okay then, once upon a time there were two young ospreys called EJ and Henry. Their eyes met across a moonlit loch and they fell instantly in love. Henry worked hard to build a beautiful home for EJ on the highest tree next to Loch Garten, a loch so blue and so deep that the happy love birds could rest assured that they would have a plentiful supply of food for the rest of their lives. Every autumn they would reluctantly say goodbye and migrate to warmer climes, vowing to return each spring to the same wonderful nest and mate. Eventually, they produced chicks and were excellent parents. Several years passed and the lovers continued to meet each spring at Loch Garten. EJ always returned to the nest on time but, over the course of a couple of years, Henry developed a tendency to return home a little . . . late.'

'Typical,' I joked.

'*Shhh.*'

'Sorry.'

'Then one year, Henry didn't arrive at all. EJ waited and waited, but no Henry. She assumed the worst. Then another male osprey appeared at the loch and wooed EJ for his own. Believing the love of her life had abandoned her, EJ mated with the new bird and eventually she laid a clutch of eggs in the very nest she built with Henry, all those years before.'

'What a tart!'

'When Henry finally returned to Loch Garten, tired and hungry, he was devastated to discover EJ had had an affair.'

'What did he do? Hit the bottle?'

'I'm coming to that – patience. He took no pris-oners. He fought off the young pretender, threw the un-hatched eggs out of the nest, and gave EJ a good telling off. She nagged him of course and said that if he hadn't been late in the first place then the whole sorry affair would never have happened. Henry put EJ's indiscretion behind him, and they went on to have many more chicks and lived happily ever after. The end.'

'That was a great story, is it true?' I asked.

'Absolutely. And the bird you just saw fishing was Henry.'

We spent two hours in the hide. Alasdair returned to sit beside me on the bench and I adapted my breathing for my photographic work. As we drove away from the loch I was aware of feeling more relaxed and contented than I had felt in a very long time.

CHAPTER 16

The car engine barely had time to warm up before the woodland opened to a clearing and a village emerged. Alasdair pulled into the car park of a grand Victorian hotel. He reached for his rucksack and pulled out a folded piece of paper. There was a complicated looking hand-drawn map on it.

'We've arrived then?' I asked, unclipping my seatbelt as I spoke.

'Not quite. I just needed to take a quick look at the directions. Okay, got it. Let's go.' We carried on up a hill.

'Are we staying at a B&B then?' Nethy Bridge was a large village but I doubted it could accommodate two hotels.

'Er, no.' His faint smile told me he was hiding something. He gestured towards the back seat. 'If you reach into the top pocket of my rucksack you'll find the details of where we're staying.' I reached to the back of the car awkwardly whilst keeping half an eye on Alasdair's face.

'Alasdair, your expression would be more fitting if it was plastered across one of Annie's livestock.'

'Eh?'

'You look decidedly sheepish.'

I felt the paper of the letter in the pocket, grabbed it, settled back into my seat and took out the booking confirmation – there was a leaflet attached.

'Rosamund thought it would be nice for you to get back to nature, so she booked a—'

I read the title of the leaflet.

'A bloody woodman's hut! What the'—I scanned through the details—'This place hasn't even got electricity. What on earth was Mum thinking of?'

'Come on, Grace. Cheer up. I thought it looked great when I scanned the details. And anyway, like you said a couple of days ago, you're a country girl at heart, so—'

I cut him short.

'I said country girl, Alasdair, not backwoodsman.' We were already driving through woodland. 'I feel like Red Riding Hood for Christ's sake . . . or Gretel!' A few minutes later Alasdair halted the car at the end of a track surrounded by woodland. The hut was nowhere in sight.

'That's that then,' I shrugged, 'you really *are* a murderer. I bloody knew it. And you've lured me to the perfect place to do the deed.' I glanced at him. 'Where are the pigs?'

Alasdair wasn't really listening; he was busy looking at the leaflet. We got out of the car and he set off into the woods. After a few paces, he noticed a building through the trees and turned to face me beaming a contagious smile.

'Come on, Gretel. It's this way.'

Moments later we stood shoulder to shoulder in silence staring, in disbelief perhaps, at our accommodation. Alasdair's shoulders shook with laughter, and after a quick glance in his direction, I couldn't help but join in. Alasdair took the leaflet from my grasp.

'Honestly, Grace, if you look at the photos properly, the place really does have a . . . what's the word . . . *rustic* charm about it.' He held the leaflet up to show me the photographs. 'There's a wood burning stove, and blankets over the chairs on the veranda.' He pointed to the real thing. 'Look – there they are, and a copper kettle and everything.' He smiled at me sweetly. 'It'll be great, I promise.'

Just one little smile was all it took for Alasdair to cajole me into resigned acceptance. I sighed dramatically.

'You're such a naive dreamer. Never view a house when the estate agent has described it as rustic. It'll be a dump, guaranteed.'

'I'll give you an hour before you're in love with the place.'

'Don't bet on it.'

We wandered over to the hut which, to be fair, once close up was very sweet and rather romantic. A hammock was slung between two pine trees.

What was my mother playing at?

'How long are we staying here by the way?' I asked.

'Three nights . . . ish.'

I flashed him a sarcastic smile.

'It just gets better.'

We stepped onto the veranda and I was forced to confess that the outside sitting area was inviting. Two chairs were positioned around a peat fire pot. I allowed my fingers to run over a tartan rug draped over one of the chairs as we passed. I took a glance at the label – Knockando Woolmill, Speyside – and decided I could warm to the place.

We stepped inside. Alasdair took his phone out of his pocket and beamed.

'A signal! Who'd have thought it!'

The hut was immaculate, cosy, surprisingly warm and exquisitely decorated. It had a home-spun, ethnic 'at one with mother earth' charm about it, and was full of texture. A scattering of soft furnishings – rugs, blankets, cushions and the most beautiful embroidered antique curtains – added not only a splash of colour, mainly russet reds, but also a touch of simple five-star luxury. There was a food preparation area in one corner (pots, pans and plates were on display on shelves above the sink), and, on the far wall, a wood-burning stove was flanked by a rocking chair and a granddad's arm chair. A small circular pine table and two further dining chairs were positioned by the door, and a violin was propped against the timber cladding. I looked towards Alasdair and smiled; my smile said, 'you're right, it is lovely'. But, there were certain other, more delicate, aspects to consider. Alasdair read my mind, picked up an A4 file from a side table and provided a précis of the relevant bits.

'Well, you'll be pleased to know that we've got running water.' He stepped over to the sink and turned the brass tap. 'The water's collected from the roof and stored in barrels on the veranda.' I joined him by the sink and assessed the water, it looked clear enough. 'But we drink bottled water. It's stored in a cupboard somewhere.' He opened a cupboard door.

'The central light is run from a battery, backed up with candles.'

Watching Alasdair explore the room was like watching a child let loose in a toyshop. He picked up and analysed the promised copper kettle. I thought of something fairly important suddenly.

'Alasdair . . .'

'Yes?'

'Where are the beds?'

For once he was flummoxed – but not for long. He began to knock against the pine panelling on the wall to the right of the door. He then made a facial expression akin to Newton at his apple moment, and opened up a secret door within the wall.

'*Ta da!*'

I poked my head inside. It was a cabin bed. The bed linen was exquisite, the skylight above the bed heavenly and the view from the front window monumental. It was the perfect setting for a couple in love – only we weren't a couple in love, and there didn't appear to be another bed. I blushed. Alasdair coughed and turned away.

'The owner said she would drop by with a blow up bed later, so we're all sorted.'

'Oh . . .'

He closed the door and stepped over to a shelf with an enamel jug and a basin positioned on it. He picked up the bowl and grinned.

'And this is for washing your—'

'Bits and pieces?' I finished for him.

'I was going to say face. But, believe it or not, oh sceptical one, there's a shower for washing your bits and pieces.'

'A shower?' I jumped up. 'Where?' We popped outside. A wooden post, similar to the kind of structure a hangman's noose would swing from, was planted into the ground. A large canvas bag with a nozzle on the end hung from the horizontal spar. A water butt was perched on a raised plinth next to the shower, and the whole contraption was enclosed by larch panelling – presumably in case a red squirrel with an eye for the ladies sauntered past.

Alasdair was trying to suppress a laugh. 'You fill the kettle from the butt, take the kettle in the hut, heat it to the right temperature, and you're away.' He glanced across a clearing in the woodland towards the mountains. 'And have you ever had a shower with such a cracking view?'

'Hmm . . .'

We carried on a few paces to another larch-clad structure. Alasdair poked his head in and out.

'Just as I expected. An eco-friendly latrine.'

'A what?'

'The loo.'

I popped my head in. To my absolute surprise, it was the most palatial toilet I had ever seen – and that included a seven star hotel in Dubai. Alasdair was right. What more could a person want? I smiled, content.

'Well, I don't suppose it'll do me any harm to get back to nature.'

Alasdair put his arm through mine and escorted me back to the hut.

'I tell you what,' he said, 'make yourself comfy on the veranda and I'll make a brew. How does that sound?'

'Wonderful.'

I followed his orders and made myself comfortable on the chair. Even though it was pleasantly warm outside, I wrapped the blanket around my shoulders, exhaled deeply, and took in the view. Although we were in the middle of a forest, a clearing in front of the hut allowed a panoramic view of the mountains – roughly ten miles away – framed to perfection by the surrounding pines.

Alasdair appeared, and promptly disappeared, into the woods.

'What are you up to?' I shouted after him. He glanced back with a smile.

'Just popping to the fridge.'

'What?'

I threw the blanket off my shoulders, jumped up

and ran after him. He stopped by a stream, glanced up and down, stepped a few paces into the water and retrieved a plastic bag. He opened the bag, took out a bottle of milk, resealed the bag and placed it back in the stream.

'Well, it saves on the electric bill I suppose.'

'How did you know where it was?' I asked. He handed me a letter from his pocket.

> To Alasdair and Grace. I have put the food you ordered in the fridge and the cupboard. The 'fridge' takes the form of a plastic bag tied onto a rock in the burn. Those extra bits and pieces you wanted are tucked away in the shed, it's not locked. Have a lovely holiday and do let me know if there is anything else you need.
>
> Valery.

I returned to my chair on the veranda and waited for the tea.

'Ah, perfect.' I took a cup and some biscuits.

'I won't join you just for now, Grace, much as I want to. I have a paper to write for my Brigadier and I need to email it off today. It'll only take me an hour or so.' I tried to hide my disappointment – unsuccessfully.

'That's a shame. But, we don't have internet – we don't even have electricity – how will you email it?'

Alasdair smiled at my disappointment. 'I can

connect to the internet through my phone – I won't be long.'

'Oh, don't worry about me,' I said, now trying to sound nonchalant. 'I'll be perfectly happy out here. In actual fact I was just about to contemplate the meaning of life, and that'll take me at least ten minutes.'

I sat back in the chair and watched Alasdair grab his laptop from the car. *This really was the life*. He hummed a happy tune as he walked up the steps and crossed the veranda.

'How long did you say it would take me to fall in love with the place, Alasdair?'

'Ooh, about an hour.'

'And how long have we been here?'

'About an hour.'

I nodded appreciatively.

'God, you're good.'

He ruffled my hair like he was patting a faithful dog.

'I won't be long, and then we'll do stuff.'

After about ten minutes of half-hearted meditation (Alasdair was right, I was a fidget) I noticed a path leading away from the hut. It was like a path in an illustration of a fairy tale, inviting a naive but inquiring mind to venture on. After grabbing my camera, I followed the path along the spongy woodland floor, stepped over a stile and was surprised to see a wooden bench positioned under a tree in a clearing. It was impossible not to notice the tree as it was quite different from the native pines and silver birch. It looked like an ornamental tree of some kind, and was completely covered in the most exquisite double white flowers. I wandered over. A laminated sheet of paper had been fastened to the bench with a string. Taking a seat on the bench, I picked up the paper and saw that it was a watercolour painting of my exact view of the Cairngorm Mountains from the bench. Underneath the painting the artist had written, 'Strath Nethy and the Cairngorms'. Further down the sheet were the words:

From left to right: Bynack More, Bynack Beag, Cairngorm, Northern Corries and the Tulloch Hills – enjoy!

I leant my head back against the uneven bark of the tree for a second, and allowed the warmth of the sun to soak into my face. I sighed, content. Despite my attempt to become a fully fledged spirit of the earth, however, after five minutes I felt a little lonely. Ignoring Mum's phone embargo, I grabbed my phone from my camera bag and switched it on. Twenty missed calls and more texts than I cared to view. It was all work: tip-offs, requests from agents. One of the texts was from Paul.

Where the hell are you?

Smiling, I text back.

Guess what? I'm in Scotland! It's great. Can't believe I've never been to the Highlands before. So far I've met an aunt I never knew I had, been rescued from certain death by Alasdair (he looks extra sexy when he's wet), and found out that Mum was in the RAF – intelligence of all things. Feeling like a stranger to Mum, but on the whole, the trip itself is top banana (as you would say). Alasdair is the perfect gentleman . . . more's the pity! Speak soon. G x

I waited for the phone to ring, but it didn't. A few minutes later an email came through to my phone.

Grace.

I'm in an editorial meeting, skulking at the back and pretending to be taking notes on my laptop.

Scotland eh? What do you mean, he rescued you? How? Why? I hate him even more now. Just don't go developing some kind of hero complex towards him. By the way, I imagine Soldier Boy to have the following: 1) A flash watch (accurate to a thousand meters below sea level). Why? Who really needs that shit? 2) A really big bastard of a pen knife (most of the blades he will never use). 3) A ridiculously powerful motorbike. 4) A jutting jaw that is so chiselled he can open a beer bottle with it. 5) Bum cheeks so tight he can crack walnuts between them – I dare you to ask him to do it!

What's his flaw by the way?

Tortoise.

I snorted at the phone. Good old Paul. I could just imagine his disdain. I hit 'reply'.

Dear Tortoise (yeah, right!)

No flaw I'm afraid, but you're probably right about the watch, it looks expensive . . . draped across his tanned, muscular forearm that is ;-) You're wrong about the knife though, it's like something a boy scout would have.

Bye for now. G x

I turned the phone off. Amusing as Paul could be, it was nice to be away from it all. Very nice in fact.

Resting my head against the tree trunk once more, I began to wonder where my life was headed; always running around the world like Mum said. Maybe it *was* time for a change.

With Mum gone, the world felt empty. I felt much older and I didn't feel rooted anywhere. And then I remembered Jake, and thought of my tree at St Christopher's, and smiled at the knowledge that I really did have roots, and they were still growing strong in Devon.

Unable to find answers to a growing number of questions regarding my future, I did something I always did during moments of disquiet: I grabbed my camera. Concentrating singularly on capturing the beauty of the tree in full blossom, I cleared my mind of doubt and worry, for a little while at least.

CHAPTER 17

Back at the hut, the little door to the bedroom was open and I noticed Alasdair was asleep on the bed. He looked content. I tiptoed to the gas stove and thought about dinner – a head-scratching moment. After opening the fridge (a five-minute round trip), I rustled up a palatable pasta dish. It was better than nothing, but only just.

I looked in a cupboard for any semblance of a dessert. Something tucked away at the back of the shelf caught my eye. It looked like a Christmas pudding wrapped in muslin. I glanced at the label – clootie dumpling – what was that? Maybe it had been left behind by people who rented the hut previously. What was the sell-by date? Last month. *Oh, it would be fine.* I noticed a bag of night-light candles under the sink – too romantic perhaps? Well, we would need more than one battery-powered lamp once it got dark. And anyway, the candles would look pretty – might make me look pretty. Yes, or maybe, no. I was having that very argument with myself when Alasdair popped his head out of the bedroom.

'Hi,' he said, rubbing his eyes.

'Hi. Good sleep?'

'Too good. I noticed you'd gone for a walk and intended to crack on with dinner while you were out, but decided on a two-minute nap – an hour ago. What time is it?'

'Just gone seven.'

'What's for dinner?' He walked across the hut to peer in the steaming pan.

'I went for the easy option I'm afraid, pasta.'

'Perfect. It's a better meal than I had planned anyway,' he said, taking the spoon from me and tasting the sauce.

'Why? What had you got planned?'

'My signature dish,' he answered confidently, 'skinheads on a raft.'

'What?'

'Beans on toast.'

After a pleasant – albeit bland – dinner he said:

'Well, time to get on with my job for the evening.'

'What's that?'

He beat his chest with his fists. 'Man chop wood, light fire.'

'You do that and I'll get back to the kitchen and rustle up pudding. The suffragettes would be mortified.'

Alasdair lit the wood burner then stepped outside to light the peat fire pot. I was more than a little apprehensive about my job. When I removed the pudding from the steaming pan, my apprehension proved to be well founded.

It was a disaster.

Seizing the opportunity to give Alasdair a bit of a laugh, I loaded a tray with two bowls, cream, coffee and – the pièce de résistance – a disastrous lump of molten rock once known as clootie dumpling. I stepped out onto the veranda and tried to keep my face straight. Alasdair sat prodding the fire.

'Oh, perfect,' he said. 'Just a minute though, it's getting dark. I'll sort the lamps out.' He shot off in the direction of the kitchen and returned a second later with matches. Two candle lanterns were hanging from the veranda trusses. Once both the lanterns and the night lights were lit, the little hut was transformed.

'What's for pudding then?' he asked, looking down at the tray. He didn't seem to notice the disaster lying prostrate in the bowl.

'Clootie dumpling,' I answered, hovering over the tray like a new mother.

'Oh? I've never seen anything like it before.'

No, he certainly hadn't!

I watched as he took a mouthful. His expression was akin to a wine taster who had just taken his first slurp; food chewed slowly, eyes raised to the stars in concentration . . .

'Mmm,' he said, 'I'm getting raisins, orange peel perhaps and maybe a little lemon juice?' He tilted his head to one side in a questioning manner.

Was he serious or what?

'And perhaps,' he continued, 'a little . . . charcoal?'

161

He swallowed a mouthful of cremated dumpling, put his spoon back in the bowl and laughed out loud.

'You're such a tease. How did you know I'd buggered it up?'

'What? You've got to be kidding. Other than the fact that it looks like it's just been spat out of a volcano? That pudding should come with a health warning – do not attempt to go swimming within two hours of consuming this product as you will, almost certainly, drown.' He flopped down onto the chair. I was in hysterics by now.

'I knew something was amiss the minute I saw your face,' he added. 'You have no poker face at all, and I take it you do know you go bright red when you're either embarrassed or trying to hide something?'

'Do I ever. I hate that.'

Alasdair cleared the dumpling away and promised to return with something a little more palatable. A couple of books were sitting on the other chair. Curiosity got the better of me. I stole a look at the covers. The first one was called *The Art of Mindfulness*. The second one was a well-thumbed book I recognised from Mum's bookshelf, *The Working Sheepdog*. I opened the front cover and was taken aback to see a message to Alasdair from Mum.

To Alasdair. I know how much you enjoyed reading this during your last stay at St

Christopher's, so it is my gift to you. You never know, it might come in useful one day. Affectionately, Rosamund. X

Instinctively, I opened the front cover of the mindfulness book – another message.

Alasdair. This may help. Time to slow down perhaps? R x

Hearing Alasdair's footsteps I closed the books and hurriedly placed them on the floor. I picked up the poker and began to prod the fire while he took a seat. I decided to come clean.

'I'm sorry,' I said, 'I hadn't meant to be nosy, but I took a quick look in your books and noticed Mum had written in them.'

He put a tray laden with coffee and biscuits on the table, picked one of the books up from the floor and flicked through the pages. I returned to my seat and wrapped the blanket around my shoulders.

'Jake gave them to me last November. It was nice of her to remember me. I've been trying to work my way through the mindfulness one, but spare time isn't something I often have. It seemed apt to bring them along this week.'

'Do you mind if I—'

He cut me short as he took a seat opposite.

'Not at all, please . . .'

I took the sheep dog book and lifted it to my

163

face to smell the paper. It was strange to hold something of Mum's again.

'I was with her when she bought this,' I said, running my fingers over the cover. 'Oh. The penny has just dropped. Is that how you knew so much about sheep farming when we were at Annie's farm?'

'Guilty as charged.'

I put the book down.

'Is working on a farm something you would have liked to have done?' I asked.

'No, not really. But I'm starting to toy with the idea of doing something completely different . . .' His words tailed off into the distance and I remembered Mum's comment in the book, time to slow down perhaps.

'Sick of all the bombs and bullets, eh?'

'Possibly. We'll see.'

I shuddered momentarily. Even though the fire was emitting plenty of warmth, my back felt cold.

'It's chilled off all of a sudden. I think a breeze has picked up.'

Alasdair left his chair and returned a second later with another blanket from inside the hut.

'Here,' he said, 'drape this over your legs. Make yourself nice and toasty.'

I picked up the second book.

'What's this mindfulness business then?' The corner of a page, about three-quarters of the way through the book, had been turned to act as a bookmark.

'I'm just figuring that out. I had a quick read while you went for your walk.'

'And you fell asleep reading it, by the look of things. I'm not surprised.' I flicked through the pages. 'It looks to be fairly heavy-going.'

'It is a bit.'

'Mum was always saying, "Just you be mindful, Grace," usually when I was being told off. Is that what this book is about?'

'No. This is about the Buddhist concept of mindfulness. If you are thinking you need to be mindful, then you are not, therefore, being mindful – so to speak.' I looked at Alasdair blankly while he played with his ear. 'It's one of those subjects that, when you're reading it, the text makes perfect sense. But afterwards, it's fairly difficult to describe.' He picked up the book, scanned the back cover and began to read aloud. It reminded me of the first time I saw him in the Olive Tree Café; the book was a tell-tale distance from his face as he read, and, yes, he definitely needed his eyes checked.

'Mindfulness is the attentive awareness of the reality of things, especially of the present moment. It is a clear comprehension of whatever is taking place – blah, blah – it is a calm awareness of one's feelings, thoughts and perceptions – blah, blah, blah. When practising mindfulness, for instance by watching the breath, one must remember to maintain attention of the chosen object of awareness, faithfully returning back to focus on that object whenever the mind wanders away from it. Any clearer?

'Actually, yes, it is,' I said. 'Mindfulness is what we were doing today at the loch isn't it?'

He nodded.

'My interpretation of it, yes. I'm not sure I got it right though.'

I took a sip of coffee. 'Well, it worked for me anyway. We were focusing on the immediate present weren't we? Aware only of our immediate surroundings and ourselves – our breathing and so on. By maintaining a focus on the loch and the birds, we were able to push out all of the cloudy inner thoughts and worries we cart around every day. You know, all the crap that clutters up the brain. I don't think you need to be a Buddhist to understand it, it's not so dissimilar from concentrating on photography really, or playing a musical instrument, or fishing even, stuff like that. I don't think you need all this Buddhist stuff Alasdair, just take up music, or basically something you have to concentrate on.' He was smiling at me affectionately. 'Is that why Mum gave the book to you, because she thought you needed to sit still for a while, push other things from your mind?'

'Probably.'

'Is that why you go to St Christopher's?'

'Yes.'

'To push some of the things you've seen and done as a marine out of your mind?'

He sighed and sat back in his chair.

'I haven't done anything I wasn't prepared to do, but yes, I suppose so. I was involved in something particularly unpleasant a couple of years ago. I couldn't get it out of my head afterwards. Your mum was the one who helped to get me back on the straight and narrow.'

'What was it, this thing you were involved in?' The question was out before I had time to think about it.

He smiled and shrugged. 'Nothing worth talking about now.'

'You must have seen some harrowing things. Have you ever been injured?' I asked, looking up from my coffee. He picked up the poker and churned the coals around in the chimenea.

'No, nothing serious anyway, unlike many people I've known, including a very good friend of mine.'

'Why, what happened to him?'

He prodded the fire with a final aggressive poke. 'He trusted my judgement and the poor sod was critically injured as a result. He now wears a prosthetic limb beneath his right knee, and that's not to mention the internal injuries he's had to recover from.' Alasdair's tone was cold; he remained transfixed with the fire as he spoke.

'That must be hard for both of you. I'm guessing from your tone you feel—'

'Guilty?' he interrupted.

'I was going to say responsible,' I offered kindly. 'They're similar words, but they have a very different meaning.'

He glanced up from the fire and smiled.

'I've always loved my job, which must seem odd considering what I've said. But talking about it is something I hate to do. Do you mind if we change the subject?'

'Of course not. Anyway,' I said, brightly, 'speaking of St Christopher's, I've been toying with the idea of eventually moving away from my photographic work – and away from London in fact.' He sat back in his seat.

'Oh?'

'Well, once all of the legal aspects of Mum's estate are sorted out, once we've finished our little trip, I was thinking it might pay to keep the retreat going – renew Mum's contract with the military. I could run it myself.' Alasdair gazed into the dancing flames.

'Maybe that's something you might consider when you're older,' he said.

'I'm surprised, Alasdair. I thought you would like the idea of the retreat staying open. I'm sure lots of people would miss it if I turned the cottage into just a home.'

'Yes, they would. But it would be a fairly remote life for you. Maybe you're too young for that kind of lifestyle, tucked away in Devon on your own.'

'I'd hardly be on my own,' I scoffed. 'And anyway, Mum was my age when she started it up, and I'm sure she didn't feel tucked away.' He smiled softly.

'I'm sure you're right,' he said. 'It sometimes pays to keep your options open, that's all.'

'Yes, of course, but I've always known I would go back to Devon eventually. I'm a home-bird deep down I'm afraid.' Alasdair stared into the bottom of his empty coffee cup.

'Hey, I know,' I said, looking to pep things up. 'I saw a bottle of wine in the fridge, let's open it.' I rose to my feet. 'Also – and you're going to love this – I've seen a cupboard full of board games. And as you know, I play to win.'

He smiled. 'That would be great, but I should warn you that we've got a big day tomorrow.'

'What's Mum got up her sleeve now?' I asked, stopping at the door.

'We're heading into the mountains. I'll get a map and show you. Let's go inside.'

'The only game with most of the pieces in the box is Scrabble,' I said, 'or we could play Guess Who?, but that's for ages three to nine.'

'Guess Who? it is then.'

He poured out the wine while I set up the Scrabble.

'Come and have a look at the map and I'll show you where we're going tomorrow.'

I picked up my glass and peered over the map while he explained.

'We'll park at Rothiemurchus'—his finger pointed to a nondescript location—'and then we'll take a saunter up the Lairig Ghru (which is a mountain pass that runs through the Cairngorms). Then we leave the Lairig Ghru and work our way up to the summit of Ben Macdui.' His finger traced the line of our walk. I sat in silence contemplating the walk then thought, *hold on a minute – summit?*

'Then it's a short-ish hop down the mountain to Loch A'an, and then back up to the top of Cairngorm Mountain, with a final jump on the funicular railway to shoot back down to the ski station – that's it.'

That's it?

'And this was Mum's idea, the route and everything?'

'Yes, it was.' He folded the map away.

'Well, Mum obviously thought I was up to it. It looks like a blooming long way though. And we're doing the whole walk in just one day?'

'No, two days. Well, one and a bit really.'

The penny dropped.

'This is going to be an ashes moment isn't it?'

'Afraid so.'

'Correct me if I'm wrong, but there didn't appear to be any *H* for hotel signs along the route. Is this one of those situations where you'll tell me halfway along the walk that there's a pub at the top of the mountain.'

'There *is* a pub at the top of the mountain, at the funicular visitor centre, but there's no accommodation so . . . we're camping.' With half a smile on his face he turned his attention to the Scrabble board.

'Camping!' My voice came out at a higher pitch than I expected. 'Don't tell me – Mum's idea again.'

'Afraid so.'

'But this place is heavenly, why leave it?'

Alasdair smirked. 'You've soon changed your tune . . .'

We turned most of our attention to the wine and slightly less attention to the Scrabble.

After a couple of defeats on my part I packed the Scrabble away while Alasdair rose to his feet and picked up the violin.

'Mind if I play something?'

I shook my head, surprised. 'I'd love it. Can you honestly play?'

He tucked the violin under his chin. 'I used to play – probably a bit rusty now, though. You'll have to bear with me.'

He tuned the strings and then began. It was a classical piece and his rendition was . . . awful.

'That was wonderful, Alasdair.'

He bowed and lowered the violin to the side with a flourish.

'An exam piece. The music teacher took a shine to me; the violin was supposed to give me . . . purpose.' He stabbed the air with the bow. 'But this bow makes a great sword for a kid, so the plan didn't really work!

'I can just imagine. It sounds like you had an interesting childhood.'

'Interesting?' He flopped onto a chair. 'Let's just say my childhood was the exact opposite of yours.'

'In what way?' Once again I hoped I could get him to open up a little, expand on Mum's letter.

'I was a bit of a tearaway, that's all. But at least my schooling wasn't all wasted, I can still knock out a tune. Mrs Bradley would be delighted!'

'I wish I had your confidence, but I was only ever average on the piano, so I don't play to an audience.'

'Why do you do that?' he asked, frustrated.

'Do what?'

'Put yourself down. I've heard you sing and I was – I don't know – enchanted. So you're no doubt better than you let on when it comes to the piano too.'

I blushed and looked at my feet.

'It's just the two of us, Grace – who cares? Okay, answer me this: I just made tons of mistakes. Did you think, Oh my God, that idiot Alasdair has just made a right old fool of himself, what an arse? Or did you think, bless him, he's had a go, just for me?'

I smiled.

'See, who cares? And the difference is, you really *are* musical, so show off a bit!'

'Okay, the truth is, when I'm singing alone, or with Mum around, or even Jake, I'm relaxed. But as soon as there is any kind of audience, even just one person, I muck up, and I *mean* muck up. I just don't like the idea of singing to people.'

'Maybe if you saw it as singing *for* people instead of *to* people then you might begin to see singing in public – or just when others are around, like now – as a different concept, as something that brings pleasure. I'll shut up, it was just an idea.'

'Possibly, I don't know. I suppose my mind is full of embarrassing memories. It was horrendous at the Academy, singing while lots of other people were hanging around. I felt physically sick roughly fifty per cent of the time.'

'Like a marine waiting for a maths test,' he joked. 'That can't have been pleasant. No wonder you left. Maybe the mindfulness book would help,' he suggested, leaning forward to pick up the book. I thought about his suggestion for a second.

'Trust me, nothing can help. And, to be honest, I wouldn't want it to.'

Once more, we parted company at a much later hour than we intended. As we said goodnight and I climbed into my bed, I shouted through the door to Alasdair who was making up the inflatable bed in the lounge.

'Just one thing, Alasdair?'

'Fire away.'

'In the car, when you asked if I wanted to go to Loch Garten, you said the ospreys were special. Why are they special to you?'

He leant against the doorframe and thought about his answer.

'I wanted to see the ospreys because, sometimes,

when I'm deployed somewhere – depending on where I am of course – I log on to the Loch Garten website and watch the ospreys at work. I suppose I find them calming. They're so free.'

'Don't you feel calm when you're away?' I asked quietly.

'Not always, not any more.'

'Well, anyway, I just wanted to say thank you.'

'What for?' he asked, looking tired but happy.

'Oh, I don't know, for everything really.'

'You're very welcome. Goodnight, Grace.'

'Goodnight.'

CHAPTER 18

After a hearty breakfast we headed off on the next stage of the adventure into the mountains. The road meandered alongside the River Spey initially, and we would catch glimpses of wader-clad fishermen casting their lines deep into the river while driving along.

'I suppose the Spey is a salmon river,' I said absently.

'Yes, these guys will have paid big money for a beat on the Spey'—and then, randomly—'Jake's a good fisherman.'

'I know he is, he taught me.'

'You can fish?' He took his eyes off the road for a moment. 'You never fail to surprise me, Grace.'

'Not so surprising really, just assume I did every-thing a boy would do in his formative years. Imagine *Swallows and Amazons* meets *Anne of Green Gables* and you're nearly there.'

'He's a good man,' Alasdair was obviously keen to finish what he wanted to say about Jake. 'You were fortunate to have him around.'

I felt tears sting my eyes.

'Yes, I know. I need to see him – things to say.

Mum was a strong character. It wasn't his fault she chose to keep me in the dark. Grief makes you behave badly – made *me* behave badly.'

After a pause, Alasdair said, '*Anne of Green Gables*? What's that?'

Saved from my emotional moment, our eyes met over the handbrake.

'A book.'

'Never read it.'

'You do surprise me, Alasdair.'

'I can just imagine you lapping up all the old-fashioned children's books when you were little. But answer me this'—he glanced across—'and it's a vital question if we're to continue to rub along together. What camp do you fall into, *Secret Seven* or *Famous Five*?'

'Oh, *Secret Seven*, no question,' I answered, laughing.

'Thank God for that!' he said, feigning relief. 'You may not be aware of this, but the civilised world is split into two categories, *Famous Five* and *Secret Seven*. You're in my camp. I would have had to kick you out of the car if not.'

We laughed.

'I do like to read my old books when I go home, although . . .'

'Although what?' he pressed.

I blushed.

'I was just going to say that Mum once caught me reading one of her saucy novels when I was sixteen. She had a penchant for erotic novels. There's quite a collection at St Christopher's.'

Alasdair beamed. 'Brilliant! Good old Rosamund. What did she say when she found you?'

'Nothing much. She just smiled, took it off me and said I could have it back when I turned eighteen.'

'And? Did she ever let you have it back?'

'She did indeed, on my eighteenth birthday. Well, that and twenty more. I was so embarrassed.'

Alasdair laughed out loud. 'So what does Ms Buchanan prefer to read now, children's books still, or have you developed a taste for something more. . . exotic, like your mum?' He flashed me a sexy smile, there was definitely a devilish twinkle in his eyes – *was he flirting or what?*

'I read both. But mainly the saucy stuff lately.' *What a fibber.*

Alasdair adjusted himself in his seat and his mouth twitched – *perfect.*

We left the forest (and the public road) behind, and travelled a mile or so up a fairly steep track and onto scrubby, open moorland. The Cairngorm Mountain Range was no longer a postcard scene in the distance, but an all-encompassing presence around us. The track narrowed and came to an abrupt end at a settlement of wooden buildings. We had arrived at Rothiemurchus Lodge, an army outdoor pursuits centre Alasdair had visited before. My heart fell to my boots. It was going to be a long, difficult walk – I could feel it. Alasdair laid the map out on the car bonnet to show me the route.

'Like I said last night, first we head up the Lairig Ghru.' He turned away from the map and pointed to a mountain pass roughly half a mile beyond the lodge to the east. 'And then we'll veer left and work our way up to the top of Ben Macdui.'

I remained silent. Rather than looking back at the map, my head remained permanently arched upwards. The mountains looked vast – and steep.

'We'll take it nice and easy, no rush,' he said casually, 'and there'll be plenty of scenery stops. I promise you, we're going to have a wonderful time. Oh, there aren't any toilets up there, so . . .'

I took the hint and disappeared to make use of the facilities in the lodge.

We started along the footpath. Thankfully, the path looked steeper than it felt underfoot. Alasdair chatted away behind me, and we worked our way methodically up the mountain pass.

'Now this is what I call perfect walking weather,' he said, 'sunny, but not hot, and with a just a bit of a breeze. Heaven.'

Half an hour after leaving the lodge I got into my stride, which was fortunate as the path veered sharply to the left and we began a much steeper ascent out of the Lairig Ghru. I felt a definite affinity with goats as we carved our way up a narrow track barely noticeable through the heather. Despite the breeze it was hot work, so I rolled up my sleeves to allow the air to circulate. I also stopped to take in the view, but the far side of the pass was all we could see at that point. Looking down the glen I couldn't believe how much height we had gained in such a small amount of time.

Alasdair was perfectly patient. There was no conversation between us, just the occasional reassuring smile when I glanced down the path.

After a final, calf-burning climb, I realised I was no longer simply looking blankly at the heather on the path in front of me, but my field of vision opened out to take in the mountains – Ben Macdui and its neighbours. The welcoming breeze gained in strength and I stood for a moment and allowed the air to wash over me. The terrain underfoot was scree rather than heather, the gradient was shallower and the climb more pleasant.

Alasdair pointed in the direction of the summit of Ben Macdui. Patches of white in a couple of gullies in the distance illustrated where the snow line began. The peaks of adjacent mountains climbed out of the landscape beyond the horizon of our own mountainside, but we were still too low to see the ultimate view Alasdair had promised – the distant mountains of the west coast. He stopped to take a look at the map.

'We'll come across a little loch soon. A nice spot for lunch, I think.'

I turned around to take in the view.

'You know, I've never been up a real, proper job mountain before,' I confessed. 'It's a brilliant feeling. Can't wait to see the view from the top.'

We carried on around the mountainside and,

just as promised, a small loch appeared to our left. Alasdair instinctively passed me my coat to sit on and his fleece to wear. I was ravenous and practically ripped the rucksack from his back to get at the picnic.

A group of four teenage boys walked past. Their shoulders sagged with kit. Alasdair presumed they were on the Duke of Edinburgh Award Scheme. I agreed but commented that, other than the one cocky joker, they were worryingly quiet for a bunch of teenagers. One of them was limping; he managed a polite 'hello' when Alasdair offered a friendly 'all right lads?'

After lunch, Alasdair delved into a side pocket of his rucksack and took out a small bottle. He sprayed the contents onto his legs. I laughed.

'Well my goodness, I've seen everything now.'

'What?' he asked, massaging the lotion into his skin.

'Let's just say I didn't have you down as a moisturising kind of a guy.' He sprayed more lotion onto his hands and rubbed it into his face.

'There's nothing wrong with wanting baby soft skin,' he proffered, but he couldn't keep up the pretence and began to laugh. 'Believe it or not, *this*,' he held up the bottle of body oil to show me, 'is the best midge repellent on the market.' He lobbed the bottle at my feet. I picked it up and read the label.

'But it *isn't* midge repellent, it's women's body oil.' I was confused.

'That may be so, but it works, so who am I to knock it.'

'Incredible,' I said, also rubbing a little onto my face and hands. 'Actually, I've been meaning to say, Alasdair, *you*, the rebel that you are, seem to be wearing shorts.' I stood to shake the crumbs from my trousers and stepped a couple of paces towards the water's edge. 'I thought you said shorts were a no-no today.'

'Ah, yes, well,' he stuttered, 'I didn't say I would practise what I preach did I? I just didn't want you to get bitten to death or sunburnt.' He flashed me his best smile.

'That's okay. I don't have any shorts with me, and anyway, I wouldn't want my socks to give me a tan line either.' I looked up at the sky. 'It's definitely warm enough to get a tan today.'

Alasdair peeled the top of one of his thick walking socks down from just below his calf to below his ankle bone. 'You're right,' he said, looking at his leg, 'I think I've gone and got myself a bit of a tan today.'

I took the opportunity to check out his legs; my head tilted to the angle of an attentive dog. Alasdair's legs were exactly the sort of pins a sculptor would create – when sculpting a piece entitled *Adonis*.

Long and lean with perfect athletic calves.

My eyes casually wandered up the rest of his body and rested on his face. He was smiling at me. Caught out, I turned away to hide my face and paddled the soles of my boots in the loch.

'What's this loch called? You, err, you never said.'

Alasdair glanced at the map.

'Lochan Buidhe. I've probably pronounced it wrong though.' He took the opportunity to have another look at the route whilst biting into an apple.

'I bet "Lochan" means *little loch* or *just a tiddler* in Gaelic,' I bent down to swish my hand in the water. 'Or it may just mean *bloody freezing.* This water feels like recently melted ice. Come and put your hand in.'

'I don't need to,' he said, laughing. 'It *is* recently melted ice, you nutter!'

We began preparations to move on. Alasdair was buckling up his rucksack when we heard a yell in the distance. The boy with the limp was hobbling frantically down the mountain towards us, flailing his arms in the process. I looked at Alasdair; my concerned expression matched his own. The boy was almost completely out of breath when he reached us.

'Please—help. One of the—group—a fall—'

'He's hyperventilating,' Alasdair said, sitting the boy down calmly.

'Are you asthmatic? Do you have an inhaler?' The boy nodded. He fumbled with the zip pocket on the side of his trousers. Alasdair unbuttoned the clothes around the boy's neck and took the inhaler from his pocket. After a few puffs, although still in a panic, he was at least able to talk.

'What's your name?' Alasdair asked.

'James – Jamie. You've got to help.'

'Right then, Jamie. Whatever the problem is, we'll sort it out. What's happened?'

'It's my mate, Charlie. There's a big patch of snow. He was running down it, for a laugh, you know. I couldn't do it – bad blisters. He couldn't stop – gone over the edge.' Jamie looked at me, panic-stricken, and added, 'What if he's dead?'

'How far from here?' Alasdair asked, anxiously now. He glanced up the path in the direction of Ben Macdui. The path worked its way up a particularly steep part of the mountain for roughly 500 feet or so, ending at a blind summit. I placed an arm around the shaking boy.

'Just over the top.'

'Will I see your mates if I stay on the path?' Alasdair asked, putting on his rucksack.

'Yeah.'

'Have you phoned 999?'

'I tried to, no signal. Remembered you two.' He grabbed Alasdair's arm. His eyes looked wild. 'Please, you've got to help him.' Alasdair glanced over Jamie's head and spoke to me directly.

'Stay with him,' he said. 'Keep him warm and take a look at his blisters.' He took his phone out of a pocket and threw blister plasters at me – ones he insisted I apply to my ankles at the hut before we departed. 'I'll either see you back here, or up with the others.'

He started at a run whilst holding the phone to

his ear. Jamie, still anxious about his friend, started to get up.

'No, Jamie.' It was my turn to be firm. 'Let's do what Alasdair said and get you sorted out first. That limp of yours, bad blisters you said.'

'Yeah, my right foot, but we really should go, they might need my help. I'm supposed to be the team leader.' He rose to his feet anxiously.

'We'll go to them in a minute when you've got your breath back. Take your boot off and we'll plaster up your ankle.' He looked up towards the rise – Alasdair was running at an impressive pace up the path.

'You'll be more use to them if you can walk,' I said, holding his arm and pulling him down onto a rock. 'And he's in very safe hands with Alasdair.'

The back of his foot was cut to ribbons. I used the time plastering his heel to gain a little more detail. They were sixth form students from Berkshire – on the Duke of Edinburgh Scheme as Alasdair had guessed – and were all seventeen.

About fifteen minutes (and a few more puffs from the inhaler later) we set off to join the others and I was relieved to find two boys standing on the path beyond the rise, just as Jamie promised. They were standing next to a patch of snow, roughly forty metres square, that cut away steeply into a gully. The slide mark the impetuous Charlie had carved through the ice was sickeningly visible. The boys didn't speak; they looked as pale as Jamie. Alasdair's rucksack lay abandoned towards the edge of the gully. It was obvious that where the snow ended a steep craggy drop would begin. It was my turn to flush with panic.

'Where's Alasdair?' I shouted, having bypassed the boys and begun to work my way down the rocks towards his rucksack. A dark-haired boy yelled back.

'He told us to wait here. He's taken his rope and first aid kit and gone down the gully to find Charlie.'

'What?' I glanced around blankly and wondered what on earth I should do. Surrounded as we were by Highland wilderness, I at once appreciated the very real danger and isolation of walking in the mountains. What if the boy *was* dead? I started to work my way towards the edge of the gully. I wanted to peer over in an attempt to check Alasdair was safe, but the dark-haired boy called after me again.

'Wait—wait!'

I turned to look at the boys. They seemed younger than their seventeen years.

'The man said you're not to go after him. We were supposed to tell you to wait with us.'

I looked towards the gully and then back at the boys. He was right. There was no point making the situation worse.

We waited for a sight or a sound from the ravine, but – nothing. I tried to maintain a positive tone with the boys, but despite our attempt to remain calm, we were crippled with anxiety. Then, what seemed to be an interminable time later, the dark-haired boy, Tom, said he could hear something. It sounded like a helicopter. The third boy, Simon, noticed a tiny grey speck in the sky.

'Get your coats and wave,' I ordered. 'With any luck it's here for Charlie.'

The speck transformed into a yellow helicopter with *Royal Air Force* written on the side. As it edged towards us I realised we were almost certainly in the way.

'Come on guys,' I shouted. 'We need to move down the path.'

Alasdair's rucksack sat on the snow-clad gully, the straps and gaping top pocket flapped as the helicopter manoeuvred into position – the port wheel and tip of the rotor blades were perilously close to the rocks. We couldn't see the pilot as the tail-rotor faced towards us. Only the winchman, who was hanging out of the helicopter looking at the scene below, was visible. Then, another man and a stretcher were lowered into the gully and out of sight.

No one spoke. I held on to Jamie's arm in an attempt to comfort us both. The other two boys stood still with their hands pressed to their faces.

A little while later, another air crewman at the top of the winch leant forward out of the open door and made hand signals. The winch was raised, the stretcher reappeared and it made its way slowly up to the helicopter. A body wrapped in a blanket lay across the stretcher. Jamie was the first to speak, but it was more like a whisper.

'He's dead isn't he?'

I noticed an orange piece of plastic at one end of the stretcher.

'No, Jamie. I don't think he is. Isn't that a head brace? I don't think they would bother with a brace if he was dead, and the winch-man was down there for ages, so he must have been taking his time applying first aid or something surely.'

The stretcher disappeared into the helicopter and the winch was lowered once more. The original air crewman appeared and, once safely in the helicopter, the side door was closed, the nose of the aircraft fell forward and the helicopter moved away up and over the mountains.

No one spoke. We returned to the patch of snow.

'Where's Alasdair?' I asked, quietly. They looked at each other in silence – clearly as confused as I was. I edged my way to the rucksack. Alasdair's shemagh had been blown onto the snow by the helicopter's downwash. There was no way I was going to let him lose it. I sat down and edged my way along the ice. I shouted out his name. What if he had fallen too, but the helicopter guys hadn't seen him? Sod it. I decided to manoeuvre myself to the edge of the gully and look down. As I made my first tentative moves I heard a voice shouting from the path.

'Grace! Don't make me come and rescue you a second time.'

It was Alasdair. He was standing with the boys. Relieved beyond words, tears began to flow. He started towards me. Our paths intercepted adjacent to his rucksack. I didn't say a word but flung my arms around him like a welcoming war bride.

'What's all this then?' he asked, stepping back and smiling. He cupped my face in his hands and used his thumbs to wipe the tears from my cheeks.

'I thought . . .' I didn't have the words.

'I left strict instructions you were to stay on the path.'

'I know but—' I pointed into the gully, but still didn't have the words to explain my emotion, and then I noticed his right forearm; it was badly grazed.

'Jesus, Alasdair; look at the state of your arm!' I held his arm in my hand and ran a finger near a deep graze. 'We need to get some antiseptic on that – and look at your watch, it's scratched to bits!'

He turned his wrist to look at his watch.

'Not to worry, it's only a knock-off thing I picked up in the Middle East.'

'What about your arm though? That must smart a bit.'

He shrugged. 'I've got another one if it falls off! I'll put something on it later.' He put his arm around my shoulders and smiled. 'Thanks for rescuing my lucky shemagh by the way, I never go anywhere without it.' I handed it back to him but, in return, he draped it like a scarf around my neck. 'Come on Rainy Face,' he joked, 'let's get going.'

CHAPTER 19

Alasdair launched the rucksack over his shoulder and we worked our way to the path to join the boys. He explained that Charlie was in a serious but not life-threatening condition. A few breaks, a leg, maybe a rib or two. Yes, Charlie's parents would be informed, and yes, the school would also be informed and finally, yes, their own parents would be informed. But there was nothing for the boys to do but to put the incident out of their minds and to carry on with the expedition.

The relief for all of them, Jamie in particular, was palpable. Tom and Simon, who I discovered was the quiet one, were given instructions to make a brew and divide Charlie's chocolate between us. Meanwhile, Alasdair insisted everyone put on extra suntan lotion, and asked Jamie to show him their route. I helped with the tea.

Jamie explained that they intended to carry on with their journey as originally planned – Ben Macdui, then down to Loch Etchachan, and camp that night at Dubh Lochan. So, once we had all calmed down and eaten a snack, we set off on the final leg of our climb – to the summit of Ben Macdui. The mountain was now nothing more than a sea of boulders. It looked like the surface of the moon.

Weighed down with kit, and with Jamie's blisters slowing down the pace, the boys dropped back a little, but Alasdair wanted the two of us to push on.

'Don't worry about the boys, they'll be fine,' he said, noticing my reticence to stride ahead. 'They need to re-establish themselves as a team rather than fall back on me for security. I've told them where we're camping if they get into any more bother.'

I nodded, waved across the boulder field to Jamie, and we pushed on.

Roughly half an hour later, beyond yet another rise, the path re-emerged out of the boulders and the way became easier underfoot. Alasdair pointed to the top of a rise, roughly a quarter of a mile ahead.

'Just this last little bit to climb and then we're there, at the top.'

I stopped, elated, and looked to the top of the rise. 'Seriously? That pile of rocks just up there is the top of the mountain?'

He smiled. 'Yep, you sound surprised.'

'I expected the top to be like a child's drawing of a mountain.' I put my fingers together in the shape of a triangle, 'you know, a triangular shape with snow on the top.' I pointed towards the summit. 'This one looks more like a dome.'

Alasdair laughed as we carried on up the path. 'Well, pointy-shaped or not,' he said, 'it's still a mountain, so you should be proud of yourself. How are your thighs by the way – burning yet?'

I rubbed my legs. 'My thighs?' I asked brightly. 'Oh, they're fine, no problem at all. I must be fitter than I thought.' I was such a liar; my thighs were on fire.

And then, after a final push, roughly two hundred yards from the summit (which was marked by a five-foot-high pile of stones – a cairn), Alasdair turned to me, grinned and said, 'You up for a race to the top?'

Run? To the top? Was he nuts?

'Sounds great,' I said, faking enthusiasm, 'but I think you should give me a bit of a head start.' I flashed him my 'I am only a weak and feeble woman' look.

It worked. He smiled knowingly.

'I'll shout back when I think I've gone a fair distance,' I said, 'you can set off after that.'

I took a last drink of water and started at a run up the hill, although it wasn't really a run, more like an enthusiastic hobble. Alasdair waited. I needed a significant head start if I was to stand a chance of winning, so I only beckoned him on once I was roughly fifteen feet from the top. With my victory assured, I was just about to clamber onto the cairn, when Alasdair shot past me, threw off his rucksack, and leapt onto the top with one last Olympian style leap (damn those Royal

Marines and their relentless training, the man must have *flown* up the bloody mountain).

He smiled down at me cheekily and held out his hand.

'Come on, there's room on these rocks for two. You can't walk to the top of a mountain and not stand on the *very* top. Well, *I* can't anyway, especially on a perfectly clear day like today.'

I reached my hand up towards his. He launched me upwards and then, in one fluid movement, hurled me onto his shoulders and all of a sudden I was on top of the world.

Views are often described as breathtaking, which is, perhaps, an overly used expression; but that one really did take my breath away. Ben Macdui was the highest mountain in the range, so any walker who scaled it not only benefited from a 360 degree panorama of the Cairngorms, but also an uninter-rupted view of the mountains of the west coast in the far distance. It was monumental.

Alasdair eventually rested me onto my feet and I glanced up at him as he continued to take in the view. He looked happy. The smile on his face was contagious and I felt an immediate desire to capture his expression, his love of the landscape, the fresh-ness of his face. I grabbed my camera and attempted to photograph the mood and texture of the place.

'So,' he said, appearing by my side, 'how do you feel now you've scaled your first mountain?'

I took a shot of him before answering. 'Actually, it's going to sound a bit over-the-top, but I feel really proud of myself. There were times, trudging up, when I wondered what the hell we were doing it for. But now I'm here, I can see why people get hooked. It's brilliant Alasdair, just brilliant.'

He smiled the warmest smile I had possibly ever seen.

'So,' he added, looking up, 'about this blue-sky theory of your mother's, what do we think? Is it a different kind of blue up here after all?'

I looked up and all around. 'Yes, Alasdair. I really think it is.'

We worked our way down from the summit and it was gone four when we sauntered, happy but hot, around a final contour, and a view of the majestic Loch A'an appeared in a cauldron-shaped glen, several hundred feet beneath us.

I remembered why I was there – Mum's letter. She must have thought Loch A'an to be quite a special place to make me walk all the way there. We stood off-centre to the head of the loch and looked down its length from an elevated position. The loch was the shape of an elongated rectangle, flanked by steep, dark crags on three sides. The far side was the only side not to be cavernously enclosed. The water was deep blue – almost black.

I noticed a small golden beach on the near-side of the loch. Alasdair explained that our camp for the night was on that beach, and so we hurried on down the slope with a lighter and faster step.

★   ★   ★

With a huge sense of achievement rippling through my aching limbs, I stepped onto the sand, slipped the straps of the water pack off my shoulders, flopped down and tipped my head back towards the afternoon sun.

Alasdair smiled down at me.

'Did you have a good day?' he asked, removing his rucksack. I beamed up at him.

'Absolutely brilliant. Thanks so much for bringing me. This place is amazing, no wonder Mum liked it here. Mind you,' I added, sitting up and taking a sniff of my T-shirt, 'I could do with a shower. I stink!'

He leant towards me and took a sniff.

'Mmm, you do whiff a bit.'

I was mortified. 'Do I? Do I really?'

He laughed and shook his head. Suddenly struck by an idea, he glanced at me – cheekily – and proceeded to drag a carrier bag out of his rucksack.

'If you genuinely want to feel refreshed, I happen to know what *the* all-time bathing experience is, and it's right in front of you.' He glanced towards the loch, then removed two hand towels from a carrier bag.

I followed his gaze.

'The loch?' I asked, incredulous. 'No way, it'll be freezing. And anyway I haven't brought a swimming costume.'

He raised an eyebrow. 'I hadn't got you down as a prude, Grace.'

Without ceremony, and with no warning what-
soever, he removed his shirt and I thought all my
Christmases had come at once. I tried to avert
my gaze, but my previous glimpse of his muscular
frame as he stepped into the shower had not
prepared me for Alasdair Finn in full, close-up,
sinuous glory.

'Come on, get your kit off woman,' he said,
throwing one of the towels at me. 'I promise I
won't look'—he winked—'well, not much.' He
slipped off his walking boots and socks. The man
had become the epitome of reckless abandon; I
hadn't seen *that* coming.

'You're serious aren't you?' I said, digging my
heels into the sand.

'Of course! There's nothing better than jumping
into a river or a loch at the end of a long sweaty
walk, I do it all the time.' He unfastened his belt.

'Alasdair!'

'What?' His face was full of fun. I glanced around
the desolate glen.

'I can't possibly just strip off to my knickers and
bra, what if someone comes?'

This comment tickled him to the core.

'*What if someone comes?*' he repeated sarcastically.
'Who the hell is going to pitch up here? You may
not have noticed, but it took several hours to walk
here. Trust me, *no one* is going to come.'

'But it's embarrassing.'

'Why? You wear a bikini at the beach don't you?
What are your bra and knickers if not a ready-made

bikini? And anyway you brought spares. I know you did, I packed them. What was it Rosamund said? *Live life, don't watch it?*'

The bugger had quoted Mum's note from the aircraft.

I glanced up at the sun, and then back to the enticing loch. The idea of jumping in the water was certainly appealing, and it would be very refreshing, wouldn't it? The deciding factor came down to one key issue – what underwear was I wearing? I peered down my top. *Oh dear God*, I remembered. I'd worn the cerise bra and knickers set Mum had bought me. Talk about 'sod's law' – I *never* wore pink underwear. But then, do men really notice that kind of thing, I wondered?

'Well, if you're sure no one will see . . .'

He smiled, held out his hand and pulled me up. 'I'm positive. Now turn away while I strip off.'

'What?'

I quickly realised his intent and turned away – the man was brazen.

Within ten seconds of turning away, there was an almighty splash in the water. I looked down at the sand. His boxers were strewn across his boots – he was naked. Alasdair the Adonis was actually naked, and only a few feet away.

'I take it you're in?' I shouted, trying to appear unfazed. 'Can I turn around now?'

'Yes, you can turn around. Hurry up if you're getting in though, it's a tad nippy. Not sure how long I'll last.'

I turned around. Alasdair was standing in the loch. The water was up to his waist – his perfect, trim waist.

'Isn't it freezing cold?' I asked, amazed. He seemed so composed.

'Of course it's cold, but the secret is to keep moving. It feels great though.' He started to swim.

Was I actually going to do this? I wondered. Was I really going to strip off to my bra and knickers and jump into a freezing loch?

I shrugged. Yep, I really was.

I stripped down to my underwear quickly. Alasdair had turned and was facing the far end of the loch, swimming breaststroke quite happily. I took a last glance at the footpath to see if anyone was coming – it was deserted. Alasdair read my mind.

'You're thinking about it too much,' he shouted. 'Just keep running into the water and don't stop. And remember, stopping at thigh level is lethal,' he tittered and murmured, 'in more ways than one!'

I was definitely seeing a new side to Alasdair.

I glanced up to the sun one final time, it was gloriously warm. The loch was certainly inviting, and I hadn't heard Alasdair yelp as he jumped in, he seemed to be having a lovely refreshing time . . .

'Keep running, don't stop,' I chanted while sprinting towards the loch, 'keep running, don't stop . . .' *SPLASH!* I really went for it and plunged in – a full, ungraceful, belly splash.

It was absolutely Baltic. I flailed around like a netted salmon and tried to scream but could only manage a hypothermia-induced pant. It was as though my entire body had been run through with a million shards of ice. I managed to stand – which was difficult as my legs had numbed in an instant – and ran straight out of the water (even faster than I had run in). Alasdair was standing on the beach, the swine must have charged out of the water as I had charged in. He was already dressed in his underwear, laughing like a drain and running a towel across his chest when I staggered onto the beach.

He threw me a towel. Although my lips had convulsed into an uncontrollable quiver, I managed to find some choice words.

'For f-fuck's sake, Alasdair! Why the f-fuck d-did you talk me into that? You're a f-fucking n-n-nutter!'

And there I stood, in front of him, in my soaking bra and knickers, shivering. My lips were almost certainly blue from the cold, my hair was glued to my face in rat's tails, and my body – in shock from the cold – was every bit as pink as my bra; I must have looked like a burns victim.

Conversely, Alasdair looked like he'd just stepped out of a Bond set on the Caribbean.

Great!

To top off my moment of bedraggled perfection, I heard cheers and wolf whistles from the direction of one of the craggy rock faces enclosing the glen. I looked up. A group of walkers – male walkers – were headed down an alternate footpath. They had obviously witnessed my little dip in the loch. I glared at Alasdair. He tried to take on a serious expression and pursed his lips – presumably trying to limit the damage by attempting to stifle his laugh; but he couldn't manage it. He burst out laughing.

'Well, I've never heard you swear like that before, you *must* be mad at me. And that was three fucks in less than ten seconds, Ms Buchanan!' He realised what he had said and raised a brow. 'If you know what I mean.' I ignored his attempt at humour.

'You're a bloody rogue!' I held the stamp-sized towel in front of me to gain some semblance of modesty. The group of walkers had almost reached the beach by then. 'You said no one would come!' I snarled. 'How the fuck am I going to get changed out of my wet knickers now that little lot have pitched up?' I glanced at him sarcastically. 'And you can take that extra fuck I just gave you and stick it up your arse.'

My last comment sent him over the edge; I actually thought he might die laughing. And then, when I realised what I had said, I couldn't help it, I also started to laugh. It was a 'throw your head back with gay abandon, I've completely lost the plot', kind of a laugh.

The men from the path skirted the edge of the beach. One of them winked. Alasdair stepped in front of me to block their free ogle. With his back to me he cocked his head to the side to speak in a murmur.

'Nice underwear by the way.'

I couldn't help but smile. I tentatively placed my fingers onto his bare, smooth – and frankly – exquisite shoulders, stood on my tiptoes and breathed into his right ear.

'Right back 'atcha.'

Alasdair put up the tent. It was one of those easy, genius tents that, once released from the outer packaging, sprung automatically into life and pegged itself into the sand.

Once dressed (and feeling more refreshed than I had felt in years – if ever), I helped to prepare a fire, which took considerable time as there was a limited amount of flammable material on offer around the beach. Alasdair refused to light it though; he said we had to wait until the sun had set. After devouring dinner – Alasdair was right, it *was* the best boil in the bag meal I had ever tasted – I made another brew. 'Come on then,' I said, 'what really happened down in the gully?'

Alasdair cleared away some of the last pieces of litter from the ration packs before he spoke. 'Let's just say young Charlie is damn lucky to be alive, that much is sure.'

'Why? What had he done? How far had he fallen?'

'He hadn't fallen far actually, but that was the

200

lucky part. What you couldn't see from the path, in fact, what was impossible to notice until you peered over the edge of the gully, was just how far a drop it was from the edge of the snow down into the gully below, a good three hundred feet.'

'Three hundred feet!' I gasped. 'How come he didn't fall the whole way then?'

'There was a ledge, no more than two feet wide, about ten feet below the edge of the snow. Amazingly he broke his fall – and his bones – as he landed on the ledge. Somehow, he managed to cling on.'

'A lucky lad then,' I surmised.

'You can say that again.'

'Was he even conscious?'

'Yes, he was, but frightened and in terrible pain. I tried to keep him talking to take his mind off the situation until the helicopter arrived.'

'Did you manage it, to keep him talking I mean?'

'Yes. Funnily enough he talked about one of the gang – Simon.'

'Oh?'

'He said he'd been moody and difficult company for the whole of the walk, bringing the atmosphere down, which is why young fellow-my-lad Charlie decided to lighten the mood with a little frolicking in the snow.'

'Simon seemed quiet, but he was okay.'

'To be fair to the lad, there's a reason behind his sullen attitude.'

'What?'

'His older brother was killed in Afghanistan last year, a Royal Marine as well apparently, poor sod.' Alasdair decided to change the subject. 'Hey, you ought to read your letter, before it gets dark.' He stood up.

'My letter? Oh, of course, my letter.'

Feeling a little apprehensive – goodness only knew what Mum was about to reveal – I glanced around our cosy camp, up to the overpowering mountains beyond, and along the silent loch, and imagined Mum there all those years before. It was a beautiful place, especially in the setting sun, but it was the absolute stillness about the place that moved me the most.

Alasdair noticed my delay in starting to read.

'Would you like me to read the letter first, précis it perhaps?'

'Thanks for the offer,' I said. 'I'll be fine.'

CHAPTER 20

The Cairngorms.

Hello My Darling.

How did you enjoy your hike? Don't you feel vibrant and totally alive? I wish I could trade places with you, just for an hour or so.

I hope you are sitting on the sand with a warm glow from a campfire on your face. I adore Loch A'an. But then I do hold a special place in my heart for the Cairngorms. In the little piece of paradise laying between Kingussie to the south and Grantown-on-Spey to the north, all of the elements seem to come together in complete harmony – it probably has some-thing to do with all that yin and yang business and so on. Where you are sitting right now is where I regard to be the most wonderful, romantic and truly peaceful place on earth. I'm sure the two of you will be completely alone. Because Loch A'an is so secluded, it rewards only the adventurous with its beauty.

On with the show.

When Geoff completed his flying training he was posted to RAF Lossiemouth, an Air Force base situated on the Moray coast, about an hour or so north of where you are now.

As luck would have it, a year or so into Geoff's tour of duty, I was also posted to Lossiemouth as the intelligence officer for a sister fast-jet squadron. It was the first time we lived together permanently as husband and wife and it was a relief to have put an end to all of the commuting. We lived in a house on the base during the working week, but at weekends we escaped to a hideaway in the Abernethy forest – the very same hut you and Alasdair are staying in at the moment.

How do you like it my love? Is it as sweet as ever? You can imagine my delight when I discovered on the internet that it's now rented out for holiday lets.

In our day, the hut was owned by a friend of Geoff's who was on an exchange posting to somewhere exotic (I can't quite remember where exactly) but the point was he gave Geoff the key and asked him to look after it. We were both fanatical hill walkers and would choose a different mountain to climb most weekends – or sometimes we would simply venture out from Nethy Bridge and meander through the forest. What else did we do? Well, we also had a Canadian canoe that we would launch from the old bridge at Broomhill, paddle down the River Spey as far as the Ballindalloch Estate, hide the canoe in the woods by the road and then hitch a ride back to Nethy Bridge. Then we would nestle up by the fire and read or idle the hours away chatting until bedtime. It was quite simply a wonderful life and no two people can ever have been more content.

Well, as the saying goes, all good things come to an end, and in the winter of 1978 the unthinkable happened. Geoff was on a training bombing run when his aircraft developed a fire in the cockpit. He couldn't extinguish the fire and had no option but to eject. Thankfully he survived, but not unscathed.

The force of the ejection combined with a particularly harsh landing had fused two of the vertebrae in his lower spine. Over the following four months he underwent two operations and was hospitalised for most of the time. Squadron colleagues were understanding, and I was given a generous amount of time to spend by his side. The surgery left him with pins holding the base of his spine together for the rest of his life. On a positive note, almost immediately after his second operation he was able to walk again and, following intensive physiotherapy, he was able (more or less) to live the active life he had previously lived. He could even continue with his love of outdoor pursuits, although not to the same intensity.

Unfortunately for Geoff, the RAF medics would not contemplate him returning to flying duties. They simply couldn't risk the possibility of a second ejection – his spine would never take the strain. So, they medically downgraded him permanently and that was the end of his flying career. Geoff was devastated. He found it impossible to come to terms with the fact that his boyhood dream had come to a crashing end. He became distant and moody. I understood why he felt so desperate, but keeping a cheery attitude around someone who is so low becomes tiresome. It wasn't his fault, poor man, but, as you can imagine, the whole business put a tremendous strain on our marriage.

I was due a posting in the summer of '79 but the RAF extended my tour on the Squadron until November so I could be at Geoff's side while he was hospitalised and afterwards, of course, for his recuperation. The main decision to be made once he was on the straight and narrow (physically if not mentally) was what to do about his career. I suggested he retire from the RAF on a medical pension and follow me from place to place; it was my duty (and my wish) to support him. He wouldn't consider my proposal. To be fair, he was only in his late twenties at this point, and adored his RAF life. So, he accepted the offer of a branch change and transferred to the RAF Administration Branch, a job he would have abhorred if it hadn't been for the clever location his more than helpful posting officer appointed him to.

There was an RAF Lodge on the west coast of Scotland where service personnel could go for adventure training. Geoff was offered the job of running the lodge on a long-term basis and he jumped at the chance. He didn't ask me what I thought of the idea before he accepted it. He was miserable at Lossiemouth after the accident and no matter what I said it was impossible to break the depression. Once he was offered the posting to Arisaig, it was like a great weight was lifted from his shoulders and he was happy again. I hadn't the heart to ask him to refuse the posting although I knew, for the sake of our marriage, it was exactly what he needed to do.

Clearly, there was no requirement for an intelligence officer at an adventure training unit, so we were faced with a dilemma. Either I left the RAF and became a wife without portfolio on the west coast, or Geoff left and followed me back to England (or wherever the job may take me). Neither one of us was prepared to do what the other one wanted. Geoff wanted the job at the lodge, and I wasn't ready to give up my career. Looking after Geoff had been mentally draining. It must sound dreadful, but I was sick of it all; we had gone from being inseparable, intimate and hopelessly in love, to awkward strangers in the space of six months. The truth is I wanted to get away. I thought that if I just had one final tour of duty, one final bit of excitement just for myself, then I would be ready to leave the RAF and spend the rest of my days in Scotland with Geoff.

And so, Geoff moved to Arisaig and we returned to a commuter marriage. The Scottish west coast is a time-consuming place to reach and, as a result, we hardly saw each other. I was offered an intelligence officer's dream posting in Herefordshire, moved to England and started a whole new chapter in my career. I didn't realise at the time how significant that particular move would be in terms of moulding the rest of my life.

Despite the time spent apart, I never stopped loving Geoff and I'm certain he still loved me dearly. Somehow we managed to put those last terrible months at Lossiemouth behind us and, on the rare occasion we saw each other, we re-established a relatively intimate and caring relationship, although nothing would ever be the same as our first wonderful year at Lossiemouth and our precious time in the Cairngorms.

So, why are you sitting on the sandy shore

of Loch A'an? I have cast my mind back to that time in my life almost every day for the past thirty years (which is a lifetime to you, but a heartbeat to me). The beach at the eastern end of Loch A'an is the place my mind drifts to the most when I'm feeling nostalgic. When I think of Geoff and I camping out, exactly where you are now, I can only remember complete happiness and contentment. Sitting out under the stars on a beautiful evening with a wonderful man at a secluded lochside, well, that is my idea of heaven. Life can be wonderful when you want it to be and that is how I would like you to think of my happiest times with Geoff – desperately in love.

When you return to the hut tomorrow I'd like you to take a little walk and look for a tree we planted there. It's a double flowering cherry. If you stand and face the hut from the front, then go down a path to the right, over a stile, you'll find it. We planted it smack bang in the middle of the clearing. I loved my father's idea of physically laying down roots in a place of significance in one's life. My 'permanent marker' in the Cairngorms was that very tree. We planted it almost as soon as we started weekending there. I imagined we would return to the hut over the course of our lifetime and watch the tree grow. But, just like my apple tree at Bridge Farm, I never did get to see it establish itself within the local landscape, my life just didn't work out that way. I hope it is still growing there, but to be honest I was never certain it would adapt to a mountainous climate. If it did, it will show that a young couple in love spent a wonderful year there and, for a short time at least, we found a place to call home and be completely happy. When you return to St Christopher's, go into the attic, have a good dig around some of the older boxes and you'll find a painting Geoff did of the hut (he was quite an accomplished artist). It's yours now my love.

Relax and enjoy the peace.

All my love.

Mum

X

PS: I asked Alasdair to download a particular piece of music onto his iPod. It's one of your audition pieces – Dvorak, Song to the Moon. You used to sing it so purely, so tenderly. Perhaps one day, when you have fallen desperately in love (as I am sure you will), you will sing it again with added maturity, as well as purity. By the way, you are in very safe hands with Alasdair, so you needn't worry about any Scottish wildcats pouncing in the night. Just in case you're wondering, the last I knew there was no girlfriend in tow . . . handsome isn't he?

Once again, my mother was a stranger to me. It wasn't a good feeling but it wasn't particularly horrific either, just odd. Alasdair had lit the fire while I read. I stepped across the sand and handed him the letter; he was becoming quite intrigued with Mum's story. Keen to gauge the expression on his face as he read the different paragraphs, particularly the last, I watched his face.

He smiled almost as soon as he began to read, had a nondescript expression for the main body of the letter, and finally, as expected, he raised his eyebrows with a playful smile towards the end, almost certainly at the part when Mum rambled on about the romance of sitting at a lochside with a wonderful man, and how she thought him to be handsome.

'She was an old romantic that mum of yours.' He handed the letter back.

'She certainly was. I'm ready for round two.'

'I'm sorry?'

'The music?'

'Oh, of course.'

He took his iPod out of his pocket and selected the correct track. I handed him an ear piece.

'Might as well listen to it together, I know the track anyway.'

We listened to the music. To be fair to my mother, it was the perfect track to listen to while sitting in the wilderness under the moon and stars.

'Nice,' he said, less than enthusiastically. 'What language is it in, Russian?'

'Czech. The woman in the song is singing to the moon. She's asking the moon to pass a message on to her lover, to tell him that she's pining for him, that kind of thing.'

He took the iPod back. 'I wonder why she wanted you to listen to that particular piece here?'

I shrugged, but I knew exactly what Mum was doing. On the one hand she was trying to entice me back into music (it was a piece of music I adored), but on the other she was telling me how she felt about Geoffrey; how she loved him. And finally, she was trying to establish a romantic ambiance between Alasdair and me (it was so transparent), and it had worked. I kept this to myself and said, 'I'm not entirely sure, probably to show how she felt about Geoffrey.'

'Ready for round three?' he asked.

I nodded. 'Yes, I might as well get it over with.'

Alasdair stepped over to his rucksack to get the tea caddy. 'You know what?' he said. 'My main thought, in fact, my *only* thought when I was down the gully with Charlie this afternoon was: "I hope that bloody helicopter doesn't blow my rucksack into oblivion, it's got Rosamund's ashes in it."' Alasdair always knew how to make me smile.

Before scattering Mum's ashes, I stepped a few paces forwards to the water's edge, turned through 360 degrees, and tried to appreciate every last drop of the shadowy glen Mum was so fond of.

With a heavy heart, I trickled the ash onto the sand.

'I'm glad you were happy here, Mum.'

I trapped the tea caddy under an arm, rested my head in my hands and let the tears flow. Alasdair appeared by my side. He said nothing but placed a supportive arm around my shoulder.

After a minute or two nuzzling into his chest, I wiped my face on the last stray tissue from my coat pocket, and we returned to our little campfire. I put every item of clothing on, including gloves Alasdair had put into the bag for me, but took off his fleece (that I found myself wearing yet again) and handed it back. He spread our sleeping bags out on the sand by the fire and handed me a steaming cup of chocolate. Face to face in the twilight, he held my gaze.

'I'm really sorry about earlier by the way,' he said softly, 'who would have thought that a group of blokes would walk past?'

'Who indeed!' I jibed, smiling.

'Seriously though, are you having a good time? Because I really want you to have a good time.' I took the chocolate from him and thought for a second about my response.

'To be honest, since we met, my life has been catapulted into one long catastrophe after another.'

He frowned.

'To begin with,' I said, 'I was blackmailed into a journey I didn't want to do, and then trundled several hundred miles away from my home. I've

213

missed out on a lucrative photo shoot and practically broken my wrist. I've stood in horror and watched a helicopter rescue a teenager from near death, and in addition to that I've nearly died of hyperthermia, twice. And finally, I've stood on a remote beach, wet through and practically naked I might add, in front of a group of strange men which is an unprecedented event in my life and something I'll probably never recover from.'

Realising I was joking, he tilted his head to one side and played with his ear lobe.

Did he know this was an irresistible habit or what?

'That's a "no" to having a good time, then?' he asked, smiling.

'Well, wait a minute,' I said. 'I should also add that, for the first time in my life, I've seen – and fallen in love with – both the Yorkshire Dales and the Highlands, I've met an aunt I never knew I had, watched an osprey fishing in the wild and I've climbed a mountain. And, most importantly,' I said, scrunching up my nose, 'I've met you. So, in answer to your question, I'm having a wonderful time, Alasdair. Thank you for asking.' With my speech complete, I stood on my tiptoes and pecked him on the cheek.

Clearly pleased with my affectionate gesture, he smiled and said, 'And we're only halfway through. Aren't you a little curious what else your mother has in store? I'm surprised you haven't asked me.'

I laughed. 'Would you tell me if I asked?

He shrugged.

'No.'

'Alasdair, if the past few days are anything to go by, then it's perhaps best I don't know what's going to happen. Mum was right, it is much more fun to just go with it. And, to be honest, I've given up even *trying* to imagine what's going to happen next.'

'Good,' he said with a cheeky grin, 'because you wouldn't believe it anyway.'

We clambered into our sleeping bags, ready to settle down for a natter over the hot chocolate – Mum was right, sitting by a fire on a remote Scottish loch with a handsome man by your side was *extremely* romantic – when the sound of distant voices penetrated the silence. Our heads turned in the direction of the footpath. Although it was almost dark, there was just enough ambient light to see three figures heading down the path. As they got closer one of them cried out: 'Grace! Alasdair! It's us. We decided to camp with you guys after all!'

The boys seemed stressed when they arrived at the beach, but once their tents were built and they were huddled round the fire with Alasdair, they noticeably relaxed.

'Anyone for a game of charades?' Jamie asked.

'Charades? In the dark?'

'Come on, Grace. No getting out of it now.'

Jamie was the first – and the last – to perform a charade. No one else had the willpower to leave the warmth of their sleeping bag. We were just looking at each other in a 'what now' kind of a way, when Tom announced we could, perhaps, sing campfire songs, to which Jamie (Mr Good Ideas Club) said, 'Grace could start us off.'

'Okay, I tell you what,' I said, with a surprising amount of confidence, 'let's sing *You Raise Me Up?* You'll probably know it, everyone does. You'll recognise it when I start.'

Alasdair looked positively gobsmacked when I offered to sing. I didn't worry about how I sounded, or what the boys thought of me, but sang quietly so my voice wouldn't resound throughout the glen. As I began the final chorus Simon began to sing and I harmonised with him. He had a soulful voice and we made quite a tuneful duet. Tom and Jamie applauded wildly and I caught Alasdair looking at me with what I thought was possibly growing affection. I was taken aback when I caught his gaze, as, just for a fleeting second, I knew without a doubt I had seen him before; was it the cap? The flashcard type memory left as soon as it arrived and Alasdair put a halt to the evening just as Tom chanted, 'More – encore!

'Time for shuteye guys,' Alasdair ordered and, without question, they stood and began to disperse. Jamie lingered, said thank you to Alasdair for rescuing Charlie, and bent down to place an affectionate peck on my cheek. Alasdair lifted his eyebrows in my direction as if to say 'he's got a crush on you,' and shooed Jamie off to his tent.

★　　★　　★

'You got the energy for a last hot drink?' Alasdair asked, once we were finally alone again.

'Yes, great idea.'

I jumped up to make the chocolate, but began to shiver once out of the sleeping bag.

'You're cold, aren't you?' he asked, concerned.

'Just a little, I'll be fine when I get back into my sleeping bag and drink my chocolate.'

'I'll get the shemagh for you,' he said, heading off towards the tent. I called him back.

'No need. I've already got it wrapped around my neck under my coat, remember?'

'Oh, well, wrap it around your head properly then, it'll be more effective that way.' I began to wrap it around my head but, not surprisingly, he took it gently from my grasp, knelt behind me and began to twist it into an Arabic turban.

'It was good of you to sing for them,' he said softly.

'Maybe the mindfulness chat has rubbed off on me, or maybe I just felt like singing.'

I looked around the glen while Alasdair returned to the warmth of his sleeping bag next to me. I thought of Mum.

'Do you think she's here with us, Alasdair?'

'Rosamund, you mean?'

'Yes.'

'Drifting around us in spirit form and having some kind of influence over present events?' he asked, a hint of sarcasm entering into his voice.

'I suppose that's what I mean, yes.'

'No. I don't believe in anything like that, sorry.' His tone was fairly abrupt.

'Well, I'm beginning to believe that there are other things going on that we mere mortals aren't aware of.'

I looked up at the stars and considered the might of the universe for a second until Alasdair burst my spiritual bubble.

'It's just this location and the letters having an effect on you, not surprising really. Sorry Grace, but when you're gone, you're gone.'

I looked at him inquisitively. 'Doesn't it frighten you?'

'I try not to think about it.'

'Well it frightens *me*,' I confessed. He remained silent but I continued and allowed my inner fears to come to the fore. 'I find difficulty in coming to terms with the fact that, once you turn your toes up'—Alasdair smiled at my analogy—'then that's it, game over, *forever.*'

'It won't matter because you won't be alive to experience the feeling of loss. You'll just be gone. It's the ones who are left behind who have the difficult job.' I wasn't sure if he was making a general comment, or referring to my situation with Mum. I tried to explain further.

'But to know that one day all of the experiences we have had'—I glanced around the desolate glen—'all the friendships made . . . it will all be over, no more life. Like I said, *that* frightens me.' Typically, Alasdair tried to give me a solution to the problem.

'See the fear as a positive thing,' he said brightly. 'You wouldn't be so worried about missing life when you're gone if you weren't enjoying it so much right now.' I nodded in agreement. 'Also, ask yourself this,' he added. 'Do you regret the life you didn't live *before* you were born?'

'I'm sorry, I don't follow.'

'Well, there was a whole heap of time that happened on earth before you came along, billions of years apparently, and you missed all of that, so—'

'Oh, I see. No, of course I don't regret not being here, I wasn't born yet.'

'If you look at death in exactly the same way – as life on earth you're simply not around to witness, like the past – then it's kind of the same principle surely.'

'Not really,' I replied. 'In the past I still had my turn to come, still had all of this to look forward to.'

'Ah, but you weren't in existence so, in actual fact, the concept of "looking forward" is something you simply couldn't do.'

I knew what he meant but it was quite a calculated way to look at things nonetheless.

'Do you think Mum is going to tell me who my father is?'

He swirled his hand in the sand. 'Do you *want* her to tell you?'

'Yes, I think I do or, no, maybe not. Oh, I don't know, mixed feelings I suppose.' I looked down the length of the loch. 'The thought of Mum revealing to me who my actual biological father is, I'm not sure how I feel about that.'

'What makes you think she's going to tell you?' he asked gently.

'Something she said in the very first letter. Oh, you haven't read that one have you?' He shook his head.

'She said there were things I *need* to know, things she *has* to tell me, so I'm guessing it's about my father. The reason I perhaps don't want to know, why I've never been too fussed about pressing her for the detail, is that if I'm a product of a one-night stand or something even worse, I would rather not know, and it doesn't look like I'm going to be Geoffrey's does it? Some things are better left in the past, I think.'

Alasdair lay back in his sleeping bag, rested his head in the sand and looked up to drink in the stars. I followed suit, and we lay there, like two cocooned caterpillars staring into the wonder of space.

It was the perfect moment to say something profound, to really impress him with my undoubted spiritual symbiosis with the greater universe . . .

'Alasdair.'

'Yes?'

'There's one thing I've never been able to work out about space.'

'What's that?' He turned to face me.

'My question is this. Which star, out of all those millions of stars'—I flung an arm out of the sleeping bag and into the atmosphere—'is actually the North Star? *And,*' I continued, 'if a person gets lost and desperately needs to find the North Star to navigate by, how does that person find the damn thing if they don't know where north is in the first place. It's like the chicken and the egg scenario. I just don't get it.'

Alasdair smiled. It was a humouring smile; the kind of smile a teacher gives to the dimmest child in the class before trying to explain something.

'It's simple – you just have to know which constellation it's near to start with. And once you know how to find it, you can use the North Star to help with navigation because it's the only star that remains constantly in alignment with north – true north that is. All the other stars appear to move as the earth turns, but the North Star stays in line with the North Pole, which is why it's also called Polaris, which is why it doesn't appear to move.'

'What?'

He laughed again.

'Edge closer and I'll show you.'

I shuffled towards him so our sleeping bags were touching. He pointed to a constellation called the Plough (it looked more like a saucepan to me so he referred to it as 'the saucepan' after that).

'And then if you use the edge of the saucepan – the opposite edge to the handle – as a sightline and look up to the first bright star, about five times the distance of the pan side, then you've found it, the North Star. Have you ever noticed if you lay still long enough, you get a tremendous sense of being on a planet that's turning, being driven by forces way beyond our control? It's quite comforting I suppose, having the North Star as a constant bearing in the universe.'

I turned to him. 'I thought you didn't believe in forces beyond our control.'

He scrunched up his nose. 'Touché!'

Glancing back at the North Star, I said, 'Maybe that's where heaven is, on the North Star, and that's why it's aligned the way it is, so the spirits up there can look down on us and make sure we're okay.'

'Possibly. But it'll be a bit crowded by now, and teeming with dinosaurs, and there would need to be a separate heaven for people from the southern hemisphere, so . . .'

And then, in a flash, it occurred to me.

'I think St Christopher's is my very own North Star. It's my constant bearing.'

He sighed.

'Maybe it wasn't St Christopher's that provided the feeling of security, but your mum.'

'Yes, you're probably right.'

'I haven't got a constant bearing,' he said bluntly. 'I don't need one.' I lifted my head to look at him.

'But without somewhere to point to in life, won't you drift around in the abyss like a broken compass, constantly looking for north?' I looked up to the stars and rested my head on the sand again. 'Maybe the marines are your constant bearing, Alasdair.'

I'd hoped he might open up a little with my last

comment, but he remained silent so I continued to chatter.

'Anyway, I think everyone needs somewhere to point to in life. Where are you sleeping tonight by the way?'

Alasdair jolted.

'*Grace Buchanan!*'

'Oh God, I didn't mean—' I sat bolt upright and floundered for a second before realising he was teasing me.

After providing him an affectionate punch, I clarified my question.

'What I *meant* to say,' I continued slowly, 'was you said something about a bivvy, but you haven't set anything up yet.'

'That's because I'm sleeping with Simon tonight,' he said, sitting up with a wink. 'Now Charlie's jumped ship I might as well bunk up with him. Speaking of which, time to turn in I think.'

He jumped out of his sleeping bag, turned to stand in front of me and held his hands out. I slipped my gloved hands into his bare ones and rose to look him directly in the face. I held the position; he gave the impression he had something to say.

'You seemed to *enjoy* singing earlier,' he whispered. 'You look happy and relaxed when you sing by the way.' I didn't rush to remove my hands from his but I didn't quite know what to say either.

'Simon seemed removed from the rest of us,' I said honestly, 'I was just trying to pull him into the group.'

Alasdair nodded in approval.

'Thanks for caring earlier by the way,' he said, referring to my tears by the snow gully. 'I don't think I've ever seen anyone so pleased to see me, not even my mum.' I wasn't sure what he expected me to say in response – if, indeed, he expected me to say anything at all.

'Well, you have the notebook,' I joked, brushing off the implication I cared. 'Mum's itinerary. I needed you – needed *it*,' I added quickly, 'to finish Mum's story.'

'Oh, I thought you might have been worried about me?' His face was only marginally away from mine and his eyes blazed with a greater light than the fire could achieve. My only defence was humour.

'Worried? Me? No. Not at all. Absolutely not. Why cart about the mountain with a Royal Marine if you can't put him to good use now and again?'

Alasdair turned his head to look around the moonlit glen. I glanced around too and noticed how utterly still and quiet the evening was without our chatter; the only noise was an occasional crackle from the dying embers. I waited for him to say something. He said nothing so I lowered my hands and stepped back.

'Promise you'll rescue me if a wildcat pounces in the night?' I whispered.

'Promise.'

CHAPTER 21

I didn't sleep particularly well by the lochside for several reasons, none of which had anything to do with wildcats or the eerie Highland glen. I had drunk far too much hot chocolate and, in the middle of the night when my bladder was screaming out for relief, I simply could not find the willpower to remove myself from the cocoon I had created in my tiny tent.

I was awoken by Alasdair at around six in the morning. He unzipped a small segment of my tent and passed a steaming cup of tea through the flap. Although the devil on my left shoulder wanted to scream, '*Bugger off you idiot, I've only just got to sleep in this freezing hellhole!*' – the angel on my right won the battle. So, I smiled serenely, took the tea and said, 'Oh, thanks Alasdair. You're a star.'

I could hear voiceless activity around our make-shift campsite – the boys were obviously up and about – but I gave myself ten minutes to drink my tea. I was tempted to stay in my cosy sleeping bag and simply *jump* my way out of the glen but, on reflection, decided to crawl out of the tent and wrap the sleeping bag around my shoulders instead.

With the camp packed away, a pan of boiling water and a small stove were the only significant items still in evidence. I refused Alasdair's offer of US Marine Corps Bacon and Beans (a decision I regretted half an hour later, of course) and accepted Jamie's offer of a cereal bar and an apple.

'Good night's sleep, Grace?' Jamie asked, dashing over to perch next to me in the sand. He was far too chirpy.

'Put it this way, I feel as though I spent the night balanced on top of a toast rack – I was freezing!' I gazed into my teacup. My shoulders were hunched with the cold.

'Oh, right,' Jamie said, totally confused by my sarcastic analogy. Alasdair, on the other hand, fell about laughing and stepped over to take my sleeping bag so it could be packed away. We played tug of war with it for a few seconds but, in the end, I had to let it go.

Within twenty minutes we were ready to move on. My early morning blues soon vanished when I remembered that this was, perhaps, a once in a lifetime experience: waking up in a remote Scottish wilderness wasn't, after all, an everyday occurrence. A thin layer of mist hung over the water, adding a ghost-like quality to the glen. I spent several minutes trying to capture on camera the one aspect of Loch A'an I found to be the most enchanting: the stillness.

The climb out of Glen A'an to the summit of Cairngorm Mountain was challenging; I wasn't cold for very long. Alasdair brought up the rear chatting with Simon, and Tom, Jamie and I recalled the dramatic events of the previous day – which we had begun to exaggerate wildly during the storytelling process. Our pace increased a notch for the last quarter of a mile, which wasn't easy as the terrain underfoot was particularly steep and constituted a sea of uneven boulders and loose scree. The cairn pinpointing the top of the mountain came into view just at the point when Alasdair shouted, 'Last one to the top makes the brew.' The competitive nature within all of us enabled a mad scramble to the top. Unsurprisingly, I was no match for three hormonally charged teenage boys and one steel-thighed Royal Marine. They were perched on the cairn when I arrived at the top, and were holding their cups out towards me expectantly. Alasdair looked the cheekiest of all, despite being twenty years their senior.

Just like the day before when we had climbed Ben Macdui, Alasdair held out his hand and launched me upwards to stand beside him, firm against the breeze, on top of the world. The boys jumped off the cairn, leaving us to enjoy a moment alone. Once again, I turned through 360 degrees to take in the view, but this time, quite unexpectedly, my eyes filled with tears. The landscape was almost too inspiring, Alasdair almost too wonderful and my heart too full of pride at what we had achieved over the past couple of days to be able to hold back an outpouring of emotion.

I turned away from Alasdair and tried to force the tears back with my index fingers. Alasdair noticed, took a tissue from his pocket, turned me towards him and dabbed my tears away.

'Come on, Rainy Face,' he said. 'We can't have tears in front of the kids.'

He bowed his head, pecked me tenderly on the cheek – at which point I thought my heart might just explode – grinned cheekily and said, 'How about a photo?'

With our photo call (and my emotional moment) complete, Alasdair took out his map, rested it on the side of the cairn and pointed out adjacent mountaintops. Simon held a corner of the map down to prevent it flailing about in the breeze.

The point of interest to catch *my* eye in particular was a building a few hundred yards down the mountain on the opposite side of Loch A'an. Alasdair explained it was the Ptarmigan Restaurant and also where the funicular railway stopped. This was excellent news, and I decided Cairngorm would always remain my favourite mountain, purely because it had a café perched practically at the top. Unfortunately, Alasdair burst my bubble almost as soon as it had inflated – it was eight-thirty in the morning and neither the café nor the railway opened until ten.

And so, with a tremendous sense of achievement on my behalf, we began our descent from the mountain. We arrived at the rear of the funicular building within minutes. A fire door had been propped open with an extinguisher, allowing the music from a funky radio station to flow out onto the mountain.

'I'll be back in a sec,' Alasdair said, flashing me a last playful wink as he threw off his rucksack and sauntered through the door. The boys arrived within a couple of minutes and asked the whereabouts of Alasdair.

'I have a feeling he may have nipped to find a loo,' I said, just as he reappeared – looking as proud as punch – through the open door.

'Come on then guys, let's go.' Alasdair's head nodded towards the open door indicating we should all enter the building. I looked at him questioningly but he said nothing, smiled his sexy smile, escorted us through the empty café (cruelly I thought) and out onto the funicular platform. A man in blue overalls greeted us at the barrier, shook hands with Alasdair, smiled and with a broad Scots accent said, 'Don't forget, mum's the word, eh?'

We were escorted through the barrier and followed Alasdair into a carriage. The boys were as shocked as I was. I looked at Alasdair and shook my head in amazement.

'What now?' he asked playfully, but he knew I was gobsmacked.

'Only *you* could have pulled this off, Alasdair. I have never known anyone with so much cheek.'

★   ★   ★

Saying a final goodbye to the boys was surprisingly emotional. They intended to loiter around the funicular base station and wait for 'the olds' to arrive, but we had a date with the bus back to Rothiemurchus to retrieve the car. I gave Jamie a quick peck – which inflamed his cheeks to the colour of burning coal – and Tom shook hands with us. But the most unexpected reaction came from Simon. He shook Alasdair's hand and then gave him the most enormous bear hug. Alasdair hugged him back, ruffled his hair and said, 'Just you remember everything we've talked about, okay?' To which Simon responded, 'Thanks for everything, Al.'

The shuttle bus arrived, we jumped on and our sojourn in the Cairngorms came to an end. I turned to wave to the boys but a lump came to my throat and I turned away; I had been trying to hold off any emotion for the final ten minutes before we departed. Alasdair must have seen the moisture build up on my lower lashes.

'You really *are* a rainy face. Come here you soppy thing.' He placed an affectionate arm around my shoulders.

'Oh, I'm fine. I just feel as though we've left the kids behind, that's all.' I searched for a tissue in my pocket. Alasdair changed the subject and withdrew his arm from around my shoulder as the bus pulled away.

'You'll be pleased to know that there are no more mountainous adventures on this trip.'

'Oh, we're not scaling Ben Nevis tomorrow then?' I asked, pulling myself together.

'Er, no. Back to the hut for some downtime today.'

'And tomorrow?'

'Well, tomorrow, Grace, we're doing something totally different . . .'

'Yes?'

'We're going to a wedding.'

I spun my head to face him. Alasdair was smiling in an *I know! It's bloody crazy* sort of a way, and we both broke down into hysterical laughter that lasted all the way back to the car.

CHAPTER 22

I fully intended to retire for a late morning nap on our arrival at the hut. But, remembering Mum's reference to the flowering cherry tree, I looked at the letter once more and went out to the clearing to make sure that it was still there. It was. I smiled. Mum's legacy at the hut was the tree I had leant on and photographed the day before. She would have been delighted that it had thrived. Such a beautiful thing; striking even. And at least someone was now aware that the tree in the clearing by the bench, where so many visitors to the hut must have sat and pondered for a while, was Mum's tree; that her time in the Cairngorms had been significant and lasting.

Alasdair appeared carrying a tray.

'I thought you might be ready for this by now,' he said, squatting down and passing me a plate. 'One bacon butty and a nice cup of tea as promised. Although, I don't actually remember promising anything of the kind to be honest.' All I wanted to do was to lean over and hug him, but then I noticed an envelope perched against a cup. I picked it up – it was addressed to me from Mum.

I expected to pull out another letter, but found myself holding an old newspaper cutting. I glanced at Alasdair perplexed. He nodded towards the paper and smiled. I opened it out and, recognising the article in question, smiled weakly, blushed and folded the cutting away. Alasdair took it from me and, despite my obvious embarrassment, began to read out loud.

'It's a hit! North Devon teenager takes Queen's Theatre by storm. Barnstaple Musical Society bowed out to thunderous applause last night following a magical performance of the classic Rogers and Hammerstein musical, *Singin' in the Rain*. Grace Buchanan, aged 18, dazzled as up-and-coming singing sensation, Kathy Seldon. With the voice of an angel and a tantalising cheeky smile, her rendition of *All I Do Is Dream Of You* was one to remember. Grace leaves for London in September to follow her musical dream—'

'Stop! Alasdair! Please, no more!' I snatched the paper from him. 'As sweet as it is that Mum saved this, she doesn't need to keep reminding me about how she felt. I get it. I'm a failure.'

Alasdair's smile faded.

'I'm sure that's not what she meant. Listen, Grace. I need to talk to you.'

He looked so serious I was certain he was going to tell me something dreadful. I put the newspaper cutting down.

'What is it? What's the matter?'

'It's about the wedding tomorrow.'

He took a seat and began to play with the tassels of a blanket as he spoke.

'What about it?'

Before he had time to answer, I added, 'Actually, whose wedding is it? I'm guessing they're friends of yours?'

He sighed and glanced across the clearing. 'The groom is the man I told you about when we were in the Dales, the man who was injured, Alex. He's a good friend, we joined up together. He was a friend of Rosamund's too.'

'How do you feel about going to the wedding? You seem apprehensive.'

'To be honest it's the last thing on earth I want to do. And he's asked me to be his best man, which seems beyond ironic.'

'Don't you want to see him?' I asked gently.

'Yes, of course.' He rubbed his temple. 'All his family will be there. God only knows what they'll think of me.' He sighed again and rested his head against the back of the chair. I gave him a moment's silence and tried to think of something to say. I wondered what Mum would say to reassure him.

'Well, I'm no expert, and I don't know the details of what happened, but surely he wouldn't have asked you to be best man if your friendship wasn't important to him.' I leant across and took his hand. The unexpected gesture startled him slightly. 'Maybe it's time to stare down this demon, Alasdair. It sounds to me as if it's all in your head.'

He nodded.

'Actually, speaking of staring down demons . . .' He paused.

'Yes.'

'The thing that I've been trying to tell you is, when Alex told your mum about his intention to marry Sarah, she suggested to him that . . .' He stopped mid-sentence.

'She suggested what?'

Alasdair's face held the expression of a doctor who is just about to pass on some terrible news.

'She told him you would sing at the wedding.'

'*What*?' I pulled my hand away and jumped to my feet. 'You have got to be joking. Why have you waited until now to tell me?'

'I wanted you to have a good time,' he said despairingly. 'That's the reason I've been asking you about your stage fright. She asked me to hand you the letter before I told you, I swear I didn't know what was in it though.'

I put my hands to my face and turned to look at the hut.

'I just don't bloody well believe it. What was Mum playing at? How dare she . . . pimp me out like this!' I threw up my arms in exasperation and turned back to face him. 'It's a terrible imposition. She actually thought I would *sing* at a stranger's wedding?'

'Basically, yes. You're not mad at *me* are you?'

His face was the epitome of anguish.

'Of course I'm not mad at you. I'm just sorry you've had the burden of telling me. Mum had

235

no right. What are they expecting me to sing anyway? An aria, modern stuff, what?'

'*Amazing Grace.*'

I dropped into the chair again, dumbfounded. Alasdair came to kneel beside me and took my hand.

'When we get there tomorrow I'll take Alex to one side and tell him you won't be able to sing. I won't make any excuses. It won't make a scrap of difference to anyone. Your mum should never have said—'

I cut him short, my voice barely audible.

'Like I told you, *Amazing Grace* is the hymn Mum used to sing to me at bedtime. She must have suggested to your friend that I sing it. Why is she putting me through all of this, Alasdair?'

He let go of my hand.

'She had her reasons I suppose, but,' he continued brightly, 'don't give it another thought. I'll sort everything out.'

'I feel bad, though. I hate to let your friend down – let *you* down. I bet they've paid for the accompaniment, a pianist or something. God, this is awful.' I dropped my head, angry at Mum *and* at myself for being such a damn wimp.

'The band is there to play throughout the evening anyway. They aren't just there for you.'

'A *band*? Are they any good?'

Alasdair laughed.

'Not bad. It's just a band he used to be part of years ago, so it's no big deal.'

'Perhaps best then,' I said brighter. 'I'm not sure I could sing along to amateurs.' As soon as the words tumbled out I realised I had expressed myself badly. Alasdair shot me an expression of shocked amusement.

'Grace Buchanan, you bloody snob!'

'No! I didn't mean it like that. I meant—oh, you know what I meant.'

We giggled while Alasdair continued to rib me as a diva. When the laughter subsided I turned to face him and said, 'I wish, more than anything, I had more confidence, but I just don't think I can do it, which is a nightmare, I know, especially considering how you feel about going.'

He leant across and took my hand again. 'Don't give it another thought.'

We sat with our own thoughts for a second, and then: 'Hey,' I said, 'incredible coincidence that we happen to be, more or less, in the same location as the wedding. What were the odds of that?'

Alasdair smiled.

'Alex is from Edinburgh and his wife is an American, so they probably—'

I jumped in, nodding knowingly.

'American? I can just imagine her. She probably jumped at the chance of a wedding with a *Braveheart* slash *Highlander* theme. Yes, that makes perfect sense.'

Alasdair stood, gave my hand a last squeeze then headed back into the hut. He turned round in the doorway and smiled his own trademark cheeky smile.

'*Singin' in the Rain*, eh? Did you jump out of a cake wearing a skimpy leotard with a pom-pom on your bum?'

I laughed.

'Yes, to my everlasting shame, I jumped out of the cake. And yes, before you ask, there were lots of jazz hands and cheeky winks, even a bum wiggle or two! But there was no pom-pom I'm afraid.'

Alasdair raised his eyebrows. His smile was irresistible.

'Grace Buchanan flashing cheeky winks and bum wiggles, now that's something I'd pay good money to see. Any chance of a rendition? Just for me?'

I turned away with a smirk and fixed my gaze on the mountains.

'Never going to happen, Finn.'

I went for a nap at lunchtime and woke ravenous at five. We replayed the events of our first night at the hut and chatted about the past forty-eight hours. It was clear that, despite the trauma, we both felt the walk was enhanced by the adoption of our boys. Eventually the cold night air got the better of us, and we retired into the hut at around eight.

'So, how come you ended up performing in a big production at eighteen?' he asked. 'I thought you hated performing.'

'I do – did. But I needed to prove my worth to get a place at the Academy. I vomited before every performance . . . nightmare!'

'And what about now? Has your fear of singing in public become slightly less intense since our sing-song with the boys? And don't jump to the conclusion that I'm trying to persuade you to sing at the wedding either.'

I smiled sarcastically.

'Singing to a few kids around a campfire is very different to performing on a stage, Alasdair.'

'I was there too, remember, and you refused to sing for me the night before so I reckon you've made a step forward.' Alasdair looked distinctly pleased at the thought.

'I was including *you* as one of the children. I've been meaning to ask though,' I said, happily snuggling in to my chair, 'Tom said, or maybe it was Jamie, anyway it doesn't matter, *one* of the boys said you told them I was a singer or could sing or something? How did that come about?'

Alasdair performed his usual trick of finding an occupation to distract attention from what he was about to say. He crossed to the wood burner.

'One of them asked what you do when I helped them to put the tents up,' he said, stoking the fire.

'And what did you say?' I wasn't sure how he had gone from photographer to singer in the few minutes he had spent on his own setting up camp with the boys.

'I told them you were trained in voice and piano at the London Academy of Music. They probably assumed you were a singer.' He turned his attention to some books on a shelf.

'A fairly natural assumption I suppose,' I continued, 'but that's *not* what I do for living. I left the Academy years ago.' I hoped I wasn't about to hear something that would almost certainly upset me.

'What did they say when you told them what I *really* do for a living?'

'I didn't tell them about your photographic work,' he answered, calmly flicking through a book with his back to me. I kept my voice low, but there was no disguising my annoyance.

'So, you didn't answer their question correctly then.'

He didn't respond. I knew the following question had to be asked even though I didn't really want the answer.

'*Why* didn't you tell them I'm a photographer?'

He turned to face me.

'Honest answer?' he asked.

'Of course, what other kind is there?'

He grabbed the book and returned to the sofa.

'I didn't say you're a photographer because I didn't want them to make incorrect assumptions about you, didn't want them to get the wrong impression.' He turned the pages of the book. I sat still for a moment, at a conversational crossroads. I could either let my annoyance pass and enjoy the evening, or I could say what I felt needed to be said. Naturally I took the second route.

'And what would those incorrect assumptions be exactly?' He stared at the book, bit his lip and said nothing. 'Alasdair! For crying out loud, close

240

the damn book and tell me. What would those assumptions be?'

He closed the book.

'Look, I just wanted to protect you.'

'Protect me? Why would I need protecting? What the hell is wrong with my job?'

'I didn't want them to have the stereotypical paparazzi image of you. Didn't want them to see you as a moped riding, cut throat, money grabber who—'

'Who *what?*'

I couldn't remember a time when I was so thoroughly angry, not because he told the boys I was a singer, but because we were getting to crunch time regarding what Alasdair genuinely thought about my job, about me.

'Okay, you *really* want to know what I think?' His voice was calm but firm. 'I have very little time for so-called photographers who sneak about the world taking hidden photographs of insignificant people doing indiscreet things, while a poor soldier has probably died on the same day and it doesn't even make the paper.'

'That's where you're wrong,' I snarled, 'because troop losses *do* make the papers. You may not have noticed but the forces have great support from the press!'

He glared at me. 'Fine, you're right! But this gossip stuff is all irrelevant nonsense and the stupid-arse general public lap it up, handing over good money just for a glimpse of tits and arse, or a peek at some obscure celebrity who happens to be sleeping with the husband of someone even more obscure. Who cares, for Christ's sake?' I hated seeing this side of Alasdair and tried to hold back the tears.

'And that's what you think of me?' I said, my turn to speak quietly. 'Is this because of the photo I took of that politician's wife in Yorkshire, because if it is—'

'I didn't say that.'

'I hadn't got you down as someone who would make rash assumptions, but you really are a judgemental, stuck-up arsehole. And you haven't got a clue what you're talking about. First of all, I'm not actually a pap – not that it would matter if I was – and second of all, my kind of photography provides a bit of light relief from the boredom of everyday life, it's like eating a bar of chocolate. You're taking it to the extreme. And perhaps you should remember that it's the very same "stupid arse" general public who buy these magazines who also fully support the troops and pay your wages by the way.'

Alasdair's face turned to thunder.

'I'm fully aware of that. You've taken what I said and twisted it.'

I rose to my feet and walked over to look out of the front window.

'Did Mum put you up to this?' I asked, looking into the forest.

'Put me up to what?' His voice sounded tired and dejected.

'I've been such an idiot falling for this ridiculous

charade. I can just imagine the scene at St Christopher's'—I mimicked Mum's voice—'Hello Alasdair love, I've got quite a favour to ask. My silly daughter Grace has got herself in with the wrong crowd. You're a sensible boy, I'd like you to make her see sense, get her back into music.'

'That's not how it was. I make my own decisions, my own judgements.'

'You don't do a very good job of it.'

I turned to face him. 'I'm sorry, Alasdair, but it's pretty obvious you're operating to Mum's agenda, using Buddhist crap to sort out my nerves'—I gesticulated towards the book lying on the floor—'from Mum's book by the way. You've been trying to persuade me to sing and manoeuvre me away from photography all along.'

'I haven't tried to persuade you to sing.'

I wasn't listening.

'God, she did a cracking job working you over.'

'I think Rosamund probably did have a number of hidden agendas behind this trip, Grace. But I would hope you know me well enough by now to see I don't operate like that.' He sounded tired suddenly. I said nothing, turned to face the forest through the window and tried not to cry.

'If I have tried to show you a way in which you might calm your nerves to enable you to sing, then it's because *I* think you have a beautiful voice, not because your mother asked me to. If I've said harsh words about your job, then it's because *I* think you're wasted. I'm absolutely certain running

243

around snapping photos doesn't make you happy. You said yourself you're thinking of moving on.'

He sat on the chair and sighed. I hadn't been able to hold back the tears. My only defence was attack.

'If we're on the subject of happiness maybe you should look a little closer to home.'

'I don't know what you mean,' he said quietly.

'Come off it, you've got more baggage than all the carousels at Heathrow's Terminal 5. Rather than trying to sort *me* out maybe it's time to look at your own life.'

I turned around to face him.

'Just like Mum, you see me as this two dimensional person, that I take snapshots of moments and never see what lies beneath. But I do see, more than most. And just so you know, I *am* happy with my life,' I lied, '*and*, I deleted that bloody photograph of the woman in the Dales, I deleted it on the same night for Christ's sake, just for you I might add'—his face softened—'Thank you for admitting what you think about me, that I'm a cut throat, money grabbing—'

'But that's not what I think about you, and just for the record, I don't see you as two dimensional, far from it. No one could sing the way you do and be two dimensional.' He started towards me but, even though I was secretly delighted with his final line, I edged towards my bedroom.

'I'll get the rest of Mum's letters from you tomorrow and we can go our separate ways. I don't want to do this any more. At least, I don't want to do this with *you* any more.'

He stepped towards me again, but I couldn't cope with the emotion and I really needed a tissue. 'Cancel my invitation for the wedding and write out everything I need to know to finish this debacle on my own.' I grabbed my bag from the floor and started delving through the contents.

'Where are you going?'

'First of all I'm looking for my bloody phone,' I glanced up, 'even though it's against the rules, and then I'm going for a walk. I want to talk to a friend.'

'I hoped I was a friend by now,' he offered quietly.

'Oh, you know what they say, there's no friend like an old friend.'

I grabbed my phone and tissues and cut through the woods towards the village, monitoring my phone as I walked. And then, finally, a signal. I sat on a bench next to a pretty iron bridge by the River Nethy.

'Hi, Grace. What's that noise? Don't tell me, you're at Niagara Falls.' Paul's familiar voice brought a smile to my face.

'It's just the noise of a river.'

'You're still in Scotland then?' he asked, trying – but failing – to stifle a yawn.

'Yes, I'm still in Scotland. You sound tired.'

'I am a bit. I've got a features deadline for tomorrow and I'm struggling with it.'

'For a proper paper or gossip stuff?'

'Proper.'

'Well. I'll leave you to it then. I was just phoning to say you were right, I found a flaw . . . in Alasdair.'

Paul perked up. 'A flaw? In Soldier Boy? Great, what is it?' It was good to hear his humour again.

'Well, the flaw is that he's an arsehole. With a capital A.'

Paul snorted. 'Oh, is that all? I thought you were going to tell me Mr Perfect had actually farted, or picked his nose. He will by the way, once you get to know him better.'

'I mean it, Paul. He really is an arsehole, and I've told him to sod off. We're supposed to be going to his friend's wedding tomorrow, but I'm going to finish the trip on my own.' A wave of guilt flushed through me as the words tumbled out. I realised Mum must have manipulated the whole event so I would be there to support Alasdair through the wedding.

'Go on then, tell me. Why is he an arsehole?'

I threw a pebble into the water and sighed.

'He thinks my job is two dimensional.'

'Your job *is* two dimensional.'

'*Paul!* I thought you of all people would be on my side.'

'Face it, you take photos of celebrities for a living. Yes, they're good photos, but hardly ground-breaking. It's just a way of earning money, like any other job. Why are you so sensitive about it?'

I didn't answer.

Paul sighed. 'Look, it doesn't matter what this bloke thinks about your job. You don't need to grub around looking for approval from others. There's nothing wrong with what you do, so long as it is, in point of fact, what you really want to do with your life.'

Silence.

'Anyway, why are you getting all prophetic on me?' I asked, sullenly. 'Where's my joker gone when I need him?'

His tone lightened.

'Don't worry, the court jester is still here for your amusement. Look, I know I take the piss sometimes, Grace – okay, most of the time – but I was getting the impression you really liked this guy. Don't go and blow it for the sake of a tiff.'

'I did – I do like him,' I said, 'but I doubt he sees me that way so it's all irrelevant.'

'Did you find out if he's single?'

'Yes, he is.'

'So what are you waiting for? From your description, if I was gay, I'd snap him up!'

I laughed down the phone.

'Believe me, he's sexy enough to turn any man gay. Oh, I don't know, it's almost like he's *too* perfect. He even rescued a boy from a mountain yesterday for Christ's sake. Then we sat round a campfire . . . it was so romantic.'

'*What!* A rescue and a campfire? I bet he set the whole rescue thing up just to impress you. And

247

the campfire thing is classic romance. Did he pull some fluff out of his belly button and use it as kindling?' He snorted. 'No, even better, I bet he created a spark to light the fire by scraping some flint across his chiselled jaw . . .'

'Stop it, Paul! I'm supposed to be angry.' I laughed again at Paul's image of Alasdair. 'Seriously though, it's like Mum's introduced me to my dream man. I suppose I'm waiting for the bubble to burst.'

'Do me a favour, Grace.' Paul's tone was stern this time. 'For once in your life just decide what it is that you want and go for it. If that means you want to get him into bed, just do it.'

'But what if he doesn't want the same thing?'

Paul laughed. 'Grace, you're a stunner. He's single, and he's a man. Trust me, he wants the same thing.'

I paused for a second, saddened a little. I knew Paul had genuine feelings for me. I skimmed the toe of my boot across the pebbly river edge.

'What do I do about the tortoise though?' I asked softly. 'I'd hate for him to be upset.'

Paul took a deep breath.

'Grace, this is the real world, not a kid's book. In the real world, the tortoise would be totally annihilated by the hare! Go to the wedding, and stop being so sensitive.'

'Okay, I will.' Tears came to my eyes. 'I love you, you know . . . in my own little way.'

'I know you do.' He cleared his throat. 'Now

bugger off and make up with Action Man; some of us have got serious work to do.'

Alasdair wasn't in the hut when I got back. His laptop sat on the chair. The screen was half-closed at an angle of forty-five degrees and the fan was whirring away. I touched the keys; they were hot. I stepped outside and shouted his name – no response.

Where the hell had he gone?

I decided to place his laptop on standby to prevent it from over-heating. An email flashed onto the screen. Despite my best efforts not to look, it was impossible not to notice the title of the email – Re: Bloody Women!

What!

Well, he already thinks I have no scruples, so I might as well just . . .

Re: Bloody Women!

Al.

Got your email. Don't worry about the singing, Sarah will understand, and I'll keep Grace's name on the list for grub, no worries.

Reference Grace – what the hell's happened to you? Your emails are usually one-liners. You're a bloody mess, man. I've never known a woman to get under your skin, and I can't believe you're prepared to reason with her – you've never reasoned with anyone in your life! The best advice I can give you is to keep her guessing, and for God's sake don't grovel, women lose all respect for men who grovel. So, in answer to your question, why not get involved? Your SF work is nearly over – my money is on promotion next year, mate!

See you in the morning. And remember, you have nothing to feel guilty about with my family. After all, without you (and the hard bastard side of your personality) my corpse would be rotting away in Afghanistan.

Alex

PS. Civilian face? You don't have one. If you pretend to be someone you're not, then it won't work in the end. Don't overthink it. No one said you had to marry the woman. Maybe she just wants a shag? (Win!)

There was way no way on earth I could resist reading Alasdair's original email. I dashed onto the veranda and shouted his name. Still no response.

Title: Bloody Women!

Alex

I've tried to phone you a couple of times, but no joy. Hopefully this email will reach you tonight if you happen to wander into phone coverage.

Well, it's your last night as a single man and I'm not there to get you drunk – shocking! It's not too late though, dude. I can have a getaway car/aircraft/spaceship pull up outside the hotel within the hour if you're having cold feet. You'll never find another woman like Sarah though, so I would stay put if I were you (how on earth did you persuade her to adore you . . . was it the limp?).

Anyway, slight change of plan. Grace isn't going to be able to sing tomorrow after all. I'm sorry I wasn't able to pull it off for you, and I know Sarah was excited, but Rosamund should never have said she would sing. Grace suffers from stage fright (proper job) and hates singing in public. I considered arm-twisting her (literally) but trust me when I say it would be unfair to push the matter (not that you could 'push' Grace to do anything, bloody woman!).

I think you were right when you said Rosamund set us up. Seriously, mate, it's a bloody nightmare. Grace is even sexier than I remembered – it's hard to stay focused when your face is inches from her backside (I've followed her up a few hills this week, and all I can say is the woman knows how to fill a pair of trousers). But she's a bit of a city girl (not my type) and she can be stubborn (ditto). She's a terrible cook, fidgets when she's nervous and she's a bit spoiled (I could go on). But on the other hand, she's up for anything, she never complains (you should have seen how great she was in the mountains – I even got her to go skinny dipping!), she's kind, doesn't spend hours putting on make-up, she's incredibly beautiful (and yet there isn't a vain bone in her body). She's genuinely caring – she even put herself at risk to save my lucky shemagh on the mountain (now that's a real woman for you!). I suppose there's just something about her that gets under my skin – arghhhh! Anyway, it's all immaterial as I've buggered it up (I'm good at that with women). Which leads me on to another reason I needed to contact you; sorry mate, but she's not coming to the wedding. I pissed her off (why do women insist on turning an innocent comment around and then throwing it back at you and then sulking?). She says she wants to carry on alone, but I'm not sure if it was one of those spur of the moment 'I don't really mean it' threats. So now I'm wondering if she meant it, or if I'm supposed to try to talk her round? Again . . . arghhh! Bottom line, can you keep her name on the seating plan for me, just in case? (This is why I steer clear of women.)

I'll try to give you a proper 'man-to-man' pep talk in the morning, but taking advice from me about marriage is like a butcher giving a brain surgeon a lesson in theatre work – I'm simply not qualified.

See you in the morning – hopefully with my little companion by my side. Seriously, though. Should I talk her round? Bollocks. Bollocks. Bollocks.

Al

PS If I could chop off my own leg and sew it on to yours, I would.

PPS Meant to say, my sabbatical has been cut short. Something's kicked off. Grace doesn't know anything about the SF side of the job and I want to leave it that way. Seriously, Alex, would it be wrong to get involved again?

I closed the screen to 45 degrees, left the fan whirring, shot into bed and ran the details of his letter over in my mind . . . *he thinks I'm beautiful . . . he thinks I'm spoiled . . . he thinks I'm beautiful . . . he thinks I'm a terrible cook . . . he thinks I'm beautiful . . .*

CHAPTER 23

The following morning after a particularly restless night, I climbed out of the bedroom and peeked around the hut. Alasdair still wasn't there. I found a note on the table.

Grace

Clearly you haven't received enough letters lately, so I decided to write you a new one. I'm not one for arguments and I have a great deal to do today, so I thought I would leave early and go to the hotel to help Alex. I'm sure you will appreciate having me out of your hair for a while. Perhaps with some time alone you will come to the conclusion that you would like us to carry on with your journey together. If you do – and I hope you do – then I have left a map giving directions to the hotel (it's on the dresser – the wedding ceremony starts at 1400). If you choose not to come then I have written out full instructions/itinerary to enable you to carry on alone, and I have also left your mother's letters for you, they are in the envelope,

which is also on the dresser, under the car keys.
You are covered on the car insurance.

  If I don't see you again, take care.

  Al

PS I have left a couple of things on the sofa which may come in handy. I know you hate to be cold.

Bloody hell, the tone of that letter was like a military memo compared to the chatty email he'd sent to Alex.

I looked across to the sofa – his fleece and shemagh were folded on the cushion. I tilted my face to the ceiling in frustration. We were having such a wonderful time and I had blown it – he had obviously taken Alex's advice.

I picked up the shemagh and sat down. How on earth had I arrived at this monumental disappointment? Resting my head onto the back of the sofa an unexpected smile emerged – Alasdair really took the biscuit. I had planned a whole reconciliation, only to find that he had pulled the rug from under my feet and buggered off. What was I supposed to do?

My thoughts turned to the wedding and to the clothes Mum had bought – the penny finally dropping regarding the fancy clothes and underwear.

I opened the suitcase and suit carrier and flicked my way through. The obvious outfit for the event was a silk, figure-skimming cowl necked dress. If

Alasdair thought I had a sexy backside in my walking trousers, he would certainly appreciate my posterior in *that* dress! I held the fabric of his shemagh to my face and wondered where in the world he had travelled to with his tatty Middle Eastern scarf; what dangers had it witnessed? It couldn't have been easy for him to leave it for me, in fact, he shouldn't have left it. What if it really did bring him luck?

I looked at my watch – it was half past nine. With only a few hours left to prepare for the wedding, I realised I needed to get a move on.

A tepid outdoor shower is not a great way to start when getting ready to go to a wedding. Add to that the lack of electricity and you have the makings of a seriously bad hair day.

On the plus side, my dress fitted perfectly. But having spent the past few days running around the hills in walking boots, it felt odd when I ripped the blister plasters from my ankles, scrubbed away the plaster marks and, Cinderella-esque, slipped strappy silver sandals onto my feet. They were a perfect fit. She had thought of everything, right the way down to perfectly shaded makeup. But there was one major item she had forgotten to include; a clutch bag. The only bag I had with me was my trusty but battered leatherwork satchel. I decided it would suffice; after all, I was going nowhere without extra makeup, tissues, a hairbrush and my camera.

By twelve o'clock I was ready to leave the hut. With flat shoes on my feet for driving, heels in one hand and clunky bag in the other, I realised to my disappointment that the image of effortless perfection I had hoped to create was dashed. Thank goodness Alasdair wasn't there.

I arrived at the hotel at around 12.45 p.m. It was a magnificent, baronial seat of utter Scottishness, complete with mountain view, turrets, kilted valet staff and the must-have loch.

On the one hand I was keen to find Alasdair – it was no fun going to a party alone – but at the same time I felt nervous at the prospect of meeting him as I had no idea what on earth I was likely to say.

The foyer was stunning. A wide, tartan-carpeted staircase with a polished oak banister swept up to the first floor, and an enormous fireplace, flanked by floor to ceiling oak panelling, covered the length of one wall. Alasdair was nowhere to be seen. The guests – and there was a considerable number of them – mingled.

Most of the men wore Royal Marine dress uniform, which consisted of a finely cut red bolero jacket, smart black jodhpurs (cut very close to the skin) and black boots. A white shirt, black bow tie and waistcoat completed the ensemble. The collective effect was impressive, and I knew if Alasdair was wearing the same get-up then I would – almost certainly – swoon.

The seating plan was pinned to a notice board. I studied it while sipping a glass of champagne. My name was shouted from across the foyer. It wasn't Alasdair calling, yet the voice was definitely familiar. It was Simon, the quiet one from Cairngorm Mountain. He rushed over to greet me, displaying a more relaxed manner than on the mountain.

'Hi, Grace.'

'Simon! What on earth? Fancy meeting you here! Are you friends of the groom?' As I asked the question I remembered his brother was a Royal Marine and figured out the link for myself.

'Dad was in the Marine Band so he knows Alex really well.' He sipped on his orange juice then stepped back to look at me. 'Wow! You look a little bit different to the last time I saw you.'

I glanced down at my dress.

'You don't think it's over the top do you?'

'You're kidding, you look great.'

He surprised me with his overnight change of persona. Alasdair's chat had worked wonders.

'Alasdair said you might not be able to come,' he said, taking a glass of orange juice from a waitress as she passed.

'Oh, last minute change of plan. I'm pleased to have bumped into you because I was just starting to feel a little bit lost. I don't know anyone here and Alasdair is bound to be busy.'

'He's out by the loch, talking to the guests. Explaining how the day is going to run etcetera, you know the sort of thing.'

'How did he seem to you this morning, Simon? Was he okay?'

'Alasdair? Funny you should ask because he seemed a bit edgy, not sure why though.'

Poor Alasdair. I should never have left him to stare down his demons alone.

I glanced around the foyer and noticed a uniformed man sitting in a wheelchair by the fireplace.

'Is the groom the man sitting in the wheelchair?' I nodded my head in their direction. He was receiving a peck on the cheek from an attractive brunette. He looked relaxed and happy.

'Yes, that's him.'

'Will you introduce me?'

'Sure.'

We hovered next to the wheelchair and waited for a suitable opportunity to speak. The brunette was monopolising his attention somewhat. Alex spun his wheelchair around.

'I'm guessing you're Grace?'

I nodded.

'You made it after all, that's great.'

I shook Alex's hand, remembered his email to Alasdair and began to stumble some lame excuse about not being able to sing. He put his hand up to stop my verbal diarrhoea.

'Don't give it a moment's thought. Alasdair explained the situation and it's no problem.'

I felt like a failure. Simon began to speak. His words and enthusiastic persistence reflected his age.

'Oh, Grace, were you going to sing? This lady has an amazing voice, Alex.'

Simon turned to me, his expression one of a pleading child.

'*Please* sing, Grace. Sarah would love it.'

I twitched for a couple of seconds while Alex chided Simon for hassling me. Respectful of his injury, I remembered Alex had been to Mum's retreat, and I knew in an instant the true message Mum was desperate to pass on to me. It was as though she was standing behind me, wagging a finger and saying, 'Grow up. Some things are more important than your pride, Grace.'

'You know what Alex, Simon's right. I really should sing something for you today.'

Alex's face lit up.

'Are you sure?'

'Of course I'm sure. Do you still want me to sing *Amazing Grace*?' I prayed he was going to say yes, I could sing it in my sleep.

'That's the one. Let's keep it as a surprise for Sarah though.' Alex's face became less cheerful all of a sudden. 'Oh, I meant to say, I was sorry to hear about Rosamund. She was a wonderful lady.'

'Yes, she was. But enough of that,' I added brightly, 'I need to rehearse. Alasdair said you've hired a band or something, but I only need a pianist.'

'The band is setting up in the ballroom. Come on, I'll show you.' He wheeled towards the ballroom. I followed on behind mouthing 'bye' to Simon.

'Also Alex, at what point would you like me to sing?' I placed my empty champagne glass on a passing tray.

'While we're signing the register was the original plan.' He turned the handle to the ballroom and pushed the heavy door open with his chair. 'Is that okay?'

'Yes, no problem.'

No problem? What the hell had I done?

'Come on then,' he said, smiling, 'let's introduce you to the Sergeant Major. He'll be pleased you're going to sing.'

'Er, Sergeant Major?'

Alex didn't answer; he didn't need to. On entering the ballroom my confusion transformed into a rude awakening. I grabbed a handle and halted his chair somewhat rudely as he tried to push towards the band. 'Alex, is this *the* Royal Marine Band?'

'A few of them, yes. Who else would we have?' He twisted his torso to look at me. 'Didn't Alasdair tell you?'

'No,' I said quietly, 'funnily enough he didn't.'

The Sergeant Major started towards us. He looked brusque and I instantly regressed ten years back to the Academy.

'Sergeant Major!' Alex exclaimed, 'Great news. Grace – you know, the opera singer – has made it after all, so it's back to plan A.'

We shook hands and I winced at the thought of being described as an opera singer.

'Wonderful news. Typical woman,' he said, 'changing your mind, but wonderful all the same.' We walked towards the bandsmen who had taken a break from warming up their instruments when I entered the room. Alex turned his chair to leave but I called after him, a sudden thought pre-occupied my mind.

'Oh, Alex, just one thing.'

'Yes?'

'About Alasdair, he's busy doing his best man thing. If you tell him I'm here, he'll probably come to find me and I have this quirk about not wanting to be disturbed when I'm rehearsing, so . . .' He nodded and carried on towards the door. 'Also Alex, sorry to be a pain, but could you put Simon on sentry duty at the door, to stop people coming in?'

Alex smiled. 'Yes, I'll get someone to stand at the door and no, I won't tell Alasdair you're here. You two need your heads banging together by the way.'

The Sergeant Major interrupted by barking an order from across the room.

'Right, let's give it a run-through,' he said. The bandsmen returned to their seats and began to prepare for rehearsal.

'Yes, I suppose that's exactly what we should do.'

I positioned myself off-centre to the front of the band and looked down the length of the room. Row after row of empty ballroom chairs stared back at me, and the smell from several bouquets of lilies made my stomach churn. I heard the rustle of paper as the Sergeant Major announced the song. He turned towards me.

'Ready when you are. Give me the nod and we'll start.'

I continued to gaze down the room. There was simply no way I could do this. My hands were soaked but I didn't want to wipe them on my beautiful new dress.

'You all right love?' He asked, trying to chivvy me along. 'Only it's 1310, and we really need to crack on.'

I glanced across at him despairingly. Noticing my distress he stepped over to speak a little more privately. He waited for me to explain.

'The thing is,' I whispered, 'I haven't sung professionally for nearly a decade, I haven't had the time to warm up my voice, and I feel physically sick at the thought of singing to over a hundred people.' He sighed and put a hand to his forehead.

'Why the hell did you say you would do it?'

'I have no idea. The thing is, I do desperately want to sing, it's just the getting going bit I find so difficult.' I looked at him imploringly, my eyes full of anguish. His expression, however, was fairly blank.

'Look, I'll tell you what,' he said. 'You nip through to the anteroom – it's through that little door there.' He pointed to a door at the far side of the room. 'No one will disturb you in there. I'll send my man Stiles through to give you some notes to help you warm up for ten minutes and then we'll have a run-through.'

'Thank you, that will probably help.'

I started towards the door but the Sergeant

Major had some last words for me. His expression was severe, his voice a little harsh.

'We'll give it a run-through at 1320 sharp. If you're good enough, I'll tell you. If you're not, I won't let you sing. Understand me?' I felt like a schoolgirl.

'Yes, Sergeant Major.' I scuttled out of the room. Stiles, the cornet player, entered the anteroom with a smile, said nothing and began to play some scales. Towards the end of the warm-up session I gazed through French doors towards the lawn and the loch. Red jackets and fancy hats merged on the grass. One particularly broad-jacketed man with a fine pair of pins caught my eye. The man turned round to speak to one of the guests. It was Alasdair, of course it was; no other man could make what was effectively 1980s ski-pants look so damn attractive. I smiled to myself whilst running up and down the arpeggio; the tone of my singing voice improved by smiling.

Looking towards the water I remembered our time at Loch Garten. I remembered focusing on the water and letting all other thoughts leave my mind. Finally, I remembered Alasdair's words, to think of singing as something to be done, not for myself, but for the pleasure of others. I closed my eyes, ran through the scales and thought of nothing but the sound of my own voice, my breathing, my heartbeat.

The door opened. It was the Sergeant Major. I didn't look at him but strode into the room and took my place in front of the band. He waited for me to start. I glanced across at him and spoke. My voice was firm and strong.

'I'd appreciate it if you played it adagio. Slow, soft and with great feeling, thank you.' They sat up straight, Sergeant Major tapped his baton and the music began. It was time to wake up, to grow up. I could bloody well sing like a star and I was not going to be cast aside by a Royal Marine Sergeant Major.

Three minutes later and the rehearsals were over. To the audience, *Amazing Grace* should sound simple and moving. As the performer, however, there is a great deal to consider, particularly the pace, and it is easy to come across as shrill when changing scale. I looked towards the Sergeant Major and waited for his decision. His face was as straight as a pole.

'Best mezzo we've ever played for. You're in. And no more of this nervous diva stuff or I'll tan your backside.' The bandsmen burst into applause. They had known I was nervous and their faces were warm as they clapped.

'Thank you, Sergeant Major. I'm going to wait in the anteroom while the guests filter in. I'll pop back just before two.'

'Okay, Dame Kiri.'

I returned to my perch by the windows and decided to try the mindfulness trick again. My eyes blurred and I fixed my gaze on my reflection in the window – my hair needed some desperate attention and a fresh coat of lipstick was begging to be applied. Relaxation was important, but not as important as looking good in front of Alasdair: I dashed to the powder room.

Freshly preened, I placed my ear against the door to the ballroom – it sounded packed. Nausea washed over me; only five minutes until Sarah appeared. There was no backing out. I stepped into the room.

From my seat by the band I could see Alasdair's side profile. He and Alex were sitting side by side – he looked more nervous than the groom. His foot tapped on the floor and he rubbed his temple. I was pleasantly surprised to see him behaving in such a way; he was usually annoyingly unflappable. He turned his head and shoulders to look about the room. What he couldn't see, therefore, was Alex's face looking up at him. His friend's expression was one of absolute affection. Alasdair's gaze found mine and relief washed through his face as he smiled at me, but then he raised his hands and furrowed his brows questioningly. I shrugged as if to say, 'what's up?' but then our silent movie gestures came to an end with the sound of Stiles' cornet. The bride had arrived.

It was perhaps the most emotionally charged ceremony I had ever attended. As the music began, Alasdair helped Alex to his feet and passed him a pair of crutches. The bride looked beautiful, angelic and blissfully happy as she drifted down the aisle, and I was spellbound with the emotion of the vows. The registrar announced they were man and wife; they kissed, we clapped and the newly married couple took their seats at a table to sign the register – *to sign the register!* I was on.

The Sergeant Major actually smiled at me as I took my position. I didn't look at Alasdair but smiled at Alex and Sarah and rallied every last scrap of self-composure in an effort to look relaxed, capable and professional. I fixed my gaze on a waiter who was standing at the far end of the room. With a final deep breath, I nodded, and the music began.

The first twelve bars are the hardest, then you're home and dry. I passed them by and realised I was enjoying myself. I wasn't thinking of technique or assessment or what other people thought of me but simply enjoyed the music.

As I held the last note I allowed my eyes to fall on Alasdair. His gaze was so enraptured I couldn't help but smile, and I realised, right then and there in my Hollywood moment, that I had fallen head over heels in love with him. What on earth would my mother say?

After just a few moments the groom led the way with a thunderous applause and I felt a wave of relief rush to the tips of my toes. It was over. I had enjoyed it, but I would be in no hurry to do it again. I turned to the Sergeant Major and mouthed, 'Thank you'. He had tears in his eyes – *surely not.*

The wedding continued with a poignant reading.

267

Then, with a final lingering kiss and yet another round of applause, the bride jumped onto the groom's knee and Alasdair wheeled them both out of the ballroom and into the anteroom. The crowd followed on behind and I mingled in, embarrassed to receive great swathes of attention and compliments.

With the exhilaration of the performance still ringing in my head, I entered the anteroom with the single-minded purpose of finally speaking to Alasdair. He was helping Alex down the steps and onto the lawn. Sarah was distracted by a crowd of ladies who chatted excitedly.

Alasdair beckoned me to join them. We faced each other in silence over Alex's wheelchair. Alex looked from Alasdair to me and then back again. He was shaking his head.

'For goodness' sake, will one of you say something or just kiss and make up?'

I shrugged my shoulders as if to say, *well, I'm game if he is.* Alasdair leant forward and kissed me tenderly on the cheek. I blushed. Alex turned to me. 'That was wonderful, Grace, can't thank you enough. I'm sure Sarah will gush all over you as soon as she's finished being mobbed. Actually, I think I'll go and rescue my wife right now, excuse me . . .'

Alasdair was about to speak when my biggest fan arrived: Simon.

'Grace, that was fantastic! Wasn't she fantastic, Alasdair?' We both looked at Alasdair. I tilted my head questioningly to one side.

'Yes, she was fantastic,' he said, 'full of surprises too. Simon, could you give us a moment please?'

I looked up at Alasdair. His face was full of mischief.

'So I just wanted to say sorry,' he said, 'you know, for being such a *judgemental arse*.' He stepped closer towards me as a waiter pushed behind him. I didn't step back.

'You forgot the "stuck-up" bit,' I jibed.

He smiled.

'And is there anything you would like to say to me in return, Ms Buchanan?'

I glanced about the room. 'No, can't think of anything.'

'I'll give you a clue,' he continued, 'it starts with I'm, and ends with sorry.'

I shrugged my shoulders. 'Okay, I may have pushed it a bit when I called you stuck-up.'

He burst out laughing and my train of thought shot off at a tangent.

'And, oh my God, Alasdair bloody Finn, I cannot believe you didn't tell me I would be singing with *the* Royal Marine Band.' I smiled what was possibly the broadest smile I had smiled in my entire life. 'Can you believe it? I. Just. Sang,' I emphasised the words, 'with *the* Royal Marine Band. How cool is that?' I looked up at him brightly, the previous day's issues completely forgotten.

'No, to be honest, I can't believe it.'

At that moment a fellow marine sauntered past, patted Alasdair on the shoulder, smiled warmly and said, 'Okay?' They chatted privately for a moment and I sobered, remembering Alasdair's concerns regarding the day.

'How's it going by the way?'

Alasdair shook his head.

'It's been fine.' Typical Alasdair; no more detail. 'Hey, I've not seen you all day,' he said, 'why don't we go down to the loch? I know you can't resist a paddle in the water . . . no skinny dipping this time though!' I narrowed my eyes at him playfully. 'My best man duties are more or less at an end – no speeches, thank God – and I'm desperate to discover what prompted you to sing.'

I nodded enthusiastically.

He sought out two glasses of champagne and I followed on, my eyes pinned to his broad shoulders, as he made his way through the guests. At the edge of the lawn a smoky female voice spoke out from behind us.

'Hello, Alasdair, is one of those glasses for me?' We turned around.

'Penny!'

It was the brunette from the fireplace. *Great!*

Penny – all teeth and smiles – took one of the glasses of champagne from Alasdair and said 'cheers' as she chinked her glass with his. She stepped onto her tiptoes to peck him on the cheek. Alasdair handed the other glass to me with a helping of an apologetic smile. She glanced in my direction, momentarily looked me up and down (only a trained female eye would notice), then turned to Alasdair and waited for an introduction. He was slow on the uptake.

'Oh, sorry. Penny, this is Grace.'

Alasdair seemed lost for words, which didn't really matter, because Penny had a whole load of them. She turned to me.

'Oh, you're the singer. Will you be singing later or are you leaving soon?'

What?

'They only wanted me for the ceremony, I'm afraid.' I handed my glass of champagne back to Alasdair. 'Well, I should leave you two to catch up.' I turned away and Penny immediately homed in on Alasdair. He called after me.

'Won't you stay? I'll nip and get another glass.'

'No, you're fine honestly.' I flashed him my best smile. 'It's a party, Alasdair. Time to mingle. And, you never know, I might take some more *bookings*.' Penny stopped mid-sip.

'Great idea, I'm sure there are lots of people here who would hire you.'

Alasdair raised his eyes at me. I turned my back to him and murmured, 'Catch you later, Al.'

The guests loitered happily for an hour in the sunshine waiting for the wedding breakfast to begin. Having played a leading role in the ceremony I was not at a loss for company or conversation, and there was always Simon. I finally spoke to Sarah. She could not have been further from the stereotypical assumption I had made while sitting on the grass at the hut.

The champagne flowed freely and I lost count of how many glasses I had consumed during the hour. I grabbed my camera and sauntered among the guests taking spontaneous shots. I focused my attention on the bride and groom and away from Alasdair, who was still talking to Penny. I did take a side profile shot of him looking particularly handsome – with Penny strategically removed from the viewfinder of course.

Alex was taking a quiet moment on the terrace in his wheelchair. He called me over.

'Having a good time?'

'Yes, the best. Thanks again for inviting me.' I crouched down next to his chair, my dress gathered on the floor. His raised glass was filled by a passing waiter while he waved at Sarah, who was having her photograph taken by the loch.

'I hope you don't mind,' he said, 'but I also know why you two have made this trip up here.'

'No, I don't mind. Did Alasdair tell you or Mum?'

'Both.' He took a quick sip of orange juice. 'We originally planned to marry in England, but when I asked Al to be the best man and told him the date, he said he couldn't make it.'

'Why?'

'I suppose he didn't want to let your mum down, and I have the distinct feeling he was looking forward to meeting you.' He glanced up at me with a grin.

'Oh?'

'Come off it, Grace. If you can't see what's crying out in front of you then, well, you must be blind.' I pushed for more.

'Hmm. But he's spent nearly an hour with that Penny woman and they seem pretty cosy.'

'Oh, that's where he is, poor chap. I should rescue him.' Alex laughed out loud and then glanced back at me. 'There's not been much room for a woman in his life since his marriage ended. If he's not working then he's busy parachuting, or abseiling, or canoeing.'

'So, let me get this right,' I said, regressing to the earlier point. 'The main reason you and Sarah married in Scotland was so Alasdair could be your best man *and* be my escort on Mum's charade?' I was flabbergasted.

'Got it in one. And so you could sing too of course. Being American, it didn't matter to Sarah where we got married, and I'm from Edinburgh originally, so it all worked out perfectly in the end. I wouldn't have considered anyone else to be my best man, we go back a long way.'

I glanced across the lawn.

'Alasdair said he was with you when you were injured.'

Alex looked surprised by my comment.

'He talked about it did he? Talked about what happened? Where we were?'

'Oh no,' I explained quickly, 'no detail. He just told me you'd been injured and that he felt . . .' I halted; this really wasn't my business. Alex finished the sentence for me. He looked at Alasdair, who was still talking to Penny by the loch.

'I know he feels responsible, but he wasn't. Alasdair's a brilliant leader – a brilliant marine – but he takes his responsibilities too far, he can't let go. The fact that I'm alive at all is down to him.'

'Do you mind if I ask what you were doing?'

Alex paused for a moment.

'Tell me, has Alasdair actually told you about his job? The finer details I mean?'

'Only that he's a Royal Marine'—I glanced around—'like everyone here it seems. Mum did pass on a little more detail, though.'

'Oh, right. Good. Well, on this particular occasion,' he pointed to his leg, 'Alasdair was leading a team of six on a surveillance job. We'd had a tip-off that some . . . people . . . would be meeting in a particular building, so we were hiding, watching it.'

'Why?' I asked, intrigued.

'Why else? So we could call in the jets and bomb the place when they went in.'

'Oh my God, who else was inside?'

'No idea. Anyway, they didn't show, so we needed to get out and get back to where British troops were.'

'Where did you hide while you were watching?'

'Me and Al were in a building opposite. Anyway, to cut a long story short, on our way back we stumbled into some bother. I took the brunt of it, including a grenade.'

'What happened?'

'Alasdair slotted the lot. There were only three of them though.'

I glanced around at the sea of red uniforms; it was a scene of dashing gentility. How very different these men must appear to their wives and families, I thought, at a wedding, in dress uniform, compared to the reality of their work when dispatched across the globe. Alex took a sip of his drink and continued with his story.

'Then he carried me to where we could be rescued, called for a helicopter, and before I knew it, I was in an American field hospital.' He glanced across the lawn to his new wife. 'That's where I met Sarah.'

'Bloody hell Alex, that's terrible – about your injury, not the fact that you met Sarah, obviously. So, why does Alasdair feel responsible?'

'Because it was his plan. His route. His team. Also, not long after we joined up as basic recruits I decided to jack it all in, but Al persuaded me to keep going. Then we both went down the SF route, so he feels—'

'Responsible,' I answered.

'Yes, but he shouldn't.'

We sat in silence for a moment. 'Has he told you he might have to go away again soon?' I said.

Alex paused and glanced across the lawn towards Sarah.

'Yes,' he answered softly. 'Listen, Grace, as much as I—'

But there was no time for Alex to finish the sentence; Alasdair appeared, alone. He cocked his head to one side and looked down at me.

'Enjoy your *mingle*?'

He could be a sarcastic so-and-so.

'Yes, thank you. Enjoy your little stroll with Penny down memory lane?'

'Yes, thank you.'

I turned to Alex.

'I've been taking some photos Alex. I'll put them on a memory stick for you. I think you'll like them. They'll be a little different from the ones your photographer is taking. More spontaneous.' I smirked at Alasdair. 'More paparazzi!'

'That's great. Sarah will love them, thanks.'

As I stood, I touched Alex's arm and whispered, 'Thank you for telling me.'

The gong sounded to announce the wedding breakfast. Alex wheeled away to find Sarah. I was dismayed to find I was sitting opposite Alasdair rather than next to him – easier for talking I supposed – but I was equally as dismayed when I discovered that the person sitting next to him was Penny (she had probably swapped our names on the seating plan). A momentary glance passed between Penny and me as we took our seats. Penny's glance said, 'I've been waiting for this man forever so just back off, bitch.' Mine said, 'Go on then, if you think you're up to it, but I'll fight you . . . To. The. Death!'

The man in uniform sitting to my right introduced himself as he pulled my seat back. He was
Captain Tristan Grant, a good-looking chap about
my age who had a sparkle in his eye and a gift for
easy chatter. He was perfect for purpose and I
made an exaggerated effort to laugh at his jokes
as the meal began. Penny began to speak; I was
sure the woman did not draw breath from dawn
till dusk.

'I'm *so* sorry to have assumed you were just the
entertainment. Alex is great, he probably invited
you to the wedding as a thank you for singing.'
She tucked into her soup and carried on talking
after the first mouthful.

'Alasdair was telling me you're a photographer
for celebrity magazines.'

I glanced up at Alasdair.

'Yes, I am, but I'm not sure for how much
longer—' She cut me short.

'So you're a paparazzo then? But you look so
angelic. It just goes to show, appearances can be
so deceptive.' She smiled serenely and carried on
with the soup – I could have thrown it over her,
especially as she had proven Alasdair's point from
the previous day. Why did everyone assume I was
a pap? Alasdair looked as though he was about to
defend me, so I stepped in.

'And what is it you do, *Penny*?'

'I'm a helicopter pilot.'

There was no competing with that.

'In the RAF?' I asked, faking interest.

'No way! Navy. I work with the marines some-times, that's how I met Alex. I've flown *him* about a few times, I can tell you.'

Yes, I thought; you most certainly *can* tell me.

She grabbed the pepper and added some to the soup. 'Hey this is nice, what is it?' Tristan picked up the menu sheet.

'Believe it or not, it's Parrot Fish Soup.'

Everyone stared into their bowl with a little consternation. Quick as a flash, thanks to the champagne, I said, 'Oh, I've had parrot fish before, but I didn't like it much because it kept *repeating* on me.'

Tristan laughed and I glanced across to see Alasdair smile. On a roll, my stand-up comedy moment in full swing, I turned to Tristan and said, 'Tell me Tristan, have you ever tried Clown Fish?'

'No, I can't say I have.' He held my gaze with a sexy smirk.

'Well don't,' I continued, 'I had it once and it tasted really *funny*.'

Once again Tristan laughed, Alasdair smiled and even Penny tittered, but then added, 'Honestly, Grace. Singer, photographer *and* comedienne. You should hire yourself out for weddings on a regular basis.'

Nothing witty came to mind immediately so I smiled and looked about the room, slightly embar-rassed. Alasdair came to my rescue. He looked at my wine glass as the waiter refilled it.

'I take it you aren't driving us home this evening, Grace.'

'Erm . . .'

Penny stepped in. '*Home*, Alasdair?'

'Oh, it's not home as such. Grace and I are staying at a woodman's hut in Nethy Bridge.' Penny's face was a picture.

'Sounds . . . cosy.'

Alasdair paused for a moment and smiled at me with unspoken affection.

'Yes, it is,' he said, 'it's wonderful.'

CHAPTER 24

If I was merry with alcohol at the beginning of the meal then I was only one or two stages from blotto by the end of it. But I could still walk, my conversation was fairly comprehensible and the room wasn't spinning.

Time for dancing!

The lights were lowered by several notches. The band retired to take a well-deserved break, which left an opening for the resident DJ. Tristan wandered off to the bar and Penny disappeared, leaving Alasdair with an opening to change seats.

'What about Tristan?' I asked, turning to look at him at the bar. He had seen Alasdair make his move and had pulled a face of mock anger.

'He'll improvise. So, what I want to know is this. What made you change your mind?'

'Change my mind about what?' I couldn't resist dragging it out of him.

'Well, first of all, about coming to the wedding. The last I saw of you at the hut you were determined to pack a little neckerchief and wander off into the wilderness alone. You wouldn't have lasted two seconds without me by the way.'

I started to interrupt but he held a finger to my lips. 'And second of all, how on earth did you come to the conclusion that you would, after all of that "I can't possibly do it, Alasdair" nonsense, stand up and sing? Thank you for doing that, by the way.' He sat back and I considered his questions.

'The answer to your first question is, I couldn't bear for you to leave your lucky shemagh behind.' I leant towards him seductively as I spoke. 'And I think you knew I would feel that way when you left it.' He smiled. 'And, you know the answer to your second question already.' I sat back.

'Oh?'

'Come off it, Alasdair "bloody know-it-all" Finn. You knew damn well that if you got me as far as the wedding, and I saw Alex with his injury, then I would decide to sing, just as Mum probably realised too. Am I right?'

He took a deep breath but didn't answer. He leant forward instead and brushed a stray twirl of hair away from my eye.

'You look wonderful by the way, and your voice, it blew me away. I heard you sing at St Christopher's and by the loch, but the way you sang today was something else.'

I would have blushed if my face hadn't already been flushed with alcohol. I let him continue.

'When I saw you in the ballroom waiting to sing I just wanted to sweep you up and take you away. But then I heard your voice and . . . and I realised there's something I really wanted to . . .'

'Hi you two.' It was Simon. The boy had an extraordinary sense of bad timing. 'So, you're going to sing for us again, Grace?'

Alasdair sat back in his chair and raised his eyes to the ceiling.

'First rule of cool, Simon,' I said, 'keep them wanting.' I glanced across at Alasdair – a smile had returned to his face. He looked relaxed, happy.

'How about a dance?' Simon asked, pulling at my hand. The DJ had moved on from ABBA to the Bee Gees.

'Okay then, but remember, these heels were not made for dancing.'

I mouthed 'sorry' to Alasdair as I rose from my chair, and found myself dancing not only with Simon but with Tristan too. Simon danced in a little world of his own (I think he had moved on from the orange juice) and Tristan took the opportunity to take my hand and jive me across the dance floor. He was quite a mover. I glanced across to see if Alasdair was watching, but he had left the table.

The pace of the music shifted down several gears for the next number. It was a typical slow-dance song and I felt embarrassed when Tristan closed in on his hold and began to smooch. We were only a few bars in when a figure appeared hovering over Tristan's shoulder. He looked back. It was Alasdair, and he had removed his jacket.

'My dance I think, Captain.'

Alasdair said the words with more raw, sexual

presence than I thought any man could ever possibly achieve. Tristan quite literally bowed out saying, 'Fair enough.'

We danced to a song that had been chosen by the DJ with Alex and Sarah in mind, but I decided it would be 'our' song for time eternal – *To Make You Feel My Love*. In truth, the DJ could have played *Smack Your Bitch Up* and I would still have found a romantic attachment to the words, but it was perfect.

The song moved on, the singer powered up, but Alasdair remained the perfect gentleman throughout – more's the pity. He lowered his head to speak into my ear.

'You seem to have spent the day running away from me. Why did you do that?'

I pulled my head back slightly.

'I didn't want to get in the way, what with you being best man and everything. And anyway, you had *Penny* for company. That woman's after you, by the way.' He shook his head with a smile and pulled me in closer. I rested my head on his shoulder and we finished the dance in silence. Alex was watching us. He smiled at me, but his expression was one of concern possibly.

Realising I was the worse for alcohol early in the evening, Alasdair called a Speyside taxi company and reserved a cab. The final farewell with the bride and groom was emotional. Alex had tears in his eyes as he said goodbye.

'Take care of yourself, dude. And no heroics this time, you listening to me?'

Alasdair shrugged, shook Alex's hand and jumped beside me in the taxi.

'Did you have a good time?' He asked as the taxi scrunched across the hotel driveway. He unfastened the top stud of his shirt as he spoke.

'It was fantastic. Just one thing though.'

I rested my head on his shoulder and yawned.

'What's that?' He put his arm around me and I nestled further into his chest – we were still tipsy after all.

'What time do we have to get up in the morning?'

'Early . . . sorry.'

'And where to this time?' I asked. 'Snorkelling in the Shetlands perchance?'

'That would be fantastic, but, not quite. Tomorrow, we fly to Zagreb.' For once I took the news in my stride; it was probably the booze.

'Oh . . . right. Well, you'd better find me some more of those blister plasters then, because my feet are bloody killing me.'

Our romantic interlude ended before the taxi arrived at the hut. Alasdair placed his jacket over me in the cold cab and, in a cosy drunken stupor, I fell asleep during the last fifteen minutes of the drive. I woke in the early hours – my throat parched as the desert – still dressed in my wedding clothes but laying under the covers. I couldn't honestly remember the car-to-bed transition, but managed to muster enough energy to abandon my dress and struggle into my pyjamas.

A glass of water sat on the windowsill next to the bed. A packet of ibuprofen rested against it. The room was uncomfortably hot so I tried to open a window, but simply could not work out how to lift the latch *and* push the sash frame down at the same time. I fell back on the bed, defeated, and realised the act of falling was a rash thing to do. The room became a whirling centrifuge machine and my head, weighing roughly the same as a diver's boots (with the diver still in them), spun around in the abyss. It was not a good feeling. I tried to fix my gaze on the stars through the Velux window . . . *were they really supposed to jump about like that?*

At 6.30 a.m. Alasdair opened the cabin bed door, leant across the bed, yanked the curtains open and put a coffee on the windowsill. I didn't move.

'Come on then diva, wakey-wakey, big day ahead. The weather's changed I'm afraid. Overcast with a little drizzle, but the good news,' he added, 'is one of the bandsmen dropped the car off so we don't need to run to the hotel.'

'Go away you horrible morning person.' My voice was muffled by the bed sheets.

'Oh good, you're alive. Breakfast served in ten minutes – sharp!'

'Not you as well.' I lifted my head and turned over to face him. 'I had enough tough love from the Sergeant Major yesterday. Just open the window will you and bugger off.'

'You know, I think it's in the mornings you are at your very best. Drink your coffee.'

Alasdair opened the window and left. I hauled my sorry carcass to the edge of the bed and looked in the mirror. A mutant panda sporting an Amazonian hair-do frowned back at me – beautiful. I put a brush to my scalp, but it felt as though a thousand acupuncture needles were being thrown randomly at my skull.

I left the security of the bed, stepped into the living area of the hut and sat down tentatively at the table. Alasdair placed a fresh mug of coffee in front of me along with cereal, toast and more ibuprofen. A battered leather-bound book sat on the table. I picked it up.

'What's this?'

Alasdair took a seat opposite.

'That thing . . . oh, it's just my journal. Your mum gave it to me. I thought it would be nice to keep a record of this trip away.'

I thought my heart was going to melt – Mum's journal, he had kept it going. I placed it back on the table and smiled.

'That's a lovely thing to have done, Alasdair.' I winked. 'Maybe I'll read it one day, learn all your secrets!'

He laughed. 'You can read it now, if you want. No secrets in there, and I'm crap at writing.'

A thought crossed my mind.

'Do you know, I had the strangest of dreams last night.'

'Really?'

He took the journal and crossed the hut to place it in his bag.

'I dreamt we were jetting off to Croatia today. How bizarre was that?'

I took a bite of toast. It didn't sit too well.

'We *are* jetting off to Croatia today, just for one night though.'

He returned to his chair and took a sip of coffee.

'Right, fine, better get ready then.'

'Hold on. What about your breakfast?' He pushed the toast towards me.

'Later, Alasdair. *Much* later.'

I rose from the table and noticed the envelope he had left for me the previous day. I took the envelope and held it in my hand – it didn't feel as though there were any letters inside, a few bits of scrunched up paper perhaps. Alasdair jumped up and snatched the envelope from my grasp.

'Probably best if *I* keep the letters,' he said, looking a little cagey.

I glanced at him, squinting.

'Just one question, Alasdair.'

'Yes?' He turned to face me sporting a cheeky grin and perched his posterior on the side of the table.

'If I was to open that envelope,' I said, pointing to his hand, 'what would I find? Mum's letters, or some bits of old newspaper?'

He shrugged and murmured, 'Erm, just some bits of old newspaper I suppose.'

'Alasdair!' I shouted, but regretted the perforating sound reverberating between my ears a moment later. 'You are unbelievable.' He shrugged and I couldn't help but laugh.

I turned to fill the kettle for my shower, but paused with my back to him as I approached the stove.

'Just one more thing, walking boots or heels today?' I heard him laugh.

'Heels. One hundred per cent.'

Once seated on the aircraft, I remembered my phone call with Paul – I really ought to have thanked him for the chat. I grabbed my phone and turned it on. Alasdair turned to me.

'What happened to the phone embargo?' he asked.

'I just need to text a friend and let him know I'm okay. He wanted me to check-in now and again.' I looked up from texting and smiled. 'Just in case you turned out to be an axe murderer.'

> *Just boarded an aircraft for Zagreb. Friends again with Soldier Boy. And guess what? I actually sang at the wedding . . . did I even mention I'd been asked to sing? Will call when back in the UK and explain. Thanks for the chat the other day. Love you loads. G x*

I turned off my phone just as the aircraft doors closed.

'He obviously cares about you, this friend,' Alasdair

said, leaning his head towards mine but holding his gaze to the front of the cabin.

'Paul? Yes, he's a very good friend.'

'Is he single?'

Where did that come from?

'Yes.'

'How do you know him?'

'He's a features journalist. We team up from time to time for work. We spend a lot of time together socially too.'

'Hmm,' he murmured, 'he's gay then?'

My jaw fell open. 'Alasdair! No, he isn't gay. And don't go getting all judgemental on me again. You made it perfectly clear how you feel about my line of work when we were in the hut, but don't drag Paul into this, he's a good writer.'

Alasdair twitched in his seat before finally turning to face me.

'Are you two an item then?' he asked gently. I smiled.

'No, we're not.'

'But he'd like it if you were?'

'Maybe . . .' I stuttered. 'Possibly. I'm not sure.'

He lowered his voice and whispered into my ear.

'Grace, he's a single, straight man who spends a great deal of time with you, and who clearly cares. Bottom line, he wants to get you into bed, it's obvious.'

I shook my head and smiled. Paul had said the same thing about Alasdair, and yet my sex life remained non-existent.

'Well,' I responded smartly, looking him straight in the eye, *'you're* a single, straight man who has spent a great deal of time with me lately and who is clearly caring, so what does that mean?' I held his gaze. His lips – achingly close – twitched into a wicked smile.

All I needed to do was to edge my face forwards and allow his lips to brush mine. But I bottled it, glanced forwards towards the hostess who was closing the overhead lockers and said, 'Anyway, do you think they provide a meal on this flight? Because I'm absolutely starving.'

PART IV

ZAGREB, CROATIA

28–29 MAY

CHAPTER 25

I felt cold as we boarded the aircraft in Scotland. Zagreb, on the other hand, basked in glorious sunshine. After grabbing our luggage from the carousel, Alasdair rushed over to the airport information desk ahead of me and spoke to the receptionist. I caught up with him and we headed to the exit.

'What was all that about?' I asked.

'Just a little surprise.'

I stopped the trolley he was pushing as we exited the terminal.

'Alasdair Finn, what the hell's bells are you up to now?'

He whistled for a taxi, turned to me and said, 'We're going to do something a little different today, right now in fact.'

'Mum's idea?'

'Oh yes. Trust me, only Rosamund could come up with this one.'

'So? What is it?'

His answer was delayed momentarily by the arrival of a taxi. Once inside, he turned to me with his trademark grin and said:

'I'm taking you on a tandem sky-dive.'

* * *

Our conversation on the way to Zagreb Flying and Parachuting School was fairly animated. It consisted of me flailing my arms about and screaming out fragments of sentences like, 'My mother is trying to kill me . . . to *kill* me for Christ's sake! The bloody woman was unhinged.' And, 'I don't care what you say Alasdair'—not that he had said anything at that point—'I'm Just. Not. Doing. It!'

The taxi halted outside the flying school. Alasdair turned to me and said, quite calmly, 'You're right. Rosamund was expecting too much. There's no way you should do it, it's not your kind of thing.'

My countenance dropped a little. I expected him to try to persuade me to do it, and was disappointed when he assumed I wasn't woman enough to take the challenge on. But really, this was crazy.

'But,' he continued, 'the jump has already been paid for, and they're expecting us at the school. I'll jump on my own and you can wait in the crew room.'

Alasdair paid the taxi driver and touched me on the arm as we climbed out of the car. 'Come on, no need to worry. You can watch.'

We were directed into an aircraft hangar. Alasdair spent much of the time talking through the jump and inspecting the kit. He handed his parachuting documentation over to the instructor – which as far as I was concerned also substituted as certified proof that he was clinically insane – and, once the instructor was happy Alasdair was capable of throwing himself out of an aircraft safely, and once

Alasdair triple checked the parachute was packed properly, he was ready to go.

I sat on my hands on an uncomfortable chair in the corner of the hangar. Alasdair's words were running through my mind. *Not your kind of thing . . . just watch.*

The more I thought about it the more disappointed in myself I became – which was exactly how I felt when I said I wouldn't sing at the wedding. But I *had* sung and it was a fantastic experience. And maybe – just maybe – I was about to miss out on something equally as thrilling. My romantic sensibilities took hold of me again, and I realised I was about to make a reckless decision.

Alasdair smiled at me from across the hangar. The instructor was helping him into a harness. He looked relaxed – a good sign surely. I could hear an aircraft running up its engines outside the hangar.

'Alasdair, wait,' I shouted. 'I'll do it.'

Within twenty minutes I was harnessed up and sitting on the aircraft side by side with Alasdair, which is when the realisation of what I was about to do hit me and blind panic set in.

The tiny aircraft was powered by propellers rather than real engines, and I half expected us to be positioned at the end of the runway and catapulted off with a giant slingshot. I expressed my concern to Alasdair as we taxied to the holding point.

'All that jetting around the world and you've never been on a prop-job before?' He leant across me to look through the window – the embodiment of calm. It was obviously a front.

'If I'd been on a "prop-job" before, then I wouldn't have jetted now would I?'

The pilot was instructed to hold the aircraft on the taxiway until a passenger aircraft landed on the runway ahead of us. I was glad of the delay.

'So, aren't you supposed to brief me on hand signals or something?' I had been trundled onto the aircraft without so much as a safety drill.

'No need. You'll be strapped to me so all you have to do is enjoy the ride'—he raised an eyebrow—'so to speak.'

Enjoy it?

If my mother hadn't been dead already I would have killed her there and then with my bare hands.

'Alasdair . . .'

'Yes.'

'How absolutely certain are you that we aren't actually going to die? Give me a percentage.'

He thought about it for a second and said, 'About ninety-nine per cent.'

'*What?* So there's a one per cent chance we actually might die? I don't like those odds.' My eyes, wide with fear, were fixed to the front of the aircraft.

'There's a degree of risk in everything we do. You don't ask me the percentage chance of death every time we get into a car, do you?'

I glanced around the aircraft anxiously.

'I feel really sick. I don't think I will jump after all. *You* do it.'

He turned his head to face me, smiled and took my hand.

'There is no reason on earth for you to do this jump with me if you don't want to. But, at the same time, there's no reason on earth for you *not* to do it either.' My eyes remained wide as he spoke. 'I promise, with every fibre of my body, that I won't let anything bad happen to you. You'll be strapped to me the whole time, and it will be wonderful. I've done this a thousand times and I'll probably do it a thousand times more.' He touched my face tenderly. 'Trust me.'

I nodded, smiled and fought back the urge to vomit.

The aircraft started on its take-off run and my hands left cartoon imprints in Alasdair's arm.

'Jesus Christ, it's loud.' I shouted, tucking my head into his chest.

The heap of tin made it off the runway – just – and we felt every little bump and tumble as the aircraft climbed slowly through clear air turbulence.

Eventually the aircraft entered into a smooth phase of the flight, and I lifted my head to face Alasdair. Slightly embarrassed by my outward display of fear on take-off, I felt the need to explain.

'I'm more of an Airbus A380 kind of a gal. I don't really like these . . . what type of aircraft is it?'

'It's a Fokker.'

I laughed out loud. 'You can say that again, I should imagine wearing a parachute is compulsory!'

And then my brief respite from bowel-loosening fear was over. The instructor stood up, Alasdair followed suit and they both looked at me pointedly as if to say, 'You too kid.'

The instructor manhandled me towards the door, then Alasdair positioned himself directly behind, as if we were standing in a queue that was a particularly tight squeeze. He didn't allow the instructor to buckle our harnesses together, but insisted on checking the harnesses himself.

Alasdair leant his head forward to speak into my ear.

'Promise me one thing,' he said.

I turned my head towards his.

'I'll promise you anything – *anything* – if it concerns staying alive.'

He took my hand and squeezed it.

'Don't close your eyes.'

And then the door opened.

Alasdair didn't give me time to catch my breath, or to look down, or to do anything at all. The sensation of having been caught with my mouth open in an air compressor manifested itself a thousand times as Alasdair pushed me forwards and I found – to my horror – that I was falling through the sky.

I wanted to scream, but found it physically impossible to do so. I wanted to enjoy the exhilaration of the free-fall phase and tried to look around the landscape as we tumbled to earth, but

I was experiencing only one emotion – fear. The only thought somersaulting over and over in my head was, 'please let the parachute open, please let the parachute open.'

It did open, but every remaining ounce of oxygen was taken away by the force with which we were whiplashed in an upwards motion as the parachute filled with air.

But then miraculously the world slowed down to a dream-like pace. We drifted gently back down to earth and I felt calm, I felt at peace, and yet, conversely, I felt the invigorating sensation of being alive at the extreme edge of living.

We landed gently, expertly, and I stood in a trance while Alasdair unclipped the harness and the parachute. I turned to face him. He was smiling the warmest smile I had ever seen.

I wanted to say a thousand things to him, but all I managed to scream as I flung my arms around him was, 'I kept my eyes open.'

We sat side by side in the back of a taxi. Somehow I managed to venture back down to earth during the ride into the centre of Zagreb. The city disappointed initially, it seemed to be no more than a Cold War concrete jungle. The taxi halted at traffic lights. A tram crossed our path on the road ahead, which is when the reality of why we had travelled to Croatia hit me.

'You're worrying about the next letter aren't you?' Alasdair asked, glancing across at me.

'Yep. She seems to be building up to something big, all that stuff about Geoffrey and her life being about to change. Also, we're getting to the point in her life when she conceived me, and I'm just wondering what giant skeletons there are in her closet, that's all.'

'I wouldn't worry,' he said, knocking my shoulder with his. 'I don't think anyone has discovered the skeleton of an actual giant yet so you should be okay.'

I laughed.

'Rosamund seems to have had a clear purpose in everything she's done so far – has made *you* do so far – so I wouldn't worry.'

We returned to our occupation of staring out of the window as the taxi moved on.

'Have you been to Croatia before?' I asked.

'Yes, but in less salubrious surroundings than this.'

I was confused momentarily but then realised what he meant. 'Ah, the Balkan thing you mean. I'd forgotten about that.'

'I was mainly in Bosnia. I came out here just after I joined up.'

'What was it like?'

'Like?'

He thought for a moment.

'Crazy. Neighbour on neighbour, years of hatred whipped up into a frenzy, nationalism, religion, economics and egos. One – or all – of those bad babies are usually involved.' He smiled across the seat at me. 'But I loved it, bizarrely. Loved being caught up in the throng, always have.' He paused, looked away from me to glance out of the window and murmured, 'Not sure what that says about me though.'

We passed through the centre of the city and headed up a slight rise. The road narrowed and the architecture altered.

'This is more like it,' I said, peering at pretty houses no more than three stories high and at least two hundred years old. Alasdair nodded in agreement.

'This must be the old town,' he said. 'Our hotel is in this area.'

The taxi came to a final halt and I was pleased that our hotel was equally picturesque. We climbed a few steps up to the hotel entrance. Alasdair looked at his watch.

'What time is it?' I asked.

'Five o'clock. Croatia is an hour ahead.'

'Five o'clock already? The day is almost over!' Alasdair smiled at my disgust that time was running away with us. He stepped aside to let me enter the door ahead of him.

The hotel foyer belied the simple 'gingerbread house' frontage. It was plush, lavishly upholstered and very shiny. I had a distinct feeling of déjà vu as we entered key cards to open the doors to adjacent rooms. Alasdair looked across at me.

'Don't worry, I can guess,' I said, 'you need to do some work?'

'I'm sorry, but I didn't check in with the guys at all yesterday.'

'There's nothing to be sorry about, you've given up so much of your time already Alasdair. Catch you later, okay?' I closed the door behind me.

A minute later and there was a knock at the door. I opened it but there was no one there. Another knock, but I couldn't work out where it was coming from. Then I noticed a door handle sticking out from the wallpaper. I pulled it open and saw Alasdair smiling back at me.

'Hey, interconnecting doors, how cool is that?' I stepped into his room for a second.

'We didn't specify a time,' he said. 'Give me an hour and then I'm yours.' He hovered at the door.

'Great. I'm going for a wander round the old town, maybe take some photographs.' I sat down on the bed. 'Actually, I'd like to read the next letter now, that way we can have a good time this evening without having to think about Mum and everything.' He considered my suggestion for a second.

'The thing is, Rosamund wanted you to go to a specific place to read the next letter and—'

I cut him short. 'So tell me where this place is and I'll go there. I am *relatively* capable, Alasdair.'

'Sorry, I know you are. Okay, I'll get the letter, and the map, but only if you're sure.'

'Of course I'm sure, now go and get the letter, there's a good lad.'

★   ★   ★

Mum had wanted me to read her letter in St Mark's Church. I was tempted to rip the letter open in the foyer and nip to the church later, but heeded Alasdair's comment regarding Mum's grand plan and found the church instead. Stepping out of the hotel into the Zagreb sunshine, dressed in beautiful clothes and wearing uncharacteristically feminine shoes, I experienced a feeling of deep happiness I hadn't felt in a very long time, if ever. The reason being, of course, was I was head over heels in love with a man who, just by looking in my direction, made my head spin and my heart leap out of my chest. Being in a romantic foreign city accompanied by a man who was attracted to me too, gave me the confidence to walk with a definite swagger.

Only minutes after leaving the hotel, the narrow street opened out onto a large cobbled square. If I thought I had entered into a fairy-tale world when I arrived in the old town, the impression was compounded tenfold when I turned a corner and saw the church. St Mark's was like a fairy-tale castle *and* a church in one. A collection of red, black and white tiles were interwoven to create a mosaic for the entire cross section of the roof that faced onto the square. Two coats of arms – also made of multicoloured tiles – were set within the mosaic. I guessed one coat of arms was the Croatian flag while the other seemed to depict a castle. I sauntered around the square for a time in an effort to capture the beauty and quirkiness of the church on camera but, just like Loch A'an in the early morning sunshine, it was difficult to capture my exact impression of the building.

I stepped inside the church with as light a foot as possible, which wasn't easy as the sound of my heels echoed awkwardly. It was dark inside, even for a church. I paused in the doorway until my eyes adjusted, walked down the aisle and headed to the font. Thankfully the front pews were illuminated sufficiently by the altar candles and, having taken a seat on a hard wooden bench, I opened Mum's letter and began to read.

CHAPTER 26

Zagreb

Hello love.

How did the wedding go? I bet you were phenomenal and looked divine. Don't stay cross at me for long, you know you enjoyed it really. How did Alasdair look in his best bib and tucker? To die for I'll bet. Did all of the ladies swoon over him?

I realise I am procrastinating. It's for a reason. This letter will be difficult to write because I have to cover a period in my life I have blocked out for many years. I have, in fact, delayed writing for a couple of weeks now. But, my illness is starting to take a significant turn for the worse, so I must get my act together. Today I feel relatively well and I'm determined to keep writing until I have conveyed all you need to know. I only hope you still regard me with love and kindness when you have finished reading. Also, Grace, the content of this letter will discuss aspects of life a mother and daughter wouldn't normally discuss – but I have to be completely honest with you if you are ever to understand why my life followed a particular path.

My last letter ended with Geoff based at the lodge on the west coast of Scotland and with my departure to Hereford. What I didn't explain was the significant turn my career took in accepting the Hereford posting. Although I was still serving in the RAF, my new job was with the special forces. I was particularly adept at photographic interpretation and had developed an outstanding reputation. One aspect of my job was to provide in-depth intelligence briefs to the guys on covert operations. I occasionally worked with MI6 and, as a result, a whole new world opened up to me. It was a fantastic opportunity, but my work took up at least eighty per cent of my time, with only twenty per cent left for my marriage – if that, to be honest. Nevertheless, Geoff and I still attempted to keep things going. I was young after all, and Geoff encouraged my adventurous spirit. Unfortunately, it was this innate sense of adventure that would lead me into a whole heap of trouble.

In the summer of 1979 I was sent on a six-month detachment to Zagreb. Remember that the '70s were a time of Cold War intrigue. Intelligence gathering was vital. One of the cells operating in Eastern Europe was using

Zagreb as its base. I would meet up covertly with operatives or contact them through other means and provide them with, well, whatever they needed really; intelligence, basic administration, the lot. I worked independently from an apartment downtown. Even though Zagreb was part of Tito's Yugoslavia, the city was vibrant. I was heady with the summer sun and every day was fresh, exciting and fulfilling. My brief from the colonel before I left Hereford was to keep my head down, merge in with the locals to the point of invisibility and provide a service to the operatives. But I'm afraid to say I became a girl about town.

About halfway through the detachment I became friendly with a writer chap who was living in an adjacent apartment block. He was an American called Sam. I initially bumped into him on the street, then in the foyer, then he popped round to see if my electric had gone off (it hadn't) and then a chance meeting at the grocer's. He was good looking, in an obvious kind of way, and fun to be with. Eventually we started to meet in the evenings for coffee or go for a stroll. Balmy summer evenings were spent chatting on the terrace at the St Catherine's Square café, all the while listening to local musicians – violinists mainly – who busked on the cobbles.

After about a month I noticed his body language towards me started to change, a delicately phrased compliment perhaps, or a supportive hand might linger in the small of my back – you can imagine the sort of thing. I thought nothing of it at first but, over time, his subtle flirtations became intoxicating, they seemed to be a natural part of the hedonistic lifestyle I had adopted. There was, however, something a little unnerving about Sam. But for that short period I had transformed into a different character altogether. I became completely self-absorbed and addicted to the thrill of the job and, I'm ashamed to say, I also became addicted to the way Sam made me feel. It sounds terribly silly now, but I felt so incredibly sexy and full of, what's the saying, joie de vivre? And so, like a ship that's lured into shallow water by a wrecker's lantern, I sailed towards the rocks.

On one particular Saturday we spent a lazy morning strolling around the old town before nipping into St Mark's Church. I thought he was going to kiss me in the church, the whole experience seemed to be shrouded in intimacy, but he didn't. We walked to St Catherine's Square for coffee and cake at our usual café. Sam splashed out on a champagne lunch 'just for the hell of it'. By the time we left the café the sexual tension between us had reached boiling point; every accidental touch was electrically charged, every glance full of sensuous expectation. Not surprisingly, something had to give. We headed back to my apartment (slightly the worse for the champagne) and within seconds of closing the door we gave in to what had become an intoxicating desire. Nothing in my life had ever felt so exhaustingly erotic. It was, quite literally, electrifying.

But, every electrical pulse must be earthed eventually and, from the moment we lay spent on the bed, I knew I had made the biggest mistake of my life – of several lifetimes in fact. There was no mutual affection, no entwined bodies in a loving embrace, just silence. All I could see in my mind was Geoff's face. All I could think of was the woodman's hut and Loch A'an and our wonderful year in the Cairngorms. I felt a desperate need to get myself clean and to run far away from Sam. If I could have run into Geoff's arms there and then and begged for forgiveness I would have done. I stood in the shower and wept while Sam dressed. I brushed my hair over and over whilst standing in front of the bathroom mirror and prayed he would have left the apartment by the time I stepped out of the bathroom.

He hadn't left; he was waiting for me in the lounge. His expression looked different somehow – it actually frightened me. I told him I had made a stupid mistake and that I loved my husband (to which he gave a sarcastic smirk). I asked him to leave. He refused. He just sat there, staring at me. I became panic-stricken and felt the need to put as much distance as possible between myself and the stranger lingering in my apartment. I couldn't even bear to look at him because doing so was an immediate reminder of my infidelity.

I grabbed my jacket and ran out of the building. I half expected him to run after me but instead he shouted in a clear and calculated voice that he would wait in the apartment for me. My head was a mess. I felt completely trapped. Sam had gone from being an object of total desire to the human embodiment of deceit and betrayal, and all within a matter of a couple of hours. I recall wandering the streets for the rest of the afternoon and into the early evening in a kind of semi-conscious daze. Even the weather turned against me. My clothes were soaked in the rain.

I considered running to friends at the embassy but what on earth would I say? 'I've just had an extramarital relationship with a man who is refusing to leave my apartment, please can you sort it out?' I would look like the absolute fool I was. I had no choice but to return, face the music and explain to Sam that we must never meet again. I was frightened though. There had been something victorious in his expression as I left, and I knew I had allowed this man to establish a powerful hold over me. If I had laughed the whole affair off and giggled afterwards I could have covered up my regret. But I hadn't been that clever. I knew when I looked into his eyes he had seen my fear. Sam was not the man I thought he was.

I plucked up the courage to head back and entered the apartment with absolute dread. The lights were off and I prayed he had come to his senses and left. I took a cursory glance in each room but there was no trace of him, so I dashed to the hall and locked the door. I left the lights off – just in case Sam had been watching from outside – and walked into the lounge in darkness.

The curtains were open but there wasn't enough ambient light filtering in from the street to cast even the slightest shadow. I tiptoed over to the window and hid behind a curtain to take a look down into the road and make sure Sam wasn't watching for me; he wasn't there. So I closed the curtains and stepped to a side table to turn on a lamp. When I turned around Sam was still in the room. I stumbled backwards with complete horror, but the true nightmare of my situation was about to become overwhelmingly apparent. Sam was dead. He had been shot in the head, his body was slouched into the chair, his head flopped down to the right. I was too petrified to scream. Actually, I did feel as though I was trying to scream, but it was impossible to convert the emotion into sound. Every instinct told me to get out of the apartment. I grabbed my purse, passport and jacket and ran for the door.

In a miraculous moment of clarity I decided my best course of action was to hide for a moment rather than run out into the street. I tried the handle of the caretaker's cupboard door: it was open, so I stepped inside, crouched down and tried to regroup my thoughts. Within five minutes I realised the decision to stay rather than run had quite possibly saved my life.

I heard agitated voices – Russian voices – in the foyer. Two men were arguing although they were trying to keep their voices low. I had picked up a little bit of the language through my intelligence work and could interpret enough to hear them say, 'Where is she?' and 'search!'

On entering the caretaker room I had noticed a tall locker in the corner. With my shoes still in my hands I closed the door behind me and crept over to the locker as quietly as I could. My heart was beating out of my chest. A couple of seconds after positioning myself in the cupboard, the door to the room opened and I could see through the grill in the metal locker that the light had been switched on. The locker was full of overalls hanging on a rail; I managed to hide behind them. One of the men walked over to the cupboard and opened the door. I really thought my number was up but, amazingly, he didn't have time to search the locker as the second man shouted for him to hurry. He left and I could finally exhale.

I spent the rest of the night hidden in the locker. I remember being unable to stop shivering – my clothes were still damp from the walk in the rain. The events of the past twelve hours were turning over in my head. I had been a damn fool falling for Sam. Had it all been some game to try and get me to talk about my work? How could it be though? I had given him the cover story that I was an administrator at the embassy. Nevertheless, there was a dead man in my apartment and, as far as I knew, the perpetrators were looking for me too.

I know you will be astonished to read all of this Grace. The story seems so ridiculously cloak and dagger, but it was terrifyingly real at the time. I must have dozed for a while but woke on hearing the sounds of local voices in the foyer. It was morning. As stiff as a post, I edged my way out of the cupboard, slipped on my shoes and took a taxi to the embassy – I will leave you to imagine the chaos and confusion that erupted over the next few hours. Police, the embassy lawyer, even the British Ambassador interviewed me. I kept my story simple. I had been out for a walk, left my door on the latch and on returning had found my neighbour (who I had seen socially occasionally) dead on my chair. I explained that I had taken cover in the caretaker's room and told them about the two Soviets.

Twelve hours after my dramatic arrival at the embassy, I found myself on an RAF aircraft headed back to England. Only three hours after landing at Brize Norton I was sitting in my colonel's office. By that time I was numb. I dreaded seeing the colonel, he had clearly held a fatherly soft spot for me since I had arrived at Hereford and had given me opportunities and experiences previously unheard of for RAF intelligence officers. I expected an almighty dressing-down and an immediate posting back to the RAF; but I was wrong. His smile was warm as I entered the office.

There were two men in the room. The colonel stood and came around to the front of his desk, greeted me affectionately and indicated I should take a seat in one of the more comfortable chairs positioned in a corner. I recognised the second man from the aircraft I had just disembarked. The colonel introduced him as Major Brown; he barely spoke for the whole interview.

I started to blither some form of an apology for the mess I had made; God knows why there was a dead man in my apartment. But, as soon as I started to make my excuses, I could tell he knew the truth. The colonel bid me to listen while he explained what he knew.

It seemed my blossoming friendship with Sam was noticed by one of our operatives working in Zagreb who had a hunch he recognised Sam from somewhere but couldn't remember where. Security checks were run on him back home and my superiors were suspicious as to the nature of his interest in me. They discovered he was, in fact, originally from Warsaw but had travelled extensively and taken on the persona of an American writer.

I was shocked, obviously. His accent betrayed no trace of his true nationality. Major Brown had travelled to Zagreb to start a surveillance operation on Sam. My stomach wrenched. I felt physically sick at the thought of how much he must know about our time together. I couldn't look him in the face.

The colonel explained that somehow, someone had cottoned on to my connection with British intelligence sources. Sam had probably been paid to get close to me and find out what I knew.

He explained that I was kept in the dark regarding their suspicions about Sam so the friendship could ride its course. They hoped to discover who he was working for and what the bigger picture was. If I had been told about the surveillance operation I might have got spooked and given the game away. I was hurt. The worst thing, of course, was I had finally succumbed and slept with Sam. I felt like a prostitute sitting with her pimp. I didn't cry. I excused myself, walked to the toilet and threw up.

When I returned to the office the colonel continued to explain what he knew. On the whole the operation had been a success. They had uncovered details of a Soviet cell working in both Zagreb and Vienna. Lastly they gave me credit for my behaviour (God, that was a joke). Major Brown made it clear to the colonel that I had let nothing slip to Sam. I confirmed this was correct but asked him how he knew, which was when I discovered my apartment and our regular café were bugged. When you consider what happened between Sam and me during the previous afternoon, you can imagine my horror on hearing this.

I was confused about why Sam was killed. They had no answer for this. It was possible he had been some kind of mercenary, or perhaps he had been working for different groups, playing one off against the other; maybe I had simply been a cover for him, they just didn't know. But the fact that his killers (if indeed that is who the two men were) had come back to the apartment building, and had been potentially looking for me, was their greatest concern.

Apparently, the 'unfortunate turn of events' (i.e. Sam's death) was unexpected and they admitted they had miscalculated the amount of risk I had been subjected to.

The colonel went on to discuss the question of my ongoing safety. I was surprised by this. Naively, as soon as the aircraft touched down in the UK, I considered myself to be on home turf. Unfortunately, my safety could not be guaranteed until more was discovered regarding the nature of Sam's death. The situation was an unholy mess.

The colonel had contacted Geoff who was given 'only minimum information' . . . we all knew what that meant. I was to be taken to Arisaig and was to lie low with my husband at the RAF Lodge. This would provide me with a degree of safety as, like any other military institute, the lodge was guarded around the clock. I boarded a helicopter for a remote landing pad at Plockton, and was then taken by car to Arisaig. I fell into Geoff's arms a broken mess. If I could have remained nestled there for the rest of my life I would have gladly done so but, yet again, fate was to conspire against me, and more devastation was not far away.

Back to the present. I told Alasdair there would be no requirement to scatter my ashes in Zagreb, I tried to put the place out of my mind a long time ago. Despite the trauma the city brought to my life, however, it is terribly important to me that you go there. I suppose I live in the desperate hope you will put yourself into my shoes, just for a few hours, and appreciate how the pretty little streets and promenades, beautiful architecture and wonderful summer weather can turn a person's head just for a moment, even if it is in the wrong direction. I hope somehow you are able to understand what I have told you and comprehend how it was possible for me to lose my way.

By the way Grace, some opportunities happen along only for one fleeting moment in a lifetime; just thought I would mention that, my love.

As ever, my darling girl.

Mum.

X

I folded up the letter, stuffed it back into my bag and sat for a while gazing up at the altar and the ornate gilded décor of the church. Mum certainly knew how to whip things up in her day. I wasn't sure what to think of it all. Disappointed in her? Quite the contrary – I was in awe of her. Mum's final words came into my mind, *once in a lifetime opportunities*. With a sudden urge to live my own life in Technicolor, I sprinted out of the church – not minding how loudly my heels clicked this time – put on my sunglasses and hotfooted it back to the hotel, humming an evocative song as I walked.

CHAPTER 27

After chasing up three flights of stairs to our rooms, I slipped off my heels and carried them down the corridor – I didn't want Alasdair to know I was back. I slipped the keycard into the door and tiptoed into the room as quietly as possible. There was a notepad and pencil sitting on the vanity desk. It was my turn to write a note:

Alasdair

I'll call for you at 7pm sharp (that's 1900 hours to you). I'm taking you out to dinner.
    Grace
    X

I wondered if only one kiss was a little standoffish. Maybe I should have put two, maybe I should have put it was a date. I folded the note in half, pushed it under our interconnecting doors, sat back on the bed and stared at the door. Placing a fingernail nervously between my teeth, I smiled and panicked at the same time. What if he didn't see the note? I should have left a tiny bit of the paper under my side of the door so I would know when he had taken it.

Crouching down on the floor I peered under the door to see if the note had gone. It would be a disaster if I called for him, all dressed up, and he hadn't read it. I was just doing my best caterpillar impression, prostrate on the floor with one eye open and peering through the crack, when another piece of paper shot under the door and hit me in the eye.

Grace

Sounds wonderful.
 Alasdair xx

Two kisses! It was definitely time for the ultimate weapon in Mum's armoury – the little black dress.

Riding high on a wave of euphoria at the excitement of our night ahead, I selected the music channel on the TV, and sang away merrily while applying my new make-up. I took in my reflection and sighed a contented sigh: my hair was silkier than usual, my skin more vibrant and my eyes shone – I was happy.

I stepped into my little dress, slipped on my shoes and heard one of Mum's favourite songs playing on the TV. A good omen, surely?

Dancing around the room I felt eighteen again, although thinking about it, I didn't want to feel eighteen – at eighteen you are still just a girl. No,

I was a *woman*; and this woman was certainly intending to push Alasdair's buttons!

I decided to try a particularly tricky dance move: a backside rotation – the type where you're supposed to slap your bum at the end of each rotation – and that's when I glanced in the mirror and an unexpected object caught my eye: it was Alasdair, he was standing at the interconnecting door and smiling at me – wryly.

There is simply no way to shrug off being caught dancing around your bedroom with a hairbrush in your hand. I flushed the colour of beetroot, grabbed the remote control and pressed mute in a manner similar to someone halting the needle on an old 45.

'Oh, don't stop on my account,' he said, hovering at the door. 'I was enjoying it.' He raised his eyebrows. 'And I mean *really* enjoying it. Although I will confess, at one point I wasn't sure if you were dancing or putting out a fire on the carpet.'

I resorted to emergency banter.

'Sod off! I was just working up an appetite for dinner, that's all.'

He picked up a cushion from the bed and slapped me on the backside with it.

'Come on; move that sexy ass downstairs. I'm starving.'

'You look great by the way,' he said as we stepped out onto the street.

For once I didn't blush. 'So do you.'

I took the lead. I knew exactly where I wanted us to go, to Mum's promenade and to the St Catherine's Square Café. It didn't take long to reach the promenade. Lanterns lined a low stone wall that edged the path as it zigzagged its way down the hillside. We paused for a second by the wall and gazed across the city. The evening light was dusky red while street lamps and office lights added a touch of sparkle to the view. Alasdair turned to face me. He propped his back against the wall, took my right hand in both of his and wrapped the span of his hand around my wrist – there was plenty of room to spare. He closed his grasp gently.

'So, how's the injury?'

'Agony,' I joked. He lowered my wrist.

'Where are you taking me?' he asked. 'The note said dinner.'

'Somewhere special, I hope.' I turned on my heels and began to walk. 'Come on, we need to find St Catherine's Square. I don't suppose you remembered the little map did you?'

'*You* have the map,' he said. 'I gave it to you to find the church.'

'Ye of little faith,' I teased. 'How difficult can it be? We don't need a map. You're just not used to someone else taking the lead that's all.'

Twenty minutes and a few false starts later, we found St Catherine's Square Café. An al fresco dining area spilled out onto the cobbles. Our waiter led us to an outside table, pulled out my chair and handed over the menus.

'So, why this place then? Good choice, by the way.' Alasdair placed an unopened menu on the table in front of him and looked around.

'Mum's letter. This was one of her haunts.' I picked up the wine menu. 'Hey, they have your favourite wine, Alasdair. Let's order a bottle.'

He flashed me his questioning look – an irresistible one.

'And?'

'And, what?'

'And, what else was in the letter? You can't freeze me out now, not at the juicy bit.' He picked up his menu.

'How do you know Zagreb is the juicy bit?' I whispered, peering over the top of the menu.

He leant forwards across the table. 'You don't need to whisper and glance around,' he said with a grin, 'who do you think is listening?' He sat back. 'Anyway, Zagreb must be the juicy bit because she told you there was going to be a change afoot at the end of the last letter, *and* because she told me not to scatter her ashes here (very suspect), *and* because we've come all the way to Croatia for one night.' He put his menu down for a second. 'Like I said, juicy.'

'You're right, it's very juicy. I'll give you the letter later, I wouldn't know where to start.'

Alasdair ordered the wine and we gave serious attention to the menu. He held it a significant distance from his face.

'I've been meaning to say, you need glasses.'

He put his menu down.

'Don't be ridiculous.'

'Yes, you do. Go on, pick the menu up again and read something without holding it at arm's length.' He picked the menu up, before putting it down onto the table again.

'How the hell is anyone expected to read anything in this light?'

We decided on the Chateaubriand. A violinist wearing traditional costume weaved through the tables. The conversation halted occasionally to accommodate applause.

As the meal neared completion and the wine took effect, Alasdair's eyes began to dance and it was time for my speciality – nervous conversation.

'I'm pleased you didn't turn out to be an axe murderer by the way,' I said casually. 'Handy that.' Alasdair struggled to swallow his wine through spontaneous laughter. I took a quick bite of my dessert and carried on.

'Although *why* we have to burden murderers with a heavy axe I will never know. For example, how many murderers throughout the world—no, that's too broad a cross-section, let's stick with the UK. How many murderers in the UK actually carry an axe? Not many I bet. Poison, yes, an actual axe, no. It might be different in Canada, for instance, lots of trees.'

Alasdair was smiling at me. 'Grace, you really are priceless.'

He sat back in his chair and looked at me with warmth; and something else perhaps?

'You know, you look so relaxed tonight. You seemed tired when we started the trip.'

He said nothing but leant forward and surprised me by taking my hand. 'Come on,' he said, gently pulling me to my feet, 'they're playing our song.'

'What? I can't hear any music. And anyway, we don't have a song.' I lied.

'There's a jukebox inside, I had a quick look when I nipped to the gents. Trust me, our song is on there.'

I glanced at him nervously.

'Don't you think it's a bit . . . 1950s.'

'No, I don't.'

Stepping into the café, I was transported into a world belonging to Mum's era: smoky, atmospheric, intoxicating.

Alasdair walked confidently over to the jukebox. He scrolled down the list of songs, turned to look at me with a cheeky grin, turned back to the jukebox and selected a song. He didn't seem to notice attention from the diners as he took me by the hand and led me to an area clear of tables.

I hoped he would have found the song from the wedding, but he chose something else entirely – *You Make Me Feel So Young*.

It was perfect – I thought I was in heaven!

We jived around our makeshift dance floor giggling like school kids and I felt utterly, utterly free. Yet despite brushing my face against his *several* times, and despite holding his gaze seductively – pleadingly – as the song ended, we didn't kiss.

What was wrong with the man?

Instead, he tipped me backwards across his arm, and our perfect moment came to a close. I retired to a bar stool to rest my weary feet while Alasdair sought out the maître d´ to pay the bill. A man crossed the room and sat on the stool next to mine. He swivelled in his seat to face me. I knew exactly what was coming.

'Where are you from, beautiful lady?' His eyes rested lazily on my legs. I had been there before; best to appease him and then walk away.

'Er, the UK. Sorry, I'm just waiting for—'

'You look like you need a good time. I can give you a good time.'

'No, thank you.'

I tried to rise from my stool but he held my shoulder and ran a finger along my leg. I was just about to wriggle out of his lecherous grasp when Alasdair appeared. He grabbed the man's wrist aggressively and held onto it. Alasdair's face held such evil menace I couldn't be sure what would happen next. The chatter in the room quietened. The man's expression was one of absolute fear; so much so that I almost felt sorry for him.

I touched Alasdair's shoulder. 'Can we go now please?' But he still didn't move; his gaze was fixed unblinkingly on his prey.

'Alasdair, please?'

He released the man's wrist and watched him

scurry away. I took Alasdair's hand and led him out of the bar into the darkness of St Catherine's Square.

'Come with me,' I said, 'I've got something I want you to see.'

I led him by the hand to St Mark's Square in silence. We paused to look at the church roof but the fabulous mosaics weren't discernible in the dark.

'Let's see if it's open.'

The church door opened with a turn of the handle. I thought of Mum and took a candle from the rack and lit it with a taper before walking in silence down to the altar. We stood still for a moment and glanced around in the candlelight.

'This is the church where Mum asked me to read her letter. I wanted you to see it before we go home tomorrow.'

He didn't respond.

Slightly disappointed, I started back down the aisle, but as I turned, he took my hand and pulled me back towards him. We faced each other by the altar. His eyes searched mine with a mixture of trepidation and absolute longing. I knew I couldn't let this moment pass. He stroked my face.

'Grace, I—' I didn't want to listen. I took a step closer and gently pressed my body against his. I thought he was going to pull away so I arched even closer to him, my lips sought his with pleading expectation. He lowered his head and allowed his lips to brush against mine.

One hand edged to the small of my back, the other to my hair. We kissed tenderly at first but our bodies ached for more. Alasdair pulled away and whispered into my ear.

'God I need you, Grace. But this isn't right.'

I wasn't listening. Desperate to feel my frame against his I allowed one hand to hover on his belt, the other on his chest. We kissed again, I knew he wanted me, but he pulled away once more.

'No. Not here, not now.' He was more assertive this time.

I looked around and giggled.

'You're probably right, it is a church after all.'

He took my hand and rushed me back to the hotel in silence. We passed his room and opened the door to mine. I turned to face him – to carry on where we left off – but he held me at a distance.

'I'm sorry, Grace, we can't do this, not now.'

He stepped a few paces away from me and raised a hand to his head. I kept my voice soft.

'Why? I thought you wanted this too. Don't you want me that way?' He turned his back to me for a moment and raised his face to the ceiling.

'Don't *want* you that way? Do you know how much self-control I've needed to get this far through without—' I was just about to step in but he turned to face me.

'When I'm not with you then I'm thinking of you. I want to hold onto you, to keep you safe. When that bloody captain was dancing with you at the wedding, I couldn't bear it. I had to walk away. And my God, when I looked across the café just now and saw that bastard touching you, I swear I was going to tear him apart. I'm desperate for you . . .' He ran his hand through his hair. 'I'm going insane. You're the sexiest woman I have ever met and you don't even know it, but I have got to hold back, I have to wait until you know the full picture, it wouldn't be fair.' He stepped towards me. 'You captivate my every waking thought, *that's* how much I want you.'

I tried to take his hand but he stepped back.

'We've only kissed, Alasdair. I'm not expecting the world.'

He stepped towards me again and took my hand.

'If I had the world to give, then I would give it to you. But I don't even have myself to give, not right now.'

'Why? Just tell me why?'

He turned towards the door.

'I don't understand, Alasdair. If this is about your job, don't worry. I know you're special forces, Mum told me in her letter.'

He looked surprised but continued to back towards the interconnecting door. I rushed to the door to face him.

'If tonight is all you can give me,' I whispered, 'I'll take it.' My eyes mirrored his distress. I couldn't believe he was leaving.

'Walking away from you right now is the hardest thing I have ever done, but staying with you would be the most selfish. I'll only let you down in the end.'

He opened the door and left.

Hell's teeth!

He wanted me – but he didn't want me. I sat down on the edge of the bed and put my hands to my face.

What a mess. Mum – with her bloody useless advice and sexy clothes.

I rose from the bed, faced the mirror and stared blankly through my reflection and into my life. After an eternity spent staring into the void, I swept my hair to one side over my shoulder, dropped my head down and reached for the fastening at the top of my dress. A hand sought mine as I reached back; our intertwined hands rested on my neck. I didn't turn, but looked up to see Alasdair's reflection in the mirror. He leant forward to whisper into my ear, his chest rested softly on my back.

'If our remaining days together were all I had to give, would you still take them?'

I didn't turn, but met his gaze in the mirror, and smiled a mischievous, intoxicating smile. Every inch of my mind and body wanted to say yes to him. I wanted to feel the smooth definition of his skin against my lips, and mine against his. Feeling his breath against my neck, I was on fire inside. I throbbed with erotic expectation. This was my moment to experience the kind of hot, passionate encounter I had only ever dreamed of, and there was no way on earth I was going to let it go.

Still holding his gaze, I raised my hands to the nape of my neck and undid the button that held my dress in place. With my arms raised above my head, I ran my fingers through my hair and arched my head backwards, inviting Alasdair to caress my neck with his lips. A shiver pulsed through me as the dress skimmed to the floor. A couple of fluid hand movements on Alasdair's behalf led to the speedy abandonment of my underwear.

I watched Alasdair's obvious delight through the mirror as he admired my naked frame, and with my back still resting against his chest, his hands mirrored each other as they stroked the curve of my hips and brushed gently across my stomach – which almost made me orgasm there and then – before he travelled in a slow, teasing strokes upwards, finally taking me onto greater pleasure as his fingers confidently aroused my nipples. His lips teased the nape of my neck while my breasts swelled and hardened under his touch.

I turned to face him. He tried to kiss me but I held him back, unbuttoned his trousers, released his erection and disarmed him of his clothes. His tongue sought mine – tenderly at first – but the desperate need within both of us led to a frenetic, lip-biting kiss. My hips pressed against his. All I wanted was to feel his length deep inside, but decided to wait. Alasdair's body was manna from heaven, and I wanted to savour it – to devour him. I wanted to give Alasdair an experience to remember me by, I wanted him to dream of this moment again, to need me again.

Still standing, I teased my way down his torso, looked up at him naughtily, and then felt the smooth shaft of his – particularly long – erection around my lips. He gasped – in a good way!

But he wouldn't let me please him for long. He lifted my chin, I rose to face him, and with powerful arms he lifted me onto his erection in one fluid motion – it was my turn to gasp.

Oh Lord . . . I'm in heaven!

And then we did it – boy did we do it. Alasdair was . . . phenomenal.

Not known for flash-flood orgasms, I came twice in ten minutes. The man knew exactly where to touch – how fast, how slow, how deep – but most importantly, he was more into me, mentally and sexually, than any man I had ever known.

Mum was right: spending the night in a foreign city with a gorgeous man (who was something of a mystery and who was desperately attracted to you too) was sensational.

PART V

ARISAIG, SCOTLAND

29–31 MAY

CHAPTER 28

Our next destination came as no surprise. Mum fled from Zagreb to the West Coast of Scotland, which was exactly where we were headed. Just like six days before, a man from a car rental company waited outside the arrivals terminal at Inverness, and, with Alasdair at the wheel, we were quickly headed south-west on the A82 towards Arisaig.

'You're quiet,' he said.

'I'm just taking in the scenery. Loch Ness isn't quite how I expected. It's big enough, but I thought the mountains around it would be more monumental. It's a little bit tame.' At that moment we entered Drumnadrochit and a giant plastic statue of the Loch Ness Monster came into view.

'Or maybe not.'

He took his hand off the steering wheel and ran a finger along my thigh. 'If it's mountains and dramatic scenery you want, then that is exactly what you will get.'

At that particular moment all I really wanted was Alasdair.

After about an hour, Loch Ness and then Loch

Lochy disappeared from the rear view mirror, and the landscape opened out somewhat. Alasdair turned to me, beaming, as a vast panorama of mountains came into view. A sign on the side of the road welcomed us to Lochaber.

'There's somewhere I don't want to pass without stopping, and it should be coming up around about . . . now.' Alasdair pointed towards a statue to the right.

Three towering figures, silhouetted against the mountains beyond, stood atop a significantly sized plinth.

'Wow, that's really striking. The figures standing on the plinth, they're soldiers aren't they?'

'Not just any old soldiers,' he answered with a smile. 'This is the Commando Memorial.'

The monument stood on an exposed spot. The wind caught me by surprise as I stepped out of the car and snapped the door out of my hand. We took a gravel path to the statue. I fought to keep my hair out of my eyes while Alasdair tucked my free hand into his coat sleeve. Pausing to point out features of significance in the landscape, he pointed towards the skyline and said, 'If you follow the eye-line of the Commandos you'll see they're looking directly at the peaks of Ben Nevis and Aonach Mor.'

I nodded, following his fingertip.

'And further on you can make out . . . let's see, they're probably the Grey Corries and, further on, the tip of the Great Glen.' His face looked fresh and alive; as strong as the statues against the wind.

'It's spectacular,' I said, still drinking in the scenery. 'Fantastic place for a memorial.'

The cloudless sky directly above us was pale blue, but the sun's rays created a rainbow as they bounced off rain falling roughly twenty miles or so down the glen.

We took some last steps towards the front of the monument.

'This area – Lochaber – is where Commando Basic Training was carried out during the Second World War,' he explained. 'That's why there's a statue here.' He gazed up at the soldiers.

Three Commandos in battle uniform, standing twenty-feet high and immortalised in bronze, stood shoulder to shoulder looking out across the Highlands. 'United We Conquer' was inscribed around the top of the stone plinth. The statue and the landscape surrounding it were in unity. Either entity would have been the lesser without the presence of the other.

Poignant, inspiring and, quite simply, perfect.

'What do you think of when you look at the monument?' He asked, stooping to pick up a piece of silver paper blowing about in the breeze.

'Let's see.'

I gazed at the statue once more and then back at Alasdair. 'I suppose it says pride, strength perhaps?' I thought for a while. 'And something else, something I can't quite put my finger on. There's something about the way the men seem to be interlinked, the three of them there, together.

There's a word to describe it but I can't think what it is.'

Alasdair smiled. 'Come on, I'll show you the memorial garden.'

We followed a path to a circular area covered in gravel and enclosed by a low stone wall. The inside boundary of the wall was lined with flowers, poppies and cards. Alasdair stopped at the entrance to the circle.

'This is where some families scatter ashes or just come to remember.' He stuffed his hands in his pockets and directed his gaze not at the memorial garden, but away, towards Aonach Mor.

I stepped into the circle and began to read the tributes. Some were for men killed during recent conflicts: fathers, sons, husbands. I could only cope with reading a few before stepping out of the circle and joining Alasdair.

'Aren't you going to read any?' I dabbed the flow of my tears with Alasdair's handkerchief; this time, he didn't call me a rainy face.

'No need. I know what they'll all say.'

He placed his arm around me and led me back in the direction of the monument. We sat at the base of the plinth in silence and looked out towards Ben Nevis. We sat there, caught up in our own thoughts, until, 'So, your turn. What do *you* think of when you look at the statue? What word would you use to sum it up?' I stood and turned to face him. Alasdair was watching the storm gaining momentum in the distance.

'The word you were searching for earlier I suppose – camaraderie.' I nodded in agreement but sensed he had more to say so remained silent. 'Soldiers travel thousands of miles, put their lives on the line for a war or for a cause they perhaps don't understand – or even worse, they may not even agree with. But you know what keeps them going, what's always kept them going in fact?' He threw some pieces of gravel across the steps.

'What?'

'Exactly what this statue stands for, each other. Well, that and the basic fact that it's what they're paid to do. I don't want you to get the wrong impression though. Forces life can be wonderful – *has* been wonderful. Just imagine how it feels to stand on the deck of a warship and sail into a home port after a long deployment. And I've done a number of expeditions to some amazing places, I've got great mates. I've got lots to be grateful for.'

I took a seat next to him on the plinth again.

'How long have you been a marine, Alasdair?'

He laughed. 'Over twenty years, man and boy.' He glanced at me. 'And we'll have no ageist jokes from you Buchanan.'

I smiled coyly. 'Actually, you're ageing particularly well, if my memory from last night is anything to go by.'

He raised his brows cheekily.

'So, thinking back,' I said. 'We've been involved

in conflict, somewhere in the world, more or less permanently over the past twenty years.'

'More or less, yes.'

I shook my head. 'No wonder you're tired. Do you think Mum was right?'

'About what?'

'About it being time for a change for you perhaps. If there is one thing I'm learning from this time away it's that life is pretty damn precious, and our time here'—I gestured to the landscape—'is kind of in layers, like my tree at St Christopher's. And maybe it's time for you – for us I hope – to start a brand new chapter, a new layer.'

'You may be right.'

'Just one more thing,' I said quietly, 'have you been told if you're definitely going away when you get back?'

He pushed a stray strand of hair away from my face tenderly. 'Yes, I'm going away.'

I sighed but said nothing. An image of Mum came to mind. I smiled inwardly at the thought of her; she gave me a much needed opportunity to lighten the mood.

'What would Mum have made of our journey so far do you think? I wonder if it's all gone to plan.'

'I think she would be thrilled. She certainly wanted us to get together.'

We both giggled.

'I know, how bad is that? I had to rely on my dead mother to fix me up with the man of my dreams.'

I blushed at the realisation of my words. Alasdair didn't let the moment pass. I knew he wouldn't.

'So, I'm the man of your dreams, am I?'

I smiled up at him.

'Maybe . . .'

We lingered for a further ten minutes while I photographed the monument before continuing on the penultimate leg of our journey. On closing the car doors, the sky darkened to black and the first spots of rain began to fall.

CHAPTER 29

We ventured on through Lochaber: Fort William passed in a blur of mist and rain, the Glenfinnan Viaduct was just a watery glance through the back window and Loch Shiel was more like a violent ocean than a sheltered inland loch. The storm reached a crescendo as we arrived at the coast; the windscreen wipers failed to match the torrent of rain being thrown in bucket loads across the car.

It was with a sense of relief, then, that we eventually arrived at our destination, the small fishing village of Arisaig. Our accommodation consisted of two rooms in a pretty hotel situated on the harbour front.

A Polish girl escorted us to our rooms.

'Oh, that's a shame,' I said with a cheeky glance at Alasdair, who was depositing the suitcases on the floor, 'there's no interconnecting door this time.'

'A minor detail,' he said. 'I'll chisel one out if necessary.'

He followed me to the window. I ran a hand through my damp hair and looked out towards the sea. At least, I thought I was looking at the sea; it was difficult to tell through the torrential rain.

'This weather has put a bit of a dampener on this evening's plans I'm afraid. Your mum didn't account for a storm.' He turned to sit on the windowsill and face me. 'So this is how tonight was supposed to work. We were *supposed* to go and sit on a little stretch of silver sand – about a mile or so from here – build a campfire, look out towards the mystic islands of Rum and Eigg—'

'Egg? As in, bacon and—'

'Yes, just listen for a second. We were going to sit on the beach and you were going to read the next letter'—he glanced out of the window—'but obviously that's not going to be possible this evening, so I'll give you the letter to read after dinner and then, well, we'll see what tomorrow brings.'

'Why don't we just enjoy this evening and I'll read the letter tomorrow,' I asked, leaning towards him playfully. 'What difference will a day make?'

He ignored my suggestion and gently pushed me away.

'No. You need to read the letter tonight.'

He picked up a strand of my damp rats-tail hair and tweaked it back behind my ear. 'We have to be somewhere in the morning, first thing, so you *have to* read that letter tonight.'

Not remotely interested in Mum's letter, and desperate to prevent Alasdair adjourning to his room, I took the only course of action left open to a harlot – I manoeuvred him onto the bed, sat astride him and arched forwards so that my lips were almost touching his.

'The thing is, Alasdair'—I allowed my hair to drape across his chest as I spoke in a low, seductive voice—'I simply haven't built up sufficient appetite for dinner. Maybe you could think of something we could do to kill an hour or so . . .'

What the hell had happened to me?

He tried not to smile but the corners of his mouth twitched, those deep blue eyes sparkled and I felt something else stir beneath his zip. It was my turn to raise my eyebrows. I began to unbutton my shirt, being careful to keep my eyes dancing with his the entire time. He laughed out loud (not exactly the response I was hoping for) and stroked my face with his hand.

'You will be my downfall, Ms Buchanan.'

Sometime later we headed out of the room and headed downstairs to order dinner.

The bar was dimly lit and cosy. Two old gentlemen propped their elbows on the bar and chatted quietly, while a middle-aged couple who had clearly been out for a walk (in *that* weather), stripped each other of their waterproof clothing at the door. We sat at a table by the fire but we weren't alone for long.

Barbara, an American of about fifty, was jolly, slightly overweight, talkative and travelling alone – tracing her Scottish ancestors in the process. I didn't mind sharing a table with her, I'd just had sex with Alasdair, the whole of Wisconsin could have asked to sit with us and I would have just smiled.

Shortly after dinner we gave our apologies to Barbara and sauntered upstairs. Alasdair went to his room to get Mum's letter. He placed it on the bed and pulled me towards him in a gentle embrace. After a tender peck on the nose he said, 'I really do have to nip next door for an hour or so and do some work, but I don't think you should read the next letter alone. Why don't you wait until I'm done and then we can read it together?'

'Why? What are you worried about? I grant you, she may be about to tell me who my father is, or was, but honestly, it's okay. I've always suspected I'd be the result of a one-night stand, although I didn't expect him to be a bloody spy! Mum's life is all in the past, I'm fine with it, don't worry.'

I sat on the bed and picked up the letter while Alasdair started towards the door.

'I'll pop back in an hour or so. We can talk about it then, okay?'

'Okay soldier – sorry, *marine*. Off you go, toodle-pip, or whatever it is you officer types say.'

His mouth smiled but his eyes did not and, as he closed the door behind him, I should have realised, right there and then, something was wrong.

CHAPTER 30

Arisaig

Hello love.

Of all of the letters you have read so far, this is perhaps the most important.

As I said, once I arrived at Arisaig Lodge I collapsed into Geoff's arms; I was so relieved to be away from the horror of Zagreb. He knew nothing of the details of my friendship with Sam but was informed by my colonel that a man had been found dead in my apartment and that, by the slightest of associations, my safety may also be in question. So, until more information came to light, I was to remain in Scotland. Geoff commented, half-jokingly, that surely I had experienced enough adventure by now and suggested I resign my commission with the RAF. I tried desperately to push the details of the past three months as far from my mind as possible and began planning my new life in Scotland, a country I adored.

The problem is the human mind cannot switch off so easily. Once ensconced in Geoff's arms I remembered how much I adored him and how happy we were together. Unfortunately though, every time he held me I felt guilty; with every kiss, a revolting, lustful image of Sam sprung into mind. It was hell. We made love on the first evening, which may shock you considering the details of my previous letter, but the cover-up game of the adulterer had already begun. We hadn't seen each other for months, we were a young couple; surely he would suspect something if I acted differently? Well, this is how my mind worked at the time. Also, bear in mind, making love to someone who you have been intimate with for years is comfortable, safe and familiar. I'm sorry to have to be so blunt but I'm desperate for you to understand. I wanted to give myself to him so I could prove we were the same as always – that life would go on just as before; but, my guilty soul couldn't cope with the strain. Silent tears slipped down my cheeks as we caressed and afterwards, as he held me tight, I knew the guilt would never leave me. It was my burden, my punishment.

Did I consider telling him about Sam in those first weeks? Of course I did. But, I kept telling myself things like, it was only one night, he would never know.

The colonel granted me compassionate leave until the finer details of my safety could be ironed out, and boy did I need it. I made a daily phone call for an intelligence update and, after a long discussion with Geoff, on the fifth day of my leave I informed the colonel of my wish to tender my resignation. He asked me to wait a couple of weeks, to let things settle.

And there we have it. I decided not to disclose my indiscretion to Geoff but to resign from the RAF and focus on building a marriage and a home life in Scotland. I breathed a deep and much needed sigh of relief.

Of course, that was not the end of the story. Nearly two weeks after my arrival, Geoff received a phone call at work from the colonel. He came home to talk to me and I knew by the look on his face something was desperately wrong. I remember thinking – Jesus Christ, he knows about Sam – but it was much worse. It was, of course, the news of my father's death. The funeral was on that very day and I had missed it. Dad was always the one I informed regarding my whereabouts; he was the sensible one who would have known how to get hold of me in an emergency. Mum and Annie fell apart after his death. A couple of days passed before someone in the village gave them the advice of contacting the duty officer at an RAF base to trace me. Then there was some confusion regarding my paperwork. The news of my father's death and the date of the funeral chased me around half of Europe before the details eventually arrived on the colonel's desk.

I was devastated. Although I had left home several years before, I had always been his special little girl and now I had no dad to run home to any more and would never see his face light up when I entered the room. All very selfish thoughts, but natural ones nonetheless and, unfortunately, the kind of feelings you can no doubt associate with now I am gone. An MOD driver and guard escorted me to the Dales. I have already told you about the horrific bombardment I received from my sister when I arrived at Bridge Farm. Perhaps you will understand now why I had neither the will nor the energy to fight back.

I returned home to Geoff and, although I looked and felt like a broken woman, my father's death did have one positive aspect; it helped to put the horror of Zagreb into perspective.

So, why did my life take a different path altogether? Perhaps you have guessed. Six weeks after I arrived in Arisaig, I realised I had missed a period. I wasn't surprised; as you know, that kind of thing can happen without any cause for concern. I didn't honestly think I could be pregnant, but decided the best thing to do was to get myself tested, to put such thoughts out of my mind and relax. There was no doctor at the lodge so I walked into Arisaig. The nurse took my sample, tested it in a separate room and then returned to give me the verdict. I was pregnant. I left the doctors surgery and walked for hours through the dunes along the coast. I ended up sitting for a while on Camusdarach beach, where you are now. Right there and then I realised that the hopelessly romantic notion I had built up over the last few weeks of living a crofter's lifestyle with Geoffrey in the Western Isles was not to be – could never be.

I know this is a horrific notion, but within the course of two or three days, I'd had sex with two different men and, remembering the date of my last period, those two days would have been around the time of ovulation. I had no way of knowing who the father was, who 'your' father was. I'm sorry Grace. Call me a tramp my darling, call me what you like, but what was done was done and the realisation hit me in terms of what I should do. My only certainty was I had to do the right thing by everyone, but most especially by you. I managed to get myself back to the lodge and immediately confessed to Geoff about Sam

– but not about the baby. I packed my bag and phoned the colonel; he arranged transport for me back to Hereford.

My darling Geoff said very little. There was no big fight, no terrible names called; we sat in the lounge in silence with my suitcases waiting by the door until the car arrived. It would have been so easy to send the car away, to tell Geoff I was expecting his baby and go on living a life together. But, when all is said and done, although I was prepared to remain married and hide my indiscretion, I was not prepared to pass another man's child on to Geoff – if indeed that was the case. But that was exactly the point, I simply didn't know. If I had stayed with Geoff the guilt alone would have sent me to an early grave, maybe it has.

What I realise now, of course, is I should have told Geoff absolutely everything and allowed him to decide whether or not he wanted me to stay. But, my father had just died and I was an emotional wreck. All I can tell you now is, at the time, I believed I was doing the right thing.

I never saw Geoff again but have thought of him often. Whenever I sit for a while by your wedding cake tree I remember the happy times, and how life can change in a heartbeat.

Speaking of your tree, there is something

else you should know. I know I always said I bought it to commemorate your birth but that isn't strictly true. The day before I left Scotland for good, Geoff had been out on a 'secret mission' to buy me a present. There was a crofter's cottage across the burn at Camusdarach that we had our hearts set on – a pretty little thing. We decided to pool our savings as a deposit and buy the place. Having planted the cherry tree at the hut (and as a wonderful gesture to the memory of my dad), Geoff had bought the wedding cake tree (a tiny pot-bound thing then) in preparation for when the house was ours. The pot was wrapped with a red bow. When the car arrived to pick me up I ran into the garden and grabbed my tree. I suppose it was my way of holding onto Geoff. I put the little red bow in an old biscuit tin and buried it within the tree's roots. It's still there. Do continue to see it as 'your' tree Grace; after all, you both put your roots down at St Christopher's in the same year.

When I arrived at Hereford I was interviewed by the colonel and told him the whole sorry tale. He didn't judge, in fact he blamed himself for deciding not to inform me about Sam, but I decided blame was fruitless. All I cared about was your safety and your future. Which I suppose brings me on to why I changed my name. Intelligence sources discovered my association with Sam had been dangerous in the extreme. He was a mercenary and had blackmailed and double bluffed his way around the Iron Curtain for a number of years. The fool of a man had become embroiled with a strand of the Soviet mafia; he owed money. He told them I was an agent and they would get their money through me. He intended to loosen my lips (metaphorically and physically) and learn valuable information regarding the British intelligence operation in Eastern Europe. Obviously I hadn't blabbed so he decided to sleep with me and then blackmail me, all quite simple really. The Soviets were growing impatient, so they decided to dispose of Sam and loosen my lips the old-fashioned way. I was lucky. Anyway, it wasn't thought likely in the end that I would be chased to the UK. I was an opportune target rather than someone of vital importance, but the colonel didn't want to take any chances. So, as an added measure, I began to introduce myself as Rosamund Buchanan (Buchanan was your grandmother's maiden name).

When you were born the name of your father was left absent on the birth certificate and the colonel arranged for your name to be Buchanan. As I was still married to Geoff, I was legally Frances Heywood. I always intended to change my name on divorce but, believe it or not, we actually never did divorce, so I remain Frances Heywood, which is why I asked Jake to deal with the death certificate directly through Grimes.

The only question remaining was what to do about my career. Clearly I needed to work to be able to support you but, in those days, women were forced to leave the armed forces on pregnancy. This is where the colonel's genius really came to light and I have been eternally grateful to him for the strings he managed to pull in order to land me with my new job.

Many of the special forces chaps and intelligence operatives were suffering from burn-out. The intelligence operation in Northern Ireland was massive and involved tremendous risk not to mention the strain of the work required in order to keep a handle on Cold War intrigue. Someone put the idea forward, albeit in a half-hearted manner, that there really ought to be some kind of retreat – a safe house – where operatives could go to for post-deployment wind down. Somehow the colonel managed to persuade a civil servant with loose purse strings to part with enough money to buy a suitable house in an inconspicuous location. Clearly, they needed someone appropriate to run the retreat – and there you have it, my new job.

However, Grace, I'm afraid this new revelation brings me to the part of my story I have been dreading telling you the most. The retreat, as you have no doubt guessed, was St Christopher's. The house doesn't belong to me my love, but I so dearly wish it did because I would give it to you in a heartbeat. I know you have always said it would break your heart if I ever sold up, and have warned me many times that you intend to kick me out in my old age. I'm so sorry I never told you; I guess I thought I would live forever, and that eventually you would meet someone and settle into a place of your own.

The retreat has given me a great deal of pleasure over the years and I feel, between us, Jake and I have been able to provide a necessary service through some difficult times. Speaking of Jake, as you know he retired from the British Army some years ago, but what you don't know is that he was my protection officer in the early days. He left the army to help me run the retreat – the soppy old fool!

By now you must feel as though I have fed you a heap of lies all of your life. I wish I had told you about St Christopher's as a child, but without wanting to sound even more melodramatic than I already must sound, St Christopher's works well because it is private and discreet. Then, as you grew older, I knew that the time would come to tell you everything, but I've hardly seen you over the past few years, and when I did, our time together has been precious, and I haven't wanted to spoil things. And now I'm dying, and I have run out of bloody time and, for a million reasons (not all to do with you) I decided that this way would be the best. The most important thing to remember is I have never purposefully lied to you, but a set of circumstances conspired to catapult my life in a totally unexpected direction. I need you to know that my over-riding concern – always – was your safety and happiness and, as Jake has reminded me a million times over the many years I have known him, I did succeed at both: you were such a happy child, I suppose I never wanted to burst the bubble.

The only remaining thing to tell you is that I have no idea who your biological father is. I'm sorry Grace, you don't look like either of them. I would hold your face in my hands when you were small and stare at you – desperate for a tell-tale sign – for any little genetic characteristic that would give me a clue as to who your father was, but the only person you resemble is my mother, you are the image of her. Sorry love, it's difficult to concentrate so I will leave you there.

I love you my darling girl.

Mum

XXX

CHAPTER 31

I looked at my watch, surprised to see it was nearly nine. The storm, which was still in furious momentum, had masked the setting sun and made the evening sky darker than usual for the time of year. My hand touched the windowpane and I traced a raindrop to its resting point on the sash.

My thoughts turned to Alasdair.

Why hadn't he told me the truth about St Christopher's at the beginning? When I thought of all the banging on I had done about going back home for good, taking over the running of the retreat. What an idiot.

I grabbed my purse and phone, shot past Alasdair's door and crept down the stairs. The weather was too ferocious to consider a walk – which is what I desperately wanted to do – so I slouched at a table around the corner of the bar. Distracted from staring at a dirty pint glass yet to be cleared from the table, I turned on my phone. There was a text from Paul:

What? You sang? And at his friend's wedding? Why would you do that? Take note of all the question marks and phone me.

I was just about to call him when Barbara appeared. She had a drink in each hand.

'Hey, looks like you could do with one of these,' she said.

Before I had time to fend her off, she put the two sloshing wine glasses down on the table and disappeared only to return a few seconds later with a chair with a cushioned seat pad. There would be no getting rid of her now.

'You two had a fight?'

'No, of course not, everything's fine. Alasdair's doing some work, that's all.'

She leant towards me and whispered, 'Sorry honey, but that sad face of yours is a bit of a giveaway.'

I shrugged my shoulders.

'It's nothing, I've just read a letter from my mum that's all. It was a bit upsetting.'

'Why, what's she done? Run off with the milkman?'

'Hardly likely Barbara, she's dead.'

'Oh, how . . .?'

I looked up from the glass.

'How did I receive a letter from a dead woman?'

Barbara nodded.

'Now that is a very, *very*, long story.' I took a drink.

'So? We've got all night, and I'm a good listener.'

'I wouldn't know where to start.'

She folded her arms across the table. Part of me wanted to apologise and walk away but, unexpectedly, it was a relief to talk.

'When Mum died I thought I would inherit her house. I've always, and I mean *always*, intended to go home forever one day, but it turns out she never owned it, so, no house for Grace.' As I said the words out loud I felt a like a child, upset to have had her best toy taken away.

'And? Anything else?'

'There's the minor fact that, after thirty-one years of never knowing my father, Mum decided to narrow it down to two men. One of them, at least, is dead.' I put my elbows on the table, covered my face with my hands and suppressed the urge to scream. 'I just don't understand why she's left it till now to tell me everything. She died so suddenly, and yet she knew she was dying, so why didn't she tell me? I'm starting to wonder if we ever truly know anyone.'

'Do you have any children?'

I shook my head.

'Well, I do honey, and if I was sick, I don't know how I'd find the words to tell my kids goodbye.' She shook her head at the very idea of it.

'That's sort of what she said in one of her letters.'

'It sounds like she was trying to protect you, but maybe a little too much.'

'I know what you're saying Barbara, but Mum should have allowed me to spend those last few months with her, look after her.' I shook my head in wonder. 'And why didn't I realise how ill she was? I saw her only a couple of months before she died and believed her story about being a bit under the weather. I feel so selfish; like I wasn't paying enough attention to her.'

She took my hand and squeezed it.

'It sounds to me like she didn't have the strength to cope with the emotion of seeing you, of telling you the truth. Grace, listen to me honey, they were *her* final months. *She* was the one having to cope with knowing she was going to die. Can you even imagine how that must feel?' Barbara shuddered. 'The poor, poor soul. Maybe you need to just respect her decision and accept it.'

Tears spilled down my face.

'You're right.'

'So,' she said brightly, 'what's the story with that lovely young man of yours?'

I dabbed my tears with her napkin. 'Oh, he's known about the house all along and never told me.'

'He seems to be a decent guy. And honey, he is to die for in the handsome stakes.' I smiled and nodded in agreement. 'Although,' she continued with a hint of sarcasm, 'you never can tell with men, but maybe he had his reasons. Let's start at the beginning, see if you and I can't iron this thing out. Your mum's house, why is it so special? Is it an ancestral seat or something? Worth a lot of money? What's the deal?'

Barbara's words hit a chord. What *was* the deal with me and St Christopher's? None of my friends expected to inherit their parent's houses. Then I realised what my obsession with Mum's cottage was all about – it was my North Star.

'I suppose I never let go of Mum's house as my proper home because it's where I feel – I felt – I belong.'

My finger traced circles around the rim of my glass.

'It sounds like your mum gave you a pretty special home when you were growing up. But, if you don't mind me saying so, maybe she made life a little bit too sweet for you.' She nudged my arm, 'Shall I pop and get some scissors so we can cut those apron strings?'

I laughed.

'You're so right, Barbara. But that's the bizarre thing. As an adult I've hardly been home. I suppose I took the old place for granted, thought it would always be there—' My voice broke. 'Thought Mum would always be there.'

'So, what's next on that list of disasters of yours?' She sat back in her chair. 'She's gone and told you who your daddy might be, that's a tough one. I wonder why she didn't tell you before?'

Once again, I knew the answer.

'I think it was because everyone concerned was happy.' Barbara smiled and waited for me to continue. 'The truth is that I was a very happy child, and I did actually have a wonderful father, a man called Jake. I wouldn't have wanted anyone else. You know what was so devastating about losing Mum, Barbara?'

'What was that?'

'The fact that she just simply had too much life in her to die. She was an amazing woman. And

361

now she's given me an aunt and . . .' I smiled and shook my head at the thought of Alasdair.

'And what, Grace?'

'And she's given me Alasdair, which is the best gift of all as it turns out.' I picked away at the frayed edge of a bar mat absently. 'Even if he is a . . .' I struggled to find the words, but not for long. Someone standing at the bar finished my sentence for me.

'A stuck-up, arrogant arse?'

I spun around. Alasdair was smiling at me so tenderly every previous emotion of anger, confusion and disappointment simply melted away.

'Are you ever going to let that go?'

'Never.'

He stood from the bar stool and gave his hand to me. Rising from my chair, I fell into his arms and rested my head on the chest that had become so familiar during the past few days. I turned to thank Barbara for the drink and the chat, but she simply raised her hand as I started to speak – winking at Alasdair – then stood and whispered in my ear, 'Honey, he's gorgeous, don't mess it up.' She sidled down the bar and introduced herself to a man in his fifties.

'Do you want to talk?' Alasdair asked. I shook my head against his chest. One burning question came to mind, however.

'This "thing" we have to do at nine tomorrow morning, has it got anything to do with Geoffrey Heywood?'

He nodded.

'Grimes has arranged for you to meet him. Rosamund wanted to give both of you the opportunity to find out for sure if you wanted to.'

'A blood test you mean?'

He nodded again. 'But you don't have to do anything you don't want to.'

'Like you said earlier, let's see what tomorrow brings.' I lifted my head from his chest to look at him, 'I think I'm beginning to understand everything. I suspect you knew the detail of every one of Mum's letters all along. Am I right?'

'More or less, although the Zagreb letter was a little more revealing than I expected.'

I felt overwhelmed by tiredness as he led me up the stairs. The issue of St Christopher's no longer seemed relevant. All I needed for the rest of the night was to hold Alasdair close, and I decided to worry about tomorrow, tomorrow.

CHAPTER 32

I woke early and noticed through the gap in the curtains that it was light outside; the sun barely had time to rest its head in Scotland at that time of year. Alasdair slept soundly by my side. I considered turning over in an attempt to lull myself back to sleep, but it was impossible. The details of the previous letter ricocheted in my mind. I crept out of bed, put on Alasdair's fleece and perched on the window seat.

The boats moored in the bay were able to rest now the storm had passed and it was a clear, still day – a perfect time for reflection.

My thoughts centred on Mum's revelation that Geoffrey Heywood was possibly my father. Bizarrely, although Sam wouldn't have been a biological descendent to be proud of, if he had been my father at least I could have drawn a line underneath the whole sorry affair.

Mum's life had inspired me up to this point in her story, I was proud of her. But no matter how difficult it would have been for her, no matter how happy we were in Mum's Devonshire paradise, I should have been given the opportunity to find out who my father was.

And yet, I simply didn't want to meet him. Finding out I had an aunt was odd, but in no way harrowing. This was different. Even if we both decided on a blood test and he proved to be my father, how could we possibly start a relationship now? Geoffrey was a stranger to me.

My mind returned to Alasdair. The man I had come to know and love over the past few days was a chameleon. Mum said Alasdair was a special forces soldier, but really, who *was* Alasdair Finn? He obviously had reservations about becoming involved in a serious relationship, and had made it clear that we only had a few days together, but it was difficult to gauge what he really wanted – he made love to me in a manner that said he didn't want to leave my life in a hurry, and his recent body language contradicted his reticence, and then there was his email to Alex . . .

I glanced across the room and noticed his journal resting inside the top of his bag. It would break any a moral code to take a peek, but Alasdair wasn't a man who was likely to open up to me in a hurry, and I needed to know – was this time away all Alasdair had to offer me, or was there a glimmer of a chance of more?

28 May, Zagreb, Croatia

Hello Rosamund.

Grace is sleeping. I'm afraid I lost the willpower to be chivalrous, but bearing in mind
you set us up, I think I've done well to get
this far before making a move (I've just
thought of something disturbing . . . I hope
you aren't looking down on us from heaven
like Grace suggested, because if you are then
you REALLY won't like what I just did to
your daughter!).

I'm looking across the room at her in the
lamp light; she has her face on the pillow and
the duvet is hurled over her shoulder like she's
in the arctic (and it's boiling in here), and even
though she's dribbling a little bit and has the
cutest snore, she still looks like an angel – my
angel, but then I thought that the first moment
I saw her.

As you know, I haven't slept well for a
very long time – the night terrors were
becoming unbearable. But during this
holiday I have slept like a baby . . . how did
you know this time away would help?
Tonight, though, I doubt I will sleep at all.

Have I done the right thing, Rosamund?
Should I have had the willpower to stay away
from Grace? I wish you were here – I might
finally talk. I've always been so certain, so

driven, but all I can think about is how much I'll hurt her in the future, and for the first time in my life, something – someone – is more important to me than my job.

By the way, it's looking like I'll be taking my team away next week. I usually clamp down and focus at this point – it was a side of my personality my ex-wife hated – but I can't concentrate. All I want to do is have fun with Grace; just run away to the hills and have a laugh and a joke forever. There's something about her that gives me the same warm feeling I experience when I'm at your house – that feeling of finally letting out a great big sigh and saying, 'That's it then, it's been a long journey but I've reached my destination – I'm home.' And yet I also have this overwhelming feeling of doom hanging over me. You won't be surprised to know that I never expected to make it to forty, yet I'm nearly there. But what if I don't make it over that final hurdle? What if I promise Grace the world and then I let her down? I've pushed my luck to the limit over the years, and I'm sure the old man upstairs must have his eye on me!

I can hear you, by the way. You're saying, 'For Christ's sake, Alasdair, just shut up and go with the flow. Now go and give my daughter a great big hug!'

And you're right. I need to stop this. Everything will be fine. I'll try the mindfulness stuff again. Grace can be my new life – I promise I'll make her happy.

Heaven can wait, after all.

Alasdair.

With my heart breaking at the realisation that, after all this time, he still wrote to Mum, I crossed the room and slid into bed beside my man, who was finally sleeping.

After breakfast we took a walk along the village front, through a small boatyard and down to the end of the jetty. We sat on the decking and allowed the soles of our boots to dangle into the water. I gave Alasdair Mum's letter to read then explained my reticence towards meeting Geoffrey. Alasdair understood.

'You know, at certain points along the way, your mum's plan has seemed to be pure genius. But at other times it's been . . .' he paused to consider. I finished the sentence for him.

'Totally insane?'

We laughed; there was no other way to describe it.

We sat in silence staring out to sea. The bay and islands beyond were stunningly beautiful, but I was too anxious to take in any of the detail.

'What time is it by the way?'

'Eight fifteen.'

I felt nauseous.

'And he's expecting us at nine?' I already knew the answer.

'Nine o'clock sharp apparently, and according to Grimes we *are not* to be late.'

There was no easy way to ask the next question.

'So, I've got a favour to ask, and I'll understand if you say no.' I kicked the heels of my walking boots against a wooden jetty leg.

'Go on.'

'Will you go to the house and tell him I don't want to see him?' Alasdair kissed me on the nose.

'Of course.'

To say I didn't want to see Geoffrey wasn't strictly true. No, I didn't want to meet him, but I did want to see what he looked like. Alasdair shook his head in disbelief when I asked if there would be a way for me to see the man without actually meeting him. He laughed and said he would 'sort it'.

According to Alasdair's notes, Geoffrey's croft was about a mile away on a beach between Arisaig and the neighbouring village of Morar. Grimes had told Alasdair to park in a particular car park and walk down the obvious path through the dunes; we would find Geoffrey's croft over a stream in front of us as we stepped onto the beach.

We found the car park without difficulty. I looked at a notice board while Alasdair locked the car.

'Blimey, Alasdair, this is Camusdarach Beach. You know, the one from Mum's letter. I wonder if Geoffrey's croft is the one they were supposed to buy together?'

Alasdair looked at his watch. 'Possibly. Come on, we need to get a move on.'

We crossed a wooden bridge and followed the path through the dunes. It was a child's paradise. The path ducked and dived this way and that, while patches of tall grass emerged through the sand and whipped at our legs as we strode on, soaking the bottom of my jeans in the process. After only a couple of minutes the dunes parted one final time and we stepped out onto the beach. It was, without doubt, the most breathtaking beach I had ever seen. The sand was the colour of pure silver and, out to sea, the Small Isles of Rum and Eigg, their iconic silhouettes black against the blue of the Highland sky, climbed monumentally out of the water.

Alasdair pointed to a cottage across a stream.

'According to Grimes' instructions this is it, this is Geoffrey's house.'

I shot behind a dune and crouched down. Alasdair looked down at me.

'What are you doing now?' he asked, a bemused smile on his face.

'I don't want him to see me, do I? Quick! Crouch down, Alasdair,' I whispered, 'he might see you talking to me.'

'I thought you wanted to see what he looks like.' He glanced at his watch again.

'I do. But he'll see me if I get any closer.'

'Get up daft arse, we can get you a lot closer than this.'

Feeling a little like a commando on a covert mission, I followed on Alasdair's heels as we crept in the prone position along the base of the dunes, skirting the outside of Geoffrey's chicken wire boundary fence as we did so. We halted at a decrepit cleft wood gate.

'Aren't you going to cover me in twigs and cover my face with green paint?' I joked in a whisper. Alasdair glanced back at me with a cheeky wink.

'Maybe later, if you're very lucky.' He yanked up a patch of grass out of the sand and stuck it behind my ear. We turned our attention to the house and I raised my head above the parapet for a clearer view.

'Right then, I'm off.' Alasdair whispered. 'I'll keep him talking at the door. Once you've had a good look at him, crawl back round to the side of the house and I'll meet you at the car.'

'Okay.'

He started at a crawl back down the fence.

'What are you doing now?' I asked, perplexed. 'I thought you were going in.' He turned his head and whispered back towards me.

'I am. But I can't just rise up out of the dunes can I? If he's watching out of the window he'll be onto us.'

'Oh yes, of course.'

He carried on crawling.

'Alasdair,' I whispered even louder this time. He

glanced back with a 'what now?' expression on his face.

'Be careful.'

He laughed, shook his head and disappeared behind the dunes. A minute later he reappeared, walked bold as brass along the beach, dropped a handful of pink sea thrift on my head, hopped over the burn and stepped through the garden gate. I peered through the long grass to achieve a clearer view of the house. The door opened almost as soon as he knocked, but my heart fell to my boots.

The plan had failed; a woman answered the door.

She glanced at her watch as she beckoned him into the house. Alasdair shook her hand, wiped his feet on the door mat and closed the door behind him.

Disappointed, I didn't retreat from my position on the dunes, but knelt up a little higher to take a closer look. There was no denying it was a pretty cottage, but Mum would have prettied it up even more. She would definitely have painted the front door a warmer colour.

And then I saw it.

A wedding cake tree – significantly smaller than Mum's – sitting in the corner of the garden. I wondered if Geoffrey had planted it. A figure appeared with his back to the front window; it was Alasdair. His arms were crossed and it looked like he was listening.

This was madness. My shoulders dropped and I sat back on to the sand. Either I could stride up to the house, walk in and hope to see the man who possibly sired me, or I could walk away. If I chose the latter then there would be no going back.

It hadn't been what Mum had wanted perhaps, but I chose the latter.

I crawled back along the fence line, stood and although it wasn't an expeditious route, walked a little way along the beach. A boulder with a flat top cried out to be sat on. I lay my sweater across the rock, sat down and, with the warmth of the sun on by back, gazed out to sea.

A myriad of 'what if' scenarios tumbled to the fore. What if Mum had chosen to stay in Scotland rather than return to her colonel? I would have known this man Geoffrey, would have had my childhood in this very spot. I would have run excitedly from the house, flinging the wooden gate open as I went, a dog barking at my feet perhaps, a little fishing net resting over my shoulder, my oversized wellingtons slowing down my progress and squelching in the sand as I ran to the sea. Geoffrey would have lifted me into his arms and cheered when I caught my first crab, taken me on a treasure hunt for driftwood and carried me home on his shoulders.

Then I thought of my real childhood, not so dissimilar and I thought of Jake; calm, kind Jake. We had done all of the fun things I could ever have imagined doing with Geoffrey – and more. He was my dependable old lion, he was my father. I smiled. It was time to move on.

I took a few seconds to soak up the sunshine and was about to head back when a damp Springer Spaniel appeared at the water's edge directly in front of me. A second later, a thick vegetative stem masquerading as a stick, with a long strand of seaweed attached to it, splashed into the water. The dog took the stem and shook his silky coat by my feet.

A man walked towards the dog; his presence gave me a much needed push to move on. The dog, still at my feet, put his elbows on the sand but kept his hind quarters raised. He barked and pounced playfully towards the seaweed until the man arrived and, on taking the dog's heavy hint, he threw the makeshift toy back into the water. The man stood next to my rock and watched the dog frolicking in the sea. I smiled politely, grabbed my sweater and began to walk away.

A voice called out, 'Grace?'

I turned around.

'I'm Geoffrey.'

I had no clue what to say, or how to behave. What was the expected behaviour of two strangers who find they have a questionable genetic link and meet by chance on a remote and achingly picturesque Scottish beach? Run into his arms? Cry? Shout, Daddy, my daddy? None of these things seemed appropriate.

'I couldn't do it,' I said, 'come to the house I mean. I'm sorry.'

'Don't be sorry. It's all such a sad state of affairs and, I have to tell you, the revelation of your existence has been . . . awkward, for me.' He leant forward with a sigh, picked up the seaweed and held it in his hand. The dog, realising his owner was distracted, lay down at his feet.

'Yes, it must have been. Do you have a partner now?'

He paused for a second. The man looked exhausted.

'I do, yes. Only, Jean isn't just my partner, she's my wife.'

'Your wife? But I thought you were still married to Mum. I don't understand.'

He leant against the rock I'd been sitting on.

'After Frances disappeared I waited for a while, thought she would simply turn up one day. Your mum could be quite . . . unpredictable.' He smiled at the thought of her, but the smile soon faded. 'But after a couple of years I realised she wasn't coming back and, what can I say, I moved on, what else could I do?'

'Didn't you try to find her, or at least *try* to get a divorce?' I asked, astounded that he had, after all, just admitted to being a bigamist.

'Yes, of course. But I kept hitting brick walls. Jean fell pregnant and I had to do the right thing.'

I stood in front of him and put my fingers to my forehead. I tried (and failed) to take it all in.

'Jean had – has – no idea I was married before.'

'So, how have you explained all of this to her

now, how has she taken the news about me?' By the fact that Alasdair was greeted by Jean at the door, I assumed she must know the whole story.

'I haven't.'

To my complete surprise my eyes filled with tears.

'But the woman at the door?'

'Is an old friend of mine who worked at the lodge. She met your mother once. She's the only person here who knows.'

'So, where's Jean?' I asked, still confused.

'Shopping in Mallaig. She'll be back soon. The thing is, if she ever found out . . .'

He rubbed his hands up and down his face in anguish. I knew what he was getting at.

'Your secret's safe with me Geoffrey.'

He smiled, relieved.

'These things, they just happen. You don't intend to be deceitful, at the time you think you're doing the right thing. I'm sorry, but if you came here to find a family, I can't. I have nothing to offer you.'

He dropped his head. I felt wretched.

'So, don't you want to find out if you're my father, not even in secret?'

He shook his head, 'No.'

There wasn't anything left to say. He lifted himself from the rock; the dog was lying by his feet and began to stretch in preparation for their departure.

'Not that it's any of my business, but I'm glad I

met your husband, a fine man – and very protective of you.' I didn't correct him regarding Alasdair's status in my life.

'Just one thing before you go, Geoffrey. The tree in your garden – the wedding cake tree – did you plant it?'

'Ha! She kept her tree then, is that how you know the significance?'

I nodded.

'I bought another one, thinking she would come back. But it's been nothing but a reminder of wasted years . . . and it's never properly taken root either, never flourished. I don't think a tree like that is suited to life here.' He kicked the sand. 'What on earth was the woman thinking of?'

Finally understanding everything my mother wanted me to learn, I leapt to her defence.

'Like you said Geoffrey, I'm sure she thought she was doing the right thing, at the time.' Bizarrely, I thought about the ospreys at Loch Garten, and how the returning mate had thrown the younger mate's eggs out of the nest.

'If she had told you she was pregnant and confessed I might not be your child, would you still have wanted me?'

He turned to face the islands.

'I can't answer that. I just don't know.'

I didn't watch him leave but turned and walked to the car. I had cried many tears over the past six months, but nothing could compare to the heart-wrenched sobs I cried during the ten minute walk through the dunes.

Alasdair was leaning against the car. He said not a word but took me in his arms and held me in silence while I wept.

'He doesn't want me. I might be his daughter, but he doesn't want me.'

'I know,' he whispered across the top of my head. 'He hasn't the strength to rock the boat with his wife. The man is an idiot. But, if you think about it, an hour ago you didn't want him either, not really.'

I glanced up at him and smiled.

'Did you tell him where I was?'

'Yes, I saw you trying to caterpillar crawl away from the croft.' He smiled at the thought. 'You're a rubbish soldier, Grace.'

'Why did you tell him where I was?'

'I felt the thing needed to be faced by both of you.'

Alasdair passed me his handkerchief. Once again I thought of Aunt Annie and tried my hardest to pull myself together. At least *she* wanted to know me.

Another thought crossed my mind.

'Are there any ashes for here?'

'Yes there are, as if you haven't been through enough already.'

'I'm not going to scatter her here, Alasdair. I know it's what she wanted, but Mum didn't know the full story. She seems to have clung on to a rose-tinted view of him. I'll take her back to Devon, to Jake.'

'Come on, Rainy Face,' he said brightly. 'I want you to listen to your uncle Al. I want you to leap up, I mean really leap, and tell yourself it's time for a change, time to put this nonsense behind you.'

I looked up at him with absolute love and affection and wiped the last of the tears away.

'There's only one thing to be done at a time like this,' he said cheerily.

I put my arms around him and looked up. 'What's that?'

'What we Brits always do when we're a bit disheartened. Go and get a nice cup of tea.'

CHAPTER 33

'So, where do we go from here?' I asked, pouring the last dregs of stewed tea between our two cups.

'We'd better talk about that away from prying ears.' He glanced around the moderately busy café.

'No, silly arse, I mean literally, where next, how long have we got here?'

He relaxed.

'Ah. We leave for Devon in the morning and then, well, that's it, you're rid of me.'

'What if I don't want to be rid of you?'

He touched my cheek tenderly and gestured to the waitress for the bill.

'Come on, let's go somewhere private.'

Arisaig was a beautiful village set within a stunning bay, but our time there had been marred by the weather, the letter and the disturbing meeting with Geoffrey. Overtaken by the desire that our last day of adventure together wouldn't be devoid of fun, I told Alasdair to carry on without me to the beach . . . it was a surprise! I had noticed a hardware shop that hired out fishing rods and sold bait. It was the perfect day for a spot of fishing.

Alasdair had rested his back against a sand dune and closed his eyes. He didn't notice me trotting along the beach towards him, loaded up with rods, bait and a net. I stood by his boots and dropped my accoutrements onto the sand.

'I don't think you get much sleep in real life.' I sat astride him seductively. 'Or am I wearing you out?'

He sat up, put his hands to the back of my neck, pulled me towards him and kissed me – good God the man knew how to kiss!

'So,' I whispered in his ear, 'time to get your tackle out.'

He looked as though all of his birthdays had come at once.

'What? Here? Right now? Okay then!'

I jumped up from his legs and stood next to him on the sand.

'Sorry to disappoint, but *this* is the tackle I was referring to.' I picked up a rod. '*Ta dah*!'

He laughed out loud and looked both disappointed *and* relieved at the same time.

'Ah.' He jumped up, still laughing. 'A fishing competition, excellent.'

'Typical bloke,' I said, picking up the gear and heading towards the rocks.

'What?' It was his turn to follow on behind.

'You have to turn everything into a competition.' I turned to look at him cheekily. 'But you'll regret it this time, because I'm going to kick your arse.'

★ ★ ★

Like a couple of garden gnomes we perched ourselves on the rocks. Alasdair left his rod on the ground and watched amusedly as I baited my hook with a wriggly maggot and adjusted the rod.

'Stop looking at me like that,' I said.

'Like what?'

'Like "Woman, know your limits! This is man's work."'

'I'm not, I assure you. Although if you start telling me the ins and outs of the Arsenal offside trap, or the benefits of a good defensive stroke in cricket, then I really will have to have a serious word with Jake.'

'There's nothing wrong with being a tomboy, Alasdair.'

'Actually, I was smiling at something else entirely,' he said with a smirk.

'What now?'

'I take it you know you stick your tongue out when you're concentrating?'

I stuck my tongue back in.

'Stop trying to put me off, this bet is as good as mine.'

'I don't think so,' he said dismissively, then nodded towards my choice of bait. 'Not while you're using maggots as bait anyway.'

I glanced into the bucket. 'Why? What's wrong with maggots? The owner of the shop was out, but the girl standing in for him said—'

Alasdair snorted. 'Girl? Well she knows diddly squat about fishing if she recommended maggots.'

This was war!

'Okay then, smartarse, what are *you* going to use for bait, fresh air?' He was just about to answer when I added, 'Don't tell me, you're going to whittle yourself a spear and dive right in.'

He laughed, flashed me a cocky *I know best* smile and stood up.

'If you must know, I'm going to turn to nature to find my bait, which – you will learn – is always the best thing to do, Missy.'

Missy?

Not caring about getting his boots wet, he stepped into the water, pulled up his sleeves, stooped down and swished his hands around under a patch of seaweed. A eureka facial expression followed and, with his hands still in the water, he flashed me his brightest smile.

'Ah, perfect,' he said, 'just as I thought.'

He stood up and held out his dripping hands to show me his prize.

Mussels?

He looked away and visually scoured the dunes.

'And all I need now,' he said, still glancing around, 'is some wool.'

And with that, he placed the mussels on a rock, and wandered off.

Mussels? Wool? The man had gone barmy.

Alasdair disappeared over a dune only to reappear a couple of minutes later with a tiny amount of scraggy-looking fleece in his hand. I nodded toward the wool.

'Did you just wrestle a sheep to get that?'

He rolled his eyes. 'Don't be daft, I got it from a fence.'

'Oh, of course.'

He sat down next to me on the rocks (looking rather smug, I thought), before twirling a stretch of wool into thin twine and placing it between his teeth. Then, he took out his knife, cracked open a mussel (which looked much slimier than the cooked version) and pierced the mussel through the hook. The wool was then wrapped round the mussel to secure it onto the hook. He flashed me an even smugger, 'super-genius' grin.

Trying to hide my worry that he may just be right about the bait, I glanced at my line (lying dormant in the sea) and said, 'Mussels and wool? You'll end up with zero reward for a lot of effort, mark my words!'

He cast his line into the water. 'We'll see young 'un, we'll see . . .'

Half an hour later, with not a tickle in sight, my thoughts turned to our surroundings.

'This place is heavenly, have you been here before?'

'Not here, no. I've been to Skye a few times though, to the Cuillins'—he nodded towards the mountains on Skye—'those big beasts over there.'

'Were you on holiday?'

He laughed.

'Not exactly no. Training in the mountains, that's

all.' He pulled his line out of the water before casting off once more.

'The island over there,' he said, 'the one that looks like a volcano?'

'Yes?'

'That's Rum, and the other one that looks like a shark's fin? That's Eigg.'

He leant back and allowed the sun to soak into his face. 'I've always wanted to take off and go island-hopping round the Western Isles. Fancy it sometime?'

'Definitely.'

It was time to do some additional fishing of my own. 'So, Alasdair Finn, my man of mystery, when you were reluctant for us to get together in Zagreb, when you said you only had a few days to give, was it because of your job, because you feel you can't commit?'

'Yes. I'm sorry.'

'Listen, you need to stop worrying about me. I've known from the outset that you're special forces, but even if you were a regular soldier, you would still spend lots of time away doing dangerous stuff. Truth is, I'd rather see you occasionally than never, and even if you were injured or—or—whatever, then I'd still be pleased that you were in my life.'

It was Alasdair's turn to take his line out of the water. He turned to me, took my hand and stroked it with his thumb. After a very deep sigh, he started to talk.

'You're right. What I do isn't so different from being a regular soldier, but I'm not often in this country, and when I am I tend to be working. I can't talk to you about what I do, can't tell you where I am for half the time, or where I'm going. Time spent together would be dictated by what precious time I have free. Just taking this time off with you for the past nine days had to be planned well in advance. It's not that I can't have a private life, but it's a limited and selfish one, which is why my marriage didn't work . . . did you know I'd been married?'

I nodded. 'Mum mentioned it in a letter – one you haven't read.'

'Ah, right. Well, as I said in Zagreb, starting something with you would be selfish of me, but as you well know – the siren that you are,' he raised his eyebrows playfully, 'I just couldn't resist. When Rosamund asked me to come away with you, every ounce of common sense told me to say no. Do you know the real reason why I said yes to her?'

I remembered his letter to Mum. 'Because she was dying? Because she helped you at the retreat?'

'No, I'm not that nice. It was because I'd seen your cracking body at St Christopher's and I couldn't get you out of my head'—he feigned a guilty expression—'I'm *that* shallow. My intelligence work won't last forever, but until I've seen it through I don't have much to offer. I want to hold on to you forever. But I don't want to be selfish either, so I'll leave it up to you.'

I was just about to step in when he said, 'Actually, you're right. Fuck it. If another man so much as lays a finger on you, I will almost certainly go instantly mad, or I'll rip his arms off – oh, and I insist on vetting this friend of yours, Paul is it? So, you're stuck with me.' He flashed me his schoolboy grin. I looked up to the sky and burst out laughing.

'Just tell me one thing. Are you actually James Bond but you just can't tell me? And, even more important than that, do you drive an Aston Martin? Because if you drive one of those, then I'm definitely sticking around.' He laughed out loud.

'If I say yes will you be my Miss Moneypenny? Or,' he added quickly with a wink, 'even better, Pussy Galore?'

'Oh God yes.' We burst into laughter.

'Sorry to disappoint,' he said, 'but my work is in no way glamorous, and I drive a clapped out Jeep . . . although I do have a pretty flash motorbike.'

I convulsed into giggles. Paul would wet himself when I told him!

'What's so funny about having a motorbike?'

I took him by surprise by leaning in and kissing him tenderly.

'I'll take whatever you have to offer Mr Finn.'

And then I got a tickle.

My rod jerked and I squealed with excitement. Thankfully, my competitive nature took control of my emotions, and I calmed down enough to reel in my catch. A decent-sized fish emerged from the water and flapped wildly on the end of the line.

'Quick, grab it!'

Alasdair opened the fish's mouth, removed the hook and balanced the prize catch across his hands. It was a pollock (according to Alasdair). My eyes travelled from the fish to Alasdair's face.

'Looks like we have a winner then,' I said cockily, 'and I think you'll find that the winner is me. Watch and learn kiddo, watch and learn.' I gave my hair a flirtatious flick and winked at him naughtily. 'Mussels and wool you reckon? Nah, maggots'll do it every time.'

Alasdair was peering at me through squinting eyes while I spoke. I tried to keep a straight face, but it was impossible. He opened the flapping fish's mouth once more, squinted to look inside, glanced back at me, and then removed a microscopic bit of wool from behind tiny teeth. He held up his exhibit for the prosecution.

'Grace Buchanan. Did you swap rods when I went for a pee?'

'Errr . . .' I bit my lip. 'When you say swap rods, could you possibly be a little more . . . specific?' I couldn't help but giggle.

Alasdair's eyes flashed bright blue – a wicked blue.

'Right! You're mine.'

I squealed and started at a pace down the beach while Alasdair crouched down and lowered the fish back into the water. He caught up with me within seconds, threw me over his shoulder, then carted me to the water's edge and dangled my backside over the sea.

'No, Alasdair. Don't! Okay, I admit it, I swapped the bloody rods.'

'I knew it! You're a little sod. Say it then, who *really* won the competition? Say it!' He lowered me down so my backside was only an inch from the water.

I screamed again. 'No! Don't get me wet . . . *pleease*!'

He lifted me a little higher, rested his forehead on mine and whispered, 'Say it then, who won the competition?'

I smiled up at him serenely. 'Okay, you did! But the mussel thing was cheating. You must have had insider knowledge.'

He lowered me to my feet but kept me wrapped in his arms.

'I'll tell you what,' he said, 'we'll call it a draw.' He tried to kiss me but I pulled away slightly.

'What's wrong?'

'Oh nothing's wrong,' I whispered, 'I was just wondering if it might be a good idea to head back to the hotel and explore that Bond theme we were talking about. After all,' I flashed him as seductive a look as I could hope to pull off, 'you already have the uniform with you.'

His eyes danced.

'Know this, Buchanan: when you *say* things like that, and then *look* at me like that—'

'Like what?' *As if I didn't know.*

'Oh, I think you know – then you risk me hauling you over my shoulder and taking you straight back to your room. And I can assure you my stamina knows no bounds. You'll be begging for mercy in the end, guaranteed.' He looked pretty pleased with himself.

'Oh, I don't know,' I said in a seductive whisper, 'I seem to remember Zagreb being pretty relentless, and one thing you should know about me Alasdair Finn, is that I never, ever, beg. Particularly for mercy.'

'Oh really?'

'Really.'

'I bet you do.'

I did.

After an energetic and somewhat enlightening afternoon at the hotel, we stepped outside to explore more of the village. We found an art gallery and I had a conversation with a local artist about the effect of light on his work. Paul's comment that my photographs were 'good but hardly groundbreaking' had got me thinking about how I might want to progress in the future, into landscape photography perhaps.

One particular painting caught Alasdair's eye.

'Hey, come and look at this,' he shouted across the shop. 'Someone has painted the two of us here at Arisaig.'

Intrigued, I thanked the artist and crossed the

gallery to find Alasdair enthralled with a beautiful painting of Camusdarach beach, the isles of Rum and Eigg silhouetted in the far distance. In the middle distance – and barely discernible to the viewer – stood a man and a woman with their backs to the artist; they were walking away from the scene.

'You're right, it *is* just like us. I'm surprised there's no dog in the painting, artists usually throw a dog into a scene like that. Who's the artist?'

Alasdair peered at a card on the wall.

'Robert Kelsey.'

'He must have known we wouldn't have a dog.'

I analysed the painting further. 'He's got the light and the perspective just right . . . clever. Have you noticed how everything seems to be in sharper focus here, without actually being in focus at all, if you know what I mean?' I studied it further before announcing, 'I'm going to buy it.'

'What?'

'The painting, I'm going to buy it – for us. It's a print so it won't break the bank.'

A cloud descended over Alasdair's expression.

'I don't think you should.'

'Should what?'

'Buy it.'

'Why not?'

'I know it sounds daft,' he explained, 'but it looks to me as though this particular couple's story is nearly over, look'—he pointed to the painting—'they're walking out of the shot, signifying their journey together is nearly over, but our journey is just beginning. Maybe he's done another painting with the couple in the foreground, let's look for one.'

I placed my hands on Alasdair's shoulders and turned him towards me.

'You're over-thinking life. Everything will be fine, I promise.'

He nodded, smiled, took my hand and we left the gallery.

I didn't buy the painting.

We idled away the rest of the afternoon exploring the coast. Alasdair took a shine to my camera and we sauntered from harbour, to rock pool, to sand dune and back again. As a result it was late afternoon before we headed back to the hotel. Alasdair closed the door to my room behind him.

'So then, I wonder what we can do to kill an hour before dinner?'

'Well, it's funny you should say that,' I said, putting my camera on the bedside table and placing my arms around his neck, 'because I've got an idea.' Alasdair's eyes danced. 'I was thinking of sexing up my *Singin' in the Rain* number, just for you . . .'

Alasdair *loved* my impromptu performance (it was probably the sexiest rendition ever performed – I had never wiggled my backside so much in my life!), and we were just getting busy on the bed when a loud beep reverberated around the room.

Alasdair sat up on the bed and took a bleeper out of his pocket.

'For crying out loud,' he said to himself, 'give a man a break!'

His eyes moved from the bleeper to me.

'I need to make a call. Sorry.'

'It's okay. I understand.'

He kissed me on the nose and left. He returned twenty minutes later and I could tell from his expression he had news I wouldn't want to hear.

'What is it? What's happened?'

He paused for a second, took my hand and led me from the bed to sit on the window seat. He knelt down next to me.

'I have to go.'

'When? Not now, surely?'

'First thing tomorrow.'

He sat back on his heels and ran his fingers tenderly through my hair; I tilted my head towards his fingers as he spoke.

'This is how my life is, Grace. Are you sure you want to be part of it?'

'Yes,' I said softly, 'I do.'

The sun was waning in the west, allowing a golden haze to be cast across the room. We lay on top of the bedcovers and held each other for quite some time while the light faded. We were shaken from our private thoughts by the sound of music.

'What the hell is that?' I asked, untangling myself from his arms. Alasdair rubbed his eyes.

'That would be Scots' night. Didn't you notice the poster?'

I went to the door; once opened the noise became deafening. I looked back at Alasdair.

'Brilliant, I bet they've got Scottish country dancing and everything.'

Alasdair walked to the door and slapped me on the backside.

'Come on, let's go downstairs. I'm starving.'

The hotel was heaving. It was an evening awash with fun, laughter and a considerable amount of booze. Before too long, Alasdair was tipsy and I had to slow down. I did not want to descend down the slippery slope to blotto again.

Four revellers from the adjacent table insisted we join them in the Dashing White Sergeant. Alasdair and I were completely useless, but no one seemed to mind as we blundered around the floor, turning left instead of right, going under when we should have gone over and generally getting the whole thing wrong.

A half hour of rib-rattling laughter passed by until the man in charge of the microphone suggested we charge our drinks and return to our seats to watch a display of Scottish dancing, after which the ceilidh band would be happy to take requests. The man finished by stating that, 'If there are any singers in the house, the band will happily oblige.'

'Now's your chance,' Alasdair said as we took our seats.

'Chance for what?'

His eyes sparkled. 'Chance to show how you've conquered your fear of singing in public. I bet they would love a bit of Grace magic here. What was it that journalist said again? *The voice of an angel, a tantalising cheeky smile*?' He leant in and kissed me seductively on my bottom lip. 'And after your performance upstairs, I have to agree with him. But I would have to add *with an outrageously sexy backside* to the description!'

'Why thank you, kind sir, but one performance per night is more than enough – I would hate to overexpose myself – except to you of course.' I held his gaze. He grabbed my hand.

'Right! That's it! Enough Scottish stuff, let's get back upstairs.'

For the very last time on our journey I put on Alasdair's fleece, wrapped his shemagh around my neck and we strolled hand in hand along the deserted village road. Instinctively, and without words, we found ourselves standing on our stretch of silver sand.

It was a perfectly still evening. The moon was bright and round, while the black of the night sky fought for space amongst a trillion stars. The gentle, melodic lapping of the receding tide was the only noise to be heard.

Alasdair took my face in his hands, kissed me tenderly and led me over to a dune. After depositing me with my back to a dune, he strolled around the beach looking for something.

'What are you doing Alasdair? Come and sit down.'

'Making a fire. I don't want you to be cold.'

'Oh, brilliant, I'll help then.'

I jumped to my feet and within ten minutes we had piled together an admirable amount of birch bark (it burns well, apparently), wood, twiggy sticks and dry grass. Alasdair spent a while building the fire to his exact specifications, reached into his jacket pocket and took out a box of matches. I dropped my head in exasperation.

'What now?'

'For the first time since I met you, I'm afraid I'm completely disappointed.'

He looked up, crestfallen.

'Why?'

'Because you've just dashed the image I have of you as a capable man.'

'Why?'

'Because you're using matches.'

He shook his head and laughed.

'Of course I'm using matches. What do you expect,' he flourished his hand, 'I'd use a wand?'

'No. I thought you would rub some twigs together or something.' He glanced at me sarcastically but I shrugged and continued to explain. 'It's just there's something incredibly sexy about a bloke who can do that kind of thing. It must be a primeval instinct for a woman to go for a man who can look after himself, and I've always wanted to be able to start a fire from scratch in case I'm ever in a survival situation.'

'Why? Are you expecting to be in a survival situation sometime soon?'

'You just never know, Alasdair.'

He sighed and put his matches back in his pocket.

'Come on then, I'll teach you how to do it. But it takes bloody ages and it was raining yesterday so the tinder might not be dry enough.'

I beamed my brightest smile and knelt next to him on the sand.

'So,' he said, 'there are three basic components necessary to start a fire: heat, fuel and oxygen.' He searched about until he found what he was looking for, and returned with a flat rock.

'What we create first is the perfect environment to sustain a fire. In our case we're sheltered out of the wind by the dune, which is good, and by placing sticks on the rock and then placing the tinder on top, the air can circulate under the fire. But this isn't going to be easy because the tinder – in our case twigs and grass – should ideally be very dry.'

He glanced up at me sarcastically as if to say *I can't believe you've got me doing this*, so I smiled encouragingly, scrunched up my nose and said, 'Well, we'll give it a go anyway. Can you do lots of this type of thing by the way?'

'What type of thing?'

'You know, set traps to catch wild animals, hollow out a dead deer and use it as a shelter, gut a seal and use it as a wetsuit, that kind of thing.'

He looked up.

'Have you been watching Bear Grylls by any chance?'

I shrugged. 'Might have . . . Jake likes it.'

Alasdair spent the next fifteen minutes twirling sticks and blowing into a birds nest type creation he had placed on the rock. No spark appeared.

'You know what, you were right, this is a daft idea. Let's get the matches out, I'm bloody freezing.'

'Just another few minutes,' he said, 'it'll ignite in a second. I'm working on the "heat" bit, have faith.'

I was beginning to regret teasing him about primeval instinct. After all, Alasdair was not the sort of man to be defeated.

'I'll tell you what,' he said, 'take my head torch and nip into the dunes and see if you can find some grass that's bone dry. That might help.'

'Okay, Boss.'

I had just disappeared out of sight when I heard him shout, 'Grace! I've got it going.' I ran back down the dune onto the beach and found him putting little strips of birch bark onto ignited tinder, protecting the embryonic flames from the breeze with his body.

'That's amazing, Alasdair. I'm impressed.'

'Well, it's a gift. Some of us have it, some of us don't.'

We spent the next ten minutes fuelling the fire before finally sitting back. I watched Mum's letter shrivel into the flames – I didn't want to keep it. For the first time since we met, I didn't sit in front of Alasdair and allow myself to be wrapped into his arms, but sat behind him and wrapped my arms around him.

We sat for a while, lost in our own thoughts, until I whispered, 'If you are wondering why I'm unusually quiet, then it's because I'm trying to think of a super-genius way to kidnap you.' My chin rested softly on the top of his head as I spoke.

He laughed and I carried on. 'I don't want you to go away. Is there no one else who could go – instead of you I mean?'

Alasdair tilted his head backwards and sighed. 'No. Anyway, the lads depend on me, and there's no way I would ever let them down.'

He seemed to be talking to himself rather than to me.

'There must be times, though, when you just don't *want* to go away – especially if you think it's all nonsense – or really dangerous or something. Aren't you ever frightened at the prospect of what you're asked to do?'

'Well, I'm not so much *asked* to do something as *told* to do it. Don't try to over-imagine what I'm going to do, you'll just worry needlessly. The general public have an impression of our work that's not necessarily correct. Try not to think about it. I'll be back before you know it.'

'Okay, I'll try not to worry, but aren't you a little

bit frightened, putting your life on the line for Queen and country I mean?'

I felt his shoulders sag a little. The cogs of his mind spun around for a few seconds before he answered.

'I fight for the man standing to my left and the man standing to my right, not the Queen.'

Alasdair stood and skimmed a pebble across the ocean with determination. He turned to face me. 'As soon as I leave here I'll have to focus on the task and put all other thoughts out of my mind, which has been easy for me until now. But I'm sure this time the thought of you – of our time here – will linger in my mind. And, in answer to your question, there's apprehension I suppose, but I'm always too busy to be frightened, and the adrenalin keeps you going. It's an addiction.' He skimmed another stone. 'The difference about this job is I've got more to look forward to when I come back.'

I stood and we kissed; boy, did we kiss.

With any other man I had ever kissed, kissing had been fun – a sexy preamble to something even more physical – but this time it was different. It was a tender union of two souls, a complete surrender of one person to another.

We returned to the fire. He rested his head on my lap and smiled up at me.

'What's your favourite tree by the way?' he asked. 'I think I've figured out everything else about you, but this one has me foxed. Is it the wedding cake tree, like your mum?'

Oh my goodness, I thought, *I'm a woman, you will never figure me out.*

'My favourite tree?' I asked with semi-serious concentration, leaning back on the dune. 'Let me see, that would have to be the olive tree. What else could it be?'

He grinned. 'Would that have anything to do with a certain café, the café where we met perhaps?'

'Maybe. What about you? What's your favourite tree? Don't tell me,' I added, 'I bet I can guess. It's the oak tree.'

'Correct answer. How did you know?'

''Cause it's such a typical bloke-type tree. You're a stereotype I'm afraid. How very disappointing.'

'Actually, Little Miss Know-It-All, the oak tree is my favourite tree because of you.'

'Oh?'

'I watched you hide in one – well, you thought you were hiding – for several days after your mum died, that's how I knew you were a fidget.'

I bolted upright.

'What?'

'I was staying at the retreat. I carved you a shepherd's crook. It's waiting for you at St Christopher's.'

I stared at him, dumfounded.

'Oh my God!' I stammered. '*You're* my old man of the woods?'

It was Alasdair's turn to be shocked. He sat up.

'*Old man*? What do you mean, *old* man?'

'So *that's* why I've been having the feeling I've seen you some place before. What was that great

401

big beard all about Finn?' I touched his face tenderly. 'Thank you for coming to the ford every day,' I added. 'You took my mind off things. Why did you do it?'

Alasdair sighed.

'Because you looked lost.'

'But why a shepherd's crook, of all things?'

Alasdair smiled. 'Because I knew you were going to the Dales, to the farm. It's a link to your identity.'

I smiled. 'Oh, nice touch.'

He lay his head on my lap again. I ran a hand through the sand and looked up towards the stars.

'Alasdair, one final thing?'

'Hmm?'

'Did you really light the fire by rubbing sticks together?'

'Of course I did!'

'I don't think so, you bloody fibber.'

'Why?'

I held my hand up in the air.

'Because I just found the match.'

CHAPTER 34

The following morning the emotional torment was similar to waiting for Mum's funeral. Alasdair explained in the car that he would walk away in the terminal building and not look back. He had to focus. I was to think only of our future life together. I was to walk away confidently, and under no circumstance was I to watch him leave.

But, no matter how I tried to be cheery and put a positive light on things, I felt sick to the core. It would have been difficult enough to say goodbye from St Christopher's – our journey together had proven to be the happiest days of my life – but this was cruel.

As we walked into the terminal building my stomach turned and my eyes brimmed with tears.

Alasdair guided me over to a corner of the bustling departure hall to say goodbye. He put down his luggage, pulled my trolley out of my hands and turned me towards him. I gazed at the floor. He pulled me into his arms, rested his head on my hair and sighed; when it came to our final moments together, words were unnecessary. He

403

pulled away and I noticed his eyes were glistening too.

'Listen, I want you to have something.' He delved into his rucksack and pulled out his shemagh.

'Oh no, Alasdair. I can't.'

He tried to wrap it around my neck but I stepped back.

'Why not? It would mean a lot to me for you to take it.'

'I know it would, but I can't. It's your lucky piece of kit, it would be like giving away a rabbit's foot or a St Christopher. No, I can't. Sorry.'

He smiled and stuffed it back into his rucksack.

'I have to go. Take good care and I'll see you very soon.'

I nodded, finally looked up at him and smiled through salty tears. He touched my face.

'Bye then, Rainy Face.'

His familiar words were all it took to send me over the edge. I struggled to find some final – meaningful – words.

'God. I've only known you for a couple of weeks, if that. This is ridiculous.'

He laughed and pulled me into his arms one final time and I knew exactly what I wanted to say.

'Just remember that, wherever you go, whatever you do, all you have to do is look up at the moon and you'll know that I'm looking at it too, thinking of you.' I laughed through my tears. 'I'll try my hardest not to pine though.'

Far from making him smile, my words disarmed him. He stepped back suddenly and held me by the shoulders.

'Listen, if it turns out that I've done the wrong thing by you, if you become unhappy . . .' His words trailed off and he shook his head. 'I just want you to be happy, and this is so unfair on you.' He stepped in again and rested his head on mine. 'You're my world now. I'm sorry I can't give you more.'

My tears became uncontrollable sobs. He lowered his head to whisper two final words into my ear.

'Love you.'

He swallowed hard, stroked my cheek gently, turned on his heels and walked away. I willed him with all of my heart to turn and flash me a final smile. But as he passed through security my heart fell even further through my shoes. He wasn't going to wave after all. It was for the best perhaps; he was right, he did need to focus.

But then, just as he was about to step out of sight, despite saying he wouldn't turn around, despite having made me promise I wouldn't watch him leave, he looked back and smiled his cheeky smile for me, one final time.

PART VI

JOURNEY'S END

DEVON AND THE DALES

CHAPTER 35

Nestled between an eleventh century church at the top of the lane and an ancient ford at the bottom there stands a stone cottage; it is, of course, St Christopher's – my haven, my sanctuary, my home.

Only it wasn't my home, not any more.

The taxi dropped me on the familiar grassy verge just off the A39. Over the years I had found it easier to walk the final half mile to the cottage; St Christopher's is such a difficult place for a stranger to find. Of course, I understood why. It was the perfect location for a secret retreat. I deposited my heavy cases and suit carrier a hundred yards or so from the house to retrieve later, and continued down a track as familiar to me as my own reflection.

At the point where the ancient cart track narrowed to a lane, I stopped for a moment at a five bar gate and looked across a patchwork of fields. Mum and I had stood at that very spot a thousand times before. It was a view that never failed to warm me to the core on a day like that one, in the May sunshine. I looked up at the sky – Devonshire blue. Mum was right, the sky *was* a different shade of blue in all the places I had been, but then the whole country had taken on a brighter perspective. And then I remembered the date. It was Mum's fake birthday, her wedding anniversary, and I smiled at the thought of Alasdair and the first time we met at the Olive Tree Café, when he told me he would deliver me back to St Christopher's on the 31st of May. Although Alasdair and I had met only eleven days previously, I felt I had known him all of my life.

I felt my phone buzz in my pocket. It was a text message, from Paul.

How's it going? Not heard from you in a few days.

I texted back.

In Devon at Mum's old house. I don't inherit after all. Long story, but I'm fine with it in the end. Tons to tell re Mum's life. Took your advice and went for it with SB. I think he's the one. I'm so happy. Back in London in a few days. Will call then x

The phone buzzed almost immediately.

Told you the hare would win. You owe me a meal by the way (and I'm pleased for you) x

Good old Paul.

★ ★ ★

I carried on down the lane. A man I didn't recognise was working in the flower border. He nodded politely as I walked past, then turned and continued with his work. The front door was freshly painted, but other than that, the house looked exactly as it had a year before.

But it seemed to be a different home entirely now; somewhere other people belonged, and I realised Alasdair was right – it was Mum, not St Christopher's, who was my North Star.

Jake was pottering in the orchard. My heart warmed at the sight of him. Trusted, reliable Jake; my rock. He noticed me standing at the gate and smiled. A man known for economy with words, he walked over and greeted me with one of his bear hugs; it felt wonderful.

'I'm so sorry, Jake,' I whispered, still in his arms. 'You mean the world to me and I've been so selfish. I shouldn't have taken everything out on you.'

'Now then, none of that. Come on in and you can tell me all about your adventure.'

He led me to the kitchen. We discussed the trip and I confessed Alasdair had become a little more to me than a friend. Jake smiled but asked for no more detail.

After two cups of tea I told him the whole sorry saga surrounding Geoffrey.

'Meeting Geoffrey was the part of your mother's plan I never agreed with,' he admitted. 'Although, to be honest, I thought the whole thing was bonkers, and I'm still not sure it was the right thing to do.'

He glanced across at a picture of Mum on the windowsill, a picture of the two of them. His eyes misted over. 'But that was Rosamund for you, completely nuts.'

'Speaking of Mum,' I said, 'I should read her last letter.'

Alasdair had given me the letter, and two sets of ashes before we left Arisaig – that included the ash I had refused to scatter on the West Coast.

'Ah, now then, before you do, I've got something for you.'

Jake left the room and returned a couple of minutes later carrying an urn.

'Your mother wanted you to read her last letter under the wedding cake tree – and then we need to do something with this.' He wasn't able to look me in the eye suddenly. I took the urn, it felt full.

'What's this?' I asked, but the realisation began to dawn.

'It's your mother.'

'*What*?'

'Like I said—'

'I know what you said, Jake. Is this *part* of her or *all* of her?'

'All of her.'

'So what have I been scattering about all over the bloody country?'

'Fire ash. Actually it was the remnants of the elder that I . . . chopped . . . up . . .' He pursed his lips and tried not to laugh. 'To be fair to your mother, at first she really *did* want you to scatter

412

her ashes all over the place. But then she was worried her soul might end up lost in torment or something, so she changed her mind. But she knew she needed something tangible to blackmail you with.'

'Did Alasdair know?'

'You're joking! He would have done his nut. Maybe you can tell him, if he ever even needs to know . . .'

I put Mum down on the table. Despite my best attempts to be mad, I couldn't keep it up and we burst into laughter. I looked at the urn:

'Mum, if you're watching right now, shame on you.'

'Actually, I've got another surprise for you.' Jake stepped into the hallway and I heard him open the bureau. Then, he opened the door to the study and returned a few seconds later holding several postcards and a shepherd's crook.

'Alasdair phoned during your trip and asked me to save these for you. He carved the crook last year – when you were hiding in your tree. The postcards are in date order – this wasn't part of your mum's plan by the way.'

My heart leapt. The postcards! I had forgotten all about them.

Yorkshire (a picture of a sheep): *Had to think on my feet a bit just now. You're right, the solicitor would want proof. Hope you enjoyed our hike up Penhill. We are just setting off to*

413

meet your formidable aunt! I'm having a great time – hope you are too. Sorry about all the white lies. Al

Cairngorms 1 (a picture of a Highland Terrier wearing a red wig): *Decided to keep the postcard thing going – you seem to have forgotten. Our hike in the Cairngorms was fantastic, haven't had fun like that in years. Hope you enjoyed our adventure with the boys. I was worried all night you might be cold. Looking forward to another night in at the hut (maybe we'll give the clootie dumpling a miss though). Al*

Cairngorms 2 (picture of a Highland cow wearing another red wig): *I may be a little tipsy. You're dancing with 'Tristan' right now. I don't like that kid. You look amazing by the way and I could listen to your voice forever. Al x*

Zagreb (picture of St Mark's Church – with a Scottish postmark): *Not sure what is happening between us, but I know I never want to let you go. Al xx*

Arisaig (picture of 'our beach'): *Thank you for the time of my life. We'll come back here one day, just jump on the ferry and see where life takes us. Sorry I had to leave you on your own. Al xxx*

I wandered out to the garden alone carrying Alasdair's crook. Before taking a seat on Mum's bench opposite her tree, I took a stroll around the old place and realised, despite everything I had discovered over the past few days, despite my disappointment in Mum, I wouldn't have traded one second of my childhood for anything – certainly not for Geoffrey. I also realised that Mum's garden was a perfectly manicured memory of the life she lived before I was born, it was her way of holding on to the past. Tulips in pots, roses, wild garlic and the apple trees – all serving as a reminder of life in Yorkshire; then there were heathers, brooms and ornamental thistles from Scotland; and finally, of course, her wedding cake tree. I ran my fingers over the smooth curve of the handle of the crook and rested it against the bench. Her last letter was printed.

CHAPTER 36

St Christopher's

My Darling Grace.

So, you've finally made it home my love. How is the garden? Is Jake keeping it just so?

Hopefully you will have come to realise what your little journey has been about – I do hope you're not disappointed in me. There is absolutely nothing I can do to rectify the situation now of course, but I have a feeling that, in the end, you will have understood. I tried my hardest all your life to be a liberal mother. I haven't nagged or cajoled (not really) so it must seem odd to you that, in death, I decided to become an interfering so-and-so. Hopefully this is the one time I can be forgiven for it.

Once I knew the cancer was terminal, my thoughts turned to you and my head filled with worrying questions. Yes, you will always have Jake, but I wanted to give you more. And so I decided to introduce you to your family, to Annie – somewhat belatedly I know. And as for Geoffrey? If the two of you want to find out for certain if he's your father, then at least now you can.

Now then, about your voice. A couple of days before I was due to leave for the RAF, my nerves got the better of me and I decided not to go. Mum sat me down and urged me to follow my dreams. She said that, although she loved us all a great deal, she sometimes wished she had followed her own dream, to learn to sing professionally (Mum had a beautiful voice). It was odd; I had only ever seen her as my mother, rather than a person with her own aspirations. And there she was suddenly, a woman with her own dreams and regrets (to be honest I'm not sure I liked it). Maybe by encouraging you with music, I've been trying to complete her life through yours. It doesn't really matter now. All I ask is that you don't put yourself in a situation where you regret anything. Please don't turn around one day and say, 'That could have been me.'

I sometimes wonder if you found difficulty in performing because, although your technique was second to none, you hadn't explored any deep emotional avenues personally and couldn't become completely lost in the music. Not that I would wish heartbreak and trauma for you my love, but I'm afraid that, without just a little understanding of the extremes of emotion, you could never realise your true potential. Whenever I hear a young voice singing the story of a more mature woman, I fail to be convinced.

You seem to have run away from life a little, always happy to stay behind the camera. But if my plan has come together then you will have climbed a mountain, sung at a wedding and skydived. I know one cannot live on an adrenalin high permanently, but I wanted you to live life on the edge for a brief moment – feels good doesn't it?

Another reason for sending you on the trip was that I wanted you to see how environmental factors play a huge part in the decisions we make in life. Would I have had an affair on a rainy afternoon in Barnstaple? Possibly not. But in sunny, magical Zagreb, caught up in a thrilling little adventure of my own, I failed to resist temptation – no excuse – but a reason nonetheless.

Speaking of sunshine, I do hope the weather stayed fine for you. Did you notice the different blues of the sky? I hope so. And what did you think of Alasdair? Oh dear, were my intentions so transparent? If the two of you didn't get it together at some point, if you aren't canoodling right now under my tree, then you must drop this letter, go to find the man and kiss him – he's crazy about you.

He may or may not have told you this, but I saw him talking to you at our tulip festival last April. He looked a little different then. Anyway, I could tell by his expression – the look in those amazing eyes of his – that he was smitten, and Alasdair is never smitten. So, when I heard you singing to yourself upstairs, I sent him to the coop for some eggs (he had to walk under the open window) and I watched him stop under the window and listen. I knew I'd cracked it. The poor soul could not take his eyes off you after that, but failed miserably to ask you out. I was so annoyed

In the process of writing everything down for your benefit, I realise I have laid my own ghosts to rest. I told Alasdair to write a journal, but should have gone through the same process myself. Nothing seems so bad – so desperate – once it is written down. If only I had gone through this process several years ago, I'm sure I could have sorted things out sooner. The secrets I have kept deep inside about my family, my affair, Geoffrey, even St Christopher's, have eaten away at my soul for years. There is a patch of Japanese knotweed across the stream, I try to pretend it doesn't exist – how could it exist in my perfect garden? But, exist it does; and no matter how much I try and chop away at the stuff, it just keeps coming back, and the rhizomes have spread like suffocating tentacles beneath the surface. My cancer has felt like the knotweed, hidden deep within. It has slowly taken a hold, killing off everything in its wake, and now I'm afraid there is simply no strength in me left to fight.

Regarding Jake (my wonderful, darling Jake), he has been my white knight. Jake and I became intimately involved when he ceased to be my protection officer – he stayed on to help run the retreat. I warned him not to become too attached to us as a family. I explained that I had a wandering spirit – that we would almost certainly move on once I knew for certain we were safe. He said nothing, just walked out. I thought he was in a huff, but then I heard the noise of a drill. He was setting up a series of horizontal wires against the front of the house. He disappeared off in the car, only to reappear an hour later with a rose in a pot – a pretty crimson thing called American Pillar. I went to the front of the house and watched him plant the rose against the wall. He stepped back, turned to me and said, 'All I ask is that you stay long enough to train this rose to the second wire. If you still want to go when it gets there, then go.' I nodded, walked back into the house and now the rose is ten feet high and covers the wall – that was when my obsession with the garden began.

And so, if I had my time again, would I live my life differently? No, I would not. After all, if I hadn't gone trotting off to Zagreb, if I hadn't had my affair (which seems like only yesterday), if I hadn't run back to Geoffrey in Arisaig, then you my darling girl would never have been conceived; and it is you, and only you, who has made my life complete.

Well, I'm so very tired, but you should know that in writing these letters I have been able to concentrate on something productive rather than count down the days to my death. In making myself focus on the past, I have been able to cope through the darkest days of my life. Is it all pre-ordained do you think? Was it always going to end this way? Or has my cancer been sparked by event or emotion I have purposefully manufactured in my life? What I'm saying is, could it have been avoided? No matter.

It's time to go now love, but before I do, I have another story from the garden for you. Do you remember in the first letter I said I was worried about my rose Alan Titchmarsh? I was going to consign him to the compost heap, but then felt I couldn't just give up on him. So, I took some drastic action. I cut him off at the knees, threw some manure at him and gave him a good, long drink; and would you believe it, the trooper has started to bud again.

What I'm trying to say is this: when nothing seems to be going your way, when you feel you have lost your bloom and you can't possibly stand tall for one more day, take a tip from the garden – get yourself a good haircut (spare no expense), have a slap-up meal and pour yourself a very tall drink (and find something saucy to read!). And although you may not feel perky by the next day, or even by the next month, trust me, by the following spring, life will turn out fine again, and you will be ready to burst into bloom once more. I wonder if you found my trees? Planting a tree is a wonderful thing to do Grace; when you have your own home you must remember to make planting a tree your top priority.

A few days ago I was staring out into the garden – reminiscing about your childhood – when one particular memory of you dancing around the garden singing a song came flooding back, and I couldn't get the tune out of my mind. It's the school hymn. I persuaded you to sing it at the Harvest Festival in the church when you were ten, remember? I took a video of you secretly from the back of the church but you always refused to watch it. Here are the words, just in case you have forgotten them:

One more step along the world I go,
One more step along the world I go;
From the old things to the new
Keep me travelling along with you.

Round the corner of the world I turn,
More and more about the world I learn;
All the new things that I see
You'll be looking at along with me.

Give me courage when the world is rough,
Keep me loving though the world is tough;
Leap and sing in all I do
Keep me travelling along with you.

And it's from the old I travel to the new,
Keep me travelling along with you.

Be happy my darling. I love you, and I'm
very proud of you. I'm so very sorry I had
to go. Mum xxx

CHAPTER 37

Smiling through the tears I sat back on the bench and gazed at her tree – such a beautiful thing. I noticed it was sending out a fresh layer. Mum would have been pleased. Although I missed my mother's company – part of my soul would always feel incomplete with her gone – the feeling of being in mourning had finally passed. Through her death – her actions – I had discovered more happiness than I thought could possibly exist. During the past ten days I had begun to realise what it was to embrace life, whatever the consequences. The reason for that, of course, was Alasdair. Thanks to Mum and Alasdair, the world was a different and better place to me.

I turned to see Jake waiting on the lawn; he held the urn in his hands and I knew what the final piece of Mum's story would be. Shoulder to shoulder, we said goodbye to my mother, under my tree – the family tree – in the garden that she loved.

I stayed on at St Christopher's for a few days and started on Mum's possessions. That was not an onerous task. Poor Mum had whittled down her wardrobe to practically nothing and had been equally ruthless with her administration.

Remembering her letter from the Cairngorms, I clambered into the loft to look for the painting Geoffrey had done of the woodman's hut; it was wrapped in a multi-coloured crocheted blanket. I washed the blanket, which was rather pretty, and decided to take it and the painting back to London.

A couple of surprises were yet to be uncovered. The solicitor – Mr Grimes – was a retired Royal Marine who had taken to the bar several years before and knew Mum from the retreat. During Jake's confession I told him that several of Grimes' toes were missing. Jake laughed and explained that the missing digits had been 'lost' to frostbite during a military training exercise in Norway. I began to appreciate that Mum's friends would, quite literally, do anything for her; but Jake confessed that they also suspected she was – ever so slightly – nuts.

On my fourth day at St Christopher's I was sitting on the window seat in the kitchen when Jake appeared, humming cheerily to himself. He threw a parcel on my knee and started to make a cup of tea.

He raised his eyes with a smile, looked towards the unopened parcel and said, 'I'd put money on that envelope being from Alasdair by the way.' My hands tore at the parcel like a five-year-old opening her first Christmas present. In it was Alasdair's shemagh – the devil had sent it after all – and a note. I held the shemagh to my face while I read.

Grace,

Can't bear the thought of you being cold so I thought you might change your mind about accepting this. Besides, the lads will only rib me if I wear it as it reeks of perfume.
Love you
Al xxx

I left my seat at the window and joined Jake at the table. The phone rang.

'Sorry love, just a sec . . .' He removed the phone from the pod on the worktop, smiled at me again and took the call. I read the note once more while listening absently to Jake's phone call.

'St Christopher's. Oh, Hello Bill, not spoken to you for ages – news, what news? Alasdair Finn yes . . .' Jake glanced in my direction before turning away to continue with the call. The person at the other end of the line spoke for some considerable time until, '—a terrible thing to happen Bill, it always is. Keep me informed – when the family have decided – yes of course—thank you Bill.' Jake's voice began to break. 'Bye Bill.'

He took several seconds before turning to face me but it felt like several lifetimes. My body – the room even – seemed to physically shrink. I didn't want him to turn around, I wanted to freeze life at that very moment; but, like Jake, the world would insist on turning.

I pushed the chair back and rose to my feet.

'What's happened?'

Jake gazed out of the window, momentarily caught in his own world, before turning and noticing the tears in my eyes. He rushed towards me.

'You don't think—Alasdair's fine, Grace.'

'But, the phone call, you said . . .'

He took a seat at the table.

'One of his team was killed. You can imagine how badly Alasdair has taken it.'

I put my hands to my face.

My immediate emotion was relief – relief someone else was dead – not Alasdair. Then I felt guilty to have even felt such a selfish emotion. Death through war was something that happened to other people, other families. I had read about troop losses and was saddened by them, but there had never been a direct personal link – even a tenuous one.

'Was he married? Kids?'

'He was married but I don't think he had children. According to Bill he was the junior man, only twenty-eight. He's never been here, I didn't know him.'

'His family must be going through hell.'

'Quite.'

'No wonder Alasdair has taken it badly,' I said, wishing more than anything I could throw my arms around him. Jake glanced out of the window again and sighed.

'He'll feel responsible of course. To Alasdair, losing this young man under his command will be like losing a son. The dead man won't be the only victim in this, they never are.'

When Alasdair and his colleagues returned to their unit several days later, Jake spoke to one of the team – Alasdair was unavailable – and the full horror of the situation came to light.

Alasdair had led a small group of special forces men on a mission to Afghanistan to rescue an aid worker who had been captured by the Taliban. They had been taken by helicopter to a compound where the man was being detained.

What should have been a relatively straightforward operation became catastrophically complicated. The intelligence available before their departure had been misleading: the rebels were organised, heavily armed and prepared for a rescue attempt. The helicopter had been bombarded with small arms fire from the moment it arrived at the compound and, once on the ground, the men had faced a bloody battle in an attempt to fight their way through the compound, during which a number of rebel lives were lost. The aid worker was found alive and, objective complete, the team retreated to the helicopter. During the final moments, however, as Alasdair had pushed his men forward to the helicopter and provided them with covering fire, the area of ground between Alasdair's colleague's position and the helicopter had become overrun with rebels. Small arms fire had pierced through the helicopter and injured two of the soldiers significantly. Grenades were launched rapidly and randomly – it was a hotbed of chaos and confusion – and it was no small miracle that the helicopter hadn't been lost. The pilot, for whom the strain of coming under constant fire throughout the operation must have been horrific, waited for Alasdair to clamber on the aircraft.

While Alasdair provided covering fire from the tail ramp, his colleague made a dash for the aircraft. It was in these final moments that Alasdair had failed to notice a lone gunman on the roof of the compound, and his junior man had been shot as he clambered on board. Despite their attempts to administer battlefield first aid en route to the camp hospital, the man had died within the hour.

I stayed on at St Christopher's hoping for some word from Alasdair – a phone call perhaps – but nothing came. I tried to draw Jake into discussing where he might be, but Jake refused to discuss the operation or provide any details regarding Alasdair's possible whereabouts. He seemed irritated simply at the mention of Alasdair's name.

A week went by, but still no word. It was hell. I had fallen hopelessly in love with a man I had no way of contacting. He had provided no address, all I knew was he had a house in Snowdonia. The number he had given me went straight to answerphone message.

He was an enigma.

And then a letter appeared via a guest at the retreat. I was in the kitchen packing away the last of Mum's possessions when Jake handed it to me with a sigh.

'It's from Alasdair,' he said quietly.

Jake put a hand on my shoulder then walked away.

Grace

You will have heard by now that the operation did not go according to plan – I shall say no more. The reason for writing is to tell you I was wrong to say I am in a position to enter into a relationship. I was in a dream. I have nothing to offer and should never have given false hope.

I cannot and will not ask you to put your life on hold just so I can see you once in a while. Turning away from you that night in Zagreb was the right thing to do, returning to your room moments later, however, was not.

I'm sorry to have told you this in a letter. It goes against everything I stand for to send it. But if I see your face or hear your voice I will want to hold on to you forever, and if I do, I will ruin your life. I'm not the man you think I am. During our time together you saw my civilian face and I'm certain you would not like the military one. I will always cherish our time together – when I told you I loved you I meant it. You are an amazing woman who deserves a full and happy life, which is something I would fail miserably to provide.

Take the very best of care, but most of all, be happy.

Alasdair.

Stunned – devastated – I threw the letter on the table in a fit of anger and ran upstairs to pack. Only I didn't pack; I sat on the bed and wondered how something so wonderful could have gone so horribly wrong, and so quickly.

Jake walked into my bedroom, sat next to me on the bed and took me in his arms, just like he used to. I nuzzled into his chest for a moment; but I wasn't a teenager any more, I was a woman – albeit a woman with a broken heart.

'Did you read the letter?' I asked.

'Yes.'

'Why is he doing this? It makes no sense. In Scotland he said we would be okay, that we'd make it work. He said he loved me.'

Jake stood, walked over to the window and stared out into the garden. It took several moments before he turned and spoke. 'I never agreed with your mother's plan to send you round the country with Alasdair. To me it was like sending a lamb to slaughter.'

'And who was the lamb in this scenario?'

'You both were. Alasdair because he was a man close to exhaustion, who already found you attractive, and who was bound to relax during your time away and start to think of another life perhaps – am I right?'

I nodded.

'And you were also vulnerable because you were grief-stricken for your mother and bound to enjoy the company of an attractive man who took the weight off your shoulders for a while. But I never thought the two of you would work out in the long-term.'

'Why?'

'Because of his job, because of who he is deep down. Men like Alasdair lead a peculiar life. You may think you'd be happy with it now, but two or three years down the line you might not be. I'll admit that many of them have normal family lives, but I know Alasdair well enough by now to know his marriage failed because he was fairly selfish.'

His harsh words surprised me.

'Don't get me wrong, I think the world of him. But he's an active man, with a whole load of adventurous hobbies. Once the excitement in your relationship calmed down, he'd go back to his parachuting or whatever else he does and you would hardly ever see him. Unlike your mother, I want more for you.'

'But maybe Mum was right, maybe I *could* fit into his lifestyle. I love him, you can't just turn that kind of feeling off. Please, please pass a message on to him, ask him to come and talk to me. Sending a letter was cruel, it wasn't like him. He must be in a mess.'

'How do you know it wasn't like him, you barely know him—'

'I *do* know him. Please, Jake, I just want to look him in the eyes, and then I'll let it go – he told me I was his world.'

Jake glanced around the room and sighed.

'You probably are his world, but it's a parallel one. Listen, there's something else, I wasn't going to tell you this . . . Alasdair arrived back in the UK a couple of days ago. I've spoken to him. I asked him to come to the retreat like he used to. He won't.'

'Why?'

'Because you're here. He can't take the emotion of seeing you, of being happy with you. It's the guilt. I've been talking to the man who brought the letter – he's staying for a few days. He was part of Alasdair's team. Apparently Alasdair shut himself down after his man died, won't talk to anyone, just concentrates on work and training . . . there's nothing you can do to make Alasdair a different man.'

'I know he must have seen some harrowing things, but so have thousands of soldiers. I'm sure they don't all bugger up their private lives because of guilt. Why should Alasdair be different?'

Jake's tone changed; he became more determined. 'Listen Grace, you need to move on. As I said before, you don't know him really, and your mother should never have led you into a relationship with a man who leads that kind of life. Alasdair may have come across to you as a certain kind of a man, a man you can depend on – lean on – but I would much rather your mother had sent you off on the journey alone.'

'I should leave then . . .'

I glanced across the room to see Alasdair's shepherd's crook leaning against the dresser.

'Do you think we ever really know a person, I mean *really* know them? I thought I knew Mum, but I didn't know anything about her as a woman, and then I thought I'd got to know Alasdair . . . and look where that got me.'

Jake took a deep breath and thought about his answer.

'I think we all create a persona as we progress through life. We create our own characters and they are influenced by loads of external factors: the job that we do, our position in the family perhaps and, to a certain extent, we stereotype ourselves . . . play out a role. We're all flawed, Grace. We all harbour dark thoughts from time to time. I've always thought that it's during the hard times that you really discover the truth behind someone's character. But a character can't be constant. Life won't allow it. Perhaps the people we know best are our own children, but even then I'm not so sure.'

'Do you regret not having a child of your own, Jake?'

He smiled tenderly.

'As far as I'm concerned, I did.'

I hugged him close, and glanced over his shoulder at the crook again. I knew in that instant where I wanted to go.

'So, are you headed back to London?' Jake asked the following day after carrying my bags down the stairs into the kitchen.

'No.'

'Where then?'

'Long-term I just don't know. But in the short-term, believe it or not, I've decided to go somewhere completely different, for a little while at least.'

'Where?'

'I'm going to go back to the Dales – to Mum's farm – to Annie. She said I could visit whenever I like and I think she meant it.'

Jake smiled.

'Sounds like a plan.'

CHAPTER 38

By the end of June my life had altered in a way that I would never have thought possible. My furniture was in storage, the flat in Twickenham sublet, contacts in the media were informed of my departure and I had said a fond farewell to my London pals with promises I would keep in touch. There was just one – extra special – friend I needed to see; I owed him a meal at the new Thai place after all. He was on good form.

'So,' Paul scooped noodles onto chopsticks as he spoke, 'you buggered off on holiday for a couple of weeks and came back determined to change your life, what a cliché. I'm not upset that you're leaving by the way, I'll give you two weeks before you hot-foot it back to London'—he pointed a chopstick at me to prove his point—'there's a limit to how much cow shit a civilised person can take, Grace.' Trust Paul to bring a dash of realism to a plan. 'And Soldier Boy?' he added. 'Has he been in touch?'

'Alasdair, his name is Alasdair, and he's a marine,' I interjected crossly. 'And no, he hasn't been in touch.'

'You found his flaw in the end then, he is an arsehole after all. And you must admit, it sounds like he was a bit of a smooth bastard.'

I glanced up and smiled, remembering.

'He wasn't smooth, and he isn't an arsehole. He's trying to protect me.'

'By leaving you?'

'Yes.'

'How does leaving you protect you?'

I pushed my tepid meal around the plate with my fork while I thought of a response. There was no way I could tell Paul, a keen-nosed journalist, the truth about Alasdair's job, or St Christopher's come to that.

'It's complicated.'

Paul put down his chopsticks.

'I know there are things you aren't telling me about him and, believe it or not, I'm not going to push, which must be a first for me. Anyway,' he added brightly, 'let's forget about him for a second and move on to something more important. Are you absolutely positive about this move up north? I know you said your mum had opened your eyes to what you really wanted out of life, but I'm worried you're just going to bounce around from place to place in the hope of finding something that doesn't exist.'

I glanced out of the window and watched a police car whizz past.

'Alasdair may have been an enigma,' I said finally, 'but he opened my eyes to living a different kind of life. Mum said in one of her letters that I was watching life rather than living it. I don't want to do that any more.'

'And you think you'll find what you're looking for in the Yorkshire Dales? Come on, it's hardly a metropolis.'

'That's exactly the point though,' I said, leaning forward in my seat, more animated now. 'I never really wanted to live a cosmopolitan life Paul, it's not who I am.'

'But if you go into landscape photography, like you said, then you'll still be watching life. Not that there's anything wrong with watching life. I watch life then write about it all the time, it works for me.'

'I agree with you,' I answered, softer now, 'but it's *what* you watch that matters, surely.' I thought of something suddenly. 'Do you know who the main influence was behind my decision to move away from my present work?'

'No idea,' he said, losing interest a little.

'Guess.'

He shrugged and scratched his head. 'Your mum? Arsehole?'

I shook my head. 'It was you.'

'*Me!* Why me? Don't lay this at my door, Grace!'

I laughed. 'When I phoned you from Scotland, you said my photos were good, but not ground-breaking. And I thought to myself, why the hell shouldn't I, Grace Buchanan, do something groundbreaking for once?'

He sighed and smiled. 'Fair enough, I'll back off. Anyway, back to lover boy. I've got one final question . . .'

'Go on.'

'How the hell did Mr Perfect get your knickers off in under two weeks, when I've spent years trying to achieve the same result and nothing, not even close.'

Despite Paul's humour, I felt unexpected tears prick my eyes at the thought of why I'd fallen for Alasdair – I knew the answer of course: 'Because it was magical, every single minute of it. And he didn't *try* to get me to fall for him Paul, it just happened. Everything fell into place. I've never lived life that way before, it was wonderful.'

Paul took my hand across the table as a tear spilled down my cheek.

'But was it *real*? It sounded unsustainable to me.'

I rested my head on the back of the chair and sighed.

'I honestly thought it was real. I'd take him back you know.'

'Even though he dumped you?'

'Thanks for that, Paul. But yes, even though he dumped me. No one will ever compare.'

He released my hand.

'So answer me this. If *I* had taken you up a mountain,' he glanced at me naughtily, 'and that's not a euphemism by the way, and then I'd strapped you onto me for the ride of your life,' he raised his eyebrows again, 'ditto'—I laughed out loud—'then would you have fallen for me in the same way?' He sat back and waited for my answer.

'Possibly,' I said stoically. 'Who knows? Like Mum said, it's all about time and place.'

'And a washboard stomach,' he murmured cheekily.

'*What?*' I tried not to laugh while drying my tears on the restaurant napkin.

'Come on, you said yourself he was an Adonis. You can bang on all you want about external factors influencing your decision to get off with him, blah blah blah, but if he'd looked like his face had just gone through a mangle, or if he hadn't had airbrushed pecks, you wouldn't have jumped into bed with him. When it comes down to it, you're just a bloody tart.'

He grinned at me warm-heartedly. I wiped away the last of my tears and smiled a wicked smile. 'You're so right, Paul.'

The sun had just begun to set behind the Dale as my car tyres scrunched over the gravel at Bridge Farm. Annie, Ted and the dogs welcomed me warmly as I stepped out of the car. Annie's tender embrace belied the basic fact that we had met only once before.

'Hope you brought your wellies,' was all she said as she ushered me into the kitchen. Meg returned to the comfort of her sofa – Alasdair's sofa – and I tried my best to concentrate on the conversation rather than drift into a world that included Alasdair. A full roast chicken and all the trimmings were waiting in the bottom oven of the AGA to be presented at a suitable juncture.

The consumption of food, or rather Annie's obsession with my daily calorie intake, became a constant battle between us and, after several weeks of pushing food around my plate in an attempt to fool Annie into believing I was eating more than the resident mouse, I was forced to concede.

The summer ticked by slowly. Jake posted Mum's aprons up to me, and I realised that growing up at St Christopher's stood me in good stead for my summer on the farm. The upkeep of the vegetable patch, the henhouse and the general welfare of the dogs became my responsibilities, but I steered clear of any four-legged object that sported horns.

It was a Sunday morning in late August when Annie sat me down at the bench under Mum's apple tree and said we needed to talk.

'I'm not going to make a big fuss about this,' she said, fidgeting uncomfortably on the bench, 'but Ted has asked me to move in with him. I'll only be down the lane.' She seemed uncharacteristically embarrassed; only Annie could have declared her intentions in such a blunt manner. I smiled but remained silent.

'His wife died ten years ago, so it seems to have been an appropriate amount of time to wait.' I thought she was joking – she wasn't.

'The thing is my love, by rights, half of this farm

belonged to your mother, which means half of it belongs to you now.'

'Well, not really,' I contested, 'Mum seemed happy to hand it over to you, so don't worry about me. It's time for me to move on anyway.' I was lying of course; the thought of moving away from that safe haven broke my heart.

'I'm not asking you to move on, Grace. What I'm saying is that you can stay here, indefinitely. One day it will all be yours anyway.'

I stood up suddenly and took a few steps away from Annie, then whirled around to face her.

'*What?* You've got to be kidding? Why don't you sell it?' She looked at Mum's apple tree, glanced around the Dale and then gestured for me to sit down again. When I slumped back on the bench beside her she reached over and took my hand.

'I don't need any money. It's what I want to do, it's the *right* thing to do.' She paused for a moment. 'Why do you think Frances sent you up here, Grace? What was her purpose?'

I shrugged. 'To meet you? To see where she grew up perhaps?'

Annie smiled. 'Perhaps. But most importantly, she sent you here as a way of passing a message on to me.'

I shrugged again.

'Listen love, Frances handed the farm over to me forty years ago, and now she wants me to hand it over to you. *I've* had my life here and now it's her turn . . . through you. That's her real message

in all of this, and she was right to send you . . .'
Annie jostled and rolled her eyes. 'It would have
been better if she'd done all this twenty years ago
of course, but we won't hold that against her.' I
smiled – typical Annie! 'To be honest love, you'd
be doing me a favour; the farm's just too much
for me now.' She let go of my hand and crossed
her arms defiantly. 'I've never been one for big
chats or arguments and I'm not going to start now.
I'm not going to hand it over straight away . . .'
she winked. 'I might not get on with that old
bugger up the lane and then I'll be back. Look,
accept it, make a go of it, live your life here. But
above all, be *happy* love.'

I thought of the sheep farming book Mum had
bequeathed to Alasdair . . . *it may come in handy.*
Had this been her plan all along?

'But I don't know the first thing about sheep
farming,' I said in a panic. 'And I'm frightened of
rams.'

She laughed out loud.

'Looks like you're going to have to learn then
lass, and quick.' I became aware that my mouth
was gaping open. I closed it. She laughed again.

'Don't worry. Ted's son will stay on and help
with the few sheep we have and you can continue
to rent out most of the land. It'll all work out, just
wait and see.' She stood up as if to go. 'He's a
nice lad; about your age . . . single too.'

She winked at me again and was just about to
retreat to the kitchen when I leapt forward and

443

threw my arms around her; luckily we both had aprons on that time to dry our eyes.

By September I had enrolled on an advanced landscape photography course at Darlington College; it was quite a drive but worth it. Then Annie volunteered my services to help with music lessons at the local primary school, and by October I was teaching music theory and piano in three separate schools. I was asked to provide singing lessons for the local amateur operatic society. I said I would. My return to music came about due to the presence of a dusty piano that sat – unloved and out of tune – in Annie's front room; it was neither unloved nor out of tune for long.

Jake phoned me in September to say he had seen Alasdair. Their paths had crossed in Scotland, at the Commando War Memorial in Lochaber, at a memorial held by the family of the man under Alasdair's command who had died. My heart ached for all of them; the dead man, his family and for Alasdair of course. Listening to Jake on the phone, I remembered Alasdair's words – that he fought for the man to his left and the man to his right – and I could only guess how Alasdair must have suffered standing with the family at the memorial.

Then Jake went on to tell me something that shook me to the core; that Alasdair had been offered a promotion and had not only refused it but had also resigned his commission. An

444

ex-colleague who was setting up a security company in the Middle East needed a partner. Alasdair had agreed to go with him once he had worked his notice with the marines. His superiors had been shocked at his decision and realised he needed help, but he refused counselling and – unusually – rather than take some time out at St Christopher's, he retreated into himself. Jake described him as a 'closed book'. Part of me wanted to rush to the Middle East and scour every city until I found him, but that would, of course, prove fruitless.

I thought of Alasdair's words on the night our friendship had turned intimate in Zagreb, 'If our remaining days together were all I could give,' he had said, 'would you take them?' Not believing at the time that he could really mean it – or, so desperate to spend the night with him I had not cared about the full implication of what he had said – my smile had confirmed that I would. Months later, I asked myself the same question. Would I have given myself to him so fully if I had known the outcome would be heartbreak? It was an easy question to answer; yes, I would, in a heartbeat.

Although I was angry with Alasdair for throwing away our future, I didn't despise him; he was clearly in a great deal of pain. Jake sent me a book about the possible effects of combat stress. I realised that Alasdair's sudden change in behaviour and his wish to punish himself for the loss of his man was not about me – or his love for me – but it concerned another issue entirely. I wished I could help him somehow, but the man had disappeared, and when a man like Alasdair disappeared there was simply no way of finding him.

Through her letters Mum had taught me to grasp every precious moment in life. She was also proof-perfect that yearning for something unattainable was a waste of time . . . precious time. Unfortunately, the heart cannot switch off so easily, and I couldn't help but grieve for the time Alasdair and I *hadn't* spent together, and regularly fantasised about what might have been in a way real life couldn't possibly have lived up to. Primarily though, I realised that one person – and only one person – carried the burden of responsibility for my future happiness . . . me. I would cherish my memories, but not be ruled by them. It was time to create more memories and to live life to the full: it was time to move on.

CHAPTER 39

November merged seamlessly into December, and we began preparations for Christmas at Bridge Farm. We were having goose (one of Ted's of course) and I realised a traditional Dales' Christmas would be something of an event.

Annie decided to wait until the New Year before moving in with Ted.

'New year, new growth, new start,' she said, but I knew the real reason she stayed on was to prevent me from being on my own at Christmas and to help me through my first winter on the farm. She needn't have worried about Christmas. Jake intended to join us for a couple of days, and Paul was also venturing up for our New Year's Eve party. He asked if he could bring his new girlfriend along. She was called Anna, and was a pole dancer originally from Kiev. Although I was fairly certain that this would prove to be another one of his jokes, and that Anna would turn out to be a copy editor from the Home Counties – when it came to Paul, one could never be certain, so I stocked up with vodka, just in case.

It was a bright but bitterly cold day in mid-December when Ted and I dedicated the whole of the morning to decorating the house. We were particularly proud of our seven-foot tree which stood resplendent by the window in the living room. Our choice of location for the tree had been contrary to Annie's wishes. She said the hall had proven to be more than good enough in previous years, and had been chosen as the correct position for the tree (by generations of our family) because it was the only place in the house that maintained a constant cool temperature (in other words, freezing). She said she would be sweeping up errant pine needles well into May if we insisted on having it in the living room. I reminded her that it would be *my* job to sweep up the needles, not hers. So, after a shake of the head (a pleading look from Ted) and a final harrumph, she eventually acquiesced.

In the afternoon, Ted drove Annie to Leyburn for a new roasting tin, which came as a shock to both of us as she adored the ancient battered one that had belonged to my grandmother, and I promised to finish the chores.

I had just sat down with a cup of coffee and a celebrity magazine (old habits die hard), when I was startled by a loud knock at the front door. Irritated, I left the comfort of cuddling Meg on the kitchen sofa, walked down the cold hallway and opened the door.

No one was there.

A parcel, wrapped up in tartan paper with a red

satin ribbon tied around it, was propped against the doorframe. I picked it up. It was a flat object, roughly a foot square in size. Bemused, I stepped into the yard but it was deserted. I closed the door to block out the cold and carried the parcel through to the lounge where I intended to set it under the Christmas tree. I assumed it was for Annie, from one of her neighbours. A gift tag was attached and I couldn't resist peeking to see who it was from.

Grace

An early Christmas present for you, I hope you like it. Robert painted it to your specifications as requested. I'll wait by the river until dark. I hope you come, but I will understand if you don't.
Alasdair
x

I nearly dropped the parcel in surprise, but then my fingers tore at the wrapping paper. It was an original oil painting and my eyes brimmed with tears when I saw the subject. It was similar to the painting Alasdair had wanted to buy in Arisaig, only this time the man and woman were in the foreground – their journey was just beginning. Alasdair must have contacted Robert Kelsey and commissioned him. I couldn't help but smile; it was such a wonderful thing to have done.

449

Meg jumped up at me repeatedly and whimpered; she seemed to know Alasdair was close by. I put the painting down on the coffee table, sat on the sofa, patted her head and glanced towards the window. I had imagined falling into Alasdair's arms a thousand times but, although I felt nauseous with excitement at the thought of seeing him, and was still very much in love, I remembered Jake's words of warning. And, as painful as it would be to watch him walk away, I wondered if the best course of action would be to let Alasdair go. Meg had scampered out of the room and was scratching at the kitchen door – there could be no doubting what *she* wanted me to do.

I grabbed the three essential outdoor items I always left on the kitchen coat hooks: my winter coat, Alasdair's shemagh and my shepherd's crook, and stepped out of the house.

The sky was a wonderful washed-out winter blue, but the sun lacked the strength to take away the chill. I stuffed my hands deep inside my pockets and headed down the field. Meg shot on ahead to the river. I had never felt so nervous in my life, not even when singing. A mixture of emotions – anger mixed with longing – fought a vicious battle. Neither emotion won.

And then I saw him.

He was by the river crouching down, making a fuss of Meg. We were only twenty yards from each other but the void felt like a thousand miles. I stopped. He looked up, tipped his head to one side and scratched his ear. My soul leapt at the sight of him, but emotional self-preservation took over. I held my position.

As he stood and walked up the field towards me, I considered my options: I could be cross, scream at him and demand an explanation, or I could simply accept, and remember that the man had been to hell and back. As he came closer, my heart ached at the sight of him. He'd lost weight, so that even under his winter jacket he seemed skeletal. The hollows beneath his eyes were dark. But what tortured me the most was, although his eyes shone with tears, the sparkle had gone.

Words were unnecessary. I held out my arms and, as I pulled him close, he emitted a sob of pure relief. He held me with such longing it seemed he couldn't get close enough.

'I'm sorry,' he whispered through my hair.

I pulled back slightly and touched his face.

'What's happened to you?'

He shook his head, speechless.

All my pent-up emotion – the grief, the longing – came to the fore and I started to cry. 'You broke my heart, Alasdair.'

He nuzzled me into his chest and spoke into my hair.

'I know, I'm sorry. I thought I was protecting you.'

I looked up. 'I thought you'd moved to the Middle East?'

His eyes also brimmed with tears. He tried to fold me into his arms again but I stepped back.

'I *was* going to go away,' he said, 'I had my tickets booked and a job ready to go. But the bloody North Star kept following me around, reminding me of you.' He rubbed fingers across his forehead nervously. 'I've been in a bit of a mess to be honest, but thinking of you, remembering all the priceless things you said and did while we were away, it's kept me going. Do you remember the night we sat on the beach by Loch A'an?'

I smiled. 'Of course I remember.'

'You said that St Christopher's was your constant bearing in life, that you'd feel like a broken compass without it.'

I nodded again and ran the back of my hand across my runny nose. Alasdair handed me a tissue from his pocket, and then continued. 'A month ago, in an attempt to pull myself together, I went home to my cottage in Wales and took off into the mountains. The weather came in. I looked down at my compass and tried to decide which path to take through the mist. The needle was pointing north . . . I know a compass needle always points to north, but it made me realise that, even if I tried to leave you alone – for your sake – and ran away to the Middle East, my heart – my inner compass – would always turn to north, to you. *You're* my constant bearing, Grace.' He laughed. 'And I've been practising that speech for a whole month while that bloody painting was being done, so it had better have worked.'

I burst out laughing – and crying again – then became indignant.

'So you've known for a whole month that you'd pitch up today? If you were so desperate to see me, why did you wait?'

'Well, walking back to my cottage, I thought, sod it! I can't live without her, I'm going to go to Yorkshire and tell her how I feel'—he touched my face—'every single day without you has been torture.'

His words softened my armour. 'How did you know where I was?'

'I persuaded Jake to tell me, he didn't want to though. Anyway, I threw some stuff in a bag and jumped in the car. But then I felt so nervous. I sat there – in the car outside my cottage – for about an hour deciding what to do for the best. After talking it through with myself I decided that, if I just pitched up and knocked on the door, you would probably throw something heavy at me and tell me to sod off.' He smiled and scrunched his nose. 'So I realised I probably needed a softener.'

'So the painting is a—a "softener"?' I asked, annoyed. Alasdair feigned his trademark sheepish grin.

'Basically, yes. I was going to buy you an olive tree, but I couldn't be sure it would survive in the Dales, so I went with the painting instead. But apparently an artist can't just knock up a painting overnight, so I had to wait. I badgered Robert to death to get it done. He's a busy man you know, I hadn't realised he was quite so . . . prominent.' He took my hand. 'Joking aside, it seemed to be a perfect way to tell you how I feel, without actually telling you, if you know what I mean.'

Still holding his hand, I stepped a little closer.

'I have to admit, it's a wonderful gesture. The painting is beautiful, thank you.'

'I'm glad you like it. Did you notice the couple are in the foreground?'

I smiled. 'Yes, I noticed.'

I gazed around the Dale. There was something I wanted to say, but I didn't quite know how to say it.

'Did you keep away because you blamed me for what happened to your colleague? Did you think I'd distracted you?'

Alasdair sighed.

'I blamed myself, not you.'

I took the shemagh from around my neck and wrapped it gently around his.

'Come on,' I said, rallying, 'there's plenty of time to talk this through. What you need is a good meal, a shave and a stiff drink. In fact,' I added with a wink, 'there's an apple pie in the oven. Believe it or not, *I* made it, with the apples from Mum's tree. So you'd better get a wiggle on or there'll be none left!'

He took my arm as I turned to run up the hill.

'I know it's a lot to ask, but seriously, I need to know – can we start again?'

I touched his face and smiled. 'It's a lot to take in, Alasdair. I'm not sure how I really feel about it all. Let's take it one step at a time . . . okay?'

'Okay.'

Not having received the answer he had hoped for, his head dropped, dejected. Despite everything he had put me through, my heart broke at the thought of hurting him, so I rolled my eyes and added, 'I *had* decided to set the dogs on you, if you ever had the cheek to show up that is. But the dogs aren't vicious enough to see you off, especially Meg, so the plan was flawed from the off.' I leant into him. 'Perhaps you should kiss me,' I whispered, 'just so I can see if the magic is still there, and then I'll make my mind up if you can stay tonight.'

He smiled his first irresistible sexy smile since his return and, just for a second, the sparkle returned to his eyes. He pressed his lips softly against mine, only to move on, fairly quickly, to a more passionate embrace.

'Well?' he asked in a whisper, pulling away. 'Do I pass?'

I stepped back, handed him the shepherd's crook and smiled. 'So tell me, just how much did you learn from Mum's book about sheep farming, because that bloody ram hates me!'

★　　★　　★

We ran away from the river, up the meadow and towards my new home. Alasdair retreated to the warmth of the kitchen, but I used the excuse of the approaching dark to bed the hens down for the night – I needed to vent some emotion.

After ushering the hens into their coop I rested my back against the rough, cold bark of Mum's apple tree and thought of her. She had been gone for a whole year, and what a year it had been. I glanced around the garden in the twilight and remembered Mum's idea of planting a tree when I found a home, so I decided to buy an olive tree to act as my permanent marker in the Dales. But then I remembered what Alasdair had said, that an olive might not be suited to life in the Dales; so I decided to plant something more fitting to the landscape instead . . . an oak tree perhaps.

I looked towards the house and through the kitchen window to see Alasdair hugging Annie. He shook Ted's hand and then bent down – presumably stroking Meg. He looked happy. I wondered what the future would hold for us. I had envisaged Alasdair as my very own English oak – strong, protective and proud. But, for all of its strength, even a mighty oak could crack. Promisingly though, I had never in my life seen a completely upended oak tree; they don't know how to give up, and I knew Alasdair wouldn't give up either. I also knew that although a wounded tree would eventually heal itself with new growth, the scar that remained on the surface would never fade away. It would be a part of the character of the tree, always.

In loving memory of Chantelle Tok 1976–2012